Shadows of the Canyon

DESERT ROSES

TRACIE PETERSON

Shadows of the Canyon

Cover design by Koechel Peterson & Associates

Published by Bethany House Publishers
A Ministry of Bethany Fellowship International
11400 Hampshire Avenue South
Bloomington, Minnesota 55438
www.bethanyhouse.com

Printed in the United States of America by
Bethany Press International, Bloomington, Minnesota 55438

Library of Congress Cataloging-in-Publication Data

Peterson, Tracie
Shadows of the canyon / by Tracie Peterson.
p. cm. — (Desert roses ; 1)
ISBN 0-7642-2517-0 (pbk.)
1. Grand Canyon (Ariz.)—Fiction. 2. Hotels—Employees—Fiction. 3. Politicians—Fiction. I. Title.
PS3566.E7717 S53 2002
813'.54—dc21 2002007789

With thanks to Jeanne Schick for her help with this project. You answered my questions faithfully and patiently and that meant the world to me. I appreciate your sweet spirit and kindness.

Also thanks goes to Janice Griffith at the Old Trails Museum in Winslow, Arizona, for her help with details related to the Harvey Girls. I appreciate your depth of knowledge on the subject and your willingness to help me.

Books by Tracie Peterson

www.traciepeterson.com

Controlling Interests
The Long-Awaited Child
A Slender Thread • *Tidings of Peace*

BELLS OF LOWELL*
Daughter of the Loom
A Fragile Design

DESERT ROSES
Shadows of the Canyon • *Across the Years*
Beneath a Harvest Sky

WESTWARD CHRONICLES
A Shelter of Hope • *Hidden in a Whisper*
A Veiled Reflection

RIBBONS OF STEEL†
Distant Dreams • *A Hope Beyond*
A Promise for Tomorrow

RIBBONS WEST†
Westward the Dream • *Separate Roads*
Ties That Bind

SHANNON SAGA‡
City of Angels • *Angels Flight*
Angel of Mercy

YUKON QUEST
Treasures of the North • *Ashes and Ice*
Rivers of Gold

NONFICTION
The Eyes of the Heart

*with Judith Miller †with Judith Pella ‡with James Scott Bell

03B

TRACIE PETERSON is a popular speaker and bestselling author who has written over forty-five books, both historical and contemporary fiction. Tracie and her family make their home in Montana.

CHAPTER ONE

El Tovar Hotel, Grand Canyon, 1923

"And in here," Alexandria Keegan announced, "are the bulk refrigerator storage areas." Alex stepped past the new Harvey House recruit and opened the door to the unit. "We keep all manner of fresh produce, fish, and . . ." She fell silent as she heard the new girl gasp.

"Oh, Miss Keegan," the girl said, blushing red and turning away.

Alex couldn't imagine what the problem was, for the girl looked positively mortified. Turning to look into the unit, Alex fully expected to see a dead rat on the floor. Such a distasteful occurrence didn't happen often, but there was that rare occasion when something unpleasant marred the Harvey restaurant's otherwise impeccable reputation.

Alex grimaced at the scene. It was a rat, all right. But this rat was the two-legged type. Worse still, this rat was her father.

Rufus Keegan, well-known for his philandering ways, was at it once again. Pressed into a compromising position in the corner of the room, one of the newer Harvey Girls appeared to be enjoying Rufus Keegan's lack of discretion.

Alex felt her cheeks grow hot as embarrassment washed

over her. How many times would she have to endure this shame upon her family? How could her father just go on humiliating her mother like this, never concerning himself with the pain he caused? Alex felt tears come to her eyes at the thought of all her mother had endured.

"Bernice, please go to the main dining room and bring Mrs. Godfrey." Alex steadied her emotions. She knew it would be better to have the dining room manager and housemother take charge of the situation.

Bernice, whose face was nearly as red as her bobbed hair, hurried off down the corridor. Alex turned to find her father smoothing the wrinkles in his clothing.

"Do you never tire of bringing shame to our family?" Alex asked, her voice a deadly calm.

"There needn't be any shame if you keep your mouth shut. Honestly, Alexandria, I don't see why you concern yourself with matters that have little to do with you."

Alex forced herself to remain silent and looked past her father to Melina Page. The girl was clearly embarrassed, but she didn't appear overly worried as she adjusted her black Harvey uniform.

"You should gather your things, Melina. I'm certain Mrs. Godfrey will have no further use for you," Alex said, staring hard at the girl.

"But you said you'd keep me from getting fired," Melina said, turning to Rufus. He only shrugged and chuckled. "But you promised!" Melina's voice raised an octave.

"He promised my mother a great many things, as well," Alex said. "But so far, he doesn't seem to honor any of those promises, either." Without conscious thought, Alex reached for the closest object—a plump, ripe, California tomato. "You are without a doubt everything the newspapers say about you and more. I'm ashamed to call you Father."

"Then don't. And don't take that tone with me. You don't have to call me Father or even acknowledge me as such, but I won't take a dressing down by the likes of you or anyone else. I don't take that tone of voice from the governor of this state! What makes you think I'll take it from my daughter?"

Shame was quickly overcome by anger, as years of betrayal seemed to culminate in this one act. Without warning, Alex threw the tomato. She picked up another tomato and then another. Hurling them mindlessly at her father, she shouted a tirade of disapproval.

"You don't care anything about my mother. You've caused her nothing but shame and anguish. Her health suffers because of you and she has no friends because you can't even give the pretense of discretion."

The ripe tomatoes splattered against the wall, against Melina's dress, and against the stun-faced Keegan.

Uncaring about the mess she was making or the vegetables she might destroy, Alex only knew that she wanted to hurt her father as badly as he'd hurt her mother. "We've suffered so much because of you. Mother can't even go to church for fear of what will be said to her!"

"Miss Keegan!"

The voice of Mrs. Godfrey caused Alex to pause. She looked momentarily at the confused woman, then picked up an apple. "My father and Melina chose to make this their trysting place." She hurled the apple, which her father barely managed to dodge before it hit the back wall with a dull thud.

Mrs. Godfrey reached out to Alex. Her grasp on Alex's left hand did nothing to waylay her from securing another apple with her right. This time she aimed for Melina.

"He doesn't deserve to get away with this." Alex nearly

screamed the words, not caring who heard.

"Hey, what's happening? I heard the hollering going on all the way down the . . ."

Alex turned, catching sight of Luke Toland. The tall, lanky cowboy had his hat pushed back on his head, his sandy-colored hair hanging down over his left brow. He appeared shocked to say the least, but Alex could take no more of her father's indiscretion.

She jerked away from Mrs. Godfrey and reached again for the nearest object. It just happened to be a large stalk of celery. Before she could throw it, however, Luke stepped in and took hold of her.

"I don't know what's happening here, but I'm sure throwing this celery isn't going to remedy the matter." He spoke softly and eyed Alex with grave concern. His gentleness was her undoing, and her tears overflowed as she collapsed against his chest and began to cry.

"He doesn't care how much he hurts us," she sobbed.

"Miss Page, please pick up your apron and follow me," Mrs. Godfrey commanded. "Your services will no longer be required by the Fred Harvey Company."

"But Mr. Keegan said . . ."

Alex lifted her gaze as Mrs. Godfrey frowned disapprovingly. "It doesn't matter what Mr. Keegan said. You are in my charge, and we do not tolerate this kind of behavior."

Melina began to cry as she passed by Alex, apron in hand. "But I need this job. I—"

"You should have thought about that before you lowered your standards of decency," Mrs. Godfrey said, leading the weeping girl from the room and down the hall.

"Perhaps if everyone lowered their standards a bit," Rufus Keegan suggested in a loud voice, "we wouldn't find ourselves answering to uptight virgins and sour old biddies."

Alex twisted in Luke's arms and started to charge for her father, wanting only to scratch the smug look off his face and clean the air of his vile words. Luke held her tight, however, and no matter how she tried to fight his hold, her actions were futile.

"Alex," Luke whispered against her ear, "it won't do any good. He doesn't care."

Alex grew still in his arms. She looked over her shoulder, his face so close it nearly touched her own. Turning back to her father, she felt her rage further ignite at the expression on his face.

"I see this wrangler knows how to handle you. Good for you, son." Keegan smoothed the sides of his mustache and trailed the stroke down to his chin. "You know, maybe if you'd spend more time keeping hold of her, teaching her the more pertinent things of life," he grinned and approached Alex and Luke with confident strides, "she'd be a whole lot happier and maybe even more cooperative." He paused as he passed by the couple. "See, I've always found that women were fairly easy to control so long as you handled them just right. Handle her with a tighter rein, cowboy. Show her who's the boss. It's about time she learned what the right man could do for her."

Alex drew back as though slapped. She could feel Luke tighten his hold on her arms, but it was the way Luke ground his teeth together that told her he'd reached his own limits with this conversation.

Reaching up to touch Luke's hand, Alex watched her father saunter down the hallway. "Like you said, Luke, he doesn't care."

"I want to put my fist through his face," Luke growled, his

grasp becoming painful to Alex.

"You're hurting me, Luke," she said, patting his hand. He released her immediately. Alex turned and looked at her dearest friend in all the world. "Thanks for keeping me from making too big of a spectacle."

Luke's expression seemed to soften as he turned to look Alex in the face. "Your pitching arm needs some work," he said with a grin. Gone was the look of rage that had just been there. Alex could see his shoulders relax.

Turning back to look at the mess she'd created, Alex shook her head. "I couldn't help myself. I saw him doing those unspeakable things and shaming my mother, and all I wanted to do was hurt him." She looked back at Luke. "I wanted to hurt him like he was hurting me . . . hurting her."

Alex felt the tears smart her eyes again. "I try so hard to be a good Christian—to keep an attitude that would be pleasing to God—but then something like this happens. Oh, Luke, I can't take much more. How can I respect a man who so clearly does not deserve such honor? My mother has been hurt so much. What if she finds out what Father has done here today? Now her health has been suffering. I want to take her away from all of this, but she won't go."

"Why not?"

Alex shrugged. "She says she could never make it on her own—that Father would strip her of everything but the clothes on her back. She won't saddle her daughters with this, either. My sister, Audra, has offered to have Mother come live with her and her family in Wyoming, but Mother says it isn't right. But, Luke, it isn't right that she suffer this humiliation every time Father decides to chase after the newest Harvey Girl or hotel maid. It seems he's exhausted his possibilities in Williams, so now he's come here to the canyon and El Tovar.

Soon there won't be a skirt in Arizona he hasn't tried to claim for his own. The management here is livid that Father would besmirch their good name."

"Why don't they forbid him entry?" Luke questioned. "After all, this is a luxury resort with plenty of important people. It's not like your father owns the place."

"No, but his political power and money keeps everyone hopping from here to Phoenix. He can pay off those who don't like his actions and cajole everyone else into doing things his way. Only the newspaper editor in Williams gives him a hard time, and that's because the owner has just as much clout as Father."

"I'm sorry, Alex."

She looked up at him, knowing he was sincere. He'd always treated her kindly in the four years since she'd come to work as a Harvey Girl at El Tovar. "I don't know what I'd do without you, Luke. Thank you for keeping me from making a complete fool of myself."

Luke grinned. "Need some help cleaning up?"

She shook her head. "No. I think the time alone will help me to cool off."

"That and closing the door," Luke motioned.

Alex had completely forgotten that they were allowing all the cold air to escape. "I should have never opened the door to begin with. Poor Bernice. She's the new girl. I was showing her around and . . . Well, the rest is pretty apparent. Anyway, I'd better get back to work. Seems like I'm always cleaning up my father's garbage."

"I really would be happy to help you. I'm done for the day and was just coming in to get a bite to eat." He seemed so eager to please her and the look on his face suggested a hopefulness that Alex couldn't ignore.

Alex patted his arm. "No. You've done more than anyone should have to do. Go eat your supper. You're a good friend, Luke." The look of pleasure left his face and was replaced with an expression of disappointment.

"Fine," he said and walked away without another word.

Alex shook her head at the hangdog manner in which he departed. Why should he be disappointed? She was saving him a great deal of messy work. Men! They were impossible to understand.

CHAPTER TWO

Luke wasn't in the mood for supper, still disgusted by the scene he'd stumbled upon in the back rooms of El Tovar's kitchen. He was also more than a little disturbed by Alex's continual use of the word *friend.*

He wanted to be more than Alex's friend. Four years of friendship had taught him that, if nothing else. He'd fallen in love with her somewhere along the way, but he couldn't put his finger on when that had exactly happened. Leaving the hotel, Luke headed down the rim path and sought solace in privacy. He ambled along just a little ways past the Lookout, a rustic creation where they offered telescopes to better view the scenic gorge.

Having spent the last ten years of his life wrangling horses and leading mule teams on various trips in the area, Luke knew the Grand Canyon like the back of his hand. He loved the canyon, and now, as he often did, Luke stared out across the vast wasteland and wondered at the glory of it all.

The sun was just starting to set in the western skies, sending slivers of orange and gold into the turquoise blue sky. The sky reminded him of Alex's eyes—eyes just the perfect shade of turquoise, with long dark lashes that, at times, gave her face a doll-like appearance. He'd memorized every inch, every feature of her face—from the high cheekbones and dark brows, to the straight nose that seemed to turn up just a bit at the tip. Her lips were full and touched with a natural blush of rosy pink that no cosmetic could ever match.

"If I ain't the lovesick cowboy," he muttered, kicking a stone over the edge. He watched the rock zigzag first this way and then that as it bounced off the rocky sentinels below.

The shadows stretched out and played games with the appearance of the canyon. The colors changed before his eyes, and only the laughter and voices from tourists strolling El Tovar's grounds reminded Luke he was not alone.

It was 1923 and this national park was getting more than its fair share of attention. Trains came twice a day, and sometimes more than that on special occasions. The cars were always filled with curious passengers who longed to see what the canyon could offer them. Few ever realized the true gift of such a majestic sight—the way the solitude could speak to their soul on a starry night, how the rush of the wind and the hum of the canyon bottom river combined to make a haunting calliope sound, or the way the scent of piñon and juniper joined with the fresh western breeze after a welcome rain.

Luke sighed. Those were the things that made this home to him. They were the wonders that made this part of Arizona a mystery to most and a heartwarming pleasure to others.

Taking off his hat, Luke wiped his brow and thought of all the changes in his life since coming to the canyon. He'd been a scrawny kid of twenty when he'd shown up looking for a job. He'd heard great things about this place all the way down in Tucson, where he'd been working as a ranch hand. He had been told the opportunity could net a man a great deal of money—enough money to start his own ranch after a year or two of work.

Luke hadn't found it quite that easy, but he had managed to set aside a good portion of his pay. While some of the other men went to Williams to spend their pay anytime they were given time off, Luke had spent his free hours at the canyon. He'd studied and educated himself on the flora and wildlife. He knew the area so well he could tell his way around in the dark . . . Well, almost.

The unmistakable sound of Alex's voice filtered through the air to reach his ears. Replacing his hat, Luke looked up to find Alex pointing the way toward El Tovar and saying something to the tourists who had stopped her. No doubt her shift had ended, and she was taking a walk to forget the scene in the cooler.

Luke deliberated for a moment. He wanted very much to ask Alex to walk with him, to spend the quiet of the evening at his side. He'd wanted that for a long time now, but he felt completely at odds as to how he could take their relationship past the point of friendship and into love. If he could just come out with the words—just tell her face-to-face that he was in love with her and wanted to spend the rest of his life with her.

Alex bid the tourists good-bye and headed toward the place where Luke stood indecisively. "I thought that was you," she said, smiling as she came to stand before him. She held a small covered basket. "Did you ever get some supper?"

"No. I just figured to get some fresh air and think a spell."

She smiled, and Luke felt the joy of it spill over him like the water at Deer Creek Falls. "Good. Then we can share my picnic."

"What?"

She held up the basket. "I packed a chicken salad sandwich, Camembert cheese, and sliced apples—instead of the applesauce that I made against the wall of the cooler." She smiled and continued. "And I have a jar of rather tart lemonade, but we'll have to share."

He smiled, knowing there was nothing in the world he wouldn't happily share with her. "Sounds wonderful."

"I thought so, too," she said, glancing around. "Where shall we share this feast?"

A great idea sprang to Luke's mind. "Let's borrow a car and get away from the area. Better yet, I'll get us a couple of horses and we can ride to this wonderful little spot I know."

Alex frowned, looking down at her uniform. "I'm hardly dressed for horseback riding. The Harvey Company hasn't seen their way to outfitting us with split skirts or trousers."

"Then we'll borrow Clancy's car," Luke said, knowing his right-hand man wouldn't begrudge him a few moments of privacy with Alex.

Alex laughed and nodded, handing the basket to Luke. "I think that sounds marvelous. My feet are sore from working tables all day long, anyway. I'm glad people love the canyon, but I do wish the management would staff more girls to help out."

They walked in companionable silence to where Luke knew he'd find Clancy feeding the mules. "Hey, Clancy, can I borrow your car? Alex thinks we need to have a picnic."

She playfully poked his ribs with her elbow. "It was his idea to borrow the car, Clancy. I had nothing to do with it. You know I've never been fond of the smelly things."

Clancy looked up and smiled, revealing a missing tooth. Just last month he'd taken a kick in the face from his favorite mule. He'd been black-and-blue for weeks, and even now the yellowed bruises were still visible in a few places.

"You can take her, just make sure you bring her back," Clancy said, straightening from where he'd been bent over the feed trough.

Luke gave his solemn promise, then ushered Alex to the car. He took them east and down a narrow road. "I know this place where we can sit and watch the sunset," he told Alex.

She said nothing but reached up to take the hairpins from her hair to let the breeze blow through her long brown curls. Luke had seen her like this once or twice before, and always it left him with a strange flutter in his stomach. She looked so very alluring with her hair down. He knew she had no idea of how her appearance affected him, and he wasn't about to tell her for fear she'd stop taking such casual liberties when she was in his presence.

Luke forced his gaze to stay on the road. In his mind he wrestled with his thoughts. *I could tell her how I feel,* he reasoned. *I could just say that she's come to mean the world to me and I'd like to court her formal-like.* Luke stole a glance and found Alex watching the road ahead. She didn't appear to have a clue as to how he felt.

Glancing at his watch, Luke pulled the car over and parked not far from the place he had in mind. "Come on. We'll walk just a bit, and if your feet are too tired, I'll carry you."

Alex laughed. "Oh, I'm sure after handling mules all day, I'd be a real treat."

"More than you know," Luke muttered under his breath.

"What did you say?"

He looked across the car at Alex and shook his head. "Nothing. Come on, we'd better get a move on if we're going to see all the colors. It's almost seven-thirty."

"That late already?" Alex questioned. "I suppose I lost track of time. Glad I got away when I did." She started to pull her hair back into a knot, but Luke grabbed up the basket and headed toward the trail.

"You haven't got time for that," he called over his shoulder. "Just leave your hair down."

His voice trembled just a bit. *Old boy, you've got it bad. Better keep quiet or you'll be making a complete idiot of yourself.*

They made their way down a narrow rocky path, angling ever closer to the rim of the canyon. Luke had a special place he liked to visit, and he knew Alex would appreciate the view, as well as the solitude. Visitors had long since headed back to the hotel and campgrounds, and they'd have the area to themselves, if Luke had judged the situation correctly. Besides, he'd never yet come across anyone who'd happened upon his secret place.

"Over here," Luke commanded. "We have to take this path."

"There's a path?" Alex teased. "Looks like a few boulders and some scrub brush."

Luke laughed. He appreciated her good mood. "See the ledge to the left?"

"You don't mean to tell me *that's* the path."

"I do." He paused and looked back at her. "You aren't going to go skittering back to the car, are you? Lost your nerve?"

Alex folded her arms against her chest. "I certainly haven't. You have the food and I'm starving. I'll follow you anywhere."

Her words hit Luke's lovesick heart like an arrow flying at full speed. "Come on, then."

He helped her around the rocks and down the last little

bit of trail. Spread out before them was the Grand Canyon in all her colorful splendor. Alex gasped in surprise.

"This is incredible. How come you haven't told me about this place before?"

"It's always been here," Luke replied, taking a seat on a rocky outcropping.

Alex joined him, her gaze still fixed on the canyon below. "I've been in this area a hundred times, but I've never been down this trail."

"My own secret haunt," he said, taking the cloth from atop the basket. "You want to serve, or shall I?"

"Let's ask the blessing first and then I'll serve you." Alex bowed her head and began to pray. "Father, thank you so much for calming my spirit with the glory of your handiwork. Thank you for Luke's friendship and his wisdom in dealing with my father. And, thank you, Father, for this food and time together."

"Amen," Luke offered, trying not to think of her reference once again to their friendship. Surely married folks needed to be friends with each other. He'd try to keep it all in proper perspective.

Alex handed him half a sandwich and added, "I meant what I said. Your wisdom probably kept me from making a poor situation worse today. I prayed a great deal while I cleaned the storage area."

Luke had never been much for prayer or Christian matters until Alex had come into his life. His mother had lived a life full of faith and love of God, but her death when Luke had been only twelve had left him doubting the hope she found in such things. For years he had listened to his older brother and sister espouse their Christian beliefs and faith. Even his father, who died only two years after his mother, kept the family Bible by the bed stand and read it religiously every night before bed. But Luke had felt God a cruel master—a strict judge who stole mothers away from children.

Alex had changed Luke's heart—or rather, God had changed it because of Alex's persistent belief in His goodness and mercy. Even now, after what had transpired with her father, Alex would no doubt speak of God's goodness. It was a faith that Luke had great admiration for and had been strengthened by.

"I found it easy to react when I saw my father with Melina, but I didn't find it so easy to pray. I'm ashamed to have acted that way in front of Mrs. Godfrey," Alex admitted. She bowed her head to take a bite of her sandwich.

"Most folks would have done worse."

Alex shrugged. "But I wasn't a good witness. I didn't show myself to be guided by God's spirit. Rather I reacted like—"

Luke interrupted. "Like anyone else would have, given the circumstance. You were hurt, Alex. There's no shame in that. Sure, you could have walked away."

"Should have walked away."

"Or you could have locked them in the refrigerator." He grinned at her and waited for her reaction. She looked up and smiled. "I see the thought crossed your mind," he added.

"Anyway, thanks for understanding. You're good at knowing what to say to me and just how to help me through a tough moment."

Luke wondered if this wasn't just as good a time as any to share how he'd been feeling. He started to comment, then held back. If she wasn't of a mind to see their relationship head toward courtship and marriage, it would ruin the best friendship he'd ever had. Was he willing to let that happen?

"Oh, look," Alex said excitedly, "the entire canyon looks like it's on fire."

Luke turned from Alex and studied the horizon. "I knew you'd like it. See the way the shadows turn all purple and gray?"

"Almost the color of lilacs in spring," she murmured.

Luke nodded. The last bit of golden sun trailed out across the landscape, touching the rocky towers and outcroppings with a light that seemed to shimmer and glow. Orange-and-red rock below transformed to hues of muted brown, while farther in the canyon the shadows grew dark, swallowing up the last bits of color.

Glancing back at Alex, Luke felt himself mesmerized by her intent study of the canyon. Her dark brown curls rippled gently in the breeze. Her turquoise eyes seemed to search for some missing piece—some subtle clue as to how it all began, how this canyon should find itself in this place, at this time. Luke leaned closer. Perhaps he'd simply kiss her and let his actions speak for his heart. He took a deep breath to steady his nerves.

She broke the spell of the moment. "I almost forgot the lemonade. Are you thirsty?"

"Huh?" He'd barely heard her words.

"I asked if you were thirsty. Do you want some lemonade?"

"Sure." Luke straightened and tried not to appear flustered. "That'd be nice."

Alex handed him a Mason jar. "Be warned, it's a bit sour."

"I like it that way," Luke said, taking a drink.

Alex picked up the conversation again. "Poor Melina was still crying when I left for the day. I don't know why women like that get caught up in the actions of men like my father.

Mrs. Godfrey was clearly as uncomfortable as I was; yet she handled the matter with such grace and refinement. I guess that's what I wish I could do. Control my temper and keep a ladylike comportment about me."

"I don't see anything unladylike about the way you reacted. You were acting on your feelings and the love you have for your mother."

Alex turned to face Luke. "I feel particularly bad for the way Father treated you." She paused as her cheeks reddened. "Those lewd comments about . . . well, I won't repeat them," Alex said, paying strict attention to her sandwich. "I'm sorry he made suggestions about you and me."

Luke nearly choked. He didn't know what to say. Clearly he couldn't speak of his love for her on the tail of her father's obviously inappropriate comments. She might get the wrong idea. Worse yet, she might think Luke felt sorry for her and was only trying to make her feel better.

"Father can't understand what you and I have together."

What do we have? Luke wanted so much to voice the question aloud. Instead, he turned his attention to the food and let Alex do the talking.

"I was serious about wanting to take mother away from here. I've been saving my money. The wages, the tips . . . all of it. Tips are always good at the canyon, so I've got a good bit set aside. Even so, it wouldn't take us far. I can transfer anywhere on the Santa Fe line. The Harvey Company would find a dozen girls happy to come to the Grand Canyon and work in my place. But . . ."

"But?" Luke questioned.

"But my father would take everything from her. He'd never allow her a single dime. I could never hope to support us both," Alex said with a sigh. "There has to be an answer."

"There always is." Luke handed the jar of lemonade back to her.

"If she'd just go stay with Audra, at least it would put her out of the reach of the humiliating comments. She can't even go to church without someone approaching her in regard to father's behavior. I try my best to encourage her, but it's just too much for her to bear. And now her health is diminishing. She's lost so much weight that nothing fits her anymore.

"If Father only cared. If he cared about her and how she feels, he could never carry on with these affairs. I've tried to explain that to him, but he's not concerned. Politics and money. That's all he wants to focus on. Not my mother. And certainly not God. He has his friends, and their political power often benefits him financially. He lies. He cheats. He destroys. It's his legacy."

"I guess just about anyone without God in his life would have a similar legacy," Luke offered.

"He and his friends find cheating so completely acceptable. I've witnessed their tomfoolery with my own eyes. It's the reason I came to the Grand Canyon from Williams. I'd worked as a Harvey Girl at the restaurant in Williams, but Father was always coming there causing problems for me. Worse yet, his friends started behaving improperly toward me."

Luke hadn't heard her talk about this before, and it angered him to think of other men treating her without the respect she deserved.

Alex shook her head. "That's why I'll never marry. I'll never trust any man to be faithful and honest. I'm not sure it's possible."

"Whoa now," Luke said, waggling his finger at her. "You can't go throwing us all in the same pot."

Alex seemed to consider his comment for a moment. "Well, I suppose present company is excluded. You'll make someone a wonderful husband . . . at least I hope you will."

"Why do you take that tone with me? Do you doubt my ability to be faithful?"

Alex shrugged and nibbled at a piece of the cheese. "I'm not doubting your ability so much as my own. I doubt my judgment of people. I've been hurt one too many times, believing someone to be genuine and honest only to find out that they're self-serving and deceitful. I remember the first time a man actually asked to court me. He was all sweet talk and flowers. He doted on me like nothing you've ever seen. Then I found out he was far more interested in doting on Father's ledgers. He figured to marry their fortunes together through me. He admitted that he didn't really love me, but rather knew it would be a beneficial union. He'd lied to me, and I caught him red-handed."

"And you think I would lie to you?"

"I don't know what to think," Alex said, her voice full of irritation. "That's the problem. That's why I'll never let my heart get caught up in such matters. I'm a poor judge of such things. Given the past, if I gave in to my heart, I'd probably end up with a man no better in his actions than my father."

"Too bad God isn't powerful enough to protect you from such a thing," Luke said sarcastically. He didn't like her attitude or the way it defeated his plans to offer her courtship and marriage.

Alex frowned and began gathering up her things. "He didn't protect my mother, so why should I think I deserve any different? It isn't that I think God incapable—it's simply that sinful man will do sinful things and good people will suffer. My desire is to help my mother—to see her through this matter. She may not be willing to impose herself in the life of my married sister, but she doesn't have that same excuse with me. I'll make her see reason. We'll go to Kansas City or Topeka or even California. We'll go far enough away that we won't have to witness my father's escapades firsthand."

She got to her feet and stared down at Luke with an expression that wavered between hurt and doubt. "I need to get back. Will you drive me or shall I walk?"

Luke got up and dusted off his jeans. "I'll drive you—that is, if you can trust me to keep my word."

"Luke, don't be like that. I didn't mean to include you. I was just talking about the men I've known in the past. I know you're not like them. I don't think of you like that." She reached out and gently touched his shoulder. "I've never seen you be cruel to anyone. I'm sorry I hurt your feelings. Please don't be angry with me."

Luke couldn't stay mad. He smiled. "Come on. Let's get you back before they send out a search party."

CHAPTER THREE

"Senator Winthrop, how marvelous you could come to El Tovar!"

The stocky man smiled in greeting. "Chester Laird, as I live and breathe. If you aren't a welcome sight for these old eyes."

Alex took in the revelry with little interest as she poured glasses of ice water. She was used to parties of the rich and influential. El Tovar seemed the perfect place for their gatherings—a respite in a luxurious setting. Not only the grandeur of the canyon beyond the walls, but the hotel itself had been a masterpiece of design. Styled in the manner of a massive Swiss chalet, the Harvey Company had spared no expense to ensure its beauty and splendor.

"How do you like our little Waldorf of the west?" Laird questioned.

"I must say, this resort is far better equipped than I had figured. My aide mentioned it was quite the popular place, very European in nature. Still, when I mentioned to my daughter, Valerie, that we were spending a month in Arizona, you would have thought I'd suggested she sell her jewels and live on the street."

"I was sorry to hear about your wife's passing," Laird said, sobering rather quickly.

"Thank you, Chester. The dear woman simply gave out. Life in the political arena was much too difficult. But Valerie does a good job—well, decidedly that! She does a superior job acting as my hostess. Speaking of which, here she comes now with my aide, Joel Harper."

Alex didn't know why, but she lifted her gaze to meet the approaching couple. Valerie Winthrop greatly resembled the actress Lillian Gish. She wore an iced blue satin gown that clung to her in a most revealing way. Typical of the elaborate evening gowns Alex had witnessed on other occasions, the neckline plunged. A choker of diamonds and pearls graced her slender throat, while a feathered stole barely covered the bare skin above the décolletage.

"Hello, Daddy," she said, leaning over to give the pretense of kissing her father's cheek. Alex knew full well her lips hadn't touched the man's face because the woman's bright red lipstick would have left its mark.

"My darling, do you remember Mr. Laird? He's an attorney in California. A powerful ally, if I do say so myself."

"Miss Winthrop, it's a pleasure," Laird said, taking hold of her extended hand. He bowed over her hand, again offering a pretense of a kiss. Alex was so mesmerized by the charade that she actually paused in her work to watch. The lengths to which the wealthy played their games never failed to amaze her. Everyone appeared to know their parts in this strange little play, yet no one was overly worried about appearing realistic or sincere.

"The pleasure is mine," Valerie Winthrop said, dripping sweetness.

"And this is my aide, Joel Harper," Winthrop announced,

turning to give Harper a mighty pat on the back.

"Harper? That's a name I know quite well," Laird replied. "I once kept company with Barrington Harper of Boston."

Alex lowered her gaze only momentarily to ensure that she'd properly tended to the table. At the rich baritone of Joel's reply, she was again drawn into the lives of her wealthy charges.

"Mr. Laird, I've heard great things about you. In fact, we met once many years ago, but of course, I was just a boy. Barrington Harper is my uncle and you were a guest in his home. As I recall, you beat him quite soundly at an especially challenging game of chess."

Laird laughed. "We've played many a challenging game over the years. Sometimes I win, sometimes he does, but always we enjoy the game. What of you, son? Do you play?"

Joel caught Alex watching him and winked before he replied. "Only to win."

Alex felt her cheeks grow hot and quickly looked away. She turned abruptly and almost ran over Bernice King, her newest trainee. "Oh, sorry, Bernice. I wasn't watching where I was going."

"That's all right, Miss Keegan." The girl shook her head and gazed around the room. "There are so many beautiful people here, I'm not sure that I'm doing anything right."

"You'll get used to it," Alex told her. "Sometimes it gets a bit overwhelming, but you have to keep your sights on what's real and important. Focus your attention on being the best Harvey Girl in the room and you'll benefit your customers as well as yourself. You might even make a tidy tip in the process."

"Oh, I hope so, Miss Keegan. I have six brothers and four

sisters at home. My ma and pa need me to send home as much money as possible."

Alex's heart went out to the younger woman. Bernice was barely eighteen and as green and inexperienced as any girl Alex had worked with. Six years Alex's junior, the poor girl had never traveled out of Missouri before going to work for the Fred Harvey Company.

"Miss, might I trouble you for a moment?"

It was the same voice Alex had heard only minutes ago. Bernice hurried away, leaving Alex with the sensation of being deserted. She turned and found Joel Harper only inches away. He stood so close, in fact, that Alex felt the need to whisper, lest she shout directly in his face.

"Yes?"

Joel smiled a very pleasant smile. He cut a dashing figure in his black tuxedo, even if his bow tie was a bit crooked. "I couldn't help but notice you watching me," he said, lowering his voice. "I believe destiny has brought us together tonight."

Alex immediately grew uncomfortable. She took a step back. "I think you're mistaken, sir. I'm the Harvey Girl who will be seeing to your table. I was merely checking to see if your party was complete. I'll be serving the salads momentarily." *Keep it professional,* she told herself. Reserved formality did more to quench ardent fires among her customers than anything else.

"Ah, but you were particularly taken when I entered the room. I felt it."

Alex had heard all she was going to take. "I thought your girlfriend looked like Lillian Gish. In fact, Miss Gish has been our guest here before, and I wasn't certain but what she had returned. I assure you, I did not mean to stare, but it was for that reason and no other. Now, if you'll excuse me . . ."

Joel took hold of Alex's arm. She stared down at his finely manicured hand in contrast to her black sleeve. Returning her gaze to meet his, Alex felt overwhelmed with the assurance that this was a man used to getting whatever he wanted. Rich and good-looking, he no doubt played the room with great expertise.

"Don't be so quick to dismiss me. I'll speak to you more about this after dinner." He let her go and turned abruptly to rejoin his dinner party.

He's just like every other man, Alex thought. *I'll have to watch myself around him. No doubt he's used to having women fall at his feet.* Smiling, Alex went about her work and saw to the needs of her other tables before forcing herself back to the Winthrop party.

Dining at El Tovar was a much more relaxed event than diners experienced at other Harvey restaurants. So many of the Harvey House Restaurants were set up with the sole purpose of feeding large quantities of train passengers in an elegant, but rapid-paced, manner. Alex had experienced an entirely different kind of work routine from the one here at El Tovar while training and serving at the Harvey House in Williams. There, the train had come in and, within thirty minutes, the Harvey Girls would feed and water the train passengers, sending no one away hungry, unless by choice. Town folk came in for meals as well, but the pacing was always set by the railroad and those passengers who paid to ride the rails. El Tovar, however, was designed for pure pleasure and leisurely enjoyment.

The evening passed in relative ease for Alex. At two of her tables, the guests ate rather hastily and hurried off to stroll the canyon rim. They tipped well, so she didn't care that they had little interest in her attention. Her other tables had minor problems or needs, but nothing out of the ordinary. Years of serving in a Harvey uniform had taught her that very little couldn't be handled with a smile and soft word.

She had anticipated trouble from Joel Harper but found him to be a perfect gentleman. He took her service and politely responded when she offered drinks or additional courses.

But while Joel had treated her with respect, Valerie Winthrop was an entirely different matter.

"Miss, this fish is cold. Take it back and bring me something else."

"Miss, I don't care for the blend of this coffee, bring me English tea."

It went on and on. Always she complained, and always Alex tried her best to pleasantly anticipate Miss Winthrop's needs.

Alex decided she was going to escape without anything too uncomfortable as the party concluded their dinner amidst conversation regarding the retired senator's return to politics. The men seemed anxious to be outside strolling and smoking and Miss Winthrop seemed somewhat bored and ready to retire to more exciting places, although where that would be, Alex was not entirely sure.

"Winston, we need a man like you for president," Laird stated as Alex began to clear away the dishes.

"Daddy will make the perfect president," Valerie added. "He's so considerate and smart. He'll know exactly what to do to keep the country strong, and with his experience and backing, he ought to easily be able to defeat President Harding."

"President Harding would no doubt find you more appealing than Mr. Harper or your father," Laird said, leering rather suggestively at Valerie's daring neckline. The feather boa had long since eased its way up around the young woman's neck, leaving her rather exposed to view.

"That's true, Val dear," Joel said rather snidely. "You know the rumors regarding Mr. Harding and his love of female companionship."

Valerie laughed and leaned forward as if to entice Laird further. "Is it true they've created a secret tunnel into the White House so that he can get his women in and out without the public knowing about them?"

"I'm sure it's well traveled if they have," Laird replied. "Perhaps if he got the Secretary of the Interior to put in a toll booth, we could write off the debts from the Great War." Laughter erupted and Alex did her level best to ignore the conversation. She'd actually heard good things about the president, and she hated to have anyone bad-mouth the country's leader. She remembered her father laughing at a quote President Harding had made. Several years earlier Harding had stated, "It is my conviction that the fundamental trouble with the people of the United States is that they have gotten too far away from Almighty God." Alex had admired him for that. Of course, she hadn't known of his philandering ways, but it didn't surprise her if such a thing were true. She only hoped that Mrs. Harding didn't suffer to the extent Alex's mother did.

Alex was so lost in thought that she missed the next round of comments. Apparently the subject had been amusing because once again they were all laughing quite boisterously.

"Excuse me," Alex murmured, reaching to retrieve an empty dessert plate.

"And if I won't?" Joel Harper questioned, reaching out to still Alex's hand. He gripped her wrist and grinned up boyishly, as if she might be impressed by his sudden attention.

"I'm afraid I must insist," Alex said, trying hard to maintain her calm. "I have a great deal of work to do."

"That's the black and white of it, Mr. Harper," Senator Winthrop said, looking as though he thought himself quite clever.

Everyone laughed with the exception of Joel. He appeared intent on keeping Alex from her duties. "Say, Val, you'd look smashing dressed as a Harvey Girl. What do you say?"

"I think they look like nuns," Valerie Winthrop replied disgustedly. "So chaste and pure."

"Well, that would leave you out, wouldn't it, darling?" Joel said, leaning toward Valerie.

Alex happened to be standing between them and found Joel's presence much too invading. Jerking away and stepping back, she picked up the last of the dinner plates and added them to her stack. Alex had just turned to head back to the kitchen when Joel reached out and pinched her backside. Whirling around to meet her assailant, Alex lost control of her tray and sent china and crystal plummeting to the floor.

Everyone at the Winthrop table broke into laughter. Alex fixed Joel with what she hoped was an icy stare. She didn't even bother to apologize. Everyone in the dining room looked up to see what had caused the disturbance.

"Is there a problem here?" Mrs. Godfrey questioned, coming up from behind Alex.

"I'm afraid I startled your girl," Joel replied before Alex could speak. "The damage is my fault. Put it on my bill."

"Nonsense," Mrs. Godfrey said with a smile. "Accidents happen. Miss Keegan, see that this is cleaned up."

"Yes, I will." Alex tried not to appear flustered as she

picked up her tray and squatted down to gather the broken pieces.

Joel leaned over to help and smiled in his dangerous way. "I'm truly sorry. I only meant to get your attention."

"Well, my name is Miss Keegan. Try that next time." Alex straightened as she picked up the last piece of china. "It generally works better than your way."

"Mine's more fun," Joel replied with a wink. "Say, why don't you meet me at the rim just beyond the rock porch. I'd like to find a better way to apologize."

Everyone watched Alex, as if to anticipate her answer. Alex shifted the tray and shook her head. With a smile she replied. "I'm afraid that would be a bad idea. I might be arrested if I joined you out there."

"But whatever for?" Joel asked, his voice lowering.

"For pushing you over the edge," Alex replied matter-of-factly before turning to head back to the kitchen. Of all the arrogant and self-absorbed men, Joel Harper had to take the prize.

Laughter rang out from the members of the Winthrop party, and Alex could hear even Joel chuckle at her response. *Let them laugh,* Alex thought. *They're too unaware of the rest of the world. All they know is their wealth and power.*

CHAPTER FOUR

El Tovar held the honor of being the prize of Harvey Hotels. The company had seen to it that every comfort could be offered. Poised not more than twenty feet from the rim of the canyon at one corner, the hotel blended rustic beauty with European refinement. The porches and supports were native stone to match the area scenery, while the bulk of El Tovar was constructed from Douglas fir logs brought in from Oregon. The four-story structure boasted nearly one hundred guest rooms—some with private baths—as well as steamed heat, hot and cold running water, electric lights, and of course, the wonderful Harvey House meals.

El Tovar was a community unto itself, with its lounges, art galleries, large elegantly set dining room, and rooftop garden. There were clubrooms, recreation rooms, music rooms—it even had its own power plant and fire safety system. The cost of construction was rumored to be upwards of $250,000, but no one seemed to question the expense. It benefited the rich, who could come and stay quite happily for about six dollars a day.

Alex felt privileged to be a part of such a fascinating place. Most of the Harvey Girls worked from around Easter until the end of summer. But some, like Alex, worked year round. There was good money to be made, especially in tips. The bulk of their customers were rich and, for the most part, liked to share the wealth. Alex's good friend Michaela Benson had managed to set aside so much money that she'd taken an extended leave of absence to travel the country. Alex knew, however, the minute Michaela wanted to come back, the Harvey Company would hire her back. It was that way with most of the experienced, popular staff.

That was also why Alex didn't worry about getting a transfer to another part of the country. Having a job, and even arranging for quarters, would be the easy part of solving her dilemma. Convincing her mother that it was the best alternative would be the difficult part. However, looking at the newly arrived Williams newspaper, she wondered if her task had just gotten easier. There on the editorial page, a cartoon once again poked fun at her family and exposed their shame.

Keegan Chooses Wrong Mount, the caption read, while a caricature of her father had been drawn alongside a mule with the branding GC, for Grand Canyon. He was running his hand over the mule's backside, while in the opposite corner, a thoroughbred mare, marked KK for Katherine Keegan, stood with her head in a haystack. The mare was contentedly ignorant of the injustice. Alex's mother would not have that luxury.

"This makes me so mad!" Alex said, flinging the paper down on Mrs. Godfrey's desk.

"I know you're not pleased to see yet another example of the paper's lack of propriety, but perhaps—"

"I'm sorry, Mrs. Godfrey," Alex interrupted, "but the paper is only drawing attention to my father's indiscretion. It's hardly their lack of propriety that disturbs me as much as everyone's lack of concern for my mother's feelings."

The older woman nodded. "I simply thought you should know about it before you had to serve luncheon. Your father is among the Winthrop party today, so I put Bernice on that table and freed you to work elsewhere. I'm sorry for the awkwardness of this situation."

"I'm the one who should apologize," Alex said, pausing at last to collapse in the chair opposite her mentor. "I have asked Father to stay away, but he refuses. Says his money is just as good as the next man's and that he helped to popularize this place. He avidly supports Winthrop's desire for the Democratic nomination for president and hopes to land himself a nice comfortable job in Washington."

"Oh, my."

Alex nodded. "Exactly. I have no desire for my mother to bear any more pain, so I must tell you that I've contemplated the idea of putting in for a transfer so that I might take her away from this."

Mrs. Godfrey didn't appear surprised. Instead, she smiled. "But, Alex, dear, you wouldn't want to rush into anything. After all, if your father is given a position in Washington, that would solve your dilemma. Perhaps he could go and your mother could remain here in Arizona."

"But that's over a year away." Alex shook her head. She'd thought all of this through more than once. "I'll just have to keep praying that God will help me to keep my temper under control in the meanwhile. I'd hate to run El Tovar short on tomatoes."

Mrs. Godfrey chuckled. "Alex, you're my best worker. You're my number one girl, and I don't want to lose you as I have Michaela. We're already two girls short. I've put in a request for at least four additional girls, especially since the

Winthrop party has announced intentions to put on quite a round of entertainment and festivities. They'll be here at least a month."

"Somehow that figures." The last thing Alex wanted to have to endure was a month of Joel Harper and her father. *Two peas in a pod,* she thought.

"Though why they chose July and August to spend at the canyon is beyond me," Mrs. Godfrey continued. "They're used to the warmth of the south, I suppose. I understand they own a plantation in South Carolina."

Alex no longer cared to hear any more about the Winthrop entourage. "Perhaps they came for the air," she said, getting to her feet. "Look, I know I'm only filling in for lunch, but I can stay and do supper as well. Just because my father is here is no reason to shelter me like a child."

"Nonsense. This was your day off. Had we not fired Melina, it would still be your day off. No, I only need the help with lunch. Then go and take some time for yourself. You need to relax. There will be enough of a burden on you in the weeks to come. With the Winthrop plans, I'm sure we'll all be working extra hours. And while I hesitate to mention it, I must say this." Mrs. Godfrey paused and fixed Alex with a sympathetic expression. "The Winthrop party has specifically asked that you be assigned them on a regular basis—especially for dinners. They're paying a premium price for a private dining room and feel you are the best on staff. I couldn't argue with them there."

"Wonderful." Alex's tone of voice left little doubt as to how she felt.

"If it helps at all, they've already given me a large sum to entice you. This is half your tip money for the month if you will continue to at least be their dinner server when you are on duty."

Alex looked at the money, then raised her gaze to Mrs. Godfrey. "There's at least twenty dollars there."

"Twenty-five, to be exact."

Alex swallowed hard. Her tips from the Winthrop table would come to more than her monthly salary at this rate. The money could help her get her mother away from Arizona that much sooner.

Alex sighed and nodded. "I'd better get to it, then."

She left Mrs. Godfrey and made her way to the kitchen. Why had the Winthrops asked for her? No doubt Joel Harper was behind all of this. Why did the world have to be filled with Joel Harpers and men like her father?

The thought of her father left a sour taste in her mouth. For years she had fought a spiritual battle as to what she owed him. She was supposed to honor him—love him. But how? How could she respect and honor a man who did nothing but dishonor his family and reputation?

Why couldn't he just disappear and leave her and her mother alone? In fact, perhaps she'd take the train to Williams and visit her mother. Maybe Mrs. Godfrey could give her the next morning off and Alex could spend the night.

Alex busied herself with her customers. She served wonderful Harvey creations, including salmon-and-celery salads and spiced herring with potato salad. Most of her fares were interested in the light lunches. The day was already warming up, making some of the customers uncomfortable, and Alex did her best to cool them down. She suggested melon platters and cold roast beef and cream cheese sandwiches. Iced tea was served in abundance, as was lemonade.

By the time her father strolled into the dining room,

comfortably settled between Valerie Winthrop and the senator, Alex had nearly forgotten the scandal of the editorial cartoon. Seeing him brought it all back in a flash, however. Alex thought she might escape unscathed, but her father motioned her to come to him and, rather than cause a scene, Alex did just that.

"May I help you?" she asked in a formal tone.

"This is my daughter, Alexandria," her father announced. "Is she the one you were telling me about?"

Joel joined them just then and grinned from ear to ear. His slicked-back black hair glistened under the casual lighting of the dining room. "That's the one. Mr. Keegan, you certainly have a charming daughter." He turned to Valerie and added, "And you thought I'd lowered my standards by falling for one of the help. Why, Miss Keegan is very nearly as well-off as you are, Val darling."

"Hardly that," Valerie said, looking at Alex as if anticipating some kind of counter reply.

"If that will be all," Alex said, looking back to her tables, "I need to finish my work."

"Well, that's *not* all," her father replied. "Joel would like you to join us this evening for dinner. I'll expect you promptly at six."

"I have plans and will not be in the area. You must pardon me now." She turned to go, but her father took hold of her and twisted her arm ever so slightly. "Don't disappoint the Winthrops, Alex. They're important to my career," he muttered for only her ears to hear.

"Father, I cannot join you," Alex replied. To the others she offered the hint of a smile and said, "I do apologize. I have a very busy schedule and my plans are already made."

"You aren't still sore because of last night are you?" Joel

questioned. "I left you a handsome tip to assure you of my sincerity."

Alex nodded. "Yes, I found your tip and was most assured of your intentions." She met his gaze and nodded, knowing at a glance that he understood her meaning.

"It takes more than cold cash to assure that girl of anything," Rufus Keegan threw in. "She prides herself in her lofty expectations. Keeps a Bible by her bed and all such nonsense. She could make a convent look impure."

"Father!" Alex exclaimed. "I will speak to you later."

She turned to go and once again found her progress halted. This time Joel was the culprit. "I beg you, Miss Keegan. Please reconsider. I'd love to have you . . ." he paused for effect, "as a guest for dinner."

Alex wasn't the least bit enticed. "Thank you, but no. Good day."

Her fists were balled by the time she got to the kitchen. To her surprise she found Luke waiting for her there. He smiled and twirled his hat in his hand. "I have the afternoon and evening off. Thought you might like to take a ride or something."

"I'd *like* to throw my father across the room," she said angrily. Pacing back and forth in front of him, Alex couldn't seem to calm her angry spirit. *Oh, Lord,* she prayed, *why do I have to let him take this kind of control over my heart and soul?*

"Alex?" Luke questioned, stepping forward. "Are you all right?"

She sighed. "No. I'm angry and on the verge of doing something stupid."

"Should I have the chef hide the tomatoes?"

She smiled and felt the tension ease a bit. "No, but I'm

not entirely certain the coconut cream pie is safe. I just may throw it."

"Don't do that—it's my favorite," Luke said, reaching out to take hold of her. "Look, forget about the problem and just come with me when your shift is done."

Alex nodded. "I suppose I could get away for a little while. I was thinking of visiting my mother in Williams. I'm worried that she's seen the morning paper."

Luke frowned. "Yeah, I heard about it."

"Well, I saw it firsthand," Alex said, trying her best to control her anger. "It just isn't fair." She stepped aside to allow the pastry chef to pass. His tray held several pies and Alex looked up to meet Luke's bemused grin. "I'll leave them alone . . . this time."

An hour later, Alex had changed into a riding skirt and allowed Luke to help her atop a lovely bay mare. She enjoyed riding and hadn't had a chance to do so in some time. She knew she might well be sore in the morning, but for now she wanted nothing more than to be free of El Tovar and her father.

"Is your father still in the dining room?" Luke asked.

"Yes, and he's responding rather excitedly to Mr. Winthrop's politics and Miss Winthrop's flirtations. It's shocking how openly they talk about inappropriate topics. I know it's part of this rather wild age, but honestly, Luke, what about modesty?"

"I'm really sorry, Alex."

Alex nodded. "I know you are. You've been very kind to me—to my mother. She thinks highly of you. She wrote me a note some weeks ago and mentioned you."

Luke eyed her curiously. "What did she say?" He climbed into the saddle and waited for her to respond.

Alex felt her cheeks grow hot and looked away rather quickly. She could hardly explain that her mother had thought he'd make a good husband and that Alex should marry and leave the area as her sister had done. Better that her daughters be able to rid themselves of their father's shame than to have the entire family continue to suffer. But Alex didn't see it that way. Luke was a nice man, but he wasn't for her.

"She just indicated that she thought well of you."

"So are you still planning to go see her?"

"No. Mrs. Godfrey can't spare me in the morning. She's not yet received any replacement staff to help out, and apparently the Winthrops are holding some kind of brunch. I'll be working all day, so I need to stay here tonight."

"Good. We won't have to hurry our ride in order for you to catch the train."

Alex nodded. "I suppose that is good."

They rode side by side, past gamble oak and pine. An ambitious gopher snake startled the horses as it left its cooler place in the shade of a rock and skirted out across the trail after a pocket mouse. The tiny mammal sensed danger, however, and disappeared into the sage.

Alex tried to calm her skittish mare, but it took Luke's strong hold to finally control the horse.

"Whoa, there. Easy, girl," he said in his soothing way.

Alex thought how very gentle, yet strong this man was. He could display such a wondrous prowess for things of nature and yet remain concerned and compassionate when it came to her feelings.

"What are you planning to do . . . I mean, will you work here for the rest of your life?" she asked without thinking.

Luke looked up, as if startled by her question. She thought

he almost looked embarrassed. "I've been saving some money. Guess I'm thinking it might be nice to buy a ranch somewhere."

Alex had never considered that Luke might actually have plans to leave. The thought distressed her, and yet hadn't she made her own plans for just such an escape? "I really love it here," Alex murmured, enjoying the quiet pleasure of their ride. "I'll hate to leave because of the beauty, but I'll happily go if it means never having to see my father again."

"Don't hate him, Alex. He's wrong, no doubt about it, but don't hate him. That will just eat away at your spirit. Remember what you used to tell me when you first started talking to me about God?"

Alex smiled. She remembered the angry cowboy from four years earlier. Luke Toland seemed mad at the world, but especially at God. "I told you what my mother always told me. 'Whoever angers you, owns you.' "

"That's right. You don't want your father to own you, now, do you?" He smiled and the warmth of it spread throughout Alex in an unexpected way.

"No, I don't want anything from that man."

"Just be a good daughter and honor him as best you can," Luke suggested.

Alex felt bile rise in her throat. "I've tried to be obedient to him, but . . . well . . . there just came a time when I could no longer follow his instructions." She remembered the times her father would come to the Harvey House in Williams. He'd come with a friend or two, and they often expressed an interest in Alex. Her father seemed unconcerned about their lewd comments, sometimes even encouraged them.

Luke halted his horse and took hold of the mare's reins to stop Alex as well. "I don't know what he did or didn't do, but he doesn't have the power to do anything to you anymore. You're independent and free of his control. You gave up a lot—the comforts of home, money, your mother's company. He doesn't have to keep hurting you."

Alex met Luke's gaze. His eyes were a rich, deep hazel color that seemed to glitter green and gold when the sunlight touched them at just the right angle. "So long as he hurts my mother, he's hurting me. It doesn't matter that he speaks lewdly or suggestively when I'm in the company of his friends. It doesn't even matter that he thinks so little of me that he encourages his friends' actions toward me. It only matters that she goes on suffering and there's nothing I can do to make it any better. I wish he . . . were dead." Tears trickled down her cheek.

Luke drew a handkerchief from his pocket and handed it to Alex. "Don't let him own you like that, Alex. You'll never know a moment's peace if you do."

"I'm trying to pray through it," she admitted, wiping her face. She folded the cloth back into a neat little square and handed it back to Luke. Smiling, she apologized. "Forgive me. I seem to be so teary these days. I'll do my best not to do this again."

"Alex, we're friends, remember? If you can't cry on my shoulder, whose shoulder can you cry on?"

Alex felt a trembling course through her. She wanted to reach out and touch Luke's face—just to thank him, just to let him know how much he meant to her. Suddenly she felt very awkward. Her feelings were getting the best of her and, rather than let the conversation continue in this intimate vein, she straightened and took up her reins. She nudged the horse forward and didn't even bother to look back at Luke when she called over her shoulder, "I didn't know coconut cream pie was your favorite."

CHAPTER FIVE

Joel Harper knew the game of politics as well as he knew the exclusive brothels of Charleston. At age thirty-six, he easily recognized Rufus Keegan's interest as being one of a man obsessed. The man wanted power and glory. It was all right with him if Keegan wanted to tag along on the coattails of Winthrop's victory, but it wasn't all right if Keegan thought he was going to replace Joel as Winthrop's right-hand man. He was a man to be watched, Joel reasoned. Keegan could either be a dangerous adversary or a powerful ally. The question was, which would he be?

"The current administration has made a mess of things to say the least," Keegan stated in a critical manner. "Just look at the problems the attorney general has made over the German alien properties. Then there's that whole question of what's happening with the federal oil reserves."

"Yes, we're watching that one closely. It appears, if my spies are correct," Winston Winthrop offered, "Secretary of the Interior, Albert Fall, is headed for just that. A fall. The man has so many underhanded dealings, he doesn't know which is which. The conservationists hate him, which is precisely why Joel thought it would do the Democratic Party well to play that ticket to the hilt. We'll show the conservationists that we care about the federal land—that we're just as appalled as they are at what's been happening in Wyoming and California. We'll promote the national parks, supporting the idea of preserving the land for posterity."

"Are you certain this will matter enough to remove Harding from office? After all, he may not have any knowledge of what Fall's been up to," Keegan replied. "It will be most important to relate the two men together."

"More importantly," Joel interjected, "we relate Winthrop to Woodrow Wilson. They were old friends and saw eye to eye on most everything. We'll focus the attention of the country on the fact that Harding rejected Wilson's League of Nations, ensuring its failure. We'll remind them that Harding did this, not to mention other things . . . things that will not bode well in the south, where we have strong support."

Keegan eyed Joel intently. The idea of scandal seemed to ignite the man's excitement. "Things such as?"

Joel wasn't about to give away all of his strategies and secrets, so he drew on one of the plans that was well-known from the previous election. No doubt it would feed the older man just enough to whet his appetite. "Southern gentlemen do not take kindly to the idea of Negroes filling positions of importance—such as the presidency."

"I seem to recall that controversy," Keegan said, stroking his chin. "Someone issued statements that suggested the president was part Negro. But then there was some sort of proof offered to nix that idea, wasn't there? Wasn't the attorney general a part of that problem as well?"

Joel nodded. "Harry Daughtery was then Mr. Harding's campaign manager. He issued public statements declaring there was no truth to the rumor of Harding's questionable lineage."

"But you have proof to suggest otherwise?" Keegan questioned.

Joel smiled. "What need do we have of proof? If the issue is brought up at the appropriate moment, with the most damaging slant, it matters very little if we have to recant our words after the election. People will remember the problem from 1920. If given in the right manner, it will eat at them, wear away their trust in the administration. This, added to other issues of trust, will soon destroy their faith in Harding."

"Gentlemen, politics is a dirty little game," Winthrop drawled in a slow, southern manner. "I do despise the use of such tactics, but sometimes these things are necessary. After all, the end results are all that matter."

"Agreed," Keegan said, nodding enthusiastically.

Joel thought the man rather ridiculous and dull. He was no different than any of the other men of means who sought to better themselves by aligning their name to that of a powerful senator or governor. But Joel couldn't fault him too much. Joel himself had come into the game by the same means. His own father had long ago disowned him for his gambling and questionable behavior. When trouble came knocking, Joel had a penchant for not only opening the door, but for making it his bedfellow as well.

"You would dance with the devil himself," his father had declared on the night he'd sent Joel from the family home.

"Only if he let me lead," Joel had called back, acting for all the world as if this dismissal from his family meant nothing at all. However, it had meant more than he'd ever allowed his father to know. More than he ever would let anyone know.

Leaving his childhood home in 1913, Joel had quickly

learned the meaning of friendship, both assumed and real. He settled himself near Washington, D.C., and made fast friends with the politicians of the area. He cut back on his gambling, or rather, he became more selective with the places he frequented. Early on, Joel realized he needed money to maintain his pretense of a wealthy Virginia son. The scheme had paid off, and Winston Winthrop found him to be a kindred spirit. Hiring the intelligent, quick-learning Joel at the age of twenty-seven, Winthrop had made no secret of the fact that he considered Joel as a potential husband for his daughter, Valerie.

Joel saw this as the ultimate revenge against his father. The Winthrops were worth millions in old money, while the Harpers were new industrial money and didn't come anywhere near the same income association. Joel's father would never let the truth of their parting be known, so for all the rest of the world, it seemed Joel was simply an independent, headstrong young man, out to further the good of the family name. And that was just as Joel wanted it.

When the time was right, when everything was in its place and Joel was the one holding all the cards, he'd make his voice known. He let the world know exactly what had happened. Joel fully intended to return to his father one day, wealthy and powerful. And then he would crush the man, just as he'd crushed Joel on that night so long ago.

"Ah, Valerie has chosen to join us," Winthrop declared, bringing their attention to the young woman across the room.

As women went, Valerie was a beauty—there was no doubt about that. But to Joel she was cold and unfeeling. She knew her father intended them to wed, but she made her own demands in order to condition her cooperation. She wanted her freedom until she was twenty-five years old. Freedom to play the field, to travel, and to do what her socialite friends were doing. Joel was a patient man. He kept close to Winthrop, protecting him from unwanted attention, while biding his time for Valerie to turn twenty-five. Now his time of waiting was over—her birthday had been last month and the day marked his victory.

He watched her cross the room, working it as she came. She stopped to talk to the older women who commented or called to her as she passed. She presented a lovely picture of health and beauty in her cream-colored dress. Joel had no notion of who the designer had been, but his ability to tuck and mold a dress to Valerie's willowy frame was sheer genius. He loved it that she chose expensive clothes and jewels. He loved it because it told every other woman in the room how much she had to waste on babbles and gowns. In turn, those very jealous matrons would tell their husbands, and they would quickly realize how very powerful and wealthy the Winthrops truly were.

Still, there was something more to his feelings for Valerie than simply her ability to show off a pricey piece of fashion ware. He wouldn't say he loved her, but he loved her possessions, and that was close enough. Not only that, but she held great sway over her father. The senator listened to his daughter, trusting her instincts and wisdom. Joel needed her to be his ally at best, or at worst to be so afraid of him that she did as she was told. He'd be satisfied either way.

Valerie appeared oblivious to his study. Her bobbed brown-black hair gave her face a waiflike quality that suggested helplessness and innocence. But Joel knew she was neither helpless nor innocent. The men got to their feet as she approached the table.

"Daddy," she said, leaning close to kiss the old man, "I do

hope you didn't wait supper on account of me."

She smiled sweetly at Rufus Keegan and then turned her charms on Joel. "My, but don't you look handsome tonight, Mr. Harper." Her southern belle simper was perfect.

"Might I return the compliment, Val darling," he said with an emphatically possessive tone.

"We're soon to announce their engagement, don't you know," Winthrop told Keegan with great pride. "I've found Joel a most beneficial man to have in my corner, and now I'll make him family as well."

"Relatives can be dangerous to trust," Keegan said, taking his seat with the others. He eyed Joel with a serious expression. "Besides, I thought you had an eye for my daughter."

"We're very progressive, Mr. Keegan," Valerie said, batting her eyelashes coyly. "No sense in settling for one pair of shoes until you've tried several pairs."

Keegan grinned and leaned forward. "And even after you've bought the shoes, there's no sense in wearing the same old pair day in and day out, eh?"

"Exactly," she said as if to encourage him further.

Joel had seen the editorial cartoon with Keegan's likeness, and it was apparent he believed in having full range of the playing field. It seemed he thought this might extend to Valerie as well, but Joel had no intention of being made the fool at their table.

"Men make the rules and, therefore, men may break them," Joel said, looking to Valerie. As if to emphasize his point, he reached under the table and put his hand casually on her thigh. She did nothing but smile sweetly and look to Joel as if waiting for him to finish his thought.

Just then Chester Laird crossed the room to join them. He brought with him two men who were obviously reporters. One man held a camera, while the other pulled a pencil from behind his ear with one hand and notebook from his coat pocket with the other.

"Senator Winthrop, I want to introduce you to two good ol' boys. These men hail from Los Angeles. They're reporters. I thought perhaps we'd have some pictures taken and a story written up for the morning edition. How about it?"

"I'm always happy to speak with the press," Winthrop replied.

Joel watched as the experienced senator went into his routine. With the other men occupied, Joel took advantage of the moment to secure Valerie's attention. Squeezing her leg, he murmured, "Where have you been?"

"Miss me?" she asked, keeping up the appearance of complete joy.

"If I find out you've been playing the field with those stable hands, I won't be easy to deal with."

"You'll do exactly what I want you to do, or Daddy will find out about the money you've been stealing from his campaign fund."

Joel eyed her seriously and drew away. "Shall we take a walk while the press interviews your father?"

"Why not."

He got to his feet and helped her with her chair. Extending his arm, he waited until Valerie put her gloved hand in his before leading her out of the room.

"We'll be back in blink, Daddy," she called over her shoulder. Then, gritting her teeth, she said under her breath, "as soon as I can get rid of this headache."

"You may think of me as a headache now, but I assure you, if you ever so much as open that pretty little mouth of yours to speak out against me in any way, I'll make sure more than your head hurts."

"Threatening me—again? How innovative. How thoroughly original."

He pulled her through the lobby of the hotel and out onto the porch of El Tovar. Grateful to see the place void of visitors, Joel whirled Valerie around and pulled her into his arms. Kissing her without any feeling of love, he released her just as abruptly and smiled.

"Just the same, I mean what I say. Don't test me. Your father and I have discussed this. Our engagement will be announced the night he announces his candidacy for president. You will wear that silver number with the modest neckline and blush at the appropriate times and appear nothing but the loving and doting fiancée."

"I'm tired of the Poiret gown. I plan to wear my new Caret. It's red and has the most delightful draping. You do want me to be properly draped, don't you?"

"The silver gown is what I want and that's what you'll give me," he insisted.

"And if I don't, you'll beat me? Is that it? Not very good for politics, Joel dear."

"There are ways to make people suffer without ever laying a hand on them," Joel replied, his eyes narrowing.

"Don't I know it," Valerie answered snidely. "You make me suffer every moment of every day. If I had my way about it, I would expose your little games and put an end to this engagement."

"But then Daddy would find out about your less-than-chaste evenings in New York. And maybe he'd even learn about your little drinking problem."

"You wouldn't!" Valerie said, taking hold of Joel's arm.

"You wouldn't ruin his chance at the presidency."

"But telling him the truth about you wouldn't ruin his chances," Joel replied very softly. "There are a lot of parties and moments of public exposure. There are also a fair number of sanitariums in the northeast. I doubt they'd care much whether your gown was Poiret or Caret. If you want to keep this situation under control, you'll stop flirting with everything in pants and pay more attention to your devoted fiancé."

"Does that mean you'll give up chasing after the Keegan girl?" Valerie asked snidely. "After all, she appears quite disinterested in your amorous attention."

"I'll do as I please. I'm a man, and a man has a right to do whatever he likes." Joel pointed the way back toward the lobby. "I'll expect your cooperation and public affection."

"Expect whatever you like," Valerie said, seeming to have regained her confidence, "but I have just as much dirt on you as you have on me. You'd better rethink your plans, Mr. Harper. You aren't packing me off to a madhouse, so just get past that notion. I'm not as naïve as you play me to be. I can bite when you least expect it."

CHAPTER SIX

Alex secured a black bow tie at the V of her white collar. Having spilled soup on her uniform during the lunch cleanup, she was required to put on a clean uniform before going about her afternoon duties. Pulling the starched white apron on over her black uniform, she sighed. The outfit was hot and the day had grown quite warm. Someone told her the temperature was nearing eighty degrees. Luke mentioned they were due for a thunderstorm, but it couldn't be any worse than the storm that was brewing at the hotel.

For days now she had waited on the Winthrop group. She'd endured Mr. Harper's undesired attention, Miss Winthrop's snobbery, and her own father's deplorable comments. Still, she worked as best as she could, putting a smile on her face and praying fervently for a kindness she did not feel.

Without warning the door to her bedroom opened up, causing Alex to whirl on her heel. "Michaela!" she exclaimed at the sight of her old friend.

"Well, if you aren't a sight for sore eyes," Michaela responded in turn. The women embraced as if they were long lost sisters.

Alex didn't know when she'd been happier to see someone. Pulling away, she wiped tears from her eyes and exclaimed, "Oh, your hair!"

Michaela put her hand up to the short bob and gave it a pat. "Do you like it?"

"It's charming, but I would never have expected you, above all people, to cut your hair. Your black curls were the envy of everyone on staff."

Michaela shrugged and tossed her bags to the bed on the opposite side of the room. "I found New York living to be a bit more expensive than I had accounted for. I ended up selling my hair to put together enough traveling money to come back to the canyon. I wired headquarters, and they told me they were desperate to have me return, so here I am."

"I'm so glad," Alex replied. Nothing else could have made her feel quite the same way. "Oh, Michaela, things have been really bad here. My father has been up to his old tricks, my mother is suffering terribly, and I've been singled out by my father and his cronies to be their private Harvey waitress. It's just madness."

"Sounds like it." Michaela instantly began changing out of her street clothes. "I told Mrs. Godfrey I'd get started right away. She told me on your day off I could fill in with the Winthrop group."

"So you already know about them?"

Michaela nodded and tossed her pink dress over the back of a chair and went to the closet. "Mrs. Godfrey told me my uniforms are still here."

"We didn't have time to worry about what to do with them. Although," Alex admitted, "it seems like you've been gone forever."

Michaela quickly retrieved the needed garments. "Oh, I

wish we had cooler uniforms. Do you know there are places along the line where the girls wear colorful skirts and peasant blouses like the Mexican girls?"

"No, but how marvelous."

"Indeed. I think we should talk to the management and suggest we have a similar uniform. Wouldn't that be grand?"

Michaela chattered on and on as if she'd only been away a few hours instead of months. Alex felt the tension drain from her shoulders and neck as her friend entertained her with stories of her trip.

"I went to Niagara Falls," Michaela said as she pulled on her black cotton stockings. "What a place. You wouldn't believe it. It was simply marvelous. You have this lovely river that moves along quite rapidly. Pretty soon there are boulders and rocks and rapids, and then the water just seems to disappear from sight and there it goes! Over the rocks and down to the river below. It was incredible."

Alex laughed. "I can tell. You sound as though the trip did you a world of good. How is your family? Did you get a chance to visit with them in Boston?"

"We had a chance to argue and screech at each other," Michaela replied, tying her shoes. "That's as close to visiting as we get."

Alex knew from past discussions that Michaela's three older sisters, all married with children, had no understanding of their younger sister's desire to be footloose and fancy-free. Her father, an elder in the church, felt that his daughter was committing a terrible sin by heading west to become a Harvey Girl. For years, the family hadn't even spoken to Michaela. Only during the last year and a half had they finally come around to being civil.

"Don't get me wrong," Michaela said, standing up ready

for work, "I'm glad we had some time together. I got to see my nieces and nephews, and my mother was actually quite interested in what I do here and what the canyon looked like."

"That's a real change," Alex commented.

"But I'm ready to get back in the saddle, so to speak," her friend replied. "I'm glad you didn't rent out the room."

Alex laughed. She'd told Mrs. Godfrey from the very start of Michaela's vacation that she hated the idea of rooming with anyone else. Mrs. Godfrey had been good to put the replacement girls elsewhere. It had worked out that Alex had kept the room to herself, a sort of perk for being Mrs. Godfrey's top waitress.

"No one else would want to room with me," Alex said laughing. "That's the only reason the room is empty."

"I can bet there's one poor cowboy who'd like to share your room," Michaela teased.

"What are you talking about?"

"Luke Toland," Michaela replied. "He's been sweet on you for years. Is he still here?"

"Yes, he's still here, but we're just good friends. You know that."

Michaela shrugged and headed out the door. "You may be just good friends, but I'm thinking Luke would like to be more than friends."

Alex shook her head and pulled the door closed behind her. "If Luke felt that way, he'd just tell me."

Harvey Girls always had more chores than just serving the customers, and one of the chores Alex enjoyed the most was polishing the silver. She usually found a quiet corner and went to work without interruption. Here, she could take time to think through her problems and spend time in prayer.

Rubbing the cloth against a large silver serving tray, Alex tried not to be overcome by her father's infidelity and her mother's misery. She couldn't fix this problem or make it go away, and knowing that made it all that much harder to deal with.

"You look lonely."

Alex looked up in annoyance. Joel Harper had sought her out in her moment of solitude.

"I assure you, I'm not," she answered with a smile.

"Miss Keegan, I get the distinct impression that you're avoiding me."

"How could that be, Mr. Harper? I'm in your company each and every day."

"Yes, but you won't come away with me so that I might get to know you better."

Alex put down the polishing cloth momentarily. "I'm sure my father has told you all about me. Let that suffice. Now, if you'll excuse me . . ."

"But I can't do that," Joel said, reaching out to take hold of her gloved hand. "Come walk with me."

"Now I'm the one who must refuse. I have duties to perform and in a few short hours I will be serving your party in the private dining room. So you see, there is no time for such distractions."

Joel eyed her seriously for a moment, then let go of her. "I'm sorry for the way your father has treated you."

Alex wasn't expecting this change of topic. She wasn't about to let Joel Harper quiz her on the intimate details of her life. "I'm sorry about it too." She took up the polishing cloth and went back to work on the tray.

"I know he's hurt you greatly." His voice was smooth and low; his manner was all charm and concern.

"It's not my feelings I'm concerned with, Mr. Harper. It's my mother." Alex didn't know why she'd shared that bit of information. Now the man would no doubt take her comment as an invitation to discuss the matter more thoroughly.

"I've been concerned for her—the senator has too. In fact, he had me wire her a dozen roses with his compliments."

"How kind."

"You say that like you don't believe me."

Alex sighed. "I believe you, Mr. Harper. I simply do not trust you, nor do I care."

"How can you be so heartless and cold? Your father told me you fancied yourself a Christian woman."

Guilty as charged, Alex thought. "Mr. Harper . . ."

"Please call me Joel."

"That would be inappropriate. You are a guest in this hotel and I am a staff member. I would be reprimanded by my superiors if I were to call you by your first name."

"I won't tell a soul," Joel teased.

"Mr. Harper, I'm sorry that my demeanor appears heartless and cold. I hold certain values dear, and among those are my beliefs in Christianity. My father, however, does not hold such beliefs and in fact mocks me at every turn. To trust someone in his company is difficult, especially when you've proven that your values are no different than his."

"How so?" he asked, moving closer.

Alex turned the tray over to continue her work. "You are engaged to Miss Winthrop, are you not? Yet you pursue me. How is that?"

"Val and I are very progressive. Surely you've noticed the turn of the world toward more liberty and freedom between men and women. It's no longer the 1800s, Miss Keegan. We needn't surround ourselves with outdated values and restrictions. Women have the vote and may make their choices. Val is exercising her rights, as am I. We may be promised to each other, but it doesn't mean we can't entertain ourselves for the moment."

"So you want to entertain yourself with me? Is that it?" Alex asked.

"Of course. You're a beautiful woman with an amazing charm. I'd find it a sheer delight to spend time with you. And I believe you'd feel the same in regard to me."

Alex finished polishing the tray and got to her feet. Clutching the heavy silver close, she shook her head. "I find you rather despicable and quite undesirable. You are no different than my father or any other man, for that matter."

Joel stood and reached out to take hold of Alex. The action surprised her—so much so that she froze in place.

"You don't know me well enough to call me undesirable. I think once you've tasted of my charms, you'll be glad for my company." Without warning he pulled her against him in a steel-like embrace. He held her head tight and kissed her hard. As he attempted to deepen the kiss, Alex dropped the silver tray on his highly polished shoes.

Joel let out a yell as he jumped away from Alex. "You did that on purpose."

Alex narrowed her eyes. "Just as you did. I would advise you to never attempt that again. I don't appreciate being manhandled, and I certainly have no interest in a man who would force himself upon a woman."

She took that moment to hurry away, barely stopping long enough to retrieve the tray. She hoped the heavy silver had broken his foot.

Joel watched Alexandria Keegan flee his presence, even as fiery pain shot up his leg. "Devil woman!" he muttered.

Limping out of the hotel, Joel glanced at his watch. He'd nearly let the time get away from him. He had a meeting in less than ten minutes.

Hurrying down the path as best he could, Joel pushed Alex from his mind. He'd deal with her later, for now he had plans to arrange. There was nothing and no one he would let come between himself and success. Right now his success depended on seeing Winston Winthrop in the White House.

Spying his man ahead, Joel slowed his pace. The man pushed his hat back and nodded as Joel approached.

"What's the news?"

"He's going to be heading to San Francisco and plans to stay at the Palace Hotel. I have a friend who works there. I can get in . . . no problem."

"Good," Joel said, trying to organize his thoughts. "The sooner we eliminate the competition, the better."

"It shouldn't be all that hard. I'll send you a wire when it's done."

"No! No further contact." Joel reached into his coat, glancing around him as he did. "Drop your hat."

"What?"

"Just do it. Drop your hat on the ground and I'll pick it up."

The man did as Joel instructed and watched in confusion as Joel bent to retrieve it. "This is the second third of your payment. The last third will be wired to your account upon my hearing the news. The papers will cover it, and that will let me know without any threat of our being discovered. There can be nothing—understand me—nothing that links us together."

The man nodded. "I know that."

Joel slipped the envelope into the hat and handed the hat back to him. "If I need you again, I'll know where to find you."

The man slipped the envelope from the hat and into his pocket. "Yeah, sure. I'll be around."

Joel watched him walk away as if bored with the entire affair. Hired assassins always seemed so easily distracted when killing wasn't the actual focus of their actions.

Glancing back toward El Tovar, Joel smiled. With any luck at all, he'd have Winthrop at the forefront of the race for president by the end of the week. And with that accomplished, he could turn his attention to more pleasurable things.

Alex's image came to mind. Perhaps he'd handled her all wrong. Perhaps there was another way to get to her. She'd obviously do anything for her mother. Maybe that was the way to a woman's heart.

Alex ignored Joel's knowing glances as she served braised duck on fine china. Risotto and buttered asparagus rounded out the entrée, and the aroma was simply heaven. Alex worried her stomach's rumblings of protest could be heard as she worked the room. She hadn't eaten supper after her upsetting scene with Joel Harper and now she regretted her decision.

The minutes ticked by amidst discussions of Washington, D.C.'s political arena. Alex listened as her father made suggestions for how he might benefit the senator. It was disgusting the way he played the room.

"I can offer a great deal to the right man," her father

droned on. "I have resources to benefit the party, that will in turn benefit me."

Alex saw the men nod knowingly as if her father had spoken some great truth.

Valerie Winthrop, dressed in a gown of silver and blue, was the only female, other than Alex, present. Alex had a feeling this was probably the way things usually were laid out, whether at the Grand Canyon or elsewhere. Miss Winthrop liked being the belle of the ball and tonight was no exception. She wore her bobbed hair slicked back under a headband of rhinestones. At least Alex presumed they were rhinestones. For all she knew, they could be real jewels. Miss Winthrop certainly wore an abundance of those, as well. Tonight her throat dripped with diamonds and emeralds and her ears were sparkling with smaller settings of the same. The glittering of her rhinestone-encrusted spaghetti straps and neckline reflected with the other stones off the highly polished paneling of the private dining room.

The room was said to have been a favorite of Teddy Roosevelt. Like other Harvey dining rooms, the furnishings were elaborate and expensive. The table, set for six this evening, could be extended to seat twelve. The fine Irish linens, glistening crystal, and polished silver would have pleased even the most discriminating taste. Even so, Valerie Winthrop appeared unimpressed.

Alex began her routine of collecting the empty plates. She thought of the extra money she was making by working exclusively with the Winthrops and wondered if it was really worth the effort. Inevitably she had to see her father on a regular basis, as well as endure Joel Harper's attention, so it seemed the money was rather hard earned.

"Bring clean glasses," her father instructed, "we're going to have a drink."

Alex said nothing but quickly retrieved six wine goblets. As she began placing them in front of each person, her father popped the cork on what appeared to be some kind of alcohol.

"No prohibition here," Joel said, rubbing his hands together. "That's the first thing we get changed when you're in the White House, Senator."

"These are wine glasses," Valerie said, holding hers up to Alex. "We're drinking champagne."

"I'm sorry, but . . ."

"There are fine, Val dear," Joel interceded with a wink. "They're bigger, after all."

Everyone laughed with exception to Alex. She longed only to be rid of the entire bunch. It wasn't that they were the first ones to imbibe in spite of alcohol being illegal, but they clearly held little regard for any rules or laws. She'd heard the lawyers who sat on either side of Senator Winthrop advise him on ways to skirt the regulations and rules of politics. She'd heard Joel agree to underhanded plans that would disgrace the opposition. Her own father had agreed to do whatever he could to discredit the senator's rivals.

They were just starting to toast their plans when Alex turned to exit the room. She would serve their desserts and coffee and hopefully leave them to discuss their futures.

"Wait, Miss Keegan," Joel said, reaching out to stop her retreat. "Share a toast with us. We're drinking to the senator's health and future."

"I don't drink champagne," she said matter-of-factly. Her father eyed her with contempt.

"Surely you can drink one small glass," Joel encouraged.

"Of course she can," her father joined in. "If she knows what's good for her."

Alex caught the meaning of his words, but stood her ground. "Senator Winthrop, I pray you will have great health and happiness."

The older man smiled. "Why, thank you, Miss Keegan," he drawled. "I know you are a woman of prayer, given your father's descriptions. I will expect that prayer to be offered up."

Alex shifted the tray of dishes. "You can count on it, sir." She cast one last glance at her father, who appeared rather confused by the exchange, before leaving the room. Pausing just outside the dining room, Alex took a deep breath and prayed.

Thank you, Lord. Thank you for getting me out of there.

"We really aren't that bad of a bunch, you know," Joel said, following her out of the room.

Alex turned with the dishes and gave Harper what she hoped was a disinterested stare. "Did you need something?"

"I need a moonlight stroll on the rim with the prettiest girl in Arizona . . . I need you."

Alex backed up a step. "I have no interest in helping you out, Mr. Harper. Now, I must go and prepare your desserts."

"I could make you happy, Miss Keegan. If you'll just give me a chance."

"I am happy. I don't need you or any other man to help me along that path."

Joel stepped forward, backing Alex against the wall. He reached out and took the tray from her hands. "I have no desire to see this dropped on my feet."

"Then mind your distance," Alex said, hurrying down the hall the moment Joel turned to put the tray on a nearby chair.

"You can't escape me," he called after her. "I'm used to getting what I want."

CHAPTER SEVEN

Luke was in no mood for the Winthrop party's nonsense. He'd been hired to take them by mule to the bottom of the canyon for an overnight stay at Phantom Ranch. Like other groups of visitors to the canyon, the Winthrop party heard of the tourist attraction and wanted to experience it. At least Joel Harper and Valerie Winthrop wanted to experience it. The stocky senator and Rufus Keegan declined, declaring no desire to spend their day aback a mule.

As best as Luke could tell, a constant gathering of supporters for the senator's presidential campaign had been pouring in throughout the week, and it was a collection of those men and women who took his time and attention now.

Luke gave his routine speech cautioning the riders of the arduous task ahead of them. "There are places," he warned, "where the narrowness of the path allows no room for error. The mules know their jobs and heed my commands. I'll expect no less from you."

A few of the party nodded solemnly, but Joel Harper chuckled and Valerie Winthrop merely batted her eyes in a flirting manner.

"The mules are generally good-natured with our guests,"

Luke stated, bringing his speech to a close, "but if you'll take a look at Clancy Franklin here, you'll understand that they can be dangerous." Clancy smiled broadly for the group while Luke continued. "About a month ago, Clancy's favorite mule gave him a swift kick in the face. The blow could have killed a lesser man—but Clancy here is hardheaded." Some of the group laughed. Luke shook his head and slapped Clancy on the back. "Clancy just lost a tooth and had his nose broke. Unless you want to follow his example, I'd suggest you do exactly as you're instructed."

With that, Luke ordered his crew to assist the travelers to their mounts. He gave a cautious glance to the entire group, for Alex had implied there had been difficulties with the Winthrop party, and Luke took that very seriously. She told him that Joel Harper pinched her backside, and then last night she'd mentioned ever so casually that Joel had been demanding her attention and seeking her for private walks. Clancy had been among the group when Alex shared her woes. He'd laughed and said that someone as pretty as Alex should expect that kind of thing. The group had teased Clancy about being sweet on Alex, and the blond-haired man had blushed a fiery red.

Luke tried not to give it a second thought, for Clancy didn't seem like competition for Alex's affections. And Alex had never implied or mentioned an interest in Clancy. Luke figured that if she had thoughts in that direction, she would have enlisted Luke's help. No, Luke was more worried about Joel Harper. He worried that there was more to this than Alex was saying. He could tell she'd been greatly disturbed by the entire matter. It wasn't like her to get her nose out of joint over a little attention, but since her father was tied to the group, Luke put it off to her distaste of Rufus Keegan. After all, she'd shared with him often enough for Luke to know that Keegan was the low-life type of scum who would sell his daughter out to the highest bidder.

He gripped the reins hard and realized his attention wasn't focused where it needed to be. His mule was sure-footed and knew the trail well, but Luke knew the folly in brooding or daydreaming over Alex. He needed to keep his attention fixed to the path ahead.

"Let's head out," he called and signaled the trip to begin.

At their first rest stop, Luke waited until the entire group had stretched and gotten a drink from their canteens before giving them a bit of canyon history.

"We left temperatures of around eighty-two degrees up on the rim," Luke began. "We'll find the canyon floor to be as hot as one hundred ten degrees, and that's why it's important to keep drinking."

"Drinking is always important, eh, Val?" Harper teased.

"I meant water," Luke threw out sarcastically. The group laughed, with exception to Joel. Valerie grinned and left Joel's side to come to Luke.

"Please ignore him, Mr. Toland, he can be a bit of a bore." She lowered her head just a bit. Looking up at him with huge green eyes, she smiled prettily and batted her lashes.

Luke ignored her and continued to speak to the group. "You'll see for yourself as we descend, the canyon is a series of layers. With each layer you'll see a good many changes. The canyon is a blend of limestone to sandstone to shale and so on. The plant life changes with the layers, as does the animal population. On the rim you might have seen gambel oaks, piñon, sagebrush, and juniper. As we head down into the canyon, this is going to change, and you'll see more yucca and mesquite, and down by the river you'll even have cottonwood and desert willow."

Luke loved the canyon for its variety and beauty. He loved to share the information he'd learned in his years at the Grand Canyon, but he could also read a group of tourists like a book. This book was clearly bored with the information. They were city folk who were used to fast-paced lives and non-stop entertainment. Asking them to slow down to the point of recognizing the differences between sagebrush and snake-weed was expecting too much.

Valerie Winthrop took hold of his arm. "So what's the ranch like?"

Luke nodded and tried to disentangle himself from her hold, but Valerie would have none of that. Giving up so as not to make a scene, Luke looked to the group.

"Phantom Ranch is a real treat. It's going to be as welcome a sight as your own home, especially after a day on mule back. We'll have a good meal for you and cabins for your comfort. The night ends up being pretty short, given how tired you're going to feel."

"Oh, surely you cowboys don't get tired," Valerie whispered.

Luke looked to her and nodded. "Even cowboys get tired, Miss Winthrop."

The rest of the trip was much the same. Luke found that anytime he stopped the group to rest, Valerie was right beside him. Harper scowled from a distance, as if trying to assess the threat and deciding what needed to be done.

"You simply must come to New York sometime," Valerie insisted. "Have you ever been there?"

"No. I've never been there."

"Then you don't know what you're missing," she gushed.

Luke continued checking the cinches on the mules. "I thought you were from South Carolina."

"I am, but I prefer the fun to be had in New York. The parties there are so incredible—why, you'd positively think you'd died and gone to heaven. And this nonsense of prohibiting liquor is hardly a bother at all. In fact, it can be quite exciting. Sometimes the police come and we all scramble like madmen out the secret passages. They have false fronts for the bar and everything. It's truly marvelous—you'd love it."

Luke looked up and studied her for a moment. "I don't think you know me well enough to know what I might love or detest. Because of this, I have to tell you you're very wrong. I wouldn't love it. I detest drinking—and drunks."

The look on Valerie's face suggested complete and utter surprise. Having finally rendered her speechless, Luke took the opportunity to move away from her to talk to Clancy.

"Well, my dear, you don't seem to be making much progress with our cowboy leader," Joel said snidely. "Good thing, too, as I specifically remember telling you to leave his type alone."

Valerie turned to meet Joel's gaze. "I'll do as I please. I don't need you telling me what to do or offering unsolicited advice."

"The only advice I've come to give is to remind you that I'll not brook this nonsense any longer. Your father agrees with me. You're much too flighty and out of control. We've been discussing your possible liability to his campaign."

"I beg your pardon?" Valerie was stunned. How could this man make her so completely miserable and still expect her to feel passion for their union?

"You heard me," Joel said, taking hold of her. He led her

away from the others, tightening his grip on her arm as he did. "Don't cause a scene with Toland," Joel continued. "If you do, you'll be sorry."

"I couldn't be more sorry than I am now," Valerie snapped.

"That's where you're wrong."

"You wouldn't risk everything you have with Daddy." She worked hard to keep her voice steady, for Joel absolutely terrified her, especially after she heard of how he had beat up a Washington prostitute. Her father's secretary had told her all the gory details, ending the tirade by telling Valerie it wasn't the first time Joel had committed such an act. She worried that it would be only a matter of time until he tried the same heavy-handed manner with her. She'd tried to talk to her father about the situation, but he'd assured her that Harper was harmless.

"Let him take out his aggressions elsewhere," her father had said, which was maddening and very much unlike her father.

That was when Valerie had begun to dig for as much dirt on Joel Harper as she could possibly find. She'd learned a little about his past, although his present was much easier to figure. Either way, she'd use it all to threaten his future.

"You don't know what I'll risk and what I won't. But I'm telling you here and now: Stay away from the men. You need to start appearing the docile little darling that everyone needs you to be. That means no more booze, no more wild parties, and no more men."

"Time to mount up," Luke called.

Valerie walked toward the group with Joel on her heel. "We haven't concluded our discussion on this matter," he whispered. "We'll talk about this more tonight."

"I have plans tonight," Valerie said with a candied sweetness she didn't feel. "They don't include you."

She hurried away from him without giving him so much as a backward glance. Once she was ready to tell Joel everything she knew about him and put her cards on the table, so to speak, he'd back away quick enough. There was no way he'd want to marry a woman who could put him in prison. Or worse yet, see him get the electric chair.

Luke finished caring for the mules and yawned. He was glad they'd made it to the canyon floor without any mishaps. Given Miss Winthrop's interest in him, Luke had feared she might well endanger them both. She insisted on being next to him whenever possible, boring him with her tales of New York or other big cities. She clearly had designs on him, but for what purpose, Luke wasn't entirely sure. He'd thought midway through the day that her actions were nothing more than a scheme to make Harper jealous, but that didn't appear to be the case.

The crisp chill of the night air revived Luke momentarily, but it only served to remind him of his dilemma. He loved his life in the canyon, but he longed for something more—to make a life with Alex, to own his own land, and support his family working for himself. Luke looked upward to the heavens. The sky seemed a million miles away down here.

Lord, I don't know what to do with my life. I want to be a credit to you, but there are a lot of things that I don't understand. He thought of Alex and her mother. He wouldn't mind having Mrs. Keegan move in with him after he and Alex married. She was a good woman—kind, considerate, even tempered. Still, it wasn't the most perfect way to think of starting married life.

If taking Mrs. Keegan into his home was the price for getting Alex as a wife, Luke knew he'd gladly pay it. The only problem was convincing Alex they were right for each other.

Deciding to call it a night, Luke headed back to the cabin he'd share with Clancy. It was smaller and less fashionable than the tourist cabins, but it was a roof over their heads. What he really wanted was a hot bath, but he figured that would have to wait until he was back on the rim.

Phantom Ranch had been designed by Mary Colter at the request of the Harvey Company. The company had been bringing tourists to the canyon floor for years, but they needed proper accommodations for overnight stays. Miss Colter had seen to that. Luke had honestly never met a feistier woman than Mary Elizabeth Jane Colter. The woman had more energy than six grown men and worked with details like an artist might when creating a painting. And in some ways, that's exactly what she'd done. She'd created an artist's rendering of a canyon ranch, with a large native-stone building and smaller cabins. There was a wonderful dining hall where folks could share a meal and their tales of the trail. There was even a recreational hall for those who still had energy to spend after the ride down. The cabins were designed with two beds, a desk and chair, and a fireplace. The finishing touch on the cabin was a large Indian rug on the floor in front of the fireplace. It was simple, yet stately, in a rustic fashion.

Mary Colter had been very particular about her design, as she was with anything she put her hand to. Luke had to admire that. He admired even more that she'd made the journey down on mule back for the opening celebration the previous year. At the age of fifty-three, Miss Colter had maintained a grace and dignity that many women half her age failed to show. Nevertheless, if she found any flaw with her creation, she was scathing and ruthless until the matter was resolved to the satisfaction of her perfectionist nature.

Yawning again, Luke opened the door to his cabin and found that someone, probably Clancy, had started a fire. The days could feel like a furnace on the floor of the canyon, but nights were chilly, often cold. Flames danced on the logs in the fireplace, warming the room and bathing it in a cheery glow. Luke fully expected to see Clancy sound asleep in his bed, but he wasn't there. In fact, the bed hadn't been touched.

Tossing his hat onto the peg behind the door, Luke stretched and went to where a pitcher of water and a bowl awaited him on a small stand. He took up a washcloth, poured a bit of water into the bowl, and began to strip away the dust of the day. Bending over the bowl, he poured more water atop his head and scrubbed momentarily to free his hair of the dust and sweat. He finished washing, stripping off his shirt and neckerchief. He rinsed out the neckerchief, but merely shook out the shirt and hung it over the back of the chair. The Harvey Company expected their employees to be well groomed, no matter the setting.

Sitting on his bed, Luke pulled off his boots and stretched his toes. He couldn't decide whether to wash out his socks in the already dirty water or just let them go. It wasn't like anyone was going to see them.

"It'll keep," he told the room and reached down to move his boots to the end of the bed. Standing, Luke had just started to unbuckle his belt when he froze in motion at the sound of a woman's scream.

The first scream sounded like a cross between laughter and hysteria. The second scream, however, flooded his cabin as a scantily gowned Valerie Winthrop burst into his room as if the devil himself were after her.

[illegible]

Sitting on his bed, [illegible] pulled off his [illegible] and [illegible] his toes. [illegible]

[illegible]

CHAPTER EIGHT

Alex knew a deep sense of satisfaction at the end of her workday. With Joel Harper and Valerie Winthrop off on an expedition to the bottom of the canyon, she had been reprieved from dealing with the party. Her father had taken the remains of their group, including the senator, into Williams for a night of entertainment. Whatever that meant. Alex found herself simply thankful to have them gone from the canyon.

Relieved of her Winthrop duties, Alex was able to work the dining room and spend more time with Michaela. Throughout the evening, they crossed paths, making comments and laughing at situations that seemed comical. Table five had a psychic who, by tasting everyone's food, could tell them in turn whether there was good fortune or bad in their future. It also saved the psychic from having to buy a meal. Table three had a honeymooning couple who seemed to hardly notice the food on their plates. Alex found it very amusing when she asked the husband if he'd like dessert and he made eyes at his wife and said he already had the sweetest confection in the world.

Surprisingly energized and happy when her shift was

over, Alex made her way to her room and peeled the hot uniform from her body. She chose a simple day dress of light blue cotton for the uniform's replacement. The dress was well-worn, although not embarrassingly so. Alex was reluctant to spend money on clothes. "I live most of my day in uniform anyway," she told her reflection as she studied the dress for any unacceptable signs of wear.

The outfit passed scrutiny, although Alex noticed that the white piping around the neckline and elbow-length sleeves had dulled considerably over the years. She wondered if she might be able to take a toothbrush and bluing to the material and lighten it.

Forgetting about her clothing for the time, Alex changed shoes and stockings and decided an evening stroll was in order. The evening was settling into a pleasantly cool temperature with barely a glow of sun still available to see by. She liked this time of night and wished Luke might be around to walk with her to discuss the events of the day and share thoughts on the days to come. The days when Luke led the two-day, overnight tours down to Phantom Ranch were her loneliest. Of course, now that Michaela was back things wouldn't seem quite so lonely.

Alex moved through the lobby, smiling at the visitors, eavesdropping on their comments. So many people marveled at the canyon's beauty. The very wealthy always seemed to come in two brands—those who had started with nothing and those who were born with everything. Those who had made their own way to financial security often seemed to care more about the things around them. They seemed to remember their origins and respected life. Those born to wealth often didn't appreciate what they had or the beauty around them. Of course, there were exceptions in each group.

People from both walks often told her that coming here had made them feel closer to God. Alex knew what they meant. She had fallen in love with the place from the first moment she'd set her gaze upon the multicolored landscape. But she'd also found a deeper commune with God as she spent days walking alone, along well-defined paths. She thought of verses in the Bible where it was noted that Jesus withdrew to lonely places. And even with its throngs of visitors, the canyon bore a certain loneliness to it.

Taking the short hike to Mary Colter's Lookout, Alex was relieved to see the place void of visitors. Most everyone had gone back to El Tovar to prepare for the next day.

With its rustic fireplace alcove and art room, the Lookout was a popular gathering place. The place had been designed to provide the viewer a good place to take photographs or make sketches of the canyon below. There were several levels for viewing, giving the visitor the best vantage for sight-seeing. There were even high-powered telescopes atop this scenic overlook that allowed the visitor to look out in more detail across the wide expanse. Alex had tried the telescopes a few times but didn't like the view as much as watching the scene with the naked eye. She could take in more sights and enjoy the play of the light and shadows—something that seemed greatly inhibited by the telescope.

Heading down the path to the lower viewing station, Alex relished the quiet and took advantage of the moment to pray. *I don't know what the answers are for the future, Lord. Sometimes the answers seem almost clear—as if I can make out the truth through a veil. But the meaning is just shrouded enough that I can neither move forward nor back. What am I to do?*

The wind picked up, moaning slightly through the trees and rock. Alex thought of Luke. He'd once taken her, along with several other Harvey Girls and employees, to the canyon floor on a mule ride. They'd had enormous amounts of fun, but Alex had enjoyed the walk she and Luke had taken that evening even more than the adventurous ride to Phantom Ranch.

As they wandered ancient paths, Luke had told her of Indian legends and folklore. How the Havasupai Indians believed the center of the world was the San Francisco Peaks, just north of Flagstaff. They believed the first people lived near a pool of water under the ground. They also had a flood story, not unlike the Bible's account of Noah and the ark.

Alex found the stories fascinating. She found Luke even more intriguing. She'd never had a male friend before. Men were liabilities in her life, and she'd never sought after their affections. Luke just seemed to sort of appear in her life and remain.

Funny, she thought, *I don't think there's anything in his nature that puts me ill at ease. If I were to seek a husband, I would want him to be just like Luke Toland.* The thought startled her. What was this nonsense about a husband? She wasn't usually given to such whimsy—why now?

"Yoo-hoo! Alex!"

Alex looked back up the rocky path. There was hardly any light to see by, save a bit of a glow from the interior of the Lookout, but Alex recognized Bernice's voice as she called, "May I join you?"

Alex smiled. "Sure, come ahead."

Bernice still wore her Harvey uniform, the white apron bearing telltale signs of dinner. "I saw you head this way and . . . well. . . ."

"Is there a problem?" Alex questioned.

"No, not really. Well, maybe. Your father is looking for

you. I thought maybe I'd better warn you."

Alex felt her entire body tense. So much for a restful night. "I thought he was spending the night in Williams. Did he say what he wanted?"

Bernice came down the trail, her red hair bobbing in the breeze. "No, he didn't say anything much at all. Just wanted to know where you were and demanded that we find you and tell you that he wanted to speak with you. Said he'd be on the north porch for an hour or so."

"Too bad," Alex muttered. "He can be there all night for all I care."

"I didn't mean to cause you pain," Bernice replied. "I only hoped to help you avoid confrontation. I thought if you knew where he was, you could keep away from that place."

Alex had lost all joy in the evening. To the west, storm clouds flickered with hints of lightning. She wondered if it would rain or simply be a dry thunderstorm. Sighing, she shook her head. "I'll not walk on eggshells just because of my father."

The wind picked up, moaning again through the rock and trees. Bernice startled at the sound. "Isn't that just awful?"

Alex lifted her head to catch the sound. "I kind of like it myself. Luke says that on the canyon floor the wind and the river make music almost like a calliope. I've never really heard it myself, but I don't travel to the bottom all the time like he does."

Bernice nodded and eyed the western skies. "Looks like we're in for a rain."

"This is our wettest month. This and August. Keeps the cycle of life going, I'm sure. I suppose we'd better head back. This thing could roll in rather quickly and we'd be drenched."

They started back up the rock-walled path to the lighted walkway above. Chattering about the day and nothing in particular, Alex realized she liked Bernice's gentle, sweet spirit. The girl was only eighteen, but with a huge family at home, she'd had to grow up quickly.

"The tips have been so much better than I could have imagined," Bernice said, beaming. "I've managed to send several dollars home to my folks, and tonight I made at least four dollars!"

"Yes, the patrons are usually quite generous," Alex agreed.

"Oh, dear," Bernice said, her voice lowering.

Alex looked to her as they came to the top of the rim walk. "What's wrong? Are you ill?"

Bernice shook her head. "It's your father. He sees you and he's coming this way."

Alex looked up the lighted path toward El Tovar. Sure enough, there he was. Striding in his anger, Rufus Keegan looked to be a man with something on his mind. Alex shivered.

"I'll stay with you," Bernice promised.

"No, I can handle him. You don't need to be in the middle of this."

Bernice looked thoughtfully at Alex. "But if I'm here, he might hold his tongue."

Alex laughed bitterly. "You don't know my father very well. He doesn't hold his tongue for anyone."

"Alexandria!"

Alex said nothing and refused to move. *Let him come to me if he needs to talk so badly.*

Rufus was slightly out of breath as he joined the two women. "I'd have a word with you—alone."

"I'll be going now, Miss Keegan," Bernice said in a voice barely above a whisper. "Unless you want me to stay."

"She does not. Be gone with you, girl," Alex's father said without giving Alex a chance to speak for herself.

"Yes, Bernice, just as I told you a few seconds ago, you needn't stay."

Her father looked miffed that she should interject her own authority in the matter, but he said nothing.

Bernice hesitantly took off in the direction of El Tovar, glancing back over her shoulder as if to make certain Rufus Keegan wouldn't rise up as some legendary monster and eat Alex alive. Alex waited until Bernice was well up the path before she turned her gaze upon her father. She knew her expression couldn't help but reveal the anger she felt inside, still she tried to keep her temper under control. "What do you want? Why aren't you in Williams, living the good life?"

Keegan leaned closer. "I'm not here to answer your questions. I'm here to give you an order. Play the game in a more cooperative manner, or pay the price."

"I'm sure I don't understand."

"And I'm just as certain you do." He leaned in closer. "You're going out of your way to embarrass me in front of the Winthrops, and I'll not have it."

"Me? Embarrass you?" She laughed and moved to walk away. "That's a bit like the pot calling the kettle black." She held up her hand. "And please don't further degrade yourself by making a pretense that you don't know what I'm talking about."

"I know all about the wrongs you suppose I've done you," her father replied, keeping pace with her for a ways. "What's happened is my business, not that of my daughter. A man does not give life to a child only to be ordered about and condemned by that same child twenty-four years later."

"I'm surprised you even know my age. The knowledge certainly doesn't come from your devoted presence in my life."

Her father reached out and stopped her. "Don't meddle in this, Alexandria. You cannot hope to win. I, on the other hand, am very good at bucking the odds. I will have my appointment in Washington with the Winthrop administration. I will have the prestige and fame accorded me."

"Wear laurels in your hair for all I care," Alex said stepping away from her father's touch. "Have your fame and glory, but leave Mother and me alone."

"You have no right to order me around. I'm here to tell you that, from now on, if anyone in the Winthrop party so much as asks you to jump—you jump."

Alex could take no more. "Why do you do this? Why not divorce my mother and let us go about our lives in an orderly and pleasant fashion? You don't need either one of us. We have no political ties to anyone and therefore merit very little of your attention. A divorce would be the simple solution."

"That's how much you know," Keegan replied, his face reddening as if he'd reached the limits of his patience.

Alex didn't care. Let him rant and rage.

"I'll never divorce her," he said flatly. "Your mother is my property and my responsibility. She'll stay at my side when I want her there and remain at home when I do not."

"But a divorce would give you the freedom—"

"No divorce!" He reached out again as if to take hold of her shoulders, but Alex was too quick for him. Shrugging, he repeated. "No divorce."

"What if mother divorces you?"

"She wouldn't dare. I'd never allow her to bring such a scandal upon us."

"Her? Bring scandal? What about you? What about 'Keegan Chooses Wrong Mount'? Everyone from here to the capital knows what you're doing and with whom. I hardly see Mother seeking a divorce to be much of a scandal."

"If you encourage her to try such a thing, I'll see that both of you suffer."

"What do you suppose we're doing now?" Alex questioned. "Do you realize I don't remember a time when I felt you truly loved me? Do you have any idea what it's like to grow up seeing other children share close relationships with their fathers, knowing you will never have the same thing?"

"Spare me your sob stories. Great men of power seldom have time for such nonsense."

"But that's the truly funny part," Alex countered. "You are neither a great man, nor a man of power. You fancy that because your bank account shows a tidy sum that you have somehow earned the respect and honor of your fellow citizens, but it isn't so. You're the laughingstock of this resort. The only reason you're even allowed here is that your money spends as well as the next man's. You were the laughingstock of Williams and probably still are, and the only reason anyone tolerates your antics is the fact that you have money, along with their insane love for a juicy piece of gossip."

"Enough! I won't be talked to in this manner. You need to remember what I've said. You may not care for the harm I cause you, but I think you'll agree that your mother is hardly strong enough to endure my wrath should I find it necessary to punish you through her."

"You had better not hurt her."

"That, my dear, will be entirely up to you," he said, sounding as though he'd regained his composure.

Alex realized the impasse. There was no way to deal with

this now. She would simply have to make her plans and steal her mother away when her father least expected it.

"Do you understand me?"

"Yes. I understand you perfectly," Alex replied. She met his dark gaze and feared for her mother's life. Would he go so far as to kill her?

"Good. There will be no divorce. Not now—nor ever."

CHAPTER NINE

Wearing nothing but a thin satin nightgown, Valerie Winthrop threw herself into Luke's cabin, screaming as she entered.

Luke stared at her in surprise, not having a clue about what to say or do.

"There's something out there," she said, backing against the wall. "I heard it. It was chasing me."

Luke went to the open door and looked out. The wind blew gently, while thunder rumbled in the distance. "I don't see anything."

He looked back to Valerie and shook his head as if to confirm it. "There's nothing out there."

"I know something or someone was out there. I could hear them saying my name—low and mournful." She rubbed her bare upper arms, the action causing the deep cut of her neckline to reveal more cleavage. She batted her lashes and pouted. "Don't send me back out there."

Luke shook his head and reached for his shirt. "I'll go check things out." He'd barely pulled the shirt on when Valerie threw herself against him. Her momentum nearly sent Luke off-balance, causing him to reach involuntarily out to

Valerie. As he grasped hold of her, she tightened her grip on him as well.

"Don't leave me," she whispered. "I'm afraid." She looked up into his face, appearing absolutely terror stricken.

"I'm sure it's all right," Luke said, trying to put her away from him as he regained his stance.

Valerie would have no part of his action and tightened her hold on him. "No! I know what I heard."

"Then someone's just playing a game with you."

Forcing her away from him, Luke pushed her back toward the bed. Pulling on his boots, he said, "Stay here and I'll go scout things out."

He headed out of the cabin, uncertain of what to do once he confirmed the safety of the area. Thunder sounded overhead. Luke wondered if they'd have rain and if that rain would make the trip back to the rim more difficult.

Seeing and hearing nothing out of the ordinary, Luke walked back to the cabin, buttoning his shirt as he went. He didn't have time to tuck it back into his jeans before he reentered the cabin to find Valerie stretched out across his bed.

Striking a seductive pose she said, "Did you chase away the boogeyman?"

"I saw no evidence that he was out there. Now come on, I'll walk you back to your place."

"Why not let me stay here with you? I won't be missed. Besides, you have two beds," she said. Then giggling she added, "But this one looks big enough for both of us."

Luke was starting to feel angry. "Ma'am, I haven't the least bit of interest in accommodating you."

"You don't like me?"

"Frankly, no." Luke motioned to the door. "Come on."

"Why don't you like me?"

"I've never cared for fast women."

"I'm not fast," she said, laughing. "I'm just purposeful. When I see something I like, I go after it."

"Well, I don't care for that kind of woman either."

"Is there someone else? Is that what this is really about? Do you have a sweetheart?"

"I wouldn't exactly say that," Luke responded, not even sure why he was bothering.

"There is someone!" Valerie sat up in the middle of the bed. "What's her name?"

"None of your business. Now get out of my bed, and let me walk you back to your cabin."

"Not until you tell me her name."

Luke had taken all he was going to take. Marching to the bed, he lifted Valerie from the mattress and set her on the floor. Again her grip on him was almost painful.

"Don't be mad at me. You and I could have a great time together. I know it."

Just then, Clancy walked through the open door. "Hey, why's the door . . ." He paused, taking in the sight.

"Miss Winthrop was sure that something was chasing her," Luke said, forcing her once again away from him. "Would you walk her back to her cabin, Clancy?"

Clancy eyed the barely clothed Valerie and then turned his gaze to Luke again. There were a dozen unspoken questions in his expression, but thankfully he didn't vocalize a single one.

"Sure thing, boss."

Luke breathed a sigh of relief, but it was short-lived. Valerie Winthrop was not a happy woman. She'd been scorned and denied, and as a rich socialite, she was probably not used to either one.

She frowned at him, her eyes narrowing as her brows came together ever so slightly. "This isn't settled between us," she whispered.

"Yes, it is," Luke replied. "Keep your distance. I don't have time for these games, and I'll not allow you to put the party in jeopardy tomorrow when we make our ascent. Keep that in mind. At the first sign of trouble, I'll separate you from the group and have Clancy escort you alone."

Valerie grew hateful then. "I can't tell you how much you've offended me. All I wanted was a little fun in this hideous place. You've made a terrible mistake."

"The error is on your part, Miss Winthrop. Good night." He hoped his firm tone would assure her of his purpose. Turning away from her, he went to the far side of the room and pretended to busy himself with poking up the fire.

"Come on, Miss Winthrop. I'll see to it that you get back safe and sound."

Luke heard Clancy's gentle tone and hoped that Valerie wouldn't take out her anger on him. Clancy was a sweet, gentle-natured fellow—Luke hated the thought of Miss Winthrop sinking her claws in him.

It wasn't until Luke heard the door close behind them that he stood and replaced the fire poker. He looked at the closed door for a long time. Why in the world had she singled him out? With the exception of two other women, both older and both obviously married, Miss Winthrop was the only female in their group. She was the obvious interest of the dozen or more men who had joined their party into the canyon.

"So why come after me?" he questioned aloud. He pulled off his shirt and draped it back over the chair. Sitting on the edge of the bed, his gaze still fixed on the door as if Valerie

Winthrop might somehow rematerialize, Luke pulled off his boots and shook his head. "Why?"

Clancy returned about that time and Luke couldn't help but feel a wash of embarrassment over the episode. Clancy looked at him, as if awaiting an explanation. Luke shrugged. "She just burst in here unannounced and threw herself at me. I'm telling you, I've never seen anything like it."

Clancy smiled. "She smells good, I've got to give her that." He closed the door and walked to his own side of the room. "She isn't very happy with you."

"I don't care," Luke said, standing to take off his jeans. He thought better of it and decided to sleep with them on. Just because Clancy was here didn't mean she might not sneak back, and if that happened, Luke intended to be at least partially clothed.

"She was crying and telling me that nobody cared about her," Clancy said, tossing his hat to a hook. "I felt sorry for her."

"Don't," Luke said angrily. "She has an entire entourage of men who would be more than happy to entertain and care for her. She's just playing games with me. The problem is, I don't know why."

"Maybe she has some kind of bet with that Mr. Harper character. They seem a strange bunch. Someone said she's engaged to Harper. If that's the case, why is she here with you?"

"Exactly," Luke said in complete exasperation. He trusted Clancy not to make a big deal out of the situation, but he felt he needed to say something. "Clancy, I'd appreciate it if you'd keep what happened here tonight just between us."

"Sure, boss."

"I don't need my reputation ruined."

"Some of the guys wouldn't see it that way," Clancy said, smiling. "They'd see you as quite the man."

"Yes, but I worry more about the truth of the matter and what God thinks." Luke sat down on the bed and rubbed his chin. "I know God knows what happened here tonight, but a Christian needs to work to be above reproach."

"What's that mean—reproach?"

"Disgrace—shame—blame. It means you live your life in such a fashion that no one can hold you accountable for things you didn't do. You keep out of situations that even look like they might be a problem."

"Like before prohibition," Clancy said, "when the guys wanted you to go to the bar in Williams. They'd tease you and say you didn't have to drink whiskey or beer."

"Exactly. I could go sit in the bar and drink nothing but water—be completely innocent—but someone might see me and believe the worst. I wouldn't be guilty of drinking, but I sure would be guilty of giving someone reason to believe falsely of me."

"But you can't be held to account for what people think," Clancy said. "Surely God doesn't expect that. I mean, you can't very well control other people's lives—especially their thoughts."

Clancy eyed him seriously, as if his words were just too incredible to believe. Luke realized that Clancy had never taken much interest in talk of the Christian walk, prior to this. Luke was aware that what he said now might very well send Clancy away from God or draw him closer. He whispered a prayer for the right words.

"You can't control other people's lives or thoughts—but you can control your own," Luke replied. "Self-control is an important part of living a Christian life. But you don't have to do it on your own. God gives you a lot of help along the way. When you're tempted to do the wrong thing, go the wrong direction, He's there for you. Just like tonight."

"How so, boss?"

"I wasn't tempted to do anything wrong with Miss Winthrop, but if I had been, this would have been a bad situation for me. It would have been hard to resist a barely clothed woman who obviously was looking for a good time. But my heart was fixed on doing the right thing. It was fixed that way because I turned my desires over to God a long time ago. Since then, I've been praying and reading the Bible, and I know a little better everyday what I should and shouldn't let myself get into."

Clancy pulled off his boots and nodded. "So because you were thinking about God, you weren't thinking about what Miss Winthrop had to offer?"

"That's partially it. It's because of my relationship with God that I also respect the people in my life. I try to treat each person as I would want to be treated—with respect and kindness. It doesn't always come out that way. I have a mean streak, as you well know."

Clancy laughed. "I've seen it a time or two."

"Well, I try to control that as well. See, a man who can control his tongue can control just about anything else. And what a man says comes up out of his heart. The Bible says so."

"I ain't never heard this religion stuff put quite this way. It makes a heap more sense than what I've known in the past."

"That's because I don't care much for religion myself. I care about God and what He wants for my life. Religions can just cause a man grief. They scatter him in all sorts of directions looking for answers to one thing and then another."

Luke walked over to his saddlebag and pulled out his Bible. "This is what counts, Clancy. The Bible has all the answers we'll ever need. It's all laid out in here."

Clancy scratched his chest and looked rather embarrassed. "I don't . . . well . . . I don't have one of those. Never saw the need, so I ain't never bought me one."

"Then have this one," Luke said, bringing the Bible to his friend. "But let me share just one passage with you first."

"Sure," Clancy said, looking at the book as though Luke were offering him gold.

Luke turned to the third chapter of John. "See here, this is Jesus talking to a man named Nicodemus—he was a ruler of the Jewish people. He tells Nicodemus, 'For God so loved the world, that he gave his only begotten Son, that whosoever believeth in him should not perish, but have everlasting life.' "

"Everlasting life? You mean, you never die?"

"Your body dies eventually—everybody's does. But when you accept Jesus as your Savior—when you believe on Him and repent of your sins—you're given eternal life for your spirit. When your body dies, your spirit will live on with Jesus in heaven."

"Seems simple enough," Clancy said, looking at the words for himself. "Is there more I have to do?"

"There are things we do out of obedience and respect to God—baptism and service, tithing and fellowship—but first and foremost, we accept that Jesus is the Son of God and we accept that He died for us sinners so that we wouldn't have to face death alone. We repent of our sins and work to never repeat our old ways. It's a new life, Clancy."

"Them are powerful words, Luke," Clancy said, looking up with an expression that suggested awe. "So what do I have to do to repent? I mean, how do I know if I did something that God considers a sin?"

"God knows your heart, Clancy. If you tell Him you're sorry for the past wrongs you've committed—if you ask Him to forgive you and to come into your heart, He will. He'll help you to understand what's right and wrong in His sight. You'll learn it by reading the Bible and you'll see, too, the deep love He has for you."

"I just talk to Him—like I'm talking to you?"

"Just so. Most folks like to bow their heads and close their eyes, but you can pray with your eyes wide open sitting atop a mule. You can pray in your sickbed and pray over dinner. It doesn't matter where you pray, it's just important that you do pray."

Clancy took the Bible in his hands and nodded. "I'd like to pray. I've been real impressed with the way you handle yourself, Luke. And like tonight, I knew in my heart you'd done no wrong with that woman. I knew it 'cause of the way you live your life the rest of the time."

"I only live my life that way because God gives me the strength to do so. I'm nothing special on my own, Clancy, but with God, nothing's impossible. He gives me the strength I need for everything."

"Then I want that too. I know you wouldn't steer me wrong."

"It's not me doing the steering, Clancy. It's God."

Clancy nodded. "That's good enough for me."

Luke smiled and slapped Clancy on the back in a hearty manner. "Then let's get down to business."

CHAPTER TEN

"So they're planning all these parties," Michaela told a group of gathered wranglers and Harvey Girls. "I've even heard it said that reporters are coming in from as far as Washington, D.C., to watch these rich ninnies fall all over themselves to see who'll be most favored to get the Democratic nomination for president."

"This is just the start. I heard they are all headed on to Los Angeles after this, and then New York," someone else threw in.

"It's all a lot of fuss for nothing, if you ask me," Luke said, eyeing Alex as she joined the little group.

"Didn't look like you minded the fuss too much last night," one of Luke's crew said snidely. "I saw that Miss Winthrop over at your cabin. Didn't look like she was fussin' much about being fully clothed. Was she campaigning?" Laughter rose up from some of Luke's crew.

"Bet she got the boss's vote for sure."

Luke had never suspected that anyone else might have seen Valerie's visit. He knew he had a confidant in Clancy, but he'd never thought to ward off this topic with the others. Looking up, he caught Alex looking at him with an expression of disbelief and betrayal. Her cheeks reddened as she realized he'd caught her watching him. She walked away from the group and headed up to the hotel without another word.

"That's not a good way to keep friends, Luke," Michaela offered without condemnation. "Come on, Bernice, we'd better get to work."

Clancy came to Luke's rescue, but not in time to help him with Alex. "Miss Winthrop got herself spooked. I took her back to her cabin. That's all that was about."

Everyone looked to Luke as if for confirmation, but all he could think of was Alex. Now she no doubt figured he'd been having some kind of clandestine arrangement with Miss Winthrop.

"Never you mind, Luke," a redheaded crew member spoke up. "There's something about the canyon that just makes women throw themselves at men."

As if to prove his point, Bernice tripped over her feet and fell into Clancy's lap. Everyone laughed in amusement at the situation. Everyone but Luke.

"If that don't beat all," Clancy murmured, helping to right Bernice. Her face turned a deep crimson, but she smiled and thanked Clancy before taking her seat in silence.

"Getting back to the parties," another Harvey Girl picked up, "I heard it said there will be a big to-do every night. The Winthrops are spending a wagonload of money on the affair. They've hired the Harvey Company to put on their best show. That means we'll be working overtime, but we'll be well compensated."

"Well, I heard . . ."

Luke only listened halfheartedly as the comments droned on about the coming events. He knew if he'd gotten up to go after Alex, everyone would have had something to say about it. As it was, it seemed wise to stay in his seat and try to catch a moment to talk to her when they could be alone.

I'm innocent here, Lord, he prayed. *I don't know why things like this have to happen to interfere in a guy's life. Alex has a hard enough time with men, and now this. It just doesn't seem fair.* He glanced across the table to where the others still carried on about the upcoming events. *Help me, Lord. Help me to find a time and place to talk to Alex. Just a quiet moment to explain.*

That moment, however, didn't come until hours later. Luke had just returned from taking a group of visitors on a rim-side trail when he spotted Alex polishing silver. She sat quietly in the most isolated corner of the room, completely lost in her thoughts

"Looks like you're gonna wear a hole in the coffeepot," he said as he came up from behind her.

Alex looked up and nodded. "It's a good task for taking out aggressions."

"And would those aggressions have anything to do with what you overheard this morning?" Alex's cheeks reddened, but she said nothing. Luke pulled off his hat and sat down at the table.

"Look, Alex, nothing happened. Miss Winthrop showed up at my cabin screaming her head off about something or someone being outside following her. She was just spooked and . . ."

"Honestly, Luke, you don't owe me an explanation. I may be naïve about some things, but I know how it is when men and women find each other attractive."

No, you don't, or you'd see how I feel about you, Luke thought to himself. He shook off the thought and instead said, "I may not owe you an explanation, but I'd like to give you one. I don't want you thinking badly of me."

Alex finally met his gaze, and Luke warmed at the sight of her turquoise blue eyes. She pierced his heart, however, with her next statement. "I don't think anything about it at all," she said. "I've seen how it can be for men, especially when a woman throws herself at them. I don't approve, and I never will, but it isn't my business or my concern how you choose to entertain yourself."

"But that's just it!" Now he was getting mad. "I wasn't entertaining myself with anything or anyone. She just burst into my cabin claiming something was after her. I checked it out and then . . ." he paused, not entirely sure how much he wanted to say.

Alex looked at him suspiciously, watching and waiting for how he would conclude the statement.

"She wanted me to let her stay, but I said no. I'm not interested in her. She threw herself at me, but I refused to be persuaded. Clancy came in about that time and I asked him to take her home. The good news in all of this is that when Clancy came back, we talked and Clancy accepted Christ as his savior."

Alex smiled ever so slightly. "That is good news."

"Especially since you're the one who helped put me back on the straight and narrow. If you hadn't given me a reason to believe again, I wouldn't have been able to share the Bible with Clancy."

"I didn't give you a reason to believe—God did that."

"Well, you let Him use you as the messenger. When I think of how much I'd hardened my heart against Him after my ma died, well, I know it wasn't easy to get through to me. I blamed God for taking her away, never thinking about the consequences of distancing myself from Him. You changed that for me. You let me see the truth."

"I just try to live out my faith," Alex said, looking embarrassed. She turned her attention back on the pot.

"Alex, I don't want you thinking poorly of me."

"I don't. If you want a . . . friendship with Miss Winthrop, you have my blessing. I promise to be civil about it. It won't affect our friendship."

"Haven't you heard a word I've said?" Luke asked, getting to his feet. He took up his hat and shook his head in anger. "I don't want a friendship with Miss Winthrop. I don't care about her. I care about . . ."

Alex looked up, waiting for him to finish his confession.

"Oh, just forget it."

He stormed out of the room to keep from saying something out of anger that he'd only regret later. He wanted to tell Alex how he felt, but if he told her in the middle of this mess, she might think he was only saying the words to get her mind off of Valerie Winthrop. Why was it his timing was always off?

Crossing the lawn, Luke stalked down the rim path, not at all certain where he was headed.

"Oh, Mr. Toland! Luke!" Valerie Winthrop called to him from where she strolled at her father's side. "Do come meet my father."

Luke felt like bolting and running in the opposite direction. Instead, he knew he needed to be amiable with the guests.

"Miss Winthrop," Luke said, tipping his hat.

"Daddy, this is Luke Toland. He was the man who led the mule trip yesterday. He's worked here for about ten years. Isn't that right, Luke?"

Luke nodded and shook the senator's hand.

"So what do you think of this park, Mr. Toland?" the senator questioned. "My daughter finds it dull and lifeless."

"Oh, Daddy, that wasn't very nice to say."

"Maybe not, but it was the truth."

Luke wanted to put an end to the conversation as quickly as he could. "I love it. The canyon is home to me. There's a great deal of peace and serenity here."

"Maybe that's why Valerie doesn't like it," Senator Winthrop replied. "She's never cared much for peace and quiet. Even as a child she enjoyed the more rambunctious games of the neighborhood boys. Could never understand why a young lady would prefer the company of ruffian boys. Still, this park is decent enough. She ought to be able to find something that catches her attention."

Valerie laughed and nudged her father. "Now, don't be boring Mr. Toland with stories about me. He knows so very much about this park that I'm sure he could really tell you a thing or two."

"I rather you tell me what your political view of the day might be." The senator appeared capable of changing subjects as fast as Clancy could change a saddle. He eyed Luke critically, as if the next words out of Luke's mouth might make or break his political career.

Luke shrugged. The conversation wasn't one he wanted to get into. "I can't say that I have a political view."

"Nonsense. We men all have views of the situation around us. This park you love so much was an act of government."

"No, sir, I beg to differ with you. This park was an act of God. The government might have set it aside as a national park, but God put it together."

"Of course, boy, but what about those groups who want to

come and destroy this fine place? The Harding administration would just as soon drill her for oil as to not."

"I put my concerns in God's hands," Luke told Mr. Winthrop. "Then I don't have to worry about it, and I can get a whole lot more done with the time I might have spent in worry."

"Sounds like you're burying your head in the sand."

"Maybe, but at least I earn my money instead of begging or demanding it, and I don't trade it for favors. Say what you will, but I see your kind of life as a real bondage."

"Yes, I'm sure your kind of folk would."

Luke felt his anger stirred. "What is that supposed to mean?"

"A lowly cowboy such as yourself can't have much interest in the things of educated men. I'm sure most of it goes way beyond your comprehension." The senator hooked his thumbs in his vest pocket and rested his hands against his portly belly. Striking such a pose, he continued. "The common man doesn't always realize that he suffers because of the decisions other people are making for him. A president should take into account that the common man most likely doesn't know what he wants or needs. In turn, the right president would choose for such people and help them to better understand their needs."

"I understand my needs fully," Luke replied, barely speaking through clenched teeth.

"But you can't. Not really. For instance, you probably believe prohibition is a good thing. Prohibition is supposed to sober the country and bring back morality and sobriety. Instead, more people than ever before are drinking. And do you know why, Mr. Toland? Poor management of this country. It's a sad and depressing event."

"Now, Daddy, there's no need to get yourself all worked up. You'll be able to make speeches later."

"Yes, I really must excuse myself. I have work to do," Luke said with as much graciousness as he could muster. He tipped his hat ever so slightly, then turned to hurry across the grounds toward the stables.

"But, Luke, we had hoped you'd join us for dinner," Valerie called.

Luke just kept going.

First Alex, and now this Winthrop character. Life at the canyon wasn't nearly the pleasant respite Luke had once found it to be. When had things gotten so crazy?

I don't have to stay. The thought came from the darker recesses of his brain. That had always been the plan. Come to the canyon, make enough money, then buy a place of his own. But he wanted to share that place with Alex, and now she thought he was just as bad as her father. Oh, she hadn't said it, but he could tell by the look in her eyes.

"She thinks I'm a no-good womanizer," Luke muttered, coming to the stable yards. He opened the gate and moved into the corral, determined to get some work done before the day was completely lost.

"She thinks I'm of such low moral character that I'd forsake my faith and fall into the arms of some city-bred flirt." He kicked at the dirt, startling the mules. Mindless of what he was doing, Luke managed to spook one of the newest recruits—a thin-faced mule with a bit of a temper.

To prove his attitude would brook little nonsense from the likes of Luke, the mule reared forward and kicked out with his hind legs.

Luke had no time to respond. He took the full blow in his left wrist, and he felt the bone snap almost instantly. Knocked backward, Luke quickly regained his footing, clutching his arm in desperate pain.

"Oh, all the stupid . . . lousy . . . things."

"Luke! You okay?" Clancy called, coming from the barn.

"I think this no good mule just broke my wrist," Luke said, gingerly feeling his forearm and hand. "Yeah, I'm sure that's what he did. Hurts like nothing I've ever had before."

"Let's get you to the doc," Clancy said, moving between Luke and the new mule. "Here," he added, taking the oversized bandana from around his neck. "Let's make you a sling."

Luke winced as Clancy maneuvered the bandana around the arm. The pain, so intense, shot up his arm and spread throughout his body. He felt sick to his stomach and lightheaded.

"Boss, don't you go passin' out on me," Clancy said, reaching out to steady Luke.

"I won't mean it if I do," Luke said, fighting the pain. "Just keep me walking—get me to the doc and I'll be fine."

"Sure. I can see that for myself. You look like you're ready to lead another group of riders to Phantom Ranch."

"I'll be all right," Luke said, biting his tongue to keep from screaming out in pain.

By this time some of the other members of his crew showed up. They watched Clancy and Luke with a curiosity that made Luke uneasy. He wasn't a sideshow at the county fair.

"Get back to work you all. Can't a man break his arm without half the state turning out to see what's going on?"

The collection of men murmured responses among themselves, but Luke couldn't hear what they were saying. It was just as well. He needed to focus his attention on keeping his feet moving down the path. He needed to keep his mind off the pain in his arm . . . and in his heart.

CHAPTER ELEVEN

"Alex!" Bernice came running into the kitchen, sliding on the still-wet floor. The boy who'd just mopped the area scowled and muttered something inaudible.

Alex looked up from the salads she'd been arranging and smiled at Bernice's enthusiasm. "What is it, Bernice? You look as if the circus has come to town."

"It's Mr. Toland!"

Alex gave Bernice her full attention, noting the look of worry in Bernice's expression. "What's happened?"

"He got kicked by a mule. He's over at the doctor's, but I heard one of his men say he's broken his arm."

"Here, take care of these salads," Alex said, not caring that it was strictly against the rules to leave her station without permission. She raced out the door and made her way to the infirmary. Visions of Clancy's broken nose and bruised face came to mind. She felt her chest tighten with worry. *Oh, God, please let him be all right.*

The doctor had finished casting Luke's wrist and hand by the time Alex arrived. A small collection of people was waiting as Luke emerged from the back room. "Well, I'm going to live," he told Clancy. He looked past Clancy and noticed Alex. He smiled.

"What happened, Luke?" Alex asked, coming from behind Clancy. "I just got here and didn't have time to ask."

Luke's brow furrowed. "I wasn't keeping my mind on my work. I backed right into one of the new mules and the crazy thing kicked me. Clancy was right there and got me up here to the doctor. I'm going to be fine. Just a few weeks in a cast and I'll be as good as new."

"No horses or mules, however," the doctor said, coming up behind Luke. "You'll need to rest for a few days and take it easy. It was a clean enough break, but there's no sense in taking chances. You'll not be able to ride for a while."

Alex saw Luke wince at that statement. Luke had grown up in a saddle. She knew riding was an important part of his life. "We'll take good care of him," she promised the doctor, taking Luke in hand. "Come on. We'll get you back to your cabin and settle you in. Then I'll get your supper and see that you have what you need for the night."

Luke grinned. "Like a mother hen, eh?"

"This is serious business, Luke," Alex chided. She didn't care how it looked or sounded to anyone else. She cared too much for Luke to let someone else take charge of him.

They walked quietly back to Luke's cabin on the far side of the stables. Alex worried about the pain he must be feeling, all the while wondering at her own feelings, which seemed much too protective and deep for mere friendship. "Does it hurt?"

"Yeah, you could say that." Now that they were alone, Luke wasn't trying to sound like his normal cheerful self.

She stumbled slightly on the uneven ground. Luke reached out to steady her, sending electrical charges up her arm and straight to the heart. She saw him grimace, however, and couldn't bear that he was hurt. Not Luke. Strong, virile, capable Luke. Why couldn't it have happened to someone else? "Did the doctor give you anything to take for the pain?"

"Yeah, but it only helps a little. He said it should stop hurting in a day or two."

"I'm really sorry," Alex said, as if somehow this had all been her fault.

"You don't need to be sorry. It was my own fool inattentiveness that brought this on. I've told my crew a thousand times, if I've told them once, you can't be daydreaming or stewing over other things while you're working with the animals. Now I'll be in this cast for six weeks, and it's going to wreak havoc with my job."

"You're in charge. Your men can get the heavy work done and you can do all the paper work and set things up for the guests. You'll see; it won't be so bad. Maybe Clancy would even let us borrow his car from time to time and we could get you out away from the hotel."

"I can't very well drive like this," he grumbled.

"Well, then I can drive us," Alex said. "It can't be that hard to learn."

Luke laughed out loud, causing Alex to halt in mid-step. "What?" she questioned as he continued to laugh. "You don't think I can learn to drive? Is that it?"

"I just don't want the rest of me broken up," Luke said, managing to contain his mirth.

"You got yourself broken up all on your own," Alex reminded him. "I have yet to break a single thing you own."

Luke sobered at this and turned away. Alex thought his attitude very strange, but said nothing. No doubt the pain and the medication given him by the doctor was enough to alter his mood.

Approaching his cabin, Luke climbed the porch steps, opened the door, and stepped inside. Alex marched in right behind him. She knew her actions would cause eyebrows to rise and tongues to wag, but she didn't care. Luke was her best friend and he needed her. *That's what friends are for,* she told herself. *They bear all things and endure all things.* Funny, that sounded vaguely familiar. Somewhere in the back of her mind she was certain she'd heard those phrases before.

She looked around the simple three-room cabin. There was a living area with a fireplace and two small windows. Luke had a worn-out sofa that Alex thought she recognized from having been in the hotel at one time. There was a desk and chair in the corner. Stacks of papers and ledgers were neatly arranged on the desktop—the organization of it surprised Alex.

On the opposite wall from the front door was another door that Alex presumed went to the bedroom or the bath. "Where's your room?"

Luke pointed to the door, and Alex nodded and asked matter-of-factly, "And the bath?"

Luke grinned. "We're already pressing propriety here. I don't think the Harvey Company would find it at all acceptable for you to see to my cleaning up."

"I wasn't suggesting that at all," Alex replied, feeling her cheeks grow hot. "I merely wanted to know where everything was. The doctor wants you to rest. I wanted to help by making the place as conducive to your recovery as possible. If I need to move things around to make it easier for you, then I have to know where everything is to begin with."

Luke yawned and Alex wondered if the medicine was making him sleepy. "I think I will lie down for a time," he said, rubbing the upper portion of his left forearm.

"I think that would be wise. I need to get back to my shift. I'll bring supper in an hour or two."

"You'll be taking care of the Winthrops tonight, won't you?"

Alex nodded. "I suppose so."

Luke seemed less than pleased with the news. "That's going to keep you longer than an hour or two, won't it?"

"I'll just do what I can to hurry them along. They love their politics," Alex said, moving to take Luke's hat from him. "Do you need help with your boots?"

"I hadn't even thought of that. Yeah, I suppose I do."

Alex motioned him to the bedroom. "Go ahead and sit down on the bed. I'll help you get them off."

Luke did as he was told, and Alex followed him into the simple bedroom. She was surprised that this rough and rugged cowboy could be such an orderly person. The bed was made, the nightstand was clear of clutter. Without a word, Alex turned down the bed for Luke, then pointed to his boots.

Luke cradled his arm and sat down on the edge of the bed. He lifted first one foot and then the other, while Alex wrestled the boots from his feet and placed them beside the nightstand. "Do you need anything else before I go?"

"No, I'm fine. I'll look forward to seeing you tonight. Might be wise to bring someone along with you. Wouldn't look good to have you visiting my cabin like this on a regular basis."

"I don't care what other people think. They already believe the worst about my family anyway."

"Yes, but they don't believe the worst about you," Luke replied. "I don't want your reputation damaged on account of me. You heard the sport they made of me over what Miss

Winthrop did. I don't want them making sport of you too."

Alex appreciated his concern. "I see what you mean. I'll do what I can. Maybe Bernice will walk with me."

Luke nodded. "Now go on back to work. I'll be just fine. Clancy is going to check in on me."

Alex was surprised at her reluctance to leave. She cared about Luke's condition and hated to think of him needing something and being unable to get to it. But it wasn't as if his legs were broken. She sighed and headed back to the hotel.

The next couple of days passed rather quickly, and as word of Luke's injury spread, he found himself pampered and spoiled in a way that he'd never have imagined. The hotel management offered him a room at the hotel, in spite of their huge influx of guests, but Luke preferred the cabin and declined the offer. Next, they suggested he allow them to bring meals to him at the cabin rather than him having to come to the hotel. This, Luke thought perfectly acceptable—especially if Alex was the one doing the delivery. Unfortunately, it wasn't always Alex. Still, she came as often as anyone else, and it always afforded them a few minutes of conversation. Sometimes she would even massage his neck and shoulders, easing the tension caused by the weight of the cast on his arm.

Clancy was a good man, hardworking and dependable, and seemed to be able to keep good enough order with the men and the tourists. Luke knew that, if and when the day came that Clancy was put in charge, he would make a good leader. The thought gave Luke a certain peace. Especially when he thought about buying a ranch of his own and leaving the Grand Canyon.

And that was the biggest trouble with being laid up. Luke had entirely too much time to think. He thought about the ranch he'd like to own. He thought about the kind of house he'd like to build. He even thought of how he'd like his wedding to be, and all of those thoughts brought him back to Alex. He was determined to talk to her as soon as she showed up with his lunch. He knew she wouldn't have much time, but then, he didn't need much time to explain his heart.

A knock on the door brought Luke to attention. That was probably her now. A little early, but nevertheless, it was a good time to talk. He threw open the door, but instead of Alex, he found Valerie Winthrop.

"Why, Mr. Toland, I nearly died when I heard what had happened."

Luke didn't know what to say. He felt so completely taken aback at her appearance that he could only shrug. Valerie seemed not to notice, however, and continued her conversation without difficulty.

"I told Daddy I was coming down here to see how you were. You positively must let us take care of you. We have an entire wing of rooms at the hotel and you would heal much faster there than here."

"Why do you suppose that?"

"Well, because I could take perfect care of you," she said, nearly purring the words. In fact, she rather reminded Luke of a cat in her white dress and formfitting bonnet. The hat was white with strips of black that stuck out away from the hat at strange intervals—almost like ears. "Well, aren't you going to ask me in?"

Luke cleared his voice and refused to move from the door. "I don't think that would be appropriate, Miss Winthrop."

"Please, call me Valerie. After all, if I'm to take care of you—"

"But you aren't," Luke affirmed. "I'm doing just fine by myself. I have good friends who come and see to my needs. It wouldn't be right for a guest to be a part of that."

"But I want to be a part of it. You're very special to me." She looked heavenward and put her gloved left hand over her heart. "When I heard what had happened, I just knew this was the fates bringing us to a more intimate relationship."

"Miss Winthrop, I'm not sure where you got the idea from me that such a thing was of interest, but I assure you it's not. I would rather you not come back here, if you don't mind."

Valerie frowned. "You're obviously still distraught from the accident. Maybe I'll come back later."

Luke heard the chatter of approaching visitors. It was no doubt Alex and maybe Michaela or Bernice. Alex was good to bring someone with her, just as he'd suggested. They always sat outside, away from the porch to afford Alex and Luke some privacy, while at the same time acting as chaperone.

Luke figured Miss Winthrop would have no choice but to leave now. "They're bringing me my lunch," he said, motioning toward the two approaching women.

Valerie leaned closer to Luke. "I could just as easily do that job."

"You have a campaign to help run and an election that will come up entirely sooner than you expect. Why not just go on back?"

Valerie leaned even closer, making Luke very uncomfortable. "I could make you very happy. I'm a rich woman and I have friends in high places."

"I doubt they're as high as my friend—God. He's the only one I need."

Valerie leaned forward and kissed him hard on the mouth. "I need you," she whispered. Her breath smelled of mint and whiskey. "Couldn't you reconsider?"

Luke pulled away from her but not before Alex noticed what was going on. He saw her cheerful countenance change in the blink of an eye. Valerie made no further scene, except for the kiss she blew back toward Luke when she was halfway up the path.

Uncertain what to say, Luke said nothing at all. What could he say? Alex had seen it all.

Bernice held back while Alex brought the tray. "I've brought your lunch," she said in a rather curt tone.

"Smells good. I'm nigh on to starving."

Alex said nothing. She put the tray on the porch table and turned to leave.

"Wait. Sit for a minute, I have something to say."

Alex looked extremely uncomfortable. In fact, she almost looked mad. The expression gave Luke cause to hope. Could it be she was jealous of Valerie Winthrop? "Why don't you send Bernice back and I'll just eat here on the porch and you and I can talk?"

"No, that's all right. I don't want to take you away from your . . . friends."

"Bernice," he called out, "why don't you go on back up to the hotel? I need to talk to Alex for a few minutes."

"Stay where you are, Bernice. I'm coming back with you."

Luke took hold of Alex. "Please stay. I need to talk to you."

Bernice had gotten to her feet. Her look of uncertainty spoke for itself. Leaning closer to Alex, Luke whispered, "Send her back so that we can talk. You aren't going to like this one bit if she overhears what I have to say."

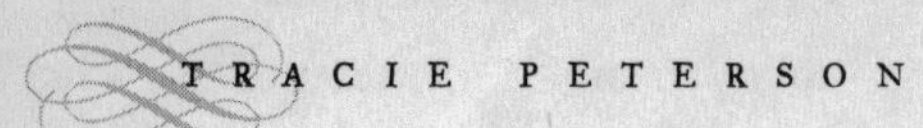

Alex studied him for a moment, then nodded. "Very well. Bernice, go ahead to the hotel."

Luke let her go and motioned to the table. "Just put the tray there and then sit down with me, if you would be so kind."

"Very well, but I don't know what this is about."

She remained haughty and distant, causing Luke to smile all the more. "You're jealous. You're jealous of Valerie Winthrop and the fact that she kissed me."

"And you've gone completely daffy. Have you been hitting some bootlegged bottle of whiskey?"

Her words sounded convincingly indifferent, but her expression was one of sheer misery. "Tell me why you're jealous." He sat down and looked up at her, "Please sit first."

Alex pulled out the chair and sat down. "I'm not jealous, and no matter how many times you say that, it won't make it true."

"That's all I want . . . the truth," Luke said, eyeing her quite seriously. "Why not tell me the truth?"

Alex felt her mouth go dry. The truth was, she didn't like seeing Valerie so capably handle her dear friend. She especially didn't like the fact that the woman was so wanton with her kisses. To be exact, she didn't like Valerie Winthrop.

"I . . . well . . . I had just hoped for time to talk to you. When I saw her here, I knew it would be of no use."

"But she's gone. She can't be a problem now. Why not just admit you're feeling jealous." Luke grinned. "Maybe you wish you were the one blowing me kisses."

Alex shook her head and lowered her gaze. Strangely enough, he wasn't that far from the mark. Her problem was that she didn't understand where these feelings were coming from. She wasn't even sure she could express her feelings in words. And, even if she could, she wasn't at all certain she wanted Luke to know how she felt. After all, it was rather embarrassing.

"I just don't think Miss Winthrop would understand the kind of friendship we have," Alex finally answered flatly.

"I'm not sure I understand it either," Luke admitted, his tone sounding rather defeated.

Alex felt the words slam against her. What did he mean, saying he wasn't sure he understood their friendship? Was he trying to tell her that he preferred the likes of Valerie Winthrop—beautiful, glamorous Valerie Winthrop?

"Look, Alex, all I'm trying to say is that my feelings for you have changed."

Alex swallowed hard and felt her breath catch in her throat. How could she lose his friendship now? Now, when she needed it most of all.

"I . . . I . . ."

"Alex!" Bernice came running in a most unladylike manner down the path. "Alex!"

Alex immediately got to her feet. Bernice had been the news bearer of nearly every bad tiding Alex had received of late. What could it possibly be this time? Refusing to look at Luke in case she broke into tears, she moved down the steps of the porch. "What is it, Bernice?" She barely managed to keep her voice from cracking.

"It's your mother!"

Alex gripped her hands together tightly. If anything had happened to her mother, Alex didn't know what she was going to do. "What's happened? What's wrong?"

"Nothing's wrong. It's just that . . . well . . . she's here. She's come to the Grand Canyon."

CHAPTER TWELVE

"Mother!" Alex exclaimed, entering the lobby of El Tovar. "I didn't know you were coming."

"I scarcely knew it myself," the petite woman replied. At fifty-two, Katherine Keegan was starting to show her age. Tiny bits of gray danced throughout her dark chocolate hair, which was stylishly arranged atop her head.

"I was just escorting Mrs. Keegan to her room," a bellboy told Alex.

"That's fine. I'll come along with you."

They walked down the hall amidst the other tourists. Alex had a million questions she wanted to ask her mother, but she wanted to wait until they had the privacy of a quiet room.

The bellboy led them to a second-floor room, handling Mrs. Keegan's four bags as though they weighed nothing at all. Escorting them into the room, the boy went about his duties, securing the bags and opening the draperies. Alex watched in silence as her mother tipped him and waited until he'd gone to remove her gloves.

"So why are you here? You do know that Father is here as well."

"Yes, I know. I plan to talk to him when the time is right."

Alex came to her mother and hugged her tightly. "I've missed you," she said impulsively. And it was so true. She'd not seen her mother in weeks and her heart had grown quite lonely for the sight of her.

"I've missed you as well," her mother said, pulling away. "Let me rid myself of this hat and jacket. It's not as warm here as it was in Williams, but the temperature is more bearable without all of this on."

Alex helped her mother out of the jacket before daring her next question. "So what is it you've come to talk to Father about?"

Her mother draped the jacket to her navy blue traveling suit across the back of the desk chair. Turning to face her daughter, she stated rather stoically, "I'm leaving him."

"What?"

"I'm getting a divorce, Alex." Suddenly it seemed her mother's strength left her. Taking a seat on the edge of her bed, she buried her face in her hands and wept softly.

Alex went to her mother and embraced her in a tight hug. "You're doing the right thing."

Her mother looked up. "Do you really think so? Oh, Alex, I'm so afraid. God hates divorce—the Bible says so. Will He also hate me?"

"No, I don't believe He will. Adultery stands as grounds for a divorce, even in the Bible."

"I just can't take any more. Rufus parades his women around me like trophies from some unnamed battle. I know I've not been the best wife to him, but his treatment of me has left me completely defeated. I'm scarcely even welcome in church, and I'm always the topic of conversation. I can't bear it any longer."

"Of course not. Don't worry about a thing. You can stay here until we figure what's to be done. I've saved a bit of money. It's not a lot, but we'll use it to set you up elsewhere."

"I have money as well," Katherine said rather sheepishly.

Alex released her hold as her mother reached for her purse. "How?" she asked.

The older woman opened her purse to reveal a great deal of cash. "I went to the bank and withdrew a good portion of our shared account."

"Father will be livid when he finds out."

"He'll be angry no matter what," her mother replied.

"That's true," Alex answered, remembering what her father had said. "He's going to be quite ugly about this—you do know that, don't you?"

"He can't hurt me any worse than he already has."

Alex studied her mother as if seeing her for the first time. She'd lost a great deal of weight, leaving her face gaunt and strained. Her clothes actually hung loose around her shoulders and waist. Alex shook her head. How many youthful dreams had been crushed and broken on the altar of Rufus Keegan's infidelity?

"Mother, Father plans to win himself an appointment to Washington. He's here to lay the foundation for that, and he won't allow us to interfere with it. Maybe it would be best if we just leave without saying a word to him."

"No, I'll have to talk to him sooner or later." She closed her purse and looked to her daughter. "I just need to know that you don't think badly of me."

"Honestly, Mother, I've thought you should leave him for ages. Father has brought shame upon this family, and now the shame should rest upon his shoulders alone. Let him suffer as we have."

"I don't want to seek revenge, Alex. I've prayed that God might just take me—pull me out of this misery so that I wouldn't have to make any choice at all—but that's not happening. I just want to be released from the pain. That alone would be enough for me."

Alex wondered if it would truly be enough. She'd like to see her father called to account for his actions. She'd like to see him stripped of the things he held dear—just as her mother had been. Her mother had little choice but to stand by and watch her dignity and social standing diminish. She could say nothing as her husband cavorted with one woman after another, all within the eyesight of the town's biggest gossips. No, Alex wasn't at all sure that merely having the pain removed was enough.

"I just need to know that God won't hold this against me," her mother continued. Getting to her feet, she paced a space at the end of the bed. "I want to be a good Christian, to be a good wife, but it's so hard. When he brought liquor into the house, breaking the law, I said nothing." Her voice broke and a little sob escaped as she continued. "When he dealt in underhanded manners with his businesses and cheated others of what is rightfully theirs, I did not condemn him. I knew God would eventually deal with him on all this and more. But if I walk away and divorce Rufus, then the blame will be mine."

Alex could sense her mother nearing hysteria. "Look, why don't you just let things lie for a time. There is nothing that says you must divorce immediately. Just take a holiday. You've come to El Tovar, so let that be the start. Tell Father you need a rest and that you're going to visit Audra. You could go there and see her and the family, while I square things away with the Harvey Company and find us a new location to live."

"Yes, but once your father learns the truth about the money . . ."

"We'll deal with that when it happens," Alex interjected. "Father is not going to immediately concern himself with such things. He's with friends—powerful friends—who can give him exactly what he wants. He won't think about banking matters for a single moment. Today, just rest. Let's just concentrate on getting through one day at a time and give the rest to God."

"I'd like that—truly I would."

A heavy knock sounded at the door, causing Katherine to jump back. "I'll get it," Alex offered. "Why don't you just freshen up a bit?" She didn't wait for a response but went to the door.

Her father pushed her back as soon as the door opened a few inches. "What are you doing here?" he demanded of his wife. He came in rather like a bull moose stomping and snorting, ready to take on his adversary.

Alex tried to think how she might intercede for her mother and create a story her father might accept, but nothing came to mind. She opened her mouth to comment, but already her mother was pulling something from her purse. With a smile on her face and a cheerfulness Alex knew her mother did not feel, Katherine Keegan handed the card to her husband.

"I came here because the Winthrops invited me to join you here. It seems they have a series of special dinners and gatherings and thought I might like to be a part of their celebration. I even purchased a new gown for the main gala. I knew you wouldn't want me to look shabby next to you."

Rufus Keegan grunted as he pulled the invitation from her hand. "You should have stayed home where you belong."

He considered the card for a moment, then glared back at his wife. "*I* didn't invite you here."

Alex stepped forward. "She's here and to send her back to Williams now would only disgrace you—the Winthrops issued the invitation personally."

Her father turned on her. "You'd better remember what I told you—I won't brook any nonsense from either one of you. I intend to see myself in Washington, D.C., working with the new president, and perhaps one day even enjoying that office myself." He turned back to his wife. "I won't tolerate your interference or scenes. If you so much as open your mouth to say the wrong thing, you'll regret it. Do you understand me?"

Alex moved between her father and mother. "Don't threaten her. She's put up with enough of your embarrassing games."

"This is no game, Alexandria. You'd do well to learn that here and now. Your mother knows her place most generally, and it isn't until she talks to you that she feels compelled to create a fuss. If you want to keep your job here, I'd suggest you learn your place as well."

Alex straightened her shoulders and leaned toward her father's face. "You have no power over me here. Of that I have absolute confidence. You cannot see me hired or fired, and that's the truth of it, so do not pretend to threaten me."

"It's not a pretense, and the threat is very real." His brows drew together as his eyes narrowed. "I fully intend to see my plan through to completion."

"Please don't argue," Alex's mother said, coming to stand beside them. "Someone might overhear."

Crumbling the invitation in his hand, Keegan threw it at Alex and stomped to the door. "You mark my words and mark them well. I won't be kept from my dreams by the likes of either one of you. I have a plan to get me where I want to be, and you'd better stay out of my way. Or else!"

"Or else what?" Alex questioned, unable to keep her mouth closed. "To what extent will you go to silence us?"

At this her father calmed, almost unnaturally so. He rubbed his mustache and actually smiled. The sinister expression on his face left Alex cold and weak-kneed.

"People die all the time, don't they?"

With that he opened the door and left the room. Alex felt frozen in place, while her mother crossed the room and quickly shut and locked the door.

"Oh, what are we to do?" she questioned. Her pale face contorted in fear and anguish.

Alex barely felt able to draw a breath. "I don't know. I wouldn't have believed him to say something so . . . so . . ." She left the words unspoken.

Her mother reached out and took hold of her. "I'm terrified, Alex. I've never seen him like this, not even when he's hit me in anger."

"He's hit you—and you stayed with him?" Alex questioned.

Her mother released her grip on Alex and walked to the window. "Alex, a married woman makes many a choice that seems irrational to others. I've done what I had to do, just as I'm doing what I have to do now."

"But, Mother, this has to stop. He must be stopped."

Her mother nodded. "I know."

CHAPTER THIRTEEN

Valerie Winthrop had never known a man she couldn't conquer. Generally all she had to do was bat her eyelashes, smile coyly, and show a spark of interest and the men came running. But in the case of Luke Toland, that simply wasn't so. Luke had no interest in her, and that could only mean one thing—another woman.

He had said as much, but Valerie couldn't find out from Luke who that woman might be. Watching him, however, she'd been able to pretty much ascertain that Luke was in love with Alex Keegan, the dowdy little Harvey Girl. Worse still, the Keegan woman also appeared to have feelings for Luke—although Valerie wasn't entirely sure the woman knew it yet. Women were such queer creatures at times, and Alex Keegan seemed the strangest of them all. For all Valerie could tell, Miss Keegan was not at all interested in the men around her, in spite of numerous comments of praise and adoration. Although why anyone would praise the creature was beyond Val. She found Miss Keegan quite boring with her spiritual interests and Biblical restrictions.

As she dressed for dinner, Valerie took special care to wear something sensually appealing. She hoped later to slip away to Luke's cabin. Poor, dear man. His broken wrist was making him quite miserable. Valerie knew just the right medicine to help him heal, and perhaps by wearing this gown, she might actually take his mind off the homely Miss Keegan.

But along with her interest in Luke, Valerie longed to have everyone's attention fixed on her. She loved the way men came to attention when she entered a room—loved the look of admiration, of longing in their eyes. She was like a prized jewel that everyone wanted, and she enjoyed the position. Her life—on her terms.

Too bad she had to contend with Joel Harper. She had grown bored and weary of his attention. He only wanted the money and power her status could afford him, and he was a bitter man with an agenda to right the wrongs done to him. Had he been even the slightest bit attentive, Valerie might have found him worthy of her affections. After all, he was handsome. He had a sort of Fred Astaire look to him.

She'd even told him so when they'd been in London earlier in the summer and had seen Astaire dance with his sister Adele. Joel had been flattered, unnecessarily so. He'd pressed for her affection after that, seeing her comment as some open door to become more intimate. But her comments had been nothing more than passing thoughts, certainly nothing to suggest she was ready for physical romance with her father's lackey.

Smoothing down the satin of her Poiret dinner gown, Valerie tried not to think about her fate with Joel. She still had her freedom for a time. A freedom that might see her happily entangled with a certain cowboy, if she could only find a way to capture his attention.

Looking at her reflection in the mirror, Valerie knew she looked rather scandalous. The pale green satin clung to her in a most daring way, while the draped neckline scarcely hid the fact that she'd chosen to wear very little under the gown. Just let Luke Toland try to ignore her now.

She rubbed her favorite scent on her bare upper arms. It had been her experience that this was most effective in drawing a man's attention. Lastly, she touched up her makeup and hair.

"Perfect," she murmured, noting her reflection one last time.

The evening had cooled considerably, but Valerie refused to take a wrap. The look she wanted would be ruined if she were to add so much as a scarf to the ensemble. Making her way to the rooftop garden, where they'd all agreed to meet prior to dinner, Valerie drew appreciative stares from every man she passed along the way. She smiled to herself. It was good to feel their approval—to sense their longing. It gave her a sensation of power.

Reaching the roof, she immediately spotted her father's stocky frame. Dressed rather uncomfortably in the tuxedo he hated, her father was already playing the room. A consummate politician, Winston Winthrop knew very well how to work the crowd to his advantage. The best thing he had going for him was his ability to listen—really listen. He could pick up details in a conversation that everyone else tended to miss. Using these details, the good senator managed to align himself with the common man. It had worked to his advantage and had seen him through thirty-some years of public office.

"The common man," he would say to Valerie, *"holds the key to success. For the common man, once influenced for you, will eagerly share what he knows with his neighbors. And, once they are convinced, they will share their opinion with their neighbor and so on. The wealthy not only care little for such matters, but rarely are willing*

to share their news with each other for fear of their powerful friends becoming even more powerful." And Valerie knew this to be true, for her father rarely spoke of important matters unless it was to press someone into service on his behalf.

"Daddy," she said softly, coming up beside the portly senator. She leaned in to kiss his cheek, stopping just before reaching face. She'd learned long ago that her father's cheek was hardly the place for her lipstick.

Joel stood just to the right of her father. His perusal of her costume seemed to come in a mix of emotions. He liked what he saw, she was sure of that. But she was just as sure that he didn't like everyone else seeing her that way.

"Sweetheart, you'll catch your death. Perhaps I should escort you back downstairs so that you can get something to put about your shoulders," Joel suggested.

Valerie loved that he was disturbed by her appearance. *Let him fret and fuss,* she thought. *I will never let him own me.*

"I'm perfectly warm, thank you." She turned away from him then and met the man at her right. "I'm Valerie Winthrop."

The man was of no special account. He was just one of the many who followed her father around like a faithful dog. Valerie pitied these men. They were like pack animals seeking out the strongest among them. Sometimes that strength came in the form of intelligence and sometimes in physical stamina, but always they sought it out and aligned themselves accordingly.

When it was time for dinner, they adjourned from the gardens and made their way to the private dining room. There were twelve of them tonight, Valerie noted. Her father had brought in several additional players, including Rufus Keegan's wife, Katherine. The petite woman was absolutely no threat to anyone. Nor was she of any interest. Mr. Keegan did nothing to hide his open admiration for Valerie, breaking away to whisper obscenities in her ear, promising her things he couldn't possibly make good on. Valerie knew him to be the worst of philanderers. Several times he had cornered her to suggest they slip away to his suite. She'd never given him serious thought, however. He was old. Much too old. And not nearly as wealthy or powerful as he liked to think. Why, she could have her pick of wealthy men from New York to Los Angeles. There was no reason to settle for the likes of Rufus Keegan.

With the additional people to serve, Valerie found that there were two Harvey waitresses at their disposal. She did her best to keep them both working. Miss Keegan seemed to realize her game, while the stocky little redhead who assisted her seemed as naïve as a schoolgirl.

"This tea is tepid," Valerie complained to the redhead. "Bring me another cup."

"Yes, ma'am."

Valerie watched Alex Keegan with a particular curiosity. What was it about her that Luke Toland should find so appealing? She wore no makeup, yet Valerie had to admit her skin was the color of peaches and cream. Her cheeks blushed naturally and her dark lashes needed no paint to make them more appealing. Even her hair, which was dark brown and wavy, had been pinned into a rather attractive style atop her head. Valerie almost envied the fact that Alex had long hair. In the city you seldom saw any woman their age still sporting long hair. Yet, Valerie had seen the men admire those few remaining souls who kept their locks long, almost as if these were the last vestiges of true womanhood. Men could be so peculiar.

Still, Alexandria Keegan couldn't match Valerie's beauty. Valerie's classic looks had been praised from London to Madrid and all across Europe. She had been toasted in New York and New Orleans. She knew the power her looks gave her. So why hadn't they yet given her the elusive Mr. Toland?

Then it dawned on her. Somewhere between the pear salad and the filet mignon, Valerie suddenly realized the attraction. Luke Toland felt sorry for Alex. His supposed love was born out of pity. The idea churned in her head as she made small talk with her father's dinner guests, and by the time éclairs and chocolate russe were served, Valerie had it all figured out.

Luke doesn't really love her, she told herself. *He sees how poorly her father behaves and knows the shame she's endured. He no doubt has befriended her thinking her a sweet, naïve young woman who would never do anyone harm. But I can change that.* After all, Valerie already knew of Joel's interest in adding the elusive Miss Keegan to his list of conquests.

As the dishes were cleared away and the coffee served, Valerie excused herself, mindless of Joel's scowl, and left the room. She had told her father she needed to powder her nose, but in truth, she knew this would be her chance to visit Luke.

Her strapped heels were hardly the proper footwear for the rocky and uneven path to the cabin, but Valerie guarded her steps. Her thoughts, however, ran away with her, suggesting all sorts of scenarios.

"First, I'll tell him I was worried about his recovery," Valerie mused. She wished she'd thought to bring him one of the chocolate-glazed éclairs. Her mother had often told her that a man's affection could often be roused with food.

She neared the cabin and smiled at the hint of light coming from behind the pulled curtains. *Then I'll pace a bit in front of him, letting him see every curve and line. That should warm his blood considerably.*

Reaching the cabin porch, Valerie slipped off her shoes and placed them on the top step. She wanted her approach to be quiet, because as a final thought she decided she wouldn't so much as knock. She'd simply walk in on him and catch him unaware.

Reaching for the doorknob, she smiled when it turned easily in her hand. She pushed open the door and found Luke rather stunned, sitting on the couch.

"What are you doing here?" he asked gruffly.

"I thought you could use some company."

"No, I'm afraid not. Clancy's coming back in a minute—he's gone to get a chessboard. We have a game to play."

"I'd be more fun to play with than Clancy."

"I doubt it. Clancy is pretty good at chess," Luke said rather dryly.

Valerie knew she'd have to act fast. Crossing the small room, she positioned herself between Luke and the fire. The warmth felt amazingly good. "That's not what I mean and you know it."

"I'm never sure what you mean, Miss Winthrop. I've never been able to figure women out. Seems to me they play a lot of games, and chess just isn't one of them."

Valerie smiled, hoping the coy look she'd perfected would give Luke reason to send Clancy packing. "I can learn to play whatever game you'd like."

"I'd like for you to leave," Luke said, getting to his feet. His broken wrist seemed to be of no consequence, and he seemed completely capable of fending for himself.

Valerie backed up a step, suddenly feeling uncertain of

her plan. Luke took hold of her arm and practically dragged her to the door. "I don't know why you came here, but don't come back. I have no interest in your kind."

Anger rose up in Valerie. "What do you mean, my kind?"

"You know exactly what I mean," Luke replied. "You know exactly what you're doing and what you're planning on getting, but you won't be getting it here—with me. Good night."

With that he shoved her out the door and locked it behind her. Valerie stood in dumfounded shock for several moments. How dare he treat her like a common trollop? Dismissing her like one of his crew members.

"You'll wish you'd played the game with me, Mr. Toland."

Valerie picked up her shoes and made her way back to the hotel. Her confidence was slightly damaged by Luke's rejection, but she pushed her feelings aside. Pausing to put her shoes back on, Valerie was taken aback when Alex Keegan came out the door.

"Good evening, Miss Keegan," Valerie said, straightening.

"Oh, hello." Alex started to walk past, but Valerie reached out and stopped her. "I'm so glad we have had a moment alone. I must tell you that despite substandard food from time to time, your performance has been remarkable."

Alex eyed her suspiciously, but Valerie knew very well how to lull her into a false sense of security. "I'm simply amazed," Valerie continued, "that you can remember what everyone has ordered and keep it all straight. You must be a very smart woman."

Alex shook her head. "No, I credit the training. Having been here for four years, the job is second nature."

"Four years? My, but that's a long time. I know when Luke told us he'd worked here for over ten years, I found it hard to believe. Of course, Daddy has great new plans for Luke, and I'm sure it is only a matter of time before his years at the Grand Canyon are behind him."

This got Alex's attention. Valerie nearly laughed out loud as the woman froze in her steps. "What do you mean?"

"Why, Daddy has offered him a position. Once he's president, Daddy won't have time to mind all his interests."

Alex's demeanor relaxed a bit as she smiled. "Luke would never take a job in the city. He hates them. Hates the noise and hubbub. And he hates politics."

"Oh, I know all of that," Valerie simpered. "He's just the dearest thing, isn't he? Anyway, Daddy has a ranching interest he's just purchased in Wyoming. He's offered Luke the job to run it as if it were his own. And who knows, if he plays his cards right—it just might be his own someday. After all, Daddy says Luke would make a wonderful husband and father."

Valerie noted the defeat in Alex's expression. Feeling good about what she'd accomplished in such a brief conversation, Valerie turned to leave. Calling back over her shoulder, she plunged the knife in a little deeper. "I'm sure Luke will be glad to leave this place. There's nothing here he'd want to stay for. He told me as much."

Alex watched Valerie Winthrop leave. For several moments, Alex felt as if her legs were made of lead. Unable to move, Alex remembered every detail of their conversation. Luke was going to work for the senator? It just didn't make sense. *He hates politics and can't abide the men who pursue such power. Why would he do this?* Then a sinking thought came to her. *He's always wanted his own ranch. Maybe he sees this as an easy way to make that come true. But at what cost?*

Making her way to the Lookout, Alex tried to rein in her

thoughts. In spite of the party going on in the main dining room, her duties for the evening had concluded. She would go to the Lookout and escape the noise and party spirit of the tourists. Hopefully, there would be very few people around.

The upper level appeared to have one or two people milling about, so Alex chose the lower level station for her respite. Hiding in the shadows under the overhead balcony, Alex tried to regain her composure. Surely Miss Winthrop was lying.

"But how do you propose to eliminate the competition?" A voice sounded from overhead, and Alex recognized it as her father's.

"By doing exactly that. Eliminating the competition," Joel Harper said snidely.

Alex pulled back even farther into the dark recesses of her hiding place. Apparently her father and Joel had left the party in order to consider their plans.

"You don't mean kill them?" her father questioned.

"I mean exactly that."

Alex put her hand over her mouth to muffle the gasp that escaped. Joel apparently talked of death as easily as someone else might talk of the weather.

"But how?

"I have some people already on the job."

"Truly?" Her father sounded completely fascinated, and Alex cringed, remembering his threats to her and her mother.

"I've been working on this for nearly a year. We do whatever we can to buy off the competition or otherwise entice them to give up the race. Those who won't be bought or put off have to be dealt with in, shall we say, more permanent manners?"

Alex felt her breathing quicken. She had to get out of

here before they discovered her overhearing the conversation. She tried to think clearly, but her heart was pounding in her ears.

"Do you see yourself eliminating the likes of John Davis and Bradley Jastrow?" her father questioned.

"It's already being worked out. Why, Davis has even decided against coming to the canyon for the celebration this week and next. We've managed to create a little problem with the American Bar Association that he must attend to. After all, he's the president of that dear organization."

"Fascinating."

Alex heard a shuffling, as if the men were moving from one side of the balcony to the other. "Look," her father continued, "I'll do what I can to aid your cause. I have no desire to be the man in the presidential chair—I'd rather be one of those who puts him there and helps to keep him there."

Liar! Alex thought. She could have called it out, too, except for what she'd already overheard.

"Good," Joel answered as they moved inside. "I knew I could count on you. Things will really start to get ugly in the days to come. As we move toward the convention in New York City next June, we need to have a solid following. That's where I'll need people like you. You will be called upon to influence your circle of friends, as well as your enemies."

"My enemies know better than to cross me, they only have . . ."

Their voices faded away as they moved indoors. Alex tried to steady her nerves as she got to her feet. "I can't let them know I was here," she whispered, her worries turning into a prayer. "Oh, God, help me to do the right thing. I wish I could talk to Luke."

In a rush of emotion, however, she realized she couldn't

talk to Luke. If she could believe Valerie, he was one of them. He was going to work for the senator. But even if it was true, her heart argued, Luke would never abide killing. She knew him well enough to realize that much. Maybe she could dissuade him from going to work for the Winthrops. Maybe if he knew the kind of things they advocated, he'd reject their offer.

Alex heard the men move out onto the rim path and head back to El Tovar. They were laughing and enjoying some great joke as they went. After a few moments of silence, feeling confident she could slip back to her room unnoticed, Alex came out from the shadows and moved up the rocky path to the top of the rim.

"Where do you think you're going?"

Joel Harper came out from the darkness of the Lookout doorway. Alex swallowed hard and tried to smile. Not that he could really see her face.

"I'm sorry, I didn't know anyone was here."

"You lie rather calmly," Joel said, standing only inches from her. "Now tell me what you overheard."

Alex knew lying was no good. He already knew the truth of the matter. "I heard it all."

"That's what I figured." He reached out and gripped her arms tightly. "If you say a word—so much as a single hint of a word about any of this—I'll see you dead."

This threat, coupled with her father's, and added to Valerie's announcement about Luke, left Alex in a state of near hysteria. Laughing, she shook her head from side to side as if to shake away the image of her nightmare. Joel pulled her down the path away from the Lookout. The area afforded them a bit more privacy.

"I'm serious. I'll kill you."

"It seems you'll have to stand in line, Mr. Harper." Alex managed to sober herself a bit. "I've been threatened all day long—all week, in fact."

"Those were most likely idle threats, my dear." He pulled her close against him and held her fast. "But my words are more than that. I'd hate to harm you—you're so lovely, so pure. We could make a great team if you'd just give me a chance."

His breath against her face reeked of whiskey, and his hands fondled her back and neck in a much too familiar way. Alex pushed against him, but he didn't release her. She began to fight in earnest and tried to scream, but he clamped his mouth upon hers without warning. The sickening taste of whiskey touched her lips as he forced himself upon her. Alex feared not only for her life, but for her innocence. She brought her foot down on top of Joel's, all while struggling to pull away.

"Fighting me is no good. I have the ability to break your neck right here and now," Joel said in panting breaths. "You need to stay on my good side."

Alex laughed bitterly and with all her strength managed to push him slightly off balance. As he let go of her to right himself, Alex hurried away. "You have no good side, Mr. Harper," she called back, not waiting to hear if there might be a reply.

As Alex neared the hotel, she tried to appear self-confident and self-assured. She wouldn't run. She'd walk very quickly and put herself near people. Surely Mr. Harper wouldn't cause a scene in front of others. She pushed aside her first reaction, which was to go to Luke. She felt safe with Luke, in spite of her anger at men in general. Luke had been trustworthy.

But Luke had said his feelings had changed, and the thought of facing Joel Harper and the Winthrops without him left her with an aching loneliness.

Oh, God, what am I to do?

CHAPTER FOURTEEN

Luke watched from a distance as Alex and Mr. Harper appeared to share an intimate moment. He watched Harper embrace Alex and pull her close. With his stomach churning, Luke looked away. He didn't want to wait and see if Harper and Alex kissed. The intimacy of the scene suggested it just might happen, and the image that flooded his head sickened him.

How had his life suddenly become so complicated? The woman he cared about was in the arms of another man. The job he loved was off limits to him because of his broken wrist. It was so frustrating.

Walking back to his cabin in the cool night air, Luke fought the need to rush back to Alex and force her away from Harper. *She can't possibly be attracted to him,* Luke reasoned. *She hates men who act as Harper acts. She despises infidelity.* He paused, stopping behind El Tovar, wondering if he had misjudged the situation. Perhaps Alex wasn't all that willing to be alone with Harper.

"Hey, Luke, I was just lookin' for you," Clancy said, coming upon him. "Your boss wants to see you. Something about coordinating several mule trips."

Luke nodded, pushing aside his concerns about Alex. "Thanks, Clancy. I didn't figure anyone would be looking for me this late."

Clancy shrugged. "Guess they've got a full party going in there and one thing led to another. You know how money talks. Someone mentioned how much fun it had been to take the ride down to Phantom Ranch, and the next thing you know everybody wants to go. This whole political thing is bringing in some real dillies, let me tell you."

Luke knew only too well. He thought of Alex with Harper. Maybe she'd aligned herself with him because of her mother. Alex was rather desperate to see her mother away from the humiliation caused by Rufus Keegan. Maybe she'd gone to Harper for help. The idea irritated him, almost more than the thought of Alex being involved romantically. Emotions could carry a gal away, making her do stupid things she'd later regret. But helping her mother was something Alex would think out—plan out. If she'd gone to Harper for help, it would be because she'd calculated the risk and the result.

"Guess I'll go see what we can figure out. You boys are going to have your work cut out for you," Luke muttered. "Wish that mule hadn't broken my arm."

"You've said that at least fifty times since it happened," Clancy grinned. "It's still broke. Wishin' it wasn't doesn't make it so."

"Tell me about it."

"God, help me to do the right thing," Alex murmured as she continued toward El Tovar. A hot bath and quiet night of rest was all she wanted. She wondered about her mother and whether she should go and check on her, but decided against it. No doubt her father had mandated that her mother not be allowed out of his sight for long. Of this, Alex felt confident.

With her mind on these things, Alex refused to give Joel Harper any further consideration. His threat was very real, but if Alex dwelled on it, she wouldn't be able to think clearly.

"I'm not done with you," Harper declared in a menacing tone.

Alex had thought herself rid of Joel Harper for the night, but instead she found him back on her heel, his anger only piqued by her attitude. He took hold of her arm and turned her back to face him. The rage in his expression was quite evident.

"I said, I'm not done with you," he growled.

"Well, I was through with you. I have no desire to be manhandled by you or anyone else. You think very highly of yourself and your effect on women, Mr. Harper, but your flattery and attention would be better shared with someone who finds such things appealing."

Joel seemed to regain control of his temper. His face relaxed just a bit, but not so his hold. "I can give you many good things."

"I have all I need."

"You could have more. I can make your life very comfortable."

"I thought you were to marry Miss Winthrop."

Joel nodded. "I am, but it needn't concern us. I find your innocence and purity quite refreshing." He tightened his hold and pulled her close. "You must have some kind of feelings for me."

Alex struggled but to no avail. "Oh, I do have feelings, Mr. Harper, but they aren't at all the kind of feelings you'd like to hear about. Now let me go."

"Just give me a chance," he said, lowering his voice to a husky whisper. He leaned closer to Alex's ear. "I have a way with women."

Alex stopped fighting against him. Her voice was flat and void of emotion. "Let me go."

"Not until you understand. I can't have you threatening our plans—my plans. But I think you can realize that much. I can make life very good for you—or very bad."

"So your purpose for this is to overwhelm me with your romantic passion so that I'll remain silent about your plans to eliminate the competition, is that it?" She asked the question very matter-of-factly, as if the answer were of no concern to her. In truth, however, she felt dizzy, almost near to fainting from fear.

"We could have a wonderful time together. And your father might even get that appointment to Washington he so badly desires. You wouldn't want to stand in the way of that, now would you?"

"So if I cooperate with you, become your mistress, you'll ensure my father's appointment? Is that it?"

"Something like that," Joel said, grinning. "I see you're beginning to think like one of us. Threats aren't always the way to get things done. Sometimes promising benefits can be much more productive."

"I don't want your promises. I prefer your threats to your sweet talk and promises, any day. You hold absolutely no appeal to me whatsoever."

"Maybe not, but you're going to have to promise me your cooperation, one way or another. I'm just saying it can either be a whole lot of fun for both of us, or it can be a misery that makes you wish you'd never met me."

"I realize the validity of your threat, Mr. Harper. I can't

make promises as to what I'll do or say, however. Lives are at stake."

Joel's expression hardened again. "You are so very right, Miss Keegan, and the very first life at stake . . ."

"I know. I know. The first life at stake is mine. Go ahead and threaten me." Alex hoped she sounded bored with the entire matter, when in truth she was praying someone would come along and interrupt this affair.

"That's not what I was going to say," Joel said, his whiskey breath hot upon her face. "The first life at stake will be your mother's."

"What?"

"I'm telling you that if you refuse to cooperate with me, I'll see your mother dead. I have many people who are willing to help me. I have men here who are at my every beck and call. They will willingly do anything for money."

"You would kill an innocent woman to have your way?"

"I will do whatever is necessary to win this election."

Alex felt her knees weaken. A trembling started in her legs and wound its way up her entire body. She had to get away from this evil man. She saw the pleasure he took in speaking of death and destruction. She could feel the cold, heartlessness of his soul in his very touch.

She tried to pull away. "Let me go."

"Stay with me," he encouraged. "I have a wonderful room and I think you and I could very much enjoy the night together."

Alex fought harder. This time, she dug her fingernails into his arm. "I said, let me go. Let me go or I'll scream." Her voice grew louder.

"Miss Alex? Are you okay?"

It was Clancy. Alex breathed a sigh of relief. Joel instantly unhanded her and stepped back a pace.

"Clancy, would you walk me back to the hotel?" she asked, looking at the ground rather than let Clancy see in the dim lighting how upset she really was.

"Sure thing, Miss Alex."

Alex said nothing more to Joel. She knew there was nothing she could say. He wouldn't listen to her, nor would he pledge to leave her mother out of the situation. Walking in silence with Clancy, Alex felt tears come to her eyes. Things had gone from bad to worse in just a matter of days. What was she to do?

"I hope I didn't interrupt anything important," Clancy said softly, almost hesitantly.

"No, Clancy, you did exactly right. Mr. Harper was out of line." She paused momentarily and reached out to touch Clancy's arm. "Please don't tell anyone what happened. It's rather embarrassing."

"I'm not sure I know just what did happen, but I won't say a word, Miss Alex. I know how things can get misunderstood. That's the way it was with the boss and that Winthrop gal. She just don't seem to like taking no for an answer. Guess her boyfriend feels the same way, eh?"

"Yes." Alex felt an overwhelming regret that she'd believed Luke might actually have encouraged Valerie Winthrop's actions. Hearing Clancy speak of it now, in the aftermath of her own forced encounter, Alex knew that Luke was innocent. Sometimes hindsight wasn't all that comforting.

Back in her room, Alex felt overwhelmed with her fears. Michaela had already made her way to bed but wasn't asleep, so Alex took the opportunity to try to better understand her own turbulent emotions by talking.

"Do you think people always mean what they say? Like

when they threaten people or talk about threatening people?"

Michaela sat up and pushed her pillow behind her. Leaning back against the headboard she shrugged. "I guess that would depend on who they are and what they have planned. Why do you ask?"

Alex took off her apron and tossed it aside. She wanted to tell Michaela everything—the talk she had with Valerie Winthrop, Joel's threats, even her confusion over Luke. Instead, when she opened her mouth she said, "My mother wants a divorce."

"Well, I would too, if I were her. The way your father treats her is abominable."

Alex undressed and pulled on a robe. "I know. He's threatened us both if we cause him trouble."

"Never mind the fact he's caused you both more trouble than you deserve," Michaela threw in.

"Exactly," Alex continued. "He's pressing for a presidential appointment, so he's sidling up to Senator Winthrop. He's probably bribing and threatening him as well." She sat down on the chair beside Michaela's bed. "Then tonight, Mr. Harper took liberties with me."

"No! What did he do?"

Alex felt the disgust well up inside. "I'd overheard him saying some things that were rather incriminating. He was talking to my father, and after my father had gone, he realized I'd overheard the conversation. He forced me to a secluded place, threatened me, then tried to woo me by touching me and kissing me. I tried to fight him off, but of course he was much too strong." She shuddered. "I just wish I'd never heard what he told my father."

Michaela leaned forward. "What did he say that was so bad?"

"He plans to eliminate the competition for Senator Winthrop."

Michaela laughed and eased back against the headboard. "Is that all? Of course he wants to eliminate them. The fewer people running against his man, the better."

"No," Alex countered. "He really wants to eliminate them—kill them if necessary."

Michaela's eyes grew wide but she said nothing, so Alex continued. "But don't you breathe a word of this to anyone." She grew silent for a moment as she contemplated the situation. "I don't know what to do."

"In what way? I mean, what is there that you have to do?"

"That's just it, I don't know. If Mr. Harper is being truthful, then someone should notify the authorities. But how can I be certain of the truth? I don't know if he's just talking big, trying to scare me and everyone else into cooperating with his plans. Then I guess I want to be helpful to my mother, but at the same time . . . well . . . I guess I'm afraid for her and for me. While I don't know what Mr. Harper is able to do, I fully understand what my father is capable of. It just scares me that I won't do the right thing . . . that someone I love will suffer because of my poor choice."

Michaela shook her head. "That doesn't sound like you. Why be afraid? God's big enough to handle this, isn't he?"

"I guess it's just a real test of my faith. I feel like crying, but I know I'd be better off praying."

"Then pray."

Alex nodded. "I guess you're right. It's just that . . . there are other things too."

"Like Luke?"

Alex looked at her friend—hesitant to reply. "I suppose he's a part of it as well. Miss Winthrop told me something tonight that didn't sit well."

"And you believed her? Goodness, Alex, you've grown into a ninny while I was gone."

Alex smiled at her friend's good-natured teasing. "Well, she said that her father was offering him quite a deal. A ranch of his own to run in Wyoming and plenty of money, and . . ."

"And?"

"And I guess he's even offering Miss Winthrop, at least that's how it sounded."

"I thought she was engaged to that Mr. Harper menace."

"She is, but she implied . . ."

"Oh, Alex, just listen to yourself. Why should you give anything the woman says a second thought? She's out there wearing next to nothing for clothes, dressing more scandalously than anyone I saw on my travels, and playing games of romance with every man she meets. Obviously she's just come to realize you're in love with Luke and wants to put a stop to that while she decides how to deal with it. Only problem is she didn't count on the fact that Luke's in love with you."

"That's crazy talk. You've said as much before, but Luke and I are just friends."

Michaela laughed. "Sure you are and I'm going to get the nomination for presidency. First woman president. Makes about as much sense as you and Luke being just friends."

Alex got up and began to pace. "I don't know how I feel about anything. I don't understand half of what's happening around me, and with my mother and father at odds the way they are, I certainly have no desire for love or romance."

"Why not? Your mother and father are no example of what happens in romance. By your own admission, you've told me about your parents and their history. Your mother was of a good family with money. Your father knew that, as an only child, she'd inherit everything and, if they married, then he'd be wealthy. And so he is. And that's the basis of their relationship. But none of that has anything to do with what you and Luke share."

"But that's just it. Luke and I don't share anything—not really—unless you count friendship."

"Friendship's a good place to start. But you and Luke have gone beyond mere friendship—and I think if you look deep into your heart and forget about everybody else's problems for a few minutes, you'll see what I mean."

Luke looked at the advertisement his brother had sent in his last letter. The notice was about a ranch for sale in Wyoming, just north of Laramie. The Broken T Ranch was well within a price Luke could afford. It wouldn't have many provisions to start with, but there was a small house and a few outbuildings and corrals. A very small starter herd was included in the price, but it would take some time to build the herd into a productive and profitable business. Of course, Luke hardly expected to walk right into a well-established business. These things took time and money.

His brother's letter explained that the man who owned the ranch had taken ill and had never been one who managed things well to begin with. His vast herd had dwindled over the years as the man battled his illness. Now, knowing his days to be numbered, the man simply wanted to sell the property and be done with it. The rest of the letter told of the family and of his brother's interest in moving to California.

Putting the letter and advertisement back in the envelope,

Luke contemplated what he should do. The answer seemed so hazy in his mind. If he left the canyon and bought the ranch without Alex as his wife, he might never see her again. Yet the ranch was a good offer, probably better than what he could get elsewhere. And if he could convince Alex of his love and commitment, he'd be able to provide her a home near to her sister. That way she'd have family close, and her mother would probably be able to travel between the two families with relative ease.

Luke pulled out his Bible to consider some of the Scripture from last Sunday's church service. He prayed there might be an answer to his dilemma, but his mind wasn't on it. Again he thought of what he had seen.

Why had Alex been with Joel Harper? What did she think to accomplish by enlisting his help? Harper was nothing but trouble, and she'd already mentioned a deep dislike of the man.

His wrist irritated him, causing Luke to leave his desk and seek the comfort of his sofa. There didn't seem to be easy answers tonight. Just frustration and misery. Why, Lord? Why did that mule have to kick me? Why do I have to be laid up like this? Why did I fall in love with a woman who has absolutely no interest in loving me back?

The questions flooded his conscious mind. If he fell asleep, no doubt they'd pester his unconscious mind as well. Why couldn't things be simple?

He thought about the advertisement. *I want a ranch for Alex and me together,* he reasoned. I want to settle down and start a family. He glanced to the ceiling. "I thought you wanted that for me, God. I mean, it sure seemed like something you were leading me to. Lord, if this isn't supposed to be the way I'm to go, then why can't you take the desire from my heart? If

I'm not supposed to marry Alex, then why don't you send me the woman I am supposed to marry?"

He mentally ran down a list of the current Harvey Girls. There wasn't a single one, except Alex, who had ever struck his fancy. He could see himself having fun with any number of women, but with Alex, he had completely different visions. He saw himself marrying and living happily with a lifelong companion. He saw himself fathering children and raising them with Alex. No matter what scenario he dreamed up, he always saw Alex in the middle of it.

"This is crazy," he said, getting up off the sofa, ignoring the ache in his arm. He crossed to the desk and took up his brother's letter. Sitting down, Luke reached for pencil and paper. He'd send a letter to the Broken T and let the owner know his interest. It couldn't hurt to just let him know. Then if it were meant to be, God would work out the details. Including Alex.

CHAPTER FIFTEEN

The morning train brought the arrival of additional political supporters and adversaries. The front contender, John Davis, had been unable to attend the party at the Grand Canyon due to complications with the American Bar Association. The reporters noted that one of the Bar's board members had somehow been charged with bootlegging and Davis himself was called to answer in regard to the matter. Joel smiled to himself to see his plans come into play.

Bradley Jastrow, a solid citizen with a war hero record and brief state representative experience in Alabama, was also a contender for the Democratic nomination for president. His appearance at the Grand Canyon sent reporters scurrying to get information and pictures for their papers. Joel thought it all rather amusing. They were like dogs running from person to person, begging scraps as they went.

Jastrow cut a rather dashing figure with his red, wavy hair and piercing blue eyes. As a lieutenant in the army during the Great War, Jastrow had led his troops against a German trench, resulting in its capture. Later he was severely wounded while single-handedly taking out a machine gun position. His wounds resulted in a lengthy hospital stay, a battlefield promotion to captain, and, if Joel's research proved correct, an addiction to morphine.

Jastrow, the eldest son of a wealthy shipping magnate in Alabama, maintained his bachelorhood at thirty-six and seemed to draw more than his fair share of feminine attention. Since women now had the right to vote, Joel needed to take his appeal seriously. Appearance had always had a certain amount of importance, but that usually lent itself to the image of the "older, wiser" contender. The man who convinced the nation of his experience and knowledge of certain matters, showing his patriotism and ability to connect to the general public, always made a strong showing. The country had always looked for father figures—a strong, steady man to stand at the helm.

Eyeing Jastrow, with his winning smile, broad shoulders, and classic looks, Joel reconsidered the matter. Women would change the political arena. Their desires and views would matter. Jastrow would appeal to the emotional, feminine voter, especially those who were single. Valerie had pointed this out, noting he had a certain charisma, especially in light of his hero status. Still, Joel felt confident that he could arrange to have the man taken care of if the need arose. There was always the possibility that Jastrow's popularity had been underestimated. Not only this, but the tide of support could easily turn from one candidate to another, depending on the mood of things across the nation.

Jastrow was very much against prohibition, unlike many of his other Democratic contenders. The attitude won him friends among those in southern society and big cities, but elsewhere he was seen with contempt. He was also very supportive of the Ku Klux Klan, which again split his support.

"So what do you think of the news that President Harding

has . . . food poisoning?" Senator Winthrop asked Joel in a low, rather hesitant tone.

Joel smiled. "Food poisoning, eh? Well, life is sometimes hard on all of us. The president certainly is no exception to that rule. The trip he made to Alaska was quite arduous. I'm of the mind that this adventure was probably too difficult. The man has heart troubles, or so I've heard." Joel wasn't about to tell the senator everything he knew. After all, there might come a time when they would be called upon to deny any knowledge of certain . . . affairs. Better the senator have no knowledge of those unpleasant matters.

"I find it more of a concern to us that Bradley Jastrow and John Davis should still have a large following of supporters," Joel added. "The others are hardly worth our time, but those two need to be watched. They will be a challenge to be sure."

The senator hooked his thumbs in his vest pocket as he was wont to do. "I welcome the challenge. I have nothing to hide and a positive record to support me. Davis was nothing more than a minor candidate in 1920. He'll be nothing but a minor candidate in '24."

Joel smiled. Winthrop could be very naïve, but it worked to Joel's advantage. "I'm sure you're right."

"Now, Jastrow's father is a well-known friend of the south," the senator continued. "We have many of the same friends. There will be supporters who will find themselves torn right down the middle. What shall we do about that?"

"I have some thoughts on the matter. I think in the long run, we won't need to worry about Jastrow. His health isn't all that great."

"But of course not. He was wounded in the Great War," Senator Winthrop added.

"Yes, but his war wounds aren't causing near the problem

his addiction to morphine is creating."

"I didn't know about this."

"And you really don't need to know more than that. I have it under control. I don't believe Jastrow will be a problem. Addictions have a way of resolving themselves," Joel said, just then seeing Rufus Keegan enter the room with Valerie at his side. He wanted to get the senator's blessing once and for all on announcing the news of their engagement, so he quickly put the issue of Jastrow aside. "Senator, I'm grateful that you would share the limelight with your daughter and announce our engagement at the main gala. I think many people will be swayed to vote for you because of the family image you'll portray."

"Nothing's too good for Val. She's my pride and joy. My life."

Joel nodded. "Yes, and the public will find that heartwarming." He watched Valerie simper over Rufus Keegan. "If you'll excuse me, Senator, I have some plans to discuss with Valerie. I see she's just come in with Rufus Keegan."

"Good man, that Keegan. He's offered me the support of all of Arizona and part of California."

"Let us hope he has the ability to deliver on such a promise."

"We should find something for him to do once the election is won. I'll need people like him. After all, when you and Valerie marry, I know your time will be divided."

Joel started to frown, then caught himself. "Nonsense, Senator. Valerie knows very well how time-consuming politics can be. She'll understand my allegiance to you."

The senator nodded, smiling. "She's a good woman. Always looking after my interests."

Joel could see Valerie toying with Keegan's tie and felt a

surge of jealousy. "Indeed," he managed to say.

Joel left the senator to his own devices and crossed the room to greet Keegan and his reluctant fiancée. "Good to see you, Mr. Keegan," Joel lied. He had so little use for the man. His overinflated sense of self-worth was an irritation to Joel. More worrisome was Winthrop's apparent belief that the man was of value. Joel would have to deal with that soon. "Hello, darling," he added, turning to Valerie. He kissed her on the cheek, surprising her momentarily. "You look positively radiant."

Valerie eyed him suspiciously but said nothing. Joel smiled and continued as if nothing were amiss. "I hope you're looking forward to tonight's party," he said to Keegan. "The senator is eager to discuss his plans for the campaign."

"I wouldn't miss it. I'm eager to hear his plans and know his mind."

Yes, I'm sure you are, Joel thought. He took hold of Valerie, however, without comment. "Val, darling, we need to discuss our plans for announcing our engagement."

"I thought you'd worked that all out with Daddy," she said rather sarcastically.

Joel laughed. "You're such a goose, Val. Of course we've worked it all out. I simply need to tell you what's expected of you."

Keegan laughed out loud at this. "Good man. Put her in her place and tell her what to do. That's the way to groom them. If you don't catch them early, they'll turn out like my daughter. Headstrong and inconsiderate of the men in her life."

"Now, Mr. Keegan, I find your daughter quite delightful. Quite . . . delightful," Joel said, emphasizing the words. "I'll look forward to her being close by in Washington should you accept the senator's position once he's installed as president."

Joel watched the man's face contort from an expression of anger and disgust to the realization that someone was actually mentioning a position for him. Joel loved to throw crumbs to the dogs that way. If nothing else, it often proved entertaining just to watch them fight amongst themselves. Of course, this time, he wanted to make clear that he considered Alex a part of the package. Keegan seemed to understand rather quickly and, as that understanding dawned on him, he nodded.

"I'm sure Alexandria would love Washington."

Valerie frowned and tried to pull away from Joel but he held her fast. "Perhaps Val and she can be great friends." Joel tightened his grip on Valerie's arm. "Ah, here comes your lovely wife, Mr. Keegan. I'm sure you'll have things to discuss with her, so if you'll excuse us . . ."

"Of course," Keegan said, giving Valerie a wicked smile. "I enjoyed our time together."

Valerie smiled in return. "As did I. Perhaps we can spend time together later. I'll expect to dance with you this evening." Her voice dripped honey, and Joel felt as though she purposefully worked to humiliate him.

"You may count on it," Keegan replied.

Joel yanked Valerie away from Keegan with the briefest acknowledgment of Mrs. Keegan. The woman looked haggard, so he offered nothing more than his greeting before forcing Valerie into a quiet corner.

"Your father's campaign is dependent upon you playing your part, my dear. I have plans for you that do not include playing the tramp with Rufus Keegan."

"What do you want from me?"

"You know very well what I want," Joel said, lowering his

voice. "And one of these days I'll tire of waiting for what I want and simply take it."

"Are you threatening me?"

"Actually, yes. I am. Now, will you be a good girl and cooperate with me?"

"I'll never cooperate with you. I'm going to speak with Daddy and see that this ridiculous farce is brought to an end. I don't love you and I have no desire to marry you. I only agreed to the matter to shut you both up for the time. Daddy may adore you, but you know only too well how I feel about you." She squared her shoulders and seemed to strengthen her resolve. "Besides that, I know things about you. Things that could see you sent to prison for a long time—if not put to death."

She adjusted her hat and turned as if to go. Joel refused to be dismissed in such a manner, and he refused to allow her to ruin his plans. "You think to threaten me and walk away? I've worked too hard for you to spoil this. What makes you think I'd ever allow you to cause me the slightest bit of trouble? I can see you put in your place rather quickly, Val. A place that would be far more frightening and worrisome than the one you're in now."

"You talk big, but you're nothing more than my father's flunky."

"If we were alone, I would slap you across the face," Joel said, clenching his teeth.

"Well, rest assured we will never be alone. I could end up like that poor prostitute in Washington." She smiled. "See? You aren't the only one capable of learning secrets."

Joel's gaze narrowed. "You think me incapable of accomplishing whatever I set my mind to, but I'd ask you to reflect back on that banker's son you made such a fuss over last year."

Valerie grew still. "Leave Andrew out of this. You know his death hurt me greatly."

"Yes, I do. That's why I arranged it."

Valerie's face drained of color. "What are you saying?"

"I'm saying you were getting out of control. People were beginning to talk. It seemed the sensible thing to do." Joel prided himself on his stoic tone and rigid stance. He loved the power he felt over Valerie. Loved the complete disbelief and heartache written in her look.

"But . . . he . . . he . . . drowned," Valerie offered weakly.

"Yes, I know. I was there." Joel loosened his hold on her arm and smiled rather contentedly. "The man was a nuisance to me. Just as you are beginning to be. Just remember, Val dear, I seldom tolerate irritations for long." He reached up and rubbed her cheek with his thumb. "Poor darling. Here you thought you could scare me with your knowledge of past events, when it's you who should be terrified. Those two deaths are just a pittance. When people annoy me, I make them go away. It's that simple. Keep it in mind, my dear. Once we're married and your fortune is mine, you'll want to be particularly well-behaved."

"I'm not afraid of you. Kill me. This misery is worse than death," she said, jerking away from his touch.

"Oh, but, my dear, I wasn't speaking of your death," he said, giving her a cold smile. "I was speaking of your dear father, our next president. It would truly be a pity if he were to die so soon after our marriage. Why, we might never know what a truly wonderful president he might make."

She stared at him openmouthed for a moment, tears forming in her eyes as she searched his face. Turning abruptly, she hurried away from him as if he'd suddenly grown horns atop his head. Joel drew a deep breath and stood awash in a sensation of nervous excitement. He'd never told anyone of his deed. It seemed risqué, bold, even adventurous. Of course, she'd say nothing about it. She'd be too afraid of how it might appear to other people. There was one thing about Valerie that Joel knew he could count on: She adored her father. And that adoration ensured his control.

Seeing the Keegans standing outside on the veranda, Joel made his way to join them. He wanted to press home his point regarding Alex. Walking outside, Joel found the warmth of the day uncomfortable, but the shade afforded them on El Tovar's porch was welcome.

As he approached the Keegans, Rufus pulled his wife behind one of the stone archway supports. Joel thought it rather strange. It looked as if Keegan was trying to hide away from the other guests. Joel smiled to himself. The Keegans apparently had things they'd rather not discuss with an audience, but that was exactly what Joel was going to give them. Stepping from the porch, Joel positioned himself just beneath the arch and well out of sight of Keegan.

"What do you suppose to gain by this?" Keegan asked his wife.

"Rufus, I have no desire to fight with you. I have simply come to tell you that I'm leaving. I want a divorce, and I mean to have one."

Joel started at this news. He pressed closer to the porch. He had to hear every word, for this could prove very beneficial.

"There will be no divorce," Keegan growled out. "You are my wife and you'll stay that way."

"You're mistaken, Rufus. I've endured a great deal

because of your escapades, but no more. Alex and I will quietly leave. There needn't be any public show."

"Ah, so Alexandria is in this. I should have known. I warned her . . ."

"Alex did nothing," Katherine Keegan interjected. "I simply came here because it seemed a good way to tell her goodbye and inform you at the same time. She has insisted I allow her to come with me, and frankly, I'm glad for her company."

"There will be no divorce! I won't tolerate it. I won't bear such public humiliation when I'm attempting to better myself with a position in Washington."

"I've borne your public humiliation for years. In fact, the final straw arrived at my door just before coming here."

"What do you mean?" Keegan asked, his rage apparent in his tone.

"I mean your child. Your illegitimate son. One of your conquests, a Miss Gloria Scott, has given birth to your son and has made it clear to me that she'll make this quite public if we do not pay her well. I have no desire to be a part of this. Divorce me and marry her, but do not expect me to stand by idly and bear even more disgrace." Her voice broke and she began to cry. "I cannot take this anymore. You must understand."

Joel thought the news rather tasty. There was a great deal he could do with something like this. Already the plans were churning in his head. He'd have to get one of his men to go check out this Gloria Scott woman.

"No divorce. I'll see you dead first." Keegan's low, ominous tone struck a chord in Joel. He recognized his own determination in Keegan's temperament.

"Do you hear me, Katherine? I'll see you dead before I let you do this."

"Then kill me," she sobbed. "Kill me and release me from this unholy bond."

Keegan laughed. "You miserable wretch. What a waste of my time. Stay out of my way. Go hide yourself in your room and leave me to work my plan."

"Please, Rufus. Please. Not just for my sake, but for Alex. She deserves happiness, even if that's impossible for us."

"It's not impossible for us, woman. I'm living it daily. You're the only one who is unhappy. But trust me, it could be much worse."

The crying grew louder and Joel backed away a bit to avoid being seen. He'd heard enough. Rufus Keegan had fathered an illegitimate child. Katherine Keegan wanted a divorce. This was rich fodder for the purposes of controlling a man—or a woman. He immediately thought of Alex. He licked his lips, anxious to pick up where he'd left off with her. Valerie would be his wife and with her would come fortune and status, but Alexandria Keegan would be his as well. It was just a matter of coordinating the details. Something Joel was very, very good at.

CHAPTER SIXTEEN

"I brought you some supper, Luke," Michaela said after he'd opened the door to his cabin. "Looks like a pretty night for a party, don't you think?"

"I guess so." Luke wasn't in the mood for small talk. "Thanks for the grub."

She put the tray on the table and turned to look Luke straight in the eye. "Are you in pain?"

"Not really. Why do you ask?"

"Because you look like you're in pain, and I just wondered if it was your arm or Alex that's causing you the most grief."

Luke felt his stomach tighten. What did she know about his feelings for Alex? Why should she even suggest such a thing as Alex causing him pain?

"Look, I know this is none of my business, Luke, but I think you probably need to talk to someone, and since I know the situation probably better than most, you can talk to me."

"Talk to you about what?" he asked, turning away.

"About being in love with Alex. About Alex being in love with you."

He turned back around at this. "Alex said that?"

Michaela laughed. "You've got it bad for her, don't you?"

"Just answer my question."

"No, Alex didn't say that she was in love with you. But I'm with her more hours of the day than not. I can tell how she feels. I can tell how you feel as well."

"How?" He watched her as she considered his question. She seemed completely at ease.

"It's the way you look at her. The way you touch her fingers when she hands you something. It's the way you speak to her. Everything about you sings it loud and clear."

"Very well. I do love Alex, but that stays right here between you and me. You may have figured me out, but I don't think you know Alex very well at all. I saw her in Joel Harper's arms last night. She can't be that much in love with me if she's carrying on like that with him."

"You don't honestly think she was in his arms because she wanted to be, do you? He forced his attentions on her, and she had to fight him off to get away."

"What? She told you this?" Luke felt sick to his stomach imagining that Alex had needed him—that she'd been in trouble no more than fifty yards away—and he'd done nothing about it.

"Luke, Alex is going through a lot right now. I can't give you all the details, but you have to understand that things aren't at all good. She's going to need you now more than ever, and I felt like I needed to speak my mind. You need to tell her how you feel about her. Don't let the days get away from you—tell her tonight."

As the sun set and a riot of color splayed out across the

western horizon, the first of the Winthrop parties began on the lawns outside El Tovar. Alex had no idea where all of these people were being housed. There were no fewer than three hundred guests gathered on the south rim of the canyon.

It appeared that the Winthrops were the perfect hosts. They had arranged the finest foods from the hotel, paid for lavish tables and decorations, and spent hundreds of dollars to orchestrate every detail. And this was only one of several parties. The main gala was not scheduled to occur for another two days.

Valerie Winthrop seemed in her element. She glided comfortably across the lawn in a flowing creation of silver and black. The look was lavish and opulent in a way that Alex could never hope to know—not that she'd want to. Yet it was amazing just the same.

A kind of silver spider's web was molded to Miss Winthrop's slicked-back hair, while long silver-and-diamond earrings hung from her ears. Diamonds were also draped, almost haphazardly it seemed, around her neck and bodice. She looked the epitome of the modern woman—seductive and alluring, tempting and mysterious.

Alex watched Valerie with a strange sort of interest. The debutante had no apparent modesty when it came to dealing with the opposite sex. She openly flirted, moving from man to man like a bee gathering pollen. The only man she seemed to completely ignore was Joel Harper, a fact that didn't appear to set too well with Mr. Harper. There was trouble in his expression, and Alex felt certain there would be a confrontation before the night was over. This thought was only compounded when Valerie attached herself rather openly to Alex's father.

Laughing in a manner that seemed much too loud,

Valerie appeared for all the world to be completely taken with Rufus Keegan. Alex's father loved the extra attention. Alex couldn't help but wonder rather crudely if her father had made Miss Winthrop his latest conquest.

Surely he wouldn't risk the possibility of losing a position in the White House. Alex stared hard at her father, willing him to see her and know what she thought of the entire matter. When he finally did look her way, however, Alex was immediately sorry. His foreboding expression said more to her than any words. Not only had he threatened her more than once, but he also had aligned himself with Joel Harper and his talk of eliminating the competition. Whether Harper had been serious or not—and Alex was becoming more and more confident that he had been—her father apparently believed such actions were necessary to gain entry to the White House. He might even be involved with the man to act on those plans, taking the life of an innocent person in order to win an election. The thought sickened Alex and made her more determined than ever to expose them both and let the law deal with them.

Moving across the well-manicured lawn to offer refreshments to the guests, Alex immediately spotted Bradley Jastrow. The handsome politician from Alabama stood near Hopi House, where guests could buy handmade Indian crafts. The Winthrops had arranged for the Indian dances to be performed during their lawn party, and Jastrow seemed quite interested in those who would dance for the event.

Alex couldn't be sure what Joel Harper and her father had planned for Jastrow, but she was desperate to warn him. Still, what could she say? *Hello, Mr. Jastrow, my father and his new friends plan to eliminate you from the race for president? Even if it means killing you?*

Maybe I could just tell him that there are rumors going around that someone plans to harm him, she reasoned. *I wouldn't have to say who told me this.*

Offering hors d'oeuvres to those she passed, Alex tried to make an inconspicuous attempt to reach the popular man. There were at least a dozen beautifully attired women who stood in a circle around him. They simpered and pouted and vied for the man's attention, all the while appearing to size up each other. It was a most unusual game they played.

Alex's only intention, however, was to warn Jastrow of the impending danger. And there was another candidate, although she'd not been told his name, who'd arrived at El Tovar for the party. Both were in danger.

First things first, she thought. *I'll tell Mr. Jastrow and then I'll seek out the other candidate.* But even as she drew near enough to hear Jastrow denounce the illegal actions of those who opposed prohibition, Alex caught sight of Joel Harper watching her.

Sweat trickled down her back. How could she possibly warn Mr. Jastrow and not arouse Mr. Harper's suspicions?

Alex looked across the crowded lawn and found her mother in conversation with Senator Winthrop. The conversation appeared all one-sided on the part of the senator, but nevertheless her mother looked every bit the captive audience. Alex couldn't help but feel proud. Her mother was a pillar of strength and managed to give a pretense at happiness that Alex would have found impossible.

Dressed in a crepe de chine gown of dark burgundy, Katherine Keegan looked almost regal—queenly in her stature and deportment. Why couldn't her father see her beauty and grace and be content with her rather than chasing after so many other women?

Jastrow moved across the lawn with several people at his side, drawn into conversations Alex had no business in. She looked back to where she'd seen Joel Harper and found him watching her. The hair on her neck stood up, and a prickling sensation climbed her spine. Harper smiled and nodded, as if knowing his effect.

Alex looked away, wishing desperately she could talk to Luke. Luke would know what to do, or at least he could give her a clearer idea of what wouldn't work. Right now Alex would settle for that alone. If she could just figure out what not to do, then maybe the proper action would present itself.

Her desperation mounted as the third contender for the Democratic nomination made his appearance. Laughter loud and shrill broke out from this new group of visitors. No one seemed to mind, however. Alex wondered if they had any idea the danger they were in. Surely not, she mused; they wouldn't be here otherwise.

Seeing her tray was nearly empty, Alex moved across the grounds, her thoughts whirling around her. Perhaps if I appeal to Mr. Harper, maybe talk to him about the importance of . . . of what? She faltered in her step, nearly falling. She turned to see if Harper was watching her, but he'd disappeared.

Frantic, Alex scanned the crowd. What if he was already putting into play some plan to eliminate the competition? She saw nothing of the man. The orchestra began to play a popular tune and people gathered onto a makeshift dance floor.

Alex's heart raced and the beat of it pounded a rhythm in her ears, threatening to leave her deaf. Hurrying from the scene, she prayed. *God, you're the only one who knows what is happening. You know the corruption here. You know what Joel Harper plans to do. Please intercede on behalf of these people.*

She picked up a full tray of lobster canapés and returned to the lawn, hoping, praying that nothing would go amiss. Scanning the grounds once again, Alex felt momentarily relieved. Mr. Jastrow seemed to be enjoying himself. Still surrounded by beautiful women, the handsome man appeared oblivious to any hint of danger. The other opponent to the senator's campaign seemed equally entertained as he helped himself to a glass of punch from Bernice King's tray.

Maybe I'm overreacting, Alex thought. *After all, nothing seems amiss. Everyone is laughing and having a good time. Maybe Mr. Harper's plans would take place only if things don't appear to be going the senator's way.* She tried to comfort herself with this idea. Surely she was making too much out of Harper's threats.

But even as she reasoned with herself, other thoughts crowded in to take away her comfort. His threats were serious. *He and my father plan to eliminate whoever gets in their way—whether it's the opposition, my mother, or me.*

Thinking of her mother, Alex quickly searched through the guests to find her. Feeling a bit panicked when her first cursory glance didn't yield her mother's location, Alex gave a more dedicated study to each area of the lawn. All the while people took food from her tray, ignorant of her growing concern.

A petite woman in burgundy could easily be swallowed up among the hundreds of guests, and Alex found herself catching a glimpse of color matching her mother's gown only to lose it in the throngs.

There were too many people. People dancing. People talking. People eating and strolling. But Katherine Keegan was nowhere to be found. *Where could she have gone?* Alex trembled, knowing her mother intended to speak about her desires for a divorce. Alex had tried to talk her out of it, but her mother was convinced that this was the way it should be. Now she feared her mother had said something and was now having to face the wrath of the man she'd borne so patiently for so many years.

Lord, I know you hate divorce, but my mother is suffering greatly. She's so frail, even sick from the worry and pain. Please help her now. Let me find her and know that she's safe.

As the skies grew darker, lights especially strung to provide a magical effect, shone down upon the crowds. Forcing herself to remain calm, Alex picked up her step as she moved through the mingling guests. *I'm getting upset for no good reason. I need to see things as they are. Mother is probably nearby or maybe she's gone back to her room. Perhaps she had a headache and retired early.* Continuing to search, Alex quickly realized her father was also missing. Was he with Joel Harper? Or was he in a confrontation with her mother? The nagging doubts resurfaced. Would he really make good on his threats?

Alex's breathing quickened. What should she do? *Oh, Luke, I wish you were here. I need you.*

Realizing how much she'd come to depend on Luke was of no comfort to her. She had prided herself on needing no one, save God. Especially no man. But right now, with every nerve in her body tingling from head to toe, Alex knew the only person in the world who could help stave off her hysteria was the one person she'd pushed away and kept at arm's length.

The orchestra ended one song and had just begun the opening strains of another when a woman's scream tore through the air. Everything stopped. The orchestra conductor put down his baton and looked to the crowd as if for a cue. Alex stared at the faces around her, frozen in time with her companions. Faces filled with fear, curiosity, and confusion stared back at her.

The woman screamed again and then there was silence.

Alex couldn't move. No matter how hard she tried. She looked at the tray in her hands, then looked to the orchestra and the people who'd been dancing. Everyone remained fixed in place, as though a photograph had been snapped of the entire group.

"Where did that come from?" someone finally questioned among a growing hum of murmured questions.

"Do you suppose it was just someone having a good time?"

"Didn't sound like a good time to me," another guest answered.

The murmurings grew to a cacophony of questioning and reasoning. Confusion settled over the crowd as they began to move again. Some moved in the direction of the scream, others went back to the food table as if to bolster their strength with refreshments.

A woman next to Alex agreed. "That woman sounded terrified, if you ask me."

This seemed to be the only encouragement Alex needed. Shoving the half empty tray into the stunned woman's hands, Alex ran at full speed across the lawn. The sound had come from the rim path, yet how far away, Alex couldn't be sure. The canyon had an eerie way of distorting sounds. Sometimes it was quite confusing.

Many of the party guests had already begun moving in the direction of the rim. Those that pushed ahead at a rapid pace were mainly the newspaper reporters.

"Someone's fallen into the canyon!" came the call.

Alex felt sickened and stopped to catch her breath. There

was a part of her that suddenly didn't want to know the truth.

Oh, God, please help me. I'm so scared. She repeated the prayer like a mantra. Forcing herself forward, she regained her momentum and pushed through the crowd.

"Someone has fallen off the edge," murmured a woman to her companion.

"No one could live to tell about that," he replied. "I took that mule ride down—that canyon's a mile into the ground. No, there won't be much left of them—whoever they are."

Alex glared at them but pressed on. The hotel had positioned additional lighting here, which seemed to only create more shadows.

"Excuse me," she said, over and over. An air of excitement enveloped the crowd, and people weren't always of a mind to move out of Alex's way. Her patience wore thin and she found herself becoming quite demanding. "I work for the hotel—get out of my way."

Finally, she cleared past the last of the onlookers and found two people standing about ten feet away. The man turned out to be Luke. Alex could see the cast on his left arm in the dim light. The woman he held was sobbing. Her face was buried against his chest, but from the look of her build and the color of her gown, Alex felt confident that it was her mother.

Two men came to stand beside Luke. One wore a park ranger uniform, while the other was dressed in a tuxedo. They were speaking in hushed tones with Luke.

Alex's legs felt weighted with lead as she pressed closer. In a hoarse whisper she asked, "Luke, what's happened?"

Luke looked up and met her gaze. She could see his expression, although shadowed. His look told her that nothing would ever be the same after tonight.

"What is it?" she pleaded. "Tell me."

Her mother pulled away and looked at Alex with tear-filled eyes. Luke released his hold on her and the ranger sympathetically took Mrs. Keegan's hand and led her to a nearby bench. Luke then turned to Alex and looked into her eyes. "I'm sorry, Alex. It's your father. He's gone over the edge."

CHAPTER SEVENTEEN

"I can't believe he's really dead," Alex said in disbelief nearly two hours later. Numb from the news, she hadn't cried a single tear. She wondered if Luke thought her cold and unfeeling.

Luke reached out and took hold of her hand. "If he'd only fallen to the first ledge, he might have made it."

"What could have happened?"

"I don't know. I came upon your mother after it'd happened. She crumpled to the ground crying. She's the only one who saw anything, and she's not talking," Luke replied, gazing at her with such tenderness. "I'm sorry you have to endure this. It's never easy to lose a loved one."

The words "loved one" slammed up against her like the time she'd stepped on the prongs of a rake, bringing the wooden handle full force against her face. She didn't consider her father a loved one. She didn't even mind the idea that he was gone—forever. Except . . . She shook her head. Except nothing. She didn't care.

Shock washed through her veins, leaving her cold. *This is your father,* she chided herself. *He's dead and you must care.* A sense of guilt crept in where the stunning news had first left her without feeling.

She tried not to think of her father, focusing instead on her mother. The poor woman had cried enough tears for both of them. Katherine Keegan now slept sedated in her suite with a ranger guarding the door outside. The canyon physician worried about her mental state and general health. There was talk, murmurings and whisperings about the accident. People were beginning to say that Katherine Keegan had killed her husband. It was all too much for Alex to take in.

"I know this is difficult for you. In spite of the way your father behaved, I know you didn't wish him dead."

Alex couldn't even look at Luke, for too many times she'd wished just that. Well, maybe not that he'd be murdered. She'd wished often enough that he'd die in his sleep and free her mother from her misery. Or that he'd die on one of his many trips to the capital. Did that make her a horrible person? Was she less of a Christian because she was glad her father had died instead of her mother? She couldn't keep from trembling.

"The rangers want to talk to you," Luke said softly. "I told them you were too upset—that they'd have to wait. But you can't hold them off forever."

She looked blankly at the wall, not seeing a thing. "I understand."

But in truth, Alex didn't understand anything at all. Joel had threatened her mother's life, but was this what he'd meant? Alex had feared he might kill her mother, but perhaps this was even worse. Had Joel Harper somehow arranged her father's death and allowed the blame to rest on her mother's shoulders? But if that were the case, if there was another person involved, then surely her mother would tell them.

Luke rubbed her hand. His warmth seemed to permeate the icy feeling that ran the full length of her body. How could it be that her father was dead? How could it be that her mother appeared to be the prime suspect?

"What's going to happen, Luke?" She looked deep into his green eyes, praying she'd find an answer she could cope with. "Are they going to blame my mother—arrest her?"

"I don't know. I wish I did—then I might feel more capable of helping you through this." He continued to hold her hand, and Alex found that she liked his touch very much.

"She's been through so much already. I don't know how she'll ever manage to get through this."

"God will give you both the strength to endure it."

She studied his face for a moment. "I need to ask you something," she said, knowing that she would know in his expression if he lied to her.

"What is it?"

"Do you think my mother killed him?"

Luke didn't hesitate. "No. I don't. She doesn't seem capable of such a thing."

"But she had plenty of motive," Alex argued, needing to hear him dispel her fears.

"True, but she's had motive for years. Why wait until now?"

"I suppose that's true. Nothing new has happened to make her act any differently."

"Are you sure nothing has happened recently?" Luke questioned. "Not that I think it would result in your mother killing him, but someone has. Perhaps a business deal went bad. Or maybe it's this whole political thing. Do you know if someone wanted to see him dead?"

Alex immediately thought of Joel Harper but dismissed

the thought. Joel and her father were like-minded. They were working together. Joel hardly seemed likely to kill off a man who was happy to do his bidding in return for an appointment in the White House.

"Miss Keegan?" a ranger questioned from the door.

"Yes, I'm Miss Keegan." Alex knew a lot of the rangers, but this man was a complete stranger. Standing picture perfect in his pressed uniform, the older man held a sympathetic expression on his face.

"I know this is a difficult time, but I need to ask you a few questions," he said rather apologetically. "It's just routine when something like this happens."

Alex looked to Luke once more. He nodded and Alex looked back to the ranger. "I suppose now is as good a time as any."

Luke got to his feet. "Do you mind if I stay here with her?"

"Yes, please," Alex said.

"I have no objection. This won't take long." The man pulled up a chair in front of Alex. "First of all, you have my sympathies. I know you must be quite taken in your grief."

Alex looked to the floor. "I'm still so shocked."

"I'm sure that's true," the ranger replied. "I understand you were working at the time of the incident."

The incident? Alex thought. How silly to call someone's death an "incident."

"Yes. I'm a Harvey employee. I work in the restaurant, and this evening I was serving at the lawn party hosted by the Winthrops."

"I understand both your mother and father were guests of the Winthrops."

"Yes. My father has been a part of the Winthrops' party

since they arrived. My mother only just arrived." Alex felt as though she were sorting through facts in her mind, trying to offer them back to the ranger in order to make sense of a much bigger puzzle.

"Why did she come to the Grand Canyon?"

"The Winthrops sent an invitation. She showed it to me. They were paying for her suite," Alex said, trying to remember everything.

"It was mentioned that Mrs. Keegan came here to confront her husband."

Alex had no intention of giving them information that they could use against her mother. "She told me she came because of the invitation." That wasn't a lie. She held her breath for a moment, trying to still her rapid breathing.

"Then you aren't aware of any problems between your mother and father?"

Alex let out her breath and shifted uneasily. Glancing to Luke, Alex felt she had no choice but to admit what everyone was already talking about. "My father was a philanderer. He had . . . ah . . . many other women in his life."

"So there were problems?"

"Yes." She bit her lower lip and prayed he wouldn't ask her to explain the fight she'd witnessed, nor tell of her father's threats. She wasn't ready to divulge this information. She first needed to talk to her mother. Tears flooded Alex's eyes and she lowered her head. She began to rub her temples where the throbbing was becoming unbearable.

"Look, why don't you wait to finish this up later?" Luke asked. "You can see she's clearly distraught. She did just lose her father."

"Yes, I understand. I suppose this can wait until morning." The ranger got to his feet and walked to the door. "Miss

Keegan, I realize this is difficult, but I'll need to speak with you first thing tomorrow."

Alex sniffed back her tears and nodded. "I'll be here."

After he'd gone, Luke moved back to sit beside her on the sofa. They were in Mrs. Godfrey's private quarters, as it seemed the only place to get away from the reporters and other busybodies.

"Alex, I'm sorry for all of this. I don't know what I can do to help, but I feel I have to offer to try."

"Luke, she couldn't have done it. My mother isn't like that. She was unhappy with my father—she has been for years. I've never known a time when he was faithful. Even when I was young he had his lady friends. I've never understood it, but Mother told me it was just the way things were. She bore it all with grace and determination. And even with all his threats . . ."

"What kind of threats?"

Alex bristled. Had she said too much? She looked to Luke and his image blurred behind her tears. How she longed to trust him with what she knew. "My father wasn't very happy that my mother had come to El Tovar. He really wanted to gain a position in Washington and he feared she might make trouble."

"How so? Everyone knew what he was doing," Luke stated matter-of-factly.

Alex got to her feet and paced the small space. "I don't know. He threatened us both."

At this Luke got up and came to her. "He threatened you? Why didn't you tell me?" He studied her a moment before reaching up to push back an errant strand of wavy brown hair. "Oh, Alex, don't you know I would have protected you? I would have talked to him at least."

His tenderness touched something deep within her. "I . . . well . . . you were busy and then you got hurt."

Luke gently touched her wet cheek. "Alex, don't you understand? I'm never too busy to care about what happens to you."

Alex could recognize the sincerity in his expression. His generally good-natured temperament had been transformed into a much more serious, more intense attitude. There was nothing casual about this cowboy. This man was all concern and . . . something else. Something Alex couldn't quite put her finger on.

His touch sent charges of electricity down her body. His gaze, so intense—demanded an intimacy from her that Alex had never shared with anyone. When he took hold of her shoulder, Alex lost herself in the moment.

"Alex, I won't let them hurt you, and if I can do anything about it, I won't let them hurt your mother."

"How did you come to be with her?"

"My arm was bothering me, so I went for a walk. I'd been walking around, trying to pray through some difficult decisions. I was headed back to my cabin when I heard her scream. I was just the first one there—the closest one to the rim."

"And you didn't see anything? No other person?"

"No. There didn't appear to be anyone else. Your mother had collapsed to her knees in complete shock by the time I got to her."

Alex began to cry in earnest. Her voice broke as she declared, "She couldn't have pushed him over. She couldn't have done it. As discouraged and betrayed as she was, she might have jumped off the ledge to take her own life, but she wouldn't hurt my father. Even if he wouldn't divorce her. . . ."

"She wanted a divorce? I thought you said she wouldn't leave him."

"I know, but . . ." Alex knew she had to tell him the truth. At least about this. "She came here . . . to . . . to tell him she was leaving him. She'd withdrawn a great deal of money from their account and had come to tell him good-bye."

"Alex, that doesn't help her situation very much. Do you suppose they fought over this?"

"Of course they fought over it," Alex replied in near hysteria. "They always fought. Father never had a civil word for Mother, and Mother had made up her mind. I'm sure they argued about it, since she had her mind set to leave."

"You'll have to tell the ranger tomorrow," he said matter-of-factly.

"I can't tell him. It would make her look bad—the wife scorned. The wife who depleted the bank account and made plans to run away and divorce her husband. None of that will help her case."

"But you have to tell the truth."

"The truth is, my mother could never have pushed my father over the edge."

"Be that as it may," Luke said gently, but insistently, "you have to tell him."

Silence fell between them as Alex tried to compose herself. The hole she'd dug herself into seemed to be collapsing around her.

"Where did she plan to go—I mean, after she left him and El Tovar?" Luke asked.

Alex drew a deep breath to steady her nerves. "We weren't sure. I was planning on asking Mrs. Godfrey to transfer me as soon as she could."

"You were going to leave with her—leave El Tovar? Were

you planning on talking to me about this?"

"I wanted to talk to you." Alex tried to compose herself, but her efforts weren't amounting to much. Her world was falling apart piece by piece and now she had to confront the possibility of another woman in Luke's life. "You were . . . were . . . busy. And Valerie Winthrop said . . ." Alex buried her face in her hands and sobbed. With his good right arm, Luke pulled her against him and held her safe. She could feel his cast, rock solid, against her side as he tried his best to pull her closer.

"Shhh, you don't have to go on. There's plenty of time to talk about this later."

Alex relished the warmth of his embrace. Luke smelled of hay and burnt wood—earthy smells that served to calm Alex's soul. Luke was her mainstay. Luke was the one she could count on when things went bad. God would always reign supreme in her life, but Luke had come to mean more to her than any other human being. Was this love? Was this, in honesty and truth, what she had hoped existed but never dared to believe in?

He stroked her hair, then gently rubbed the back of her neck. "It's going to be all right. You'll see. God is bigger than this. He'll let the truth win out."

Alex pulled away just enough to see Luke's face. "But, Luke, what if the truth is more than I can bear?"

He gently cupped her chin. "Alex, no matter what the truth is, God will see you through. Remember, you've shared those very words with me. Bad things happen, but God is still there for you. He still loves you."

"I just don't know what to do anymore," she cried.

His face was only inches from hers and, looking up, Alex found herself wondering what it would be like to kiss him. She didn't have to wonder for long. Lowering his mouth to hers, Luke kissed her long and passionately. The warmth of his touch and the depth of his kiss were enough for Alex to completely forget the moment. She put her hand up to feel the stubble on his jaw, her heart racing madly. This felt so right.

As he tightened his hold on her, Alex melted against him. They fit so well together, as if they'd always been intended for each other. If only this moment could go on forever. But like everything that offered comfort to Alex, this too had its end.

"Alex," Luke whispered, "there's something I need to tell you." This time, he was the one to pull away.

His words were like a slap in the face. Alex immediately realized what they'd just done and stepped back. What had she been thinking? "I . . . I . . . don't know what came over me."

She continued to back away as images of Luke and Valerie crept into her memory. She had to let go of her feelings for him. Even if those feelings were . . . very possibly . . . love.

"You're upset," Luke said, moving toward her. "I didn't mean to take advantage of that. I don't want you to think badly of me, but I have to tell you why I . . ." He stopped when he saw her intense gaze.

"Luke, I heard all about the ranch in Wyoming."

"How could you possibly know about that?" He seemed confused, speechless.

It was true—everything Valerie had said. He was turning his back on everything she had thought he stood for. Alex felt sick.

"I can't say," she replied. "I just do."

"Well, that's part of what I want to talk to you about."

Alex didn't want to hear about his plans with Valerie Winthrop. Not now. Not after what they had shared. "I can't stay here anymore. I need to see if they'll let me see my mother. I can't just leave her to their mercy." Alex reached for the door handle.

"Wait. We need to talk."

"Not now, Luke. I just couldn't bear it." She opened the door and stepped into the hall. Walking toward the stairs, she was immediately set upon by reporters.

"Is it true your mother killed your father because of his affairs?" one man questioned.

"No!" Alex replied. They were like wolves circling prey.

"Is it true your father sired an illegitimate child and that the woman was making demands on your mother?"

"No! How can you say such things?"

"Did your mother confess to pushing your father into the canyon?"

Alex tried to move away from them, but it wasn't until Luke pushed his way through the crowd that she had any success.

"Miss Keegan has been through a lot this evening. She's not up to answering any more questions."

"Say, aren't you the cowboy who found her?"

"Yeah, that's him, he's got a broken arm."

"Did you see what happened when Mrs. Keegan pushed her husband into the canyon?"

Luke fairly growled as he pushed Alex ahead of him. "I said, no more questions."

Taking hold of Alex, Luke maneuvered her down the hall. When they came to her mother's room, he paused momentarily. Alex thought he seemed reluctant to let go of her, but finally he released his hold. "Alex, I have to talk to you. I won't press you tonight, but tomorrow, we need to talk—it's important."

Alex faced the idea with sheer dread. Nevertheless, she nodded. "All right. Tomorrow."

Tomorrow her world would further unravel, but tonight . . . tonight she would force a stay of execution in the memory of his kiss.

That night in his cabin, Luke poked up the fire and stared absent-mindedly into the flames. Nothing in his life had prepared him for the experience of kissing Alex Keegan. He felt weak and powerful all at the same time. He knew in that moment, sharing their kiss, that she cared for him as he did for her. She wouldn't admit it, but he knew it just the same.

The night had brought about more than one revelation, however. Luke couldn't help but remember Katherine Keegan's sobbing hysteria and the words, "Rufus went over the edge."

Luke had been helpless to do much more than get Katherine to her feet. He held her against him while she cried, much as he had with Alex, but no other word from her was forthcoming. When the crowd arrived and others had taken over so that he could comfort Alex, Luke wondered quite seriously if they would simply haul Katherine to jail. She was the only one there when he arrived. She was the prime suspect, and yet Luke felt certain she hadn't done the deed herself.

Still, who else would want Rufus Keegan dead?

CHAPTER EIGHTEEN

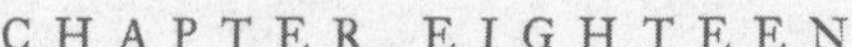

The mood of the hotel guests the following morning was more than somber—it was very nearly mournful. Luke ate his breakfast in haste, anxious to get away from El Tovar and back to the stables. He had told Mrs. Godfrey that he'd take his meals at the hotel from this point on, eating with his men in the employee dining area. She'd assured him that it was no trouble to have the girls bring meals to his cabin, but Luke felt otherwise.

Walking through the lobby of El Tovar, Luke's only desire was to talk to Alex. When he reached her mother's room the ranger told him that Alex and her mother were not taking visitors. He'd insisted the man ask Alex to step outside to speak to Luke, but when the ranger returned, he reiterated that Miss Keegan was speaking to no one.

Feeling a deep sense of frustration, Luke headed downstairs. If he couldn't talk to Alex, maybe he could find Michaela. Instead, he found himself face-to-face with Joel Harper. The man stared at him with an expression that suggested contempt, and Luke wondered if his own face revealed his intense dislike for the man. Ever since talking with Michaela, Luke had wanted to put Harper in his place.

"Mr. Toland." Harper's greeting was low, almost inaudible.

"Harper," Luke replied. "I'd like a word with you."

"Oh? I heard about your involvement in last night's affair. Are you in some kind of trouble?"

"No, but you will be if you don't stay away from Alex Keegan."

Joel Harper's upper lip curled and his expression took on a decidedly sinister quality. "And since when do employees make demands of hotel guests?"

"Since you found it acceptable to force yourself on hotel employees. I know all about your actions with Alex, and I won't tolerate it. If you doubt me, we can take this outside right now."

"Are you threatening me, Mr. Toland?"

"It's not a threat—it's a promise. If you don't leave Alex alone, I'll take the matter into my own hands."

"Is that what you did with her father?"

Luke's eyes narrowed. He'd never wanted to hit a man more than he wanted to hit Joel Harper. "I don't know what you're implying, but I've got no interest in discussing Keegan's death. I want to make clear that you understand you aren't to touch Alex again. Do you understand?"

"I think that mule must have kicked more than your arm. Are you sure you haven't loosened something in your head? Really, Mr. Toland, you should watch what you say to powerful men."

Luke stepped away lest he be tempted to give the man a sound beating. "If I see a powerful man, I'll do just that."

"You don't want to be on my bad side, Toland. You truly don't."

"I don't see that there's any other side when it comes to

you, Harper. Just remember what I said."

Luke stalked off in anger. He'd never intended to let the man get the best of him, but still, he had. Why was it so hard to remain calm and rational when dealing with the matter of Harper? *It's because he keeps bothering Alex,* Luke reasoned. Michaela said he forced himself on Alex, and that was reason enough to resent him.

The worst of it was that he wasn't half as frustrated with Harper as he was Alex. Why wouldn't she talk to him? After last night, he felt there was so much he needed to say. He couldn't help but wonder if she didn't feel the same way.

Luke wondered if the rangers had talked to her again. They would need to get all their information together in order to figure out what had happened. Alex had nothing to do with her father's death, of that he was certain, but he also felt she wasn't telling the full truth. Luke believed she was holding back more than the fact her mother wanted a divorce, but he didn't know what it could be. It wasn't like Alex to lie, even to protect someone she loved. Still, nothing like this—nothing this horrible—had ever happened to her before.

Walking along the rim path, Luke tried to make sense of everything that had happened. Keegan's death. The kiss he'd shared with Alex. Her unwillingness to talk to him. *How did she know about the ranch I want to buy? And why should it upset her so much?*

The park seemed uncommonly quiet. He saw a few visitors walking the pathways around the rim, but they made special effort to stay away from the edge. Where yesterday people had joked and teased each other by standing as close to the edge as possible, today they were guarded and sober. Keegan's death had reminded them of their own mortality. Reality had once again set in.

Another thing Luke noticed was an almost morbid curiosity to go to the place where Keegan had fallen. Not that there was much to see. There were no railings along the edge at this point, so it would have been very easy for a person to be pushed over. But could Katherine Keegan have done the deed? Luke seriously doubted it.

Rufus Keegan was a good-sized man. He probably outweighed his wife by at least a hundred pounds. He could have easily fended her off, even if she'd thrown her full body weight against him. No, Luke didn't believe for a moment that Mrs. Keegan had killed her husband. But if not her, then who? Someone wanted Rufus Keegan dead and Katherine, having been with him until the end, had to know who it was.

Luke studied the shadows on the canyon walls. Someone must have killed Keegan. He was too ambitious to have risked his own life by dallying on the edge. Rufus Keegan was no one's favorite character. He'd hurt people, stolen their livelihoods away, carried on affairs with women both single and married. Perhaps an irate father or husband had caught up with him. And the man's business dealings, by Alex's account, were far from fair or aboveboard. His death was probably a relief rather than a tragedy for most people. It would feel that way especially to Alex.

Alex. Luke felt better just knowing that Alex had been busy with her duties last night and had witnesses to prove her whereabouts. As much as she despised her father's actions, she would never plan out his murder—she wasn't capable of that. But he'd also seen Keegan get the best of Alex's gentle nature. Especially when the man insulted or hurt her mother.

If Alex had come to him saying that she'd fought with her

father and pushed him over the edge, it wouldn't really have shocked Luke all that much. Keegan had long ago killed off any affection Alex had for him. His infidelity had left her doubtful of all men—even men who didn't deserve the same reputation, like himself.

Luke kicked at the dirt. *Alex did not kill her father,* he reminded himself. Though she might have wanted to as she labored with her anger and hate, she didn't do the job. She didn't want him dead—just out of her life. Luke only wished he knew who had wanted the man dead. If he could figure that out, he could save them all a whole lot of grief.

Luke walked back to the hotel, lost in his thoughts. He'd not gone far from the place where Keegan had died when he heard his name being called.

"Mr. Toland—Luke!"

Luke looked away from the canyon and found Valerie approaching from the hotel.

"I was hoping we might talk. Do you have some time?"

"Not really," Luke said, feeling uncomfortable as she closed the distance between them. He crossed his arms against his chest as if to put a wall between them. Valerie Winthrop knew no walls, however. She gently touched his arm.

"Please. Last night was . . . so . . ." Tears filled her eyes and her voice broke.

Luke felt sorry for her, but not enough to offer any physical comfort. He hesitated to send her away, however. "I suppose I can talk for a minute."

She sniffed daintily and dried her eyes with a lacy handkerchief. Luke thought for a moment that her tears were just put on, but she seemed genuinely upset.

"What is it you wanted to talk about?" Luke questioned. The flowery scent of her perfume assailed him, and her nearness bothered him. He wasn't attracted to her in the least, but he feared what other people might begin to think if they found him alone with her, standing so close, appearing so intimate.

"I'm afraid," she finally said. "Last night . . . it proved to me that life is definitely unpredictable."

"True enough," Luke replied. "That's why a person needs to know where he stands with the Lord. You could be talking to a person one minute and the next minute find they're gone."

Valerie nodded. "That's exactly what happened. Mr. Keegan and I were talking at the party. We were laughing and making plans for the future. Daddy had invited him to South Carolina—to our home. He was to come and bring his family and share our southern hospitality. The next thing I know, he's dead." She paled a bit and turned away from Luke to gaze at the canyon. "What a terrible place." She rubbed her bare arms as if the sun had suddenly gone out of sight and the day had turned cold.

"It isn't the *place* that killed Rufus Keegan."

"I know, but if that big canyon hadn't been there, he might yet be alive. Not only that," she paused, looking around to make certain she wasn't overheard, "my father . . . well . . . I fear for him."

Luke didn't make the connection. "But why? He seems healthy enough. Safe enough."

Valerie drew close again. "I think someone may want to kill him. This campaign is so ugly. There are things going on that you can't begin to know about. I just want to keep Daddy from harm."

"He's going into a business that hardly allows for that. You can't keep people from disliking his politics and him. He'll be in one type of danger or another for the rest of his life."

"My point exactly," Valerie said, taking hold of Luke's hand. "You must help me."

"I don't understand."

"I want to hire you. I want you to be Daddy's bodyguard."

"Why me?" Luke asked, pulling away. He didn't want to appear rude, but her touch was making him very uncomfortable. "I've got a busted wrist. I'm hardly going to be able to fight off ruthless attacks."

"You won't be in that cast forever. You don't even need a sling anymore, so I know it must be healing fast. You're a good man, Luke. You have scruples. That's not something you often see, especially in political arenas. If I hired you to watch over Daddy, I know you'd do the job without reservation. You'd give it your all."

Luke managed to move away from her enough to raise his casted left arm. "I'll be wearing this for weeks. I'm telling you, even if I wanted the job, I wouldn't be of any use to you or your father."

"Don't say that. You're still strong and capable," she gushed, moving toward him again. This time she threw herself against him and wrapped him in her embrace. "Please, Luke. I need you to do this for me. I couldn't bear it if something happened to Daddy."

Luke pushed her back none too gently. "That's hardly called for, Miss Winthrop."

She started to cry again. "Don't be cruel. I'm not trying to make a scene, I simply don't want anything to happen to my father." She paused and looked at him quite soberly. "I thought you were a Christian. Aren't Christians supposed to be kind to people? Aren't they supposed to lend a helping hand and offer comfort?"

"I suppose they are," Luke said, feeling caught between the canyon and her wiles. "But that doesn't mean I must sacrifice a job I love simply because you ask me to. I'm trying to show you Christian charity just by talking with you and listening to your concerns. But you're making this really difficult. People in my world don't just throw themselves all over another person. You seem to make a practice of it, and I don't like it."

"You just don't care," she said, sobbing into her handkerchief. "I have no one who cares."

"What about Mr. Harper? You two are supposed to marry, aren't you?"

Valerie shook her head. "I don't want to marry him. I don't trust him. Joel is deceptive and devious. He does all sorts of underhanded things and threatens me all the time. I don't dare talk to him about this, for he might very well be in on the plan to harm my father."

Luke's eyes narrowed. He looked at the woman in front of him, praying to discern if she lied. "There's a plan? Do you have proof?"

Valerie wiped her eyes once again. "No, but I know something's going on nevertheless."

"How?"

"There have been people in and around my father—around his room—who have no purpose being there. Daddy is always drawing the coattail crowd."

"The coattail crowd?" Luke questioned.

"You know, those people who plan to make it big or get rich by riding his coattails to the top. Daddy is so giving, so generous, he never sees harm until it's too late. I've heard rumors and—"

"Look, you can't go acting on rumors," Luke interjected.

"If you don't have proof, the authorities aren't going to be able to help you."

"But I'm not going to the authorities. I've come to you."

Luke shook his head and started back up the path. "You need to talk to the authorities. If there is a problem, they're the ones who can help keep your father out of trouble. They can even post a guard on him while he's here at the canyon."

"Please don't leave me, Luke. Please don't say no. Don't leave me all alone in this."

Luke stopped and looked at her for a moment. She seemed so delicate, so vulnerable and lost. "Miss Winthrop, if you would turn to God, you would find you're never alone. Pray about this and ask His guidance. God will surely show you what to do."

"I don't need religion—I need you."

"No, you don't. You hardly even know me," Luke replied firmly.

"But I'd like to."

"Miss Winthrop, I can't help you, except to pray for you." He didn't know if it was God's stirring or his own personal discomfort, but Luke felt an overwhelming need to escape. "Good day," he added rather abruptly.

Luke walked away, leaving the crying woman to her own devices. He wasn't interested in anything she had to offer, and the pricking of his conscience seemed a foreboding of things to come.

The Winthrops were bad news for the entire area. He didn't want to get involved with them on any business or personal level, yet they seemed to impose themselves on people. They represented everything Luke disliked: power, money, fame, and politics. They were of the world. They were the world.

The Winthrops and their kind used people. Used them no matter the cost. If a person proved useful, they were brought in as the best of friends. Once they'd served their purpose, however, and that person was no longer needed, they were disposed of as neatly as . . . Luke stopped in his thoughts.

"As neatly as Rufus Keegan was pushed over the edge," he murmured.

The slender build of Valerie Winthrop came to mind. She'd admitted to spending part of the evening with Keegan. Maybe she knew something. After all, it was entirely possible that, short of the confrontation that sent Keegan to his death, Valerie Winthrop was the last person to speak to him.

"But she'd probably only lie," Luke surmised. He hated to judge her harshly, but each encounter with her seemed to bring trouble.

Luke contrasted her to Alexandria Keegan. Alex's gentle spirit and quiet, unassuming manners made Luke feel protective and loving. Valerie Winthrop just irritated him.

The need to see Alex, to hold her and tell her how he felt, grew stronger with each passing moment. Luke knew it was poor timing given the situation, but each time he had put off telling her of his love, things only seemed to get worse.

"I'd like a few words with you, Mr. Toland."

Luke looked up to greet the stern expression of the ranger who'd tried to talk to Alex the night before. His counterparts had already asked Luke a couple dozen questions related to Rufus Keegan's death, but he had figured they were far from done.

"Sure," Luke said nodding. "What do you want to know?"

The man's eyes narrowed. "Did you have any reason to want Rufus Keegan dead?"

Valerie Winthrop had never felt more alone in her life. She watched Luke walk away and hook up with another man. No doubt another friend—a part of his life at the Grand Canyon.

It seemed everyone had someone they could trust—but she had no one. Even her own father was so focused on his campaign and his desire for the presidency that he couldn't see anything else. Oh, she knew he loved her, but she was something more ornamental than useful in his eyes. Her father trusted her to host his dinner parties, but not to pick her own husband. Her father had never denied her anything, but on the issue of Joel Harper he seemed blind and deaf.

Drying her eyes, Valerie looked out over the canyon. It would be easy enough to jump to her death. Die in the flash of a moment—like Rufus Keegan. The thought of him dying sent chills up her spine. She remembered his suggestions the night before during their walk along the rim. She could almost recollect the feel of his hands upon her—touching her, demanding things of her she didn't want to give. She shuddered and refused to think about it. There was nothing she could do about it now.

She had thought her lie about someone trying to kill her father would cause Luke to care about her. She'd thought that if her looks couldn't bring him to his knees, then perhaps the idea of being her rescuer and protector would. But Luke hadn't been interested in this role either. He puzzled her like no other man ever had. Usually all she had to do was bat her eyelashes or wave her money and men were at her beck and call.

Even as she thought this, the idea left her more lonely than ever. Would anyone ever love and care about her—for herself? She'd played so many games acting the coquette, the wild rebel, the sweet, attentive daughter. She wasn't even sure who she was anymore. Her life in Charleston was one of privilege and elegance. She was a daughter of the South—highly respected, belonging to that elite world of modern southern belles.

She'd been born to this, taking her mother's place in society, serving as she had served. Valerie generally saved her wild behavior for times when she was away from her home. New Yorkers didn't care how she conducted herself. They didn't mind her wearing scandalous clothes and being seen entering speakeasies. They turned a blind eye to her flirtations and drinking.

Valerie only wished she could turn a blind eye to herself. She didn't like herself very much. For all the confidence of her position, somewhere along the way Valerie had lost sight of the truth.

"I have no clue as to what the truth is anymore," she whispered.

Luke had said she needed God, but Valerie had tried church and religion. It left her hopeless and burdened with its many rules and regulations. She could never hope to be the pure and innocent person that religion demanded. She could never be good enough—not with her problems and life-style.

There has to be something else, she thought. *Something more than this emptiness.* The vast emptiness of the canyon seemed to mirror how she felt inside. It would take an awful lot to fill up the Grand Canyon, but surely that would be simple compared to Valerie trying to fill the hole in her heart.

God would be big enough to fill that space, she thought, then quickly pushed the thought aside.

Ignoring the acquaintances who looked her way, Valerie

went back to her suite on the third floor of El Tovar. She had no desire to mingle and make small talk. Luke's words continued to haunt her—his talk about how a person needed to know where they stood with God. But how was a person to know something so vast as that? It wasn't as if God would come down and speak to a person face-to-face. Was it?

She thought of the whiskey she'd hidden in her dresser. The idea of drinking herself into oblivion appealed to her greatly. Let them all dine and party without her. She wasn't feeling well. Her father or Joel could make her excuses. The alcohol wouldn't solve her problems, but it would make them go away for at least a few hours. Or rather, it would make her no longer care about their existence.

Entering her room, she immediately locked the door behind her. She wanted no one to disturb her.

"I saw you with Toland," Joel stated.

Valerie turned with a start, her hand clasping the collar of her dress. "How did you get in here?"

"That's unimportant," he said, getting up from the bedside chair. "What is important is that I saw you with Toland just now."

"So what?" Valerie said, trying hard to be brave. "I happened upon him while I was walking and we talked."

"Is that what you call it when you wrap yourself around someone?"

Valerie recognized his jealousy. It was almost enough to make her laugh. Almost. But the anger in his expression drew her up short. "I've been greatly upset since last night's events. Not that I would expect you to understand."

Joel watched her with an odd sort of expression, one which Valerie found completely unnerving. He wore his dark brown suit, the one she'd helped him pick out in Charleston.

The tie was also one she'd helped him choose. His entire appearance, quality through and through, should have pleased her, but instead it left her feeling cold and disinterested. Next to a man like Luke Toland, Joel seemed boring and lifeless.

"Things have gotten out of control," Joel announced, crossing the room to look out her window. "Unscheduled events are taking place, and it's causing me a great deal of trouble."

"I'm sure I don't know what you mean," Valerie said, taking off her straw hat. She wished Joel would simply leave her alone but knew full well he'd come with something or someone on his mind. The sooner he got it out for her consideration, the better off they'd both be. "Maybe you should explain," she finally added, coming hesitantly to sit on the edge of her bed. She hoped her calm approach would soothe him.

"This election means everything to me. To your father as well," he said, turning from the window. "There is a great deal at stake, and no one will be allowed to ruin that. Not the Keegans. Not John Davis or Bradley Jastrow. Not even you." He lowered his voice a bit before adding, "Especially not you."

Fear washed over her, and the loneliness she'd felt earlier seemed to magnify. "Why don't we go downstairs for a bit of lunch?" she suggested. "You can tell me all about this over one of those lovely salads." She got to her feet, but Joel quickly crossed the room and stood between her and the door.

"You aren't going anywhere, my dear. There is much we need to consider—to take charge of. I'm going to need your help in order to see my plans to completion. You do want to see your father elected as president, don't you?"

Valerie bit her lower lip and backed up a step. "It's hardly proper for us to discuss it here."

"Why not? I'm sure you've had many other men here for . . . discussions."

"That's not true," Valerie countered. "You shouldn't be here."

"But we're engaged, my dear. Tomorrow night we'll make it official. Surely there can be no harm." He smiled in that self-confident manner she'd come to hate.

"It's not proper. People will talk."

"People are already talking, Val. They're saying things like, 'How is it that Miss Winthrop should act so freely with other men?' Or 'Didn't I hear that she's engaged? What must her fiancé think?' Those are the kind of things people are saying. You're making me the laughingstock of our social circles."

"It hasn't been intentional. You and I both agreed that we should enjoy ourselves with other people," Valerie protested in her defense.

"I believe we had both agreed to be discreet. You have obviously given no regard to that agreement. All last night you hung on one man's arm or another. I believe you made the circle to include everyone—everyone but me, that is." His eyes narrowed as he stepped toward her. "I would certainly hate to have people believe my soon-to-be wife was a woman of loose moral character."

"You've never cared what anyone thought," Valerie said, backing away from him. "Why concern yourself now?"

"Because I intend to win this election for your father. I intend to see us married and my future secured." He paused.

"I intend to have access to the Winthrop fortune—that's all I care about."

Her reached out to her and Valerie cringed and closed her eyes. When his touch didn't come, Valerie opened her eyes and noted his expression. It seemed a mix of frustration, disgust, and maybe even hurt.

"Please go," she whispered, barely able to get the words out.

Joel shook his head. "No. I intend to have what you so freely give to everyone else. Your days of denying me are over."

"Don't do this, Joel. You'll regret it, I promise."

He took hold of her dress at the neckline and tore the material down the bodice. "The only regret I have is that I didn't do this sooner."

"It's not what you think," she pleaded. "Joel, I've never been with a man. I swear it. You may have all your jealous thoughts, you may imagine the worst—but I swear it's true."

He stopped, looking at her oddly. "I don't believe you."

Panic swept through her like a fire. "I'm not lying. I'm a virgin. I may not act the part, but I've always remained that way—I do have my scruples."

"Saving yourself for marriage, eh?" His voice took on a sarcastic tone. "Well, consider this your wedding day."

Hours later, Joel left Valerie's room in a sense of euphoria. Who would have believed the woman was chaste? Not that it mattered now. She was his. Now she'd have to marry him or face the embarrassment of her ruined reputation. He might have even managed to get her pregnant. What a delight that would be. She'd have to marry him in a hurry or lose her precious social standing in Charleston. Perhaps Joel would push for a Christmas wedding. That would give them enough time to finish this trip and settle back into a more normal routine.

He could see it all now—a beautiful Charleston wedding with all the right people in attendance. He would never be fully accepted as one of them because he was a Yankee and there still existed long, wounded memories of the War Between the States. Still, with Winthrop backing him, society would play their part. They might talk about him behind his back, but to his face they would be the epitome of graciousness.

Smiling to himself, Joel felt as though he could move a mountain. Rufus Keegan had proved a rather unpleasant inconvenience, but that was behind him now. Keegan could no longer cause him trouble or make threats. He shook his head and frowned, remembering the man's audacity. Keegan had said he would relay damaging information to the senator should Joel not bring him into their folds immediately instead of waiting for the election. Foolish man. No one threatened Joel Harper and got away with it.

Systematically, Joel would take care of each problem and see his life put in order. Tomorrow night would bring him victory—sure and sweet. He had Valerie where he wanted her. He had the senator eating out of his hand. And now Keegan was out of his way.

He paused at the top of the steps to glance back at the door to Valerie's room. He thought he might feel some small measure of regret, but none came. He'd only taken what was rightfully his to take. There'll be no more Luke Tolands or Rufus Keegans or Andrew . . . what was his name? Shrugging, Joel smiled. It didn't matter what his name had been. He wasn't a problem anymore.

CHAPTER NINETEEN

Valerie stared up at the ceiling and wondered how her life had ever come to such a tragic place. She had no idea how long she'd lain there. Minutes? Hours? Days? Still too stunned to move, she nevertheless felt the pain and misery of her encounter with Joel. Closing her eyes against the images, Valerie wished herself dead.

How could anyone be so hateful and cruel? Joel had taken her innocence with hardly any more concern than if he'd been stepping on a bug. He'd appeared only momentarily stunned to realize she had been truthful about her claims of purity. But it didn't stop him. He'd laughed then, and she could still hear the sound ringing in her ears.

He had told her, even as he raped her, that she was a worthless and stupid woman. He told her that he only placed himself in her life in order to get what he wanted from her father. Then he threatened her with worse if she dared to breathe a word of his admission.

Valerie was used to using others, used to moving them like pawns in her game, but this time she'd been on the receiving end. And it wasn't at all the innocent act she'd thought it to be.

For years, she had convinced herself that the goal justified her poor behavior. Now she knew that wasn't true. It had taken Joel's attack to make her see the lie, however.

Rolling to her side, Valerie simply wanted to hide away in her room until her father decided it was time to leave the Grand Canyon. How she hated this place! Her entire life had ended here—nothing would ever matter again. The parties no longer offered her their magical illusions. Those wonderful moneyed people she often kept company with were of no interest. They couldn't make things right again—not that a single one of them would ever care.

She wept softly into her pillow. A parade of faces came to mind—Andrew, Luke, and so many others. She'd played with them, teasing them with her flirtations. She'd visited Luke in his cabin—knowing full well he'd never take advantage of her. She'd known she could take the game as far as she wanted with him, and that he'd stop when she told him to. Unlike Joel.

She cringed, still feeling his breath upon her. Sometime during his attack he'd had the audacity to tell her that she needed him.

"You'll see it in time, my dear," he had whispered against her ear. *"You'll see how much you need me."*

But she didn't need Joel or anything he had to offer. Luke had said she needed God, but she was certain God didn't need her. Especially not now.

"You've brought this on yourself," Joel had said as he dressed to leave her. *"I might have reconsidered if I'd truly believed in your innocence. Of course, there's nothing to be done now, but when you look in the mirror, you'll see exactly who brought this to pass."*

For all her flirtations and wild encounters, Valerie had always managed to get away from difficult situations just in time. There was a certain thrill to her game. She would take herself almost to the point of no return, then turn and flee before life and its mongers could take from her what they would. Now all of that had changed. Joel was right. She'd brought this on herself, and now she had to live with the consequences. Or die with them.

She dozed off and on, refusing to get out of bed. The shadows of the day shifted, changing as the hours passed. Nightmares robbed her of any peaceful sleep. She couldn't close her eyes without seeing Joel Harper staring back at her.

Hearing someone at the door to her room, Valerie held her breath and stifled her sobs. The door opened and the image of her nightmare took shape. Had he come to hurt her again?

"What are you doing just lying there? Have you been there ever since I left?" Joel questioned, turning on a light. "You're hosting a party in less than an hour's time. Get up and make yourself presentable."

"I'm not going," she answered flatly. There was nothing else he could do to her. She wasn't about to cower in fear.

"Oh yes, you are," he said, coming to the bed. Reaching out, he grabbed her arm and pulled her from the bed. She collapsed on the floor at his feet, clutching at the tattered remains of her dress. "Get up!" he commanded. "Get up and stop acting like a child."

Valerie could hardly think, much less make sense of his purpose. "Why are you here? Haven't you caused enough damage?"

"I haven't begun to cause damage," Joel said with a laugh. He crossed the room to her wardrobe and pulled open the doors with great flourish. "Oh, here, wear the scarlet gown. That suits you perfectly."

"I'm not going."

"Yes, you are. You aren't going to give me any more trouble," Joel stated, walking to where she sat on the floor. "You think I've done the worst thing to you—worse than anything else I could do—but let me assure you, my dear, that's hardly the case."

She looked up at him and met his hateful gaze. "I despise you."

"And I despise you. You're a willful, spoiled child who's had everything handed to you on a silver platter. You may have Daddy wrapped around your little finger, but you don't have me in such a position."

Valerie felt anger surface where numbness had been only moments before. Surprising them both, she leaped to her feet and raised her hands to Joel's face. She would have scratched his eyes out, but he took hold of her wrists.

"Good to see you back among the living."

"I wish it had been you who'd died instead of Mr. Keegan," she said, trying to pull away from his hold.

"No doubt that is true. It certainly would make your life less complicated, eh?" He narrowed his eyes, his brows pulling together. "Now get ready for the party. You have exactly half an hour and then I drag you out, dressed or not."

"I need a bath."

"Then take one, but be quick about it," he said, releasing her and pushing her away from him. "Oh, and one other thing, Val darling," he said sarcastically, "I know I mentioned it earlier, but I'm concerned that you might not have been paying attention. Say nothing about what happened here today."

Valerie lifted her chin defiantly. "Why? Are you afraid Daddy might send you packing if I tell him the truth?"

"I'm afraid something might well happen to *you*. You see, we mustn't let anything upset this campaign. We must keep your father in the forefront as the most positive and beneficial candidate for the job of the presidency. Having a lunatic daughter won't help his cause. Although having a dead daughter just might."

Valerie tried to keep the fear from her voice as she replied, "I suppose having a raped daughter would only cause problems for the rapist. Perhaps Daddy could receive public sympathy over the fact that his aide not only raped his campaign treasury, but his daughter as well."

"And who would believe such fabrications? After all, most everyone here, as well as elsewhere, knows full well that the daughter in question has lived life in a most provocative manner. You're already known to do as you please, with whatever man you please to do it with."

"I was a virgin. You stole that from me," she managed to say.

"And who would believe that?" he questioned. "You dress in such a manner to suggest yourself quite free and easy with your favors. You hang on the arm of every man who shows you attention—you let them handle you in ways that make decent people turn in disgust. Who would ever believe such a nonsensical declaration?"

She shook her head, tears forming in her eyes. "You know it's true."

He grinned in wicked delight. "Yes, of course, but I'm the only one who does know it for sure. And if pressed, I'll certainly say nothing of the fact—rather, I'll take the public's admiration and even sympathy for agreeing to marry such a promiscuous woman. I can manage to produce a dozen witnesses who will all swear to having been your lovers.

"No one will ever believe you, Val. If you declare me to be a rapist, I'll merely speak to the issues of your sanity and bring in my friends to declare you quite the liar. Were sexual freedoms not already a somewhat socially acceptable thing in certain circles, you might already be facing four walls in a sanitarium—or perhaps some quiet little convent in Europe. Just remember that. Remember, too, I can produce enough information on you to prove whatever I need to prove. Even to give reason, after your father's successful election to the office, for why his darling only child should end up miserably taking her own life."

Valerie shuddered. "You're mad. You've caused the death of people and you have no remorse whatsoever."

Joel shrugged. "It's rather like being hired to remove vermin. I do the job and eliminate unpleasant and nonproductive people from the world. Generally people don't want to know the details of what I do, and neither do they care. They simply want the job done. I'm needed, my dear, for there will always be vermin."

"Too bad you can't eliminate yourself," she muttered in reply.

"Now, Val, you don't mean that." He smiled at her as though he thought himself to have some special power over her.

"I hate you," she blurted.

"The feeling is mutual. I've never loved you and probably never will," Joel said matter-of-factly. "You've been nothing more than a stepping-stone to what I want. If I could kill you and still have what I want, nothing would give me greater pleasure."

Val felt as though he'd struck her. She'd never believed

him to really care, but she'd never anticipated such hate. "You'll be sorry."

"Not nearly like you will be if you dare to interfere with me again." Joel took a step toward her, and Val, still clutching her torn dress, backed up against the wardrobe. "After all, you forget I know all of your little secrets. *All* of them. Do we understand each other?"

Valerie trembled from head to toe. "I understand. Better than you can imagine."

Joel smiled. "Good. Then we should get along famously."

Val took up her toiletry items and headed into the private bath, defeated. It was more than the rape. It was the knowledge that she would have to face every day of her life with this monster as her master.

Closing the door between them, Valerie began to cry anew. There was no hope. Everything was gone. Everything had suddenly become very ugly. Death would be so much easier.

Alex looked at her mother in exasperation. "Why can't you tell me what happened?"

Her mother looked back toward the window. Her petite form seemed swallowed up in the nearly floor-length gray dress she wore. "I don't want to talk about any of it."

Alex had pleaded with her mother for answers all day long, and always, it was the same answer. Alex tried to stress the urgency of the situation once again. "But, Mother, they could put you in jail for murdering Father. If you continue to refuse to tell them what they need to know, they'll send you away from me."

Katherine Keegan looked back to her daughter. "I can't

talk about it. Please don't ask me to."

Alex went to her mother and hugged her close. "I'm sorry, Mother. It's just that there is so much that needs to be explained. No one understands what happened. I know you didn't push Father over the edge. I know that within my heart. But if you won't talk to them and tell them the truth of who did murder Father, they'll presume you guilty. You could even face death yourself." She pulled back and looked into her mother's face.

"There are worse things than death," her mother replied. She moved away from Alex and turned back again to the window.

"I love you, Mother. It hurts so much to see you suffer. Just like it hurt all those years watching Father—"

"Don't speak ill of the dead, child. He can't hurt anyone any more."

Her words were cold, almost emotionless. Alex felt a shiver run up her spine. "Mother, how can I help?"

"There's nothing anyone can do now. I'm a prisoner here, I'm sure."

"But if you weren't?"

"Then I'd rather be away from all this fuss."

"I'll arrange it then," Alex said, suddenly getting an idea. "We'll hide you away while the entire matter is investigated. I know of a cabin—it's been closed for repairs so none of the staff is living there. It doesn't have electricity, but there is a small bathroom. We'd have to put up thick blankets at the windows so that you could light a candle or lamp, and I could bring you food."

Her mother turned around to face her. "Do you really think that's possible?" It was the first real interest she'd shown all day. "I'm weary of the reporters."

"I'll arrange everything," Alex replied, hoping she wouldn't regret her words and get her mother in more trouble for her exploits. Perhaps Alex could even speak with those in charge of the investigation. "I'll go now and see what I can manage." She kissed her mother on the cheek and hurried to find the ranger who'd questioned her the night before.

"I can pretty well guess who gave you the idea that I might have something to do with Keegan's death," Luke said, barely keeping his temper under control. "Joel Harper feels that I've overstepped my bounds by telling him to stay away from Alex Keegan. He imposed himself upon her, and I put him in his place."

"It doesn't matter who brought the accusation to our attention," the stiff-backed ranger said. "The fact is you've always been a suspect because you were there when the others arrived. With Mrs. Keegan refusing to cooperate, you are next in line."

"I didn't kill Keegan," Luke said flatly. He stretched his jean-clad legs out in front of him and tried to relax. He had nothing to hide. He needed only to rest in the Lord and wait for the truth to be revealed. "If anything, I think you should seriously consider Joel Harper."

"Why?"

"Because he seems the type to eliminate obstacles. Keegan might very well have been giving him trouble."

"If that's the case, why would Mrs. Keegan remain silent on the matter?"

Luke shrugged. "I have no idea. I would imagine the woman is pretty lost in her grief and shock. This wouldn't be the kind of thing a person would get over easily."

"Was Rufus Keegan alive when you came to the canyon rim last night?"

"I don't know. He wasn't there, if that's what you're asking. I heard the screams and came to see what the trouble was. When I got to the rim, I found Mrs. Keegan alone. She'd collapsed to the ground and was crying. I helped her up and she told me, 'Rufus has gone over the edge.' Then she said nothing more—she just cried."

"How is it that you know her so well? Well enough that she'd allow you to comfort her?"

Luke leaned forward again at this. "She was in shock. She'd just seen her husband fall off the edge into the Grand Canyon. I doubt seriously she would have cared who held her while she cried. Nevertheless, she knew me through her daughter Alex. We're good friends and have worked together for the last four years."

"Did you have any reason to want Rufus Keegan dead?" The man narrowed his eyes as if to ascertain the truth in what Luke was about to say.

"No. I hardly knew the man."

"I understand you'd had an encounter with him some time back. An encounter that revealed him in a compromising situation with one of El Tovar's Harvey Girls."

"I did." Luke refused to offer any more information. If the man was going somewhere with this line of questioning, then Luke would let him do the leading.

"Did he threaten you then?"

"I don't recall that Mr. Keegan has ever threatened me."

"What did he say to you?"

Luke shook his head. "I don't recall word for word. He made some suggestive comments about his daughter and me."

The ranger seemed to perk up at this. "Comments that made you mad?"

"They certainly didn't make me happy."

"Were you mad enough to kill him?"

"No." Luke had reached the end of his patience. "You know, I've willingly answered all your questions. I'm not of the habit of lying and, while I realize you know very little about me, there are plenty of people here who can vouch for my character—many of them wear ranger uniforms." He got to his feet. "I wouldn't see killing a man as the solution to anything. Human life is valuable in the eyes of God—no matter who that human life belongs to. Therefore, I value it as well. Now, if you'll excuse me, I need to get back to work."

"As long as you're a suspect in this investigation, I'll need to advise you that you cannot leave the area."

Luke turned and frowned. "What did I do to deserve that mandate?"

"You were in the right place at the wrong time," the ranger said matter-of-factly. "And right now things aren't looking all that favorable for you—after all, as you pointed out, Mrs. Keegan is a small woman hardly capable of manhandling her husband. You, on the other hand—"

"I have a broken wrist," Luke interrupted, holding it up as if to offer evidence.

"It wouldn't keep you all that encumbered, Mr. Toland. Besides, Mrs. Keegan could have helped you as well."

"This is outrageous," Luke said. "You may have a job to do, but I'm innocent and expect you to treat me as such. The real killer is out there. That's where your focus needs to be."

"Just the same, you need to keep me apprised of your whereabouts. You aren't to leave the South Rim."

"I don't like the idea of moving her," the ranger told Alex. "I can't see why it should matter."

"It matters because she's withdrawing from everyone. She feels as though everyone is watching her every movement. The reporters are hounding her in spite of your men's efforts to keep them at bay. Why, this afternoon one of the men from Los Angeles threw rocks at her window until we were sure he'd break the pane."

The older man looked sternly at Alex. "Where would you move her?"

Alex quickly told him of the cabin. "You could post a guard in a discreet location. Somewhere in the trees where no one would see him watching the cabin. He could even be posted inside the cabin for that matter. Don't you understand? She's not about to leave without permission. She's a delicate old woman in a fragile state of health."

"I realize that. It's the only reason she hasn't been sent to the jail in Williams. By her own admission, she was alone with your father at the time of his death."

Alex felt her stomach tense at this reference. "Look, I don't care what the situation looks like, I know my mother didn't kill my father."

"She's not telling us who did," the man replied.

"I know," Alex said, feeling defeat wash over her. Perhaps it was a bad idea to suggest moving her mother. Maybe she would have been better off if they had taken her to Williams. At least in jail the reporters wouldn't have as much of a chance to pester her.

"I just want to protect her. Not from having to provide the truth, but from accusation and unnecessary grief. She's mourning my father's death and the reporters will not let her be. She's become a tourist attraction. If you need to move her to Williams, then do so. Either way, I just want to give her some peace."

The man studied her for a moment. "She'd have to have a guard. The sheriff is on his way and until we conclude our investigation or additional proof is given to refute what currently appears to be true, she's our prime suspect."

"I understand, but she's not guilty. I promise you that much. Please . . . please, just help her."

He sat in silence for several minutes. His gaze never left Alex's face. Finally he cleared his throat. "Look, I'm going to let you do this," the ranger announced, "but only because the reporters are making my life just as miserable. How do you propose to move her without the press knowing her whereabouts?"

Alex could hardly believe her ears. "I've got an idea."

After explaining her plan to the ranger, Alex went in search of Michaela. Within the hour Alex, Michaela, and Bernice had managed to arrange everything. Taking Bernice with her while Michaela kept watch on the back stairs, Alex put her plan into action.

"What is this?" her mother asked as Bernice came into the room carrying a Harvey uniform.

"We're going to sneak you out of here," Alex said. "I've even managed to get the ranger's permission."

"You what?" Katherine questioned, a look of hope filling her expression.

"I told them how difficult it's been for you here. They've agreed to let you move to a secluded cabin. A guard will be posted in the cabin with you, but otherwise they will endeavor to leave you alone until they decide what's to be done."

Katherine looked to Bernice and then back to Alex before sitting on the edge of her bed. Just as quickly as the hope had come, it seemed to flee. "What do you suppose is to be done?"

Alex went to her mother and knelt on the floor in front of her. "Mother, you have the public's sympathy. People are even protective of you. The mayor of Williams is here and stated publicly that you could not possibly have caused your husband harm—that you're a pillar of the community. The entire staff of El Tovar believes in your innocence, and I've heard it rumored that the Winthrops are even hiring a private investigator."

"No!" Katherine exclaimed. "No more investigators."

Alex studied her mother's face. She seemed almost panicked. "Mother, what is it that you aren't telling me?"

In spite of Bernice's presence, Katherine reached out to take hold of Alex's shoulder. "There are things that are better left unsaid. I can't talk about this. Please try to understand."

"But I don't," Alex said flatly. "You are suspected of causing Father's death. It's only because of your friends and public opinion that they haven't already whisked you away to Williams and jail."

"Alex, whatever happens, you must understand that I've done what I felt best. Just trust me, please."

It was then that Alex knew for certain her mother was hiding the truth. Before, Alex had told herself the moments of the murder were just too horrific for her mother to face. Better still, that her mother hadn't even been there when the murder had happened. She'd tried to convince her heart that her mother had said nothing to the officials because she had nothing to tell. But now she could see for herself that wasn't the case.

Nodding slowly, Alex spoke. "I'll try to do as you ask, but if it all begins to turn against you, you must tell them the truth. God would want no less from you."

"I know," her mother answered sadly.

Alex helped her mother dress in a Harvey uniform and planted a large straw hat upon her head.

"Keep your face down and stay in the middle of us. If we pass other people, just keep looking to the ground. Hopefully they won't be able to tell the difference."

When the coast was clear, they hurried down the back stairs. The guard had just forced several newspapermen to the top of the stairs and was to follow later in order to throw off any suspicions about the women.

Alex heard the ranger reprimand the press for interfering in his job. The men protested loudly demanding their rights to report the truth. Alex pushed her mother past the stairs, laughing and murmuring something inaudible to Bernice.

Michaela joined them outside, giving the appearance of a friendly group of co-workers out for a stroll. It was a scene often observed at El Tovar, and they figured this to be the best way to avoid suspicion. Whenever they passed by hotel guests or reporters, they giggled like schoolgirls and put their heads close together, as if telling secrets. Alex saw the fear in her mother's eyes, but she kept moving forward.

It was agreed between the three Harvey Girls that each one would take turns bringing food and supplies to Katherine Keegan and her guard. Alex could only pray they wouldn't need to leave her there for long. The place was positively dingy, and Alex feared it would only add to her mother's depressed spirits.

"I have to go work at the party the Winthrops are giving now," she told her mother. "In fact, I'm already late. You remain here and I'll come to you as often as I think it safe."

"There's no need to fuss over me, dear. I'm not running

away or going anywhere. I don't wish for anyone to worry after me. I'm sorry for the trouble," she stated, saying more than she had since Alex's father had died.

Alex hugged her mother, wishing to herself that she could turn back time and spare her mother this misery. Yet at the same time, Alex felt guilty because she wasn't all that sorry her father was gone. She was sorry he'd died without Jesus in his life. She was sorry he'd been so mean and adulterous. And she was sorry that she'd never known a time when she felt her father had really cared about her. But she wasn't sorry he was dead.

Leaving her mother safe and secure, Alex headed back up to the hotel at a run. She knew she needed to get back to the matters at hand. She needed to make an appearance at the party and assure people that all was well. She needed . . .

"Whoa, there!" Luke said, reaching out to steady Alex with his one good arm. "I don't think I've ever seen you run like that."

"Sorry . . . I . . . didn't see . . . you there," Alex panted.

He continued to touch her, rubbing his fingers along her upper arm. "I'm glad we ran into each other." He grinned. "I've needed to talk to you."

"I know, but things have been so crazy. I'm late for the party," she said, her voice steadied a bit.

"Surely they don't expect you to work—your father just died."

"Mrs. Godfrey tried to force me to take time off, but I can't. I'd go mad sitting there thinking of everything that has happened."

"They might see you as unfeeling—maybe even involved in the murder if you don't show some sorrow in his passing," Luke suggested. "I don't want them to get the wrong idea about you, Alex." He reached up and gently touched her cheek.

Alex's breathing and heartbeat continued to race. Luke's touch ignited feelings in her that she had never thought herself capable of. All she could remember was his kiss, his touch, his scent.

She dared herself to look into his eyes. What was happening to her? Why were all these feelings coming to the surface now, after he said his feelings had changed? Would he go away with Valerie Winthrop? Was there no hope of a future for them?

"I don't care what anyone else thinks," she managed to whisper.

"But you should. You don't want to give them cause to turn the light on you."

"Let them!" Alex declared, finding her voice. "I haven't done anything wrong. I may not show all the proper etiquette of mourning, but I've done nothing I should be ashamed of."

"They think I'm a suspect," Luke threw out.

This instantly sobered Alex. "But why?"

"Because I was there."

"But you didn't come until after the screams. Just like the rest of us."

"But it's my word against theirs."

Alex shook her head. "You can't be serious."

"I am. Joel Harper—at least I'm pretty sure it was him—suggested that I might have reason to want your father dead."

"No!" Alex gasped. She saw Joel Harper disbanding her support of friends and family, piece by piece. Had the world gone suddenly mad? *God, where are you in all of this?* First her mother, now Luke. How many more would have to suffer before the truth was brought to light?

CHAPTER TWENTY

On the horizon, storm clouds brewed and churned in the early morning light. Alex noticed the ugly blackness from her window and silently prayed it would rain all day and night. Tonight the gala party to end all parties was planned by the Winthrops, and already the idea wearied her to the bone. The events the night before were sedate and small, compared to what she would face tonight. Tonight, the candidates would each announce their desire to receive the nomination for president, and their cronies would expound on their capabilities and positive qualities.

Even more guests were pouring in on special trains, and Alex knew it would be impossible to pause for a moment's rest once her workday began. Not that she wanted to rest. The night had been impossibly long, and knowing her mother was the prime suspect in her father's murder, with Luke a close second, did nothing to offer her comfort. Once again her father was ruining her life.

Father. Alex had tried not to think of her father, for it was a painful chore she'd tried to avoid. She had so long wished him out of her life—out of her mother's life—but now that he was, she felt rather confused. What plans should they make? Would her mother be freed to go about her business and live out the rest of her life, or would they assume her guilt and jail her? If freed, would her mother want to remain in Williams or go elsewhere? And always in the midst of these thoughts, Alex felt guilt overcome her peace. She'd never cared enough to share the Gospel with her father. Never cared enough to approach him with anything but her anger.

"You can't hand your daughter over to your vulgar friends and expect anything but anger," she said to the room. Her words reverberated off the windowpane right back at her, even as thunder rumbled in the distance.

Turning from the window, Alex felt a sense of loss. Her spiritual peace felt ripped to shreds. The truths she'd known and honored for most of her life seemed little comfort. Her father had wounded her so often that Alex had lost count. He didn't deserve to be mourned or cared about. He didn't deserve her love or sorrow.

She sat down at her writing desk and brought her hands together in her lap. She tried hard to muster up some feeling other than anger, but short of bitterness and regret, she found nothing she could give in the wake of her father's passing. Mrs. Godfrey had offered her time away from her job to tend to her mother and deal with her father's death, but Alex had declined. Her father's death still seemed unreal. She had hardly known anything of the man.

"God, I don't mean to be so hardhearted," she whispered. "You know that has never been my desire. Every time I had an encounter with Father, I tried so hard to remain at peace with him. I tried to respect his position in my life, even if I found it nearly impossible to respect the man himself.

"I wanted to have a close family. I wanted to believe he could change and remain faithful to my mother, but instead he only grew worse." She blinked back tears. "He hurt my mother so much, Lord. How do I forgive that? How do I put this to rest and let go of my hatred and bitterness? How?"

Alex joined her co-workers as they met to discuss the day's events and the evening party. Mrs. Godfrey seemed rather frazzled, even though the hour was still quite early.

"We have a few additional staff coming from along the Santa Fe line here in Arizona. The girls will act as hostesses on the lawn," Mrs. Godfrey explained. "Michaela and Alex will be in charge of the lawn teams. There will be five girls in each group. A supper is to be given, as well as refreshments after the speeches. As I understand it, there will be festivities until well past midnight."

Several of the girls groaned, Alex included. Her job required she get up at five every morning as it was. Now they were suggesting she work until midnight or one and still have enough sleep to pull a full shift the following morning. Politicians and their madness had corrupted the gentle beauty and peace of her canyon park. The entire thing only served as one more incident to deeper harden Alex's resentment toward the Winthrops and Mr. Harper.

"You'll all help with breakfast here in a few minutes," Mrs. Godfrey announced, "then after the morning rush, Michaela and Alex, along with whomever they choose to help them, will see to the lawn tables. I have lists of necessary articles," she said, leaning forward to hand Alex a piece of paper. "This entire event will run smoothly and without problems, if you adhere to the list."

When the meeting broke up, Alex went to the private dining room and made certain her table was set properly for breakfast. She adjusted pieces of silverware and replaced a chipped plate before leaving the room to retrieve steaming pots of coffee. This was the routine with the Winthrop party. They would no doubt want the same thing today as they had on all the other days.

True to habit, the Winthrop party, this time minus Valerie, showed up at exactly seven o'clock. Joel Harper seemed to be in particularly good spirits, talking in rapid-fire to the man on his left, laughing and gesturing as they took their seat at the table. Alex wondered what could have the man so gleeful at this hour, but she didn't care enough to position herself close enough to overhear the conversation.

"Miss Keegan," the senator said, taking her aside, "I am so very sorry about your father. He seemed a good man, and I would have enjoyed having him on my staff."

"I'm sure he would have enjoyed that as well," Alex said, feeling hard-pressed as to how she should reply.

"I'm also sorry about the nonsense with your mother being held suspect. I'm certain such a dear sweet woman could have had nothing to do with such an ugly act." His drawled words were soothing.

"Thank you, Senator Winthrop. I'm certain of her innocence as well."

"I've decided to help the matter as best I can. I've hired a trustworthy man I know to do a private investigation for us. He lives in Dallas, but he should arrive by train this afternoon."

She was touched that a stranger should care so much about her mother's innocence as to spend his own money on seeing her name cleared. She also remembered her mother's panic at the thought of additional investigators. It didn't make sense to Alex, but she wouldn't say anything about it.

Her mother wasn't thinking clearly—that was all. "That's kind of you, Senator," Alex replied.

"Not at all. Not at all." He hooked his thumbs in his vest pockets and smiled. "The real interest here is truth. We want the truth to be told so that we can lay your father to rest without this stain upon your family's good name."

Alex nodded and excused herself to begin taking the breakfast orders. Most everyone stuck to a routine of the same type foods. One man always ordered dry toast and iced, poached eggs. Another wanted three grapefruits and a banana. They were as eccentric in their food orders as they were in their choices of companionship.

The meal ran smoothly, without so much as a raised voice until a panic-stricken man in a wrinkled blue suit appeared at the door to the dining room. "I'm . . . sorry . . . to interrupt," he said, gasping for breath. "I just got the news and knew the senator would want to know."

"What is it?" the senator asked, while everyone grew silent to see what the trouble was. The scene mesmerized even Alex. She stood frozen, a pot of coffee suspended from her hand.

"It's President Harding," the man said, his breathing coming in a steadier pace. "He's dead."

"What!" several men called out in unison.

The murmuring between them started out low and built quickly into loudly expressed comments of disbelief. Only Joel sat in silence, a smile touching the corners of his mouth, and in that moment Alex knew that he'd somehow had something to do with the president's death. His gaze met hers and refused to let her go. Alex felt the malice of his soul reach across the table as if to take hold of her.

"Do they say what killed him?" Winthrop asked, pushing back from the table.

"They aren't certain. He grew ill several days ago. They thought food poisoning might be to blame. It was rumored he'd eaten cherries and milk on his journey down from Alaska."

The senator nodded solemnly. "A deadly combination to be sure. Still, it seems unlikely that the president of the United States would have no one to warn him of such matters." The senator looked to his comrades in the room. "I suggest we adjourn and see to this news. If this proves to be true, we will need to postpone our announcements and party until another night."

Alex watched as the men filed out one by one, following after the senator as though they were sheep to a shepherd. Joel got up from the table at a leisurely pace, but instead of following the entourage, he moved toward Alex with a smug expression of satisfaction.

"You see, I told you I had ways of dealing with troublesome situations. You should have no doubt about the harm I could cause you, should you bring even the tiniest hint of trouble my way."

A thought suddenly came to Alex. She put down the coffeepot and braved her question. "Did you murder my father?"

Joel laughed, then moved closer and lowered his voice. "I wish I could take credit for that. I had planned to push Jastrow over the edge of the canyon—but then, you probably overheard that mentioned when I spoke to your father that night. Keegan's death ruined my plans, for you can hardly have two people fall within days of each other—especially from the same gathering of politicians.

"Besides, what do you care? You hated the man. Even now I see the contempt you hold for him written in your expression. Why should you care who did the deed so long as it's done? You could just as easily have pushed him over the edge as your mother."

"My mother is innocent. She had nothing to do with Father's death!" Alex protested loudly.

Joel put his finger to her mouth and pressed against her lips. "Shhh, darling, you don't want to raise the suspicions of others. If they hear you speaking of death, those ink slingers will hardly care what the truth is. They're after a story—the more sensational, the better."

Alex stepped back and pushed his hand away. "They're hardly going to care about my father's death, now that they have the president to contend with."

"But then, you hardly care about his death either," Joel said snidely. "Funny thing, you hated the man, made clear your utter and complete distaste for him, yet the two of you were so much alike. Dealing with you was like dealing with a younger version of him. Ruthless. Cold. Calculating."

Alex slapped Joel hard across the face, then backed away. "Don't *ever* compare me to him again." She started to leave, but Joel took hold of her and pulled her close.

"You're really disgusted by such a comparison, aren't you? Poor Alex. Didn't you ever see the truth for yourself? You're just like him. You're strong, just like he was. You're opinionated and bold, just like he was. You're ruthless and care little for things that don't concern you, and you rush to judgment about anything that doesn't fit in your perfectly ordered little world."

His words hit her hard. The truth of them scared Alex in a way that she'd never experienced. *I am like him,* she thought. *I am as horrible and awful a person as my father.*

"Let me go," she said, not even bothering to fight back.

Joel seemed surprised by her reaction and released her. "You think that I've just insulted you, but frankly, it's a compliment. I'd like to win you over to my side. There's a great deal I could do with a woman like you. Let me move you to Washington once we've won the election, and I'll show you just what I'm talking about."

Alex shook her head. "You sicken me. You arrange the death of the president, then talk of making me your mistress? Have you no soul?"

"None that I'm aware of—thankfully," Joel mused.

Alex felt a cold shiver rise up the back of her neck. "Leave me alone, Mr. Harper. I have no desire to even speak with you. Light has no communion with darkness."

"But what of shadows and shade?" he questioned. "Might those two compliment each other? The contrast of such brings beauty and grandeur to the canyon—might it not do the same for a man and woman?"

Alex felt sickened. She picked up her tray and left the dining room without another word. Harper stayed where he was, not following her for once. But it didn't matter. His words followed Alex, and they were enough to haunt her throughout the day.

The parties were canceled, and within an hour after breakfast, a storm moved in and poured monsoonal rains on the canyon park. Alex busied herself helping with lunch and then found other odd jobs that needed her attention. By the time the storm moved out in the late afternoon, leaving the canyon and El Tovar washed clean, Alex still struggled to find peace. Approaching the kitchen a few minutes before she was scheduled to work the evening shift, Alex heard Mrs. Godfrey call her name.

"Miss Keegan, would you please join me in the office?"

Alex put down the tray, her hands trembling as she moved to join her supervisor. Joel's comments rang over and over in her head. *"You're just like him."*

"Miss Keegan, this is Mr. Stokes, the investigator hired by Senator Winthrop, and Sheriff Bingham. They've come to ask you some questions about your father."

If I were given to fainting, now would be the time, she thought. The stern expressions of the men standing before her, coupled with Joel's startling revelation and added to the events of the last few days, were enough to send anyone into a faint. But Alex stood firm, though she now found herself full of doubts.

"Whatever I can do to help," Alex replied, "but my shift is about to start."

"Don't worry, Alexandria. I have someone taking your place. You're to have the remainder of the day off. You may use my office as long as necessary, gentlemen," Mrs. Godfrey said, moving to the still-open door. "I'll be seeing to my girls. If you need anything, just ask Miss Keegan for help. She knows the place nearly as well as I do."

"Thank you for your hospitality," Mr. Stokes said.

His frame reminded Alex of one of the tall cactuses she'd seen near Phoenix. Slender of build and rather gangly of limb, the man maintained a gentle countenance that put her at ease. The sheriff, on the other hand, seemed so tense and observant that he made Alex feel as though she were under a magnifying glass. He frowned at her as if she'd just done something rather disgusting. The expression reminded her of a time when she'd been a young girl of twelve. She'd taken an interest in a boy at church. Her mother thought it amusing, but her father was put out by the entire matter. He'd looked at her just as the sheriff did now, declaring the boy and his family far beneath the Keegans. Worse still, he'd caused the boy's father to lose his job and the family eventually had to move away.

"Please have a seat, Miss Keegan. We know you're no doubt mourning your father's loss, but if you would be so kind as to help us for a few moments, I assure you it would be to your benefit."

"I don't mind helping you. I am anxious to clear my mother of any suspicions."

"And you wouldn't help us if it didn't clear her name?" the sheriff asked.

"I didn't say that," Alex replied coolly. If they thought to catch her in lies, they might as well save their breath. With the shock of her father's death still wearing on her and her mother's unwillingness to cooperate, Alex felt she had no other choice but to be open and honest. At least to the best of her ability.

She took a seat in one of three chairs that had been arranged in front of Mrs. Godfrey's desk. The sheriff surprised her by walking to the chair behind the desk rather than taking one of the other two chairs beside her.

"Miss Keegan, I understand you were working the night your father died," Mr. Stokes began. He took the chair beside her, turning it so that they faced each other, more or less.

"Yes. I was serving in the capacity of hostess to the Winthrop lawn party and dance."

"And your hours of service for this event?"

"We were called to the kitchen by five-thirty and began arranging tables for the affair within the hour. The party was set to begin at eight o'clock and I was either on the grounds or in the kitchen the rest of the evening."

"And of course there were witnesses to verify this?" Stokes asked.

"Yes."

"And at any time did you leave your post to meet in private with your father?" the sheriff questioned.

Alex turned to the man. "No. My father and I did not get along, and I had no desire to seek him out."

"Why was it you didn't get along?" Stokes interjected the question in his calm, soothing tone before the sheriff could react.

"My father was a womanizer. He was also a cheat and liar. He scoffed at the beliefs held by my mother and I—beliefs of faith and high morals. He had little use for either one of us or our ideals and, in turn, I had little to do with him."

"Did you want him dead?" the sheriff asked, not to be outdone by Stokes.

Alex thought for a moment, searching her heart for the truth. She slowly shook her head. "No, not really. I wished him to be out of my life and out of my mother's life. But in all honesty, I didn't want him to die in order to accomplish that."

Stokes picked up the interrogation again. "Did your mother feel the same way?"

"I don't really know. My mother is a very private person. Whenever I tried to encourage her to leave him, she refused. She always held on to the hope that he would change. When she came here to El Tovar, I knew something was different. She was now telling me that she wanted a divorce."

"I see. And what was your father's response?"

"He didn't want one," Alex replied, feeling that she had

to tell them the entire truth of their encounter. "What he did want was a post in Washington. He supported Senator Winthrop's nomination for the presidency and planned to ride along on his success. He didn't want anything to hinder that, and a divorce would have cost him an unwelcome scandal. He threatened my mother and me and told us to let the matter drop."

"Threatened you? How?"

"He didn't really say. I threw out a comment, asked what he would do to keep us silent, and he said that people were likely to die every day or something like that. It was the first time he'd threatened my life, and it stunned me."

"You and your mother are very close, aren't you?" Stokes asked gently.

"Yes, we are. I care a great deal about her welfare."

"Which is why you asked the rangers here to let you move her to an undisclosed location?"

"Yes."

Stokes nodded. "I suppose the attention from the reporters and such was starting to be a problem."

Alex had no idea what the man wanted from her. She didn't appreciate his around-the-bush questions and said so. "Look, if you want to ask me questions, then please just ask them. If you want to know if I think my mother pushed my father into the canyon, then the answer is no. My mother weighs all of ninety pounds and my father must have weighed at least two hundred, maybe more. She's frail and unhealthy and there is no way she could have caused him that kind of harm."

"But she did have a motive," the sheriff said flatly.

"We all had a motive," Alex answered angrily. "My mother had motive. I had a motive. Half the people here at El

Tovar—forget that—half the people of Arizona had a motive for wanting my father dead. But someone is responsible and I cannot tell you who that person is. I'm not even convinced my mother can give you that name. She and I have talked, and she hasn't divulged anything beyond the pain she's enduring."

"Is that because she can't or because she won't?" the sheriff asked, his eyes narrowing as if he might scrutinize the answer from her.

Alex shrugged. "I honestly don't know." She remembered Joel and her father conspiring and, although the Winthrops had paid for this investigation, she hoped the sheriff was impartial enough to want to hear the truth. "I do know, however, because I overheard the conversation myself, that Joel Harper and my father were plotting and planning against the senator's competition. Mr. Harper talked of eliminating the competition in whatever manner necessary. My father agreed. Mr. Harper has since implied to me that he has caused problems for other candidates and will stop at nothing to get his man elected."

Instead of getting angry, both men smiled at her. "Miss Keegan, that certainly doesn't imply murder," Stokes said. "I can understand you're filled with worry over your mother's situation. So much so, no doubt, that you would say anything to keep her from going to jail for your father's murder."

At this Alex decided she'd had enough. She'd hoped they might listen, but she could see that they believed her to be nothing more than a faithful daughter lying for her guilty mother. Getting to her feet, Alex looked first to the sheriff and then to Mr. Stokes. "I'm a Christian woman. I am not in the habit of lying. I've answered your questions as best I can. Good day." She crossed to the door and opened it.

"Miss Keegan, please sit down. We're not finished with you yet," Stokes said sternly.

Alex felt the room close in as the sheriff got to his feet. "There are some important questions that we, as of yet, do not have answers for."

"Such as?"

"Well, for starts, it's been suggested that you or your mother might have hired someone to kill your father."

CHAPTER TWENTY-ONE

Alex froze in place, unspoken words stuck permanently in her throat. She looked at Mr. Stokes, unable to read from his expression whether or not he took the comment seriously.

"Please sit down, Miss Keegan, you look rather pale."

She shook her head, almost afraid that if she did as she was told, they might actually find a way to accuse her and judge her guilty.

"Someone remembered you threatening Mr. Harper," the sheriff threw in. "You said something about pushing him over the edge. Do you remember that?"

Alex thought back to her first encounter with Joel Harper. The night he'd pinched her and caused her to break a tray full of dishes. He'd wanted her to join him at the rim after dinner, and she'd said . . . The memory sickened her. She'd joked about pushing him over the edge. Someone in Winthrop's party had obviously shared that little story with the sheriff and Mr. Stokes. No doubt that someone was Joel Harper or Valerie Winthrop. Both had reasons to implicate her.

"Miss Keegan, you must admit it looks rather suspicious

that you would suggest such a thing in regard to Mr. Harper, only to have it later happen to your father," Stokes said softly. "Given the things your father did to bring embarrassment and disgrace on you and your mother, perhaps you felt you needed to take matters in your own hands, eh?"

"I can't believe this," Alex said, finally finding the words. "I would never hurt anyone. I can't even imagine resolving my problems in such a manner."

The sheriff laughed in a humorless manner. "You imagined it quick enough when putting Mr. Harper in his place."

"People have fallen over the edge before. The canyon is full of dangers and it is something often spoken about amongst the workers here. After all, we live with this danger on a daily basis. I wasn't serious about what I implied, I was trying to defuse a rather testy moment. Mr. Harper was being too free with his hands and needed to be put in his place. As for the similarities, hear me once and for all. I didn't kill my father, nor did I hire it done. I resent that you would question my character when you know nothing of me."

"We can only go on what we've been told in our investigation. Do you have someone who can vouch for your character?"

Alex could scarcely believe this line of questioning.

"I, for one, can vouch for the character of this woman," Luke Toland said, joining the party uninvited. "But since I'm also a suspect in this whole sordid affair, that probably doesn't hold much weight. I'm sure Mrs. Godfrey and at least a dozen other people, however, could vouch for Miss Keegan. I heard what you just said, and I can tell you from my knowledge of her over the past four years, there's no way in the world she'd even consider such a thing. Now, I'd personally like to talk to whoever is telling such lies."

Luke took a protective stand at Alex's side. In spite of his casted forearm, he looked for all purposes like a lion about to spring should anyone threaten his lair.

"Now, mister, don't go getting all uppity and stickin' your nose in where it don't belong," the sheriff said, coming from around the desk. "This is a private matter."

"Hardly," Luke replied, the anger building. "I'm Lucas Toland. I was summoned here to speak to a Mr. Stokes, and I'm supposing that's one of the two of you."

"I'm Stokes."

"Yeah, well, I'm not impressed. Is it your plan to badger my friend and her mother? Because if it is, I'm going to have to put a stop to it."

"I'm sorry, but this young woman and her mother are suspects in this investigation. By your own acknowledgment, you are also a suspect, Mr. Toland. After all, you were with Mrs. Keegan when the murder was discovered. For all I know, you and Mrs. Keegan were lovers and you did the old man in so that you could run away together. Or perhaps you were paid by Miss Keegan and her mother to kill Rufus Keegan."

"Of all the low down . . ." Luke stepped forward, grabbing Stokes by the lapels of his suit. His broken wrist seemed to cause him little trouble in getting his point across. "You have no right to talk in such a vulgar manner—especially in front of a lady."

"You seem awfully upset and defensive for someone who is claiming innocence," the sheriff said, reaching out to push Luke back.

"I ought to deck the both of you, and were I not a Christian, I might do just that."

"And you'd go to jail too," the sheriff said. "I'm Sheriff Bingham, and I won't tolerate any cowboys coming between me and truth. I've dealt with your kind before, and I can see to it that you're no trouble to me at all."

Alex felt as though she were watching a play. Worse yet, she felt she had been pulled from the audience and forced into a part she didn't know. She waited for someone to tell her what her lines should be—where she should stand—but no one said a word.

Without warning her eyes filled with tears and a sob broke from somewhere deep in her chest. Her breath came in ragged gasps. "Stop!" she screamed. "Stop it now!"

She turned and ran down the hall and out the hotel. She didn't stop running until she was well down the rim path, past the Lookout, past the studios. She was nearly to the Bright Angel Trailhead when Luke caught up with her and took hold of her. Spinning her around, he pulled her into his arms with such force that he nearly knocked the wind out of her as she slammed against his chest.

Spending her tears against his well-worn shirt, Alex didn't fight his hold. She felt such hopelessness, such despair. Luke was keeping her from throwing herself over the edge—maybe not literally, but certainly figuratively.

"I can't believe this is happening," she said, clinging to him tightly, almost afraid he'd push her away.

"I know, darlin', and I'm sorry."

"It's just too much, given everything else."

Luke gently tipped her chin up so she was forced to look into his eyes. "As much as I love holding you, why don't we sit down and talk this out? I want you to tell me everything. I want to talk about us."

His words brought back her biggest fears. Fears of Luke going away. Fears of him siding with the Winthrops. She loosened her hold and her words tumbled out. "I don't know if I can. I don't know that it would be a good idea. I know you have plans. Plans that will take you away from here—from me."

"They don't have to, Alex."

She looked up and met his warm expression. "But I know about the ranch—about Valerie Winthrop and her father."

"What are you talking about?"

Alex shook her head. "You don't have to hide it. You don't have to worry about my feelings. I already know. Miss Winthrop told me everything."

"Then maybe somebody better tell me, because I don't have a clue as to what you're talking about."

Alex had never known Luke to lie to her. She studied him for a moment, then raised her apron to dry her eyes. Swallowing hard, she drew a deep breath. "Miss Winthrop told me her father had offered you a ranch in Wyoming—a ranch that you would manage as your own. She said the senator thought you would make a good husband and . . . father. . . . I just figured . . ."

"You figured wrong," Luke said. He reached out and took her face in his hands.

The hardness of the cast's molding around his left hand rubbed against her cheek, but she didn't care.

"Alex, you figured this all wrong. I should have straightened this out weeks ago when I had the chance. Maybe even months ago."

Alex felt her heart race, and a tingling started where he had touched her cheeks. The sensation edged along her neck and spread throughout her body. *What's happening to me? Is this love? Am I in love with Luke Toland?*

She moaned slightly at the thought. *I can't be falling in*

love—not now. "But you said . . . I mean when I mentioned the ranch you didn't deny it."

"I'm buying my own ranch," Luke replied. "My brother sent me an advertisement about a ranch in Wyoming. It was just about the right size and already had a place to live and outbuildings. It had nothing to do with the Winthrops."

"But Miss Winthrop said . . ."

"Miss Winthrop is a liar," Luke said firmly.

He continued to rub his thumbs against her cheeks. Alex felt as if her face were on fire. "But you're still going away."

"Not without you," he replied, lowering his mouth to hers. "Not ever."

His kiss was slow and sweet. He pressed his right hand against the back of her head as if to pull her more deeply into the experience. Alex felt herself yield to the warmth and sensation of falling. Nothing like this had ever happened to her, not in all her life.

He lingered over the kiss, then pressed his lips against her cheek, her nose, her eyes. "Ah, Alex, do you know how long I've waited to do this? How much I've longed for this . . ." His voice trailed off as his mouth came back to hers. He kissed her again, then pulled away.

Alex, lost in the feeling of free falling, felt as though she'd landed rather abruptly. Opening her eyes, she looked at Luke, struggling to regain control of her breathing.

"Alex, I'm buying the ranch in order to offer you a home. You and your mother, if she'll join us."

"I don't think that would . . . I think . . ." She shook her head. "I can't think."

Luke laughed and wrapped her in his embrace. "You don't need to think right now. Just say yes."

"Yes? Yes to what?"

He laughed even harder. "I guess I never did ask you, did I?"

She shook her head again, not at all sure she understood what was happening.

"I'm asking you to marry me, Alex."

Her thoughts cleared with those few words. Suddenly ugly memories of her father's infidelity came rushing back. Other images came too. Valerie Winthrop with her arms wrapped around Luke. Joel Harper's unwelcome advances. It was too much, and Alex pushed Luke away and started to walk up the path.

"Wait! What are you doing?"

"I don't know," she said, refusing to stop or even look at him.

"Then come back here and talk to me."

"I don't think I can."

Luke took hold of her arm and drew her back around. "I think you'd better."

"It's just that . . . oh, Luke, you've been a dear friend to me. You've been the only man I could talk to and feel safe with."

"So what's the problem?" Luke asked, his brows knitting together in worry.

"Marriage is built on trust and love. I don't know that I could ever trust any man. That's why I've always avoided any kind of relationship. Any kind except the friendship I have with you."

Luke grinned. "Let's deal with one thing at a time. First, you said marriage is built on trust and you struggle with that. But I notice you didn't say anything about struggling with the love part."

Alex felt her cheeks grow hot. "I can't talk about love

when I can't figure out the trust issue. I mean, what about the past? What about my father and people like him?"

"Do you think I'm like him?" Luke asked seriously.

"I . . . never . . ." She looked away. "I don't think you're like him, but you're a man. Flesh and blood. Men have been unfaithful since the beginning of time. There are all kinds of examples in the Bible."

"Alex, I don't deserve your distrust based on the actions of someone else. If that were the case, I could say that you were just like Miss Winthrop or those trollops your father dallied with. I saw you in Joel Harper's arms the other night. I could accuse you of throwing yourself at him, and in fact, I did worry that maybe you'd gone to him for help, but Michaela set me straight."

"You'd really think me capable of—"

He put his finger to her lips. "I was wrong to suspect without any basis for the truth. I let presumption push me to suspicion. Just as you're doing with me."

His statement struck a nerve and hit her heart straight on. She'd never considered how it might be if someone perceived her on the same scale. She suddenly felt very ashamed of her attitude. Every man deserved to be dealt with as an individual. They weren't all men like her father . . . or Joel Harper.

"Oh, Luke, I'm sorry. Of course you're right. I never thought of it that way. It's just that I've been so surrounded with men who—"

"The past is not important, Alex. I'm asking you to put the past behind you and build a future . . . with me."

She looked into Luke's eyes and saw the love reflected there—love for her. It wasn't fair to believe him to be like her father or his cronies. It wasn't right to anticipate that he would cheat on her should she marry him. But the problem wasn't with Luke, she realized. The problem was with herself.

"I'm sorry, Luke. I've been so unfair to you. I don't deserve your kindness or your . . . your . . ."

"Love?" he asked, reaching up to touch her cheek. He gently stroked the smooth skin of her face, mesmerizing her with gentleness.

"Yes," she whispered.

"Alex, I don't love you because you deserve it, although you do. I love you because of who you are and who I am with you. I'm a different man with you, a man I can live with. My heart used to be all hard and bitter before you came into my life. Now I know God really cares about me, and I believe He's brought us together for a reason."

He moved to draw her into his arms once again. The cast felt cold against her shoulder, but his embrace warmed her to the core. How could she possibly walk away and never experience this warmth again?

"Alex, give me a chance to prove to you that I can be worthy of your trust. Give me a chance to show you that not all men do the things your father did. Please . . . give us a chance. Please trust me."

Alex thought of all the misery she'd endured since coming to the Grand Canyon. It was always Luke who transformed her day from bad to good. She thought of the way he'd kept her secrets—he deserved her trust.

She took a deep breath. "I overheard my father talking with Joel Harper. I think Mr. Harper has schemed to kill Mr. Jastrow, along with anyone else who plans to compete against Senator Winthrop—including President Harding."

He looked at her in disbelief. "You truly believe Harper has had something to do with the president's death? That seems unlikely. He's been here all along."

"They accused me of hiring someone to kill my father. Why does it seem so farfetched that Mr. Harper could hire someone to kill the president? After all, he has plenty of money to use for whatever he needs." Alex felt better for having told Luke the truth, for trusting him, but she had no idea where her words would lead them.

Luke pulled away, the expression on his face betraying his concern. "If this is true—if he's not just trying to sound threatening to you and the others—this is a whole lot worse than I'd imagined."

"I would guess that Mr. Harper does nothing to merely sound threatening, Luke. I think he's very dangerous, and it wouldn't surprise me at all if he was the one responsible for my father's death."

"But your mother was there when it happened. She surely wouldn't try to protect Harper."

"Not unless he was threatening her," Alex countered. "But I don't honestly know what he could use against her. He might have known about the fact that she wanted a divorce, but everyone would have found out about that sooner or later. No, if my mother had witnessed Mr. Harper killing my father, she wouldn't have a single reason to keep it from the authorities."

"That's not true," Luke said, looking even more worried than he had before. "She'd have one very good reason . . . you."

CHAPTER TWENTY-TWO

Nothing was going right for Joel Harper. The grand gala to announce Senator Winthrop's candidacy for president and Joel's engagement to Valerie was to have been the culmination of everything he had worked for, but now all that had changed.

"I think for the benefit of the nation and for our good name, we should return to South Carolina," the senator told his group over breakfast. "The death of our president should be properly mourned."

Joel couldn't repress a laugh. "Two days ago we were talking about how incompetent the man was. Now we're going to pretend to care about his death?"

"No pretense, Joel. I do care about his death. I care about his family and the pain this loss will cause them. I care about the vast number of supporters who will be devastated at this news," the senator replied.

"The immoral women of Washington, D.C., are the supporters who will miss him most," Joel said with a sneer. "No doubt those wretched creatures will have to find some other means of support."

"That's enough, Joel. There's nothing to be gained by

such talk," the senator commanded. "We'd be seen as worse than opportunists if we were to continue with a party and politics as usual. It would ruin our campaign."

"I agree," Laird said. "I never cared for the man one whit, but I won't be accused of refusing him the respect due the office. My secretary is securing our train passage at this very moment."

"As is my daughter," Winthrop replied.

So that's where she is, Joel thought. He'd figured her to be hiding in her room, cowering away, avoiding him. The thought had given him great pleasure.

"I instructed her to get us tickets for the first available train," Winthrop added.

Joel wasted little time asserting his views. "It will take time to gather our things, pay the bills, see to our entourage."

"Exactly so," the senator replied. "We'll leave someone here to see to it all."

Joel shook his head, trying desperately to think of a way to buy time. "It will be difficult to bring everyone together in one place again. This is a prime opportunity, and we'll be less than responsible to our supporters if we walk away from the campaign now."

"No one is walking away from the campaign," the senator said firmly. "There are plans to be in Los Angeles in October and, of course, we can always reschedule our own event either here or back in South Carolina."

"But it's not the same. The momentum will be lost," Joel said, fearing his plans would completely unravel. He wanted to eliminate Jastrow before leaving the canyon, but he could hardly explain that to this group.

"The momentum is already lost," one man at the table threw in.

Joel narrowed his gaze, marking the man as an enemy. "The people are shocked, naturally. But this is the time to move forward and remind them that Calvin Coolidge will take the office of president and that we need to—"

"No, Joel. I generally agree wholeheartedly with you," the senator interjected, "but this time, I must object. Proper etiquette demands we show our respect."

"But you can't leave without letting the people know your intentions," Joel said, quickly trying to think of how he might convince the senator to at least give one last party. "You may desire to save your official announcement for the presidency, but the people who've come here deserve to hear you say something about this entire matter."

Joel could see the senator's expression grow thoughtful and felt a small twinge of victory. "Remember," he added, "the people are rather like sheep waiting to be herded and told what to do. You've instructed them to come, and come they have. Now you want to just leave them to their own devices. That would certainly spell disaster for you."

"Well, I suppose you have a point, Joel. When I discussed this with Valerie, she said we should head for home immediately," the senator drawled in his slow southern manner. "But I suppose she wouldn't object to a brief gathering, one in which we could share our condolences with our supporters. Maybe even give them some idea of our future arrangements."

Joel began to breathe a little easier. He'd deal with Valerie later—punish her for attempting to thwart his plans with her influence over her father. But for now he'd help the senator decide what was to be done, and then he'd step up his plans for Jastrow.

Two Harvey Girls entered the room to serve breakfast and

Joel immediately noticed neither one was Alexandria Keegan. It was as if the entire world was attempting to foul up his day. His feelings of elation over what he'd managed to accomplish with the president were fading fast in the face of these minor defeats. He toyed with a fork while waiting for the dark-haired Harvey waitress to serve his plate.

"Where is Miss Keegan?" he questioned.

The woman eyed him with a look of disbelief. "Her father was murdered."

"Yes, I know that. She was about her business yesterday, so I presumed she was attempting to keep busy."

"I believe she and her mother are planning the funeral," the girl offered and said nothing more.

"Remind me to send her an extra bonus," the senator told Joel. "Her work was exemplary, and I want to reward her."

Joel nodded but said nothing. He pushed the food around on his plate and tried to calculate what needed to be done to control the most damage and return order to his plans.

With the others talking amongst themselves, the senator leaned over to talk in a hushed whisper. "Joel, I know you're disappointed, but there are several factors we must consider. Our public will expect us to offer them comfort and hope. You see, what happened to President Harding could just as easily happen to the next president. We must be prepared to show them our strength, without looking as though we have no feelings for the situation at hand."

Winthrop drew a deep breath and continued. "There are also matters we need to discuss privately, between the two of us."

"You and me?" Joel questioned, not liking the idea.

"Yes. You see, I'm concerned about Valerie. She's not feeling well—in fact, the last few days she's been most unhappy. I'm not at all comfortable with forcing her to announce her engagement when she's feeling so poorly."

His words came as a blow to Joel's ego. "She's just succumbing to the heat and excitement. She might even be struggling with the tragedy that has occurred here."

"Nevertheless, we'll wait a week or two and let her recover."

The words were given without room for protest. The senator didn't even wait for a response as he turned back to his companions to offer his ideas for the evening's event. Joel felt his temper rise, but there was no way he could let it become evident.

"If you'll excuse me," Joel said, putting his napkin aside, "I believe I could use some air."

He exited the room, narrowly missing the Harvey Girl who entered bringing coffee. He pushed back several tourists and made his way through the hall and up the stairs. Taking the steps two at a time, he made his way to Valerie's floor and proceeded to her room. Taking the key he'd managed to buy off one of the bellboys, Joel opened the door to find the room completely deserted. The bed stood pristine, in freshly made order. The nightstand was void of Valerie's book and other accessories.

A search of the wardrobe and bath revealed the same. She had removed all evidence of her presence. Where had she gone? What kind of game did she think she was playing?

He slammed the door behind him and stood in the hall momentarily. His own room was at the end of the corridor, with Winthrop's suite situated between his room and Valerie's. He walked toward the senator's door, thinking to knock and see if Valerie had hidden herself in her father's room, but just as he approached a maid came out from the room.

"Excuse me," Joel said, smiling and putting on his best display of charm. "Could you tell me if Miss Winthrop is inside?"

"No, sir. There's no one in there."

"Do you mind if I look for myself?"

The woman shook her head. "I can't let another guest inside the senator's suite."

Joel pulled several bills from his wallet. "Not even for this?"

Luke knew he had no conclusive evidence to prove Joel Harper's plans, but armed with Alex's information and his own suspicions, he intended to meet with the rangers. Most of these men knew him well after ten years at the canyon. They knew his character and the way he conducted business. If they were going to learn the truth about Harper, someone was going to have to listen to reason.

He had nearly reached El Tovar when he spotted Valerie Winthrop coming back from the direction of the train depot. Luke thought momentarily to hide from sight, but then reconsidered. The woman might very well be willing to offer up information vital to his task. After all, who would know Joel Harper better than the woman he intended to marry?

She spotted him and smiled. Gone was the enthusiastic greeting and flirtatious temperament Luke had been forced to deal with on so many occasions.

"Hello, Mr. Toland," she said softly. She actually looked past him, rather than at him.

Luke noted that she had dressed conservatively in a brown tweed skirt and jacket. A peek of a turquoise-colored blouse could be seen at the top of the jacket, but otherwise there was no other hint of color. It was a far cry from the flamboyant and daring fashions she'd worn before.

"How are you today, Miss Winthrop?"

She surprised him by refusing to meet his gaze. It was almost as if she was embarrassed. "I suppose I'm as well as one can be, given the news."

"Yes, it's quite a blow to hear about the president."

She finally turned her gaze upon him. "You know, I've been thinking about the things you said."

Luke started at the change of subject. "What things?" He knew his tone sounded suspicious, but Valerie Winthrop had been a real thorn in his side.

"The things about God. I suppose hearing about the president's death and, of course, Mr. Keegan's . . ." She shuddered. "Well . . . I guess . . . I just wondered about what you'd said. You talked about turning to God and never being alone."

"That's right." Luke pushed aside his suspicions. If she wanted to know about a relationship with God, he needed to be open to that.

"Well, it just seems that my life is rather . . . well . . ." She sighed and looked past him to the canyon. "I feel like nothing is going right. I feel alone, and yet there are so many people who play a part in my life." She shook her head. "I know none of this probably makes any sense to you."

"It makes perfect sense, Miss Winthrop." Luke prayed for the right words. "Without a rightness to God, nothing is ever really put in order. We're just going through the motions. We get up in the morning and go about our affairs, meet with our friends and deal with business, but something is always missing."

She looked rather shocked and nodded. "Yes. Yes. It's exactly that. I know I've been rather outspoken and the manner in which I've treated you has been inappropriate, but I really want to better understand what you're talking about. My mother—she was religious. I know she spoke about God, but I never listened. My father insists we go to church every Sunday, but I'm not sure that it's for God's sake so much as for the sake of public approval. After all, everyone goes to church."

"Not everyone, Miss Winthrop. But even so, going to church isn't enough. It's not about being religious, either."

"Then what?"

He kicked at the dirt and chose his words carefully. "It's about putting your trust in God. It's about letting Him take control—putting the past behind you and seeking a newness in Him."

Several guests approached, talking in animated conversation about the death of the president. Luke stepped aside in order for them to pass by. He tipped his hat at the ladies and received their nods, while the men in the party did likewise for Valerie Winthrop. Luke was surprised to watch her acknowledge them briefly, then turn away. Gone was any hint of a desire to flirt and be the center of attention. In fact, if Luke hadn't known better, he'd have believed she would just as soon have been swallowed up by the earth.

Once the visitors had passed, Valerie let out a long breath. Luke could see she was relaxed to be once again alone with him. What did it all mean?

"Can God care about someone like me, Luke?" she asked, forgetting her earlier formality of calling him Mr. Toland.

"Of course He can. You aren't the worst sinner to ever walk the earth, neither are you the least. We're all just sinners to God, and He deals with each one of us as an individual child."

"Yes, but I've done things in my life, things that will have lasting consequence." Her lower lip quivered and tears came to her eyes. "You know how I've acted. Does God know too?"

Luke felt sorry for the lost woman. "He does, Miss Winthrop. He knows how you've acted and He knew how you would need Him. He knew it long before you were even born."

"That's hard to believe."

"But true."

She looked him square in the face. "But aren't there times when you feel lonely? When you feel like the rest of the world has deserted you and you're all alone?"

At one time Luke might have perceived such questions as a come-on, but not now. He realized she was searching, nearly crying out for understanding.

"I used to feel that way. I felt like I was all alone after my mother died. I didn't understand why God would take away someone I needed and loved. But you know, over the years, now that I've put things right between God and me, I don't feel that way. I might feel a sense of being by myself and maybe want to be with other people, but I'm never lonely. I know God is there for me. I know He's walking right beside me."

"But there are so many people I've wronged. You included."

Luke smiled and pushed back his hat. "I forgive you."

"You do?" she questioned. Her tone was one of disbelief.

"I do," Luke assured.

"But I lied to your . . . to Miss Keegan. I made her believe . . ."

"I already know about all of that," Luke admitted. "And I still forgive you."

She looked at him with an expression of wonder. "And God does the same thing?"

"When you ask Him to, and you're truly sorry, then God forgives you. You can ask Him to help you not make the same mistakes again."

Additional groups of tourists were on the lawn now, some heading down the path toward them. Valerie grew noticeably uncomfortable, and Luke couldn't help but glance over his shoulder to note Joel Harper was heading down the rim path toward the Lookout studios.

"I have to go," she whispered. She moved toward the hotel.

"Sure." Luke didn't try to stop her. "I'll be praying for you, Miss Winthrop."

She stopped and turned around at this. "Would you, please? Will you truly pray for me?"

Luke felt awful inside at the realization that he should have thought of this a whole lot earlier. "Of course I will. Alex will too."

Valerie bit her lip and nodded. "Thank you." She started to turn, then surprised Luke by coming back to him. "Might I further impose?"

"I suppose that depends on what you need." He smiled, trying to appear lighthearted about the whole thing.

"Would you mind meeting me this evening? I'd like to talk to you more about these God matters."

Luke shook his head. "I don't think it would be appropriate for us to meet alone."

Valerie nodded. "I wasn't suggesting that. I'm not entirely sure what my father plans. We were to head home today, but the trains are booked. We can't head out until tomorrow morning. With the cancellation of the gala, there doesn't seem to be much purpose in continuing our stay. At least that's what he and I decided this morning. Hopefully Mr. Harper hasn't changed Daddy's mind. I think it would be in the poorest of taste if we were to continue campaigning in the wake of the current president's death."

"I can see what you mean."

"Anyway, if there is to be some sort of gathering, I'll send you word. I'd like you to be my guest. Otherwise, let's simply meet after supper in the lobby. There should be plenty of people there."

"All right," he said, hoping it was the right thing to do.

"Thank you."

She seems sincere enough, Luke thought. He watched her enter the hotel quickly and disappear from sight. *Lord, I don't know what's gotten into her, but I'm sure it's for her good. Let her understand the truth about you. Let her desire to know you more.* His prayer seemed such a pittance. *I should have been praying for her all along. Instead of being angry with her or worried about my relationship with Alex, I should have concerned myself with Miss Winthrop's eternal soul.*

Realizing he'd forgotten his meeting with the rangers, Luke refocused his energies. He would continue to pray for Miss Winthrop, but for now he needed to speak with the authorities and see what could be done to figure out the murder of Rufus Keegan and what, if anything, Joel Harper might have had to do with it. If the man had a hand in killing the president of the United States, surely he'd have no problem at all in eliminating a man such as Keegan.

CHAPTER TWENTY-THREE

"Mother, you must tell them what you know. If not them, then tell me and I'll tell them," Alex pleaded. "You can't let the responsible party get away with murdering Father." Alex had just been given the word that the authorities were going to take her mother to Williams and formally charge her with the murder of Rufus Keegan. The fact that they were giving up on the investigation simply because there were no other viable options or suspects was tearing Alex apart.

"You don't know what you're asking, Alexandria," her mother replied.

Alex felt only a marginal sense of achievement. At least her mother hadn't dismissed the matter completely.

"I know they're talking about moving you to the jail in Williams. You're the prime suspect and they mean to charge you with Father's murder if you can't prove otherwise."

Alex took ahold of her mother's hand. "Please, Mama, don't let them send you to jail for something I know you didn't do. If Joel Harper is responsible for this, then you must tell the authorities. If he's threatened you or me, you must ignore it and let the law deal with him."

Her mother shook her head and looked down at the

floor. "Mr. Harper is in no way to blame for what happened."

"How can you be sure? If it was another man who pushed Father, then perhaps Mr. Harper hired it done. The man is ruthless. He would stop at nothing to see his precious campaign won."

"It wasn't Mr. Harper's doing," her mother insisted. "Please, just let it be."

Alex stepped away from her mother and tried to figure another path of reasoning. "There was someone else there that night, wasn't there? You weren't alone."

Her mother said nothing but turned uncomfortably, glancing at the door. The ranger had agreed to wait outside while they talked, but his presence was very evident.

Determined to have an answer, Alex confronted her mother. "Who are you protecting?" Alex questioned.

Katherine Keegan put her hand to her mouth as if to keep the words from flowing out. Alex's knees trembled. Her mother really was protecting someone. All this time, Alex had only guessed that it could be one of many possibilities. She feared that her mother had been threatened and that this was the reason for her silence.

"Mother, please."

Her mother lowered her hands, twisting them together anxiously. "I can't. Now that you've guessed this much, please understand. I can't say anything more."

Alex walked the rocky path back to El Tovar, more frustrated and worried than ever. Her mother was protecting someone, but whom? Why would her mother be willing to go to jail for a murderer? There were few people—Luke and Clancy, Mrs. Godfrey, Michaela, and a few other Harvey Girls—who showed her mother the slightest bit of respect or courtesy. It just didn't make sense for her mother's loyalty to run so deep. Alex knew she wouldn't rest until the truth came out for everyone to see.

Then Alex began to let her imagination run wild, and for just a moment Luke's image came to mind. Was her mother protecting him? Could it be possible he had taken Alex's frustrations and pain and decided to put an end to her father's life?

"No," she said, shaking her head vigorously as she entered the kitchen.

"What did you say?" Michaela questioned.

Alex looked up and realized several Harvey Girls as well as two of the kitchen staff were watching her as if she were about to impart some great truth to them.

"Nothing. I'm just muttering to myself."

"Well, when you get done with your own company," Michaela teased, "Mrs. Godfrey has asked to see you in her office."

Alex nodded and took off down the hall to see what Mrs. Godfrey required. Knocking on the open door, Alex peeked her head inside. "You wanted to see me?"

Mrs. Godfrey nodded. "Come in and close the door."

Alex eyed her curiously for a moment, then nodded. Closing the door behind her, Alex walked to the desk. "What's this all about?"

Mrs. Godfrey handed her an envelope. "Senator Winthrop brought this by earlier."

Alex took the envelope and opened it. "Oh my." She counted at least a hundred dollars more than she'd been promised from the Winthrop group. "What's this all about?"

"The senator praised your work, sympathized with your circumstances, and said he wanted you to have this. He was very complimentary and said that in spite of knowing you often faced difficulty with his group, you were the epitome of graciousness and charm."

Alex sat down opposite Mrs. Godfrey and shook her head. "I've never hated working with a group of people more than I have the Winthrops. It was only the love of God that kept me on the job."

"Perhaps the senator understood your misery."

"Maybe. I don't know that he could really focus on anything other than his campaign and his plans for the presidency."

"People are often deluded, blinded even, by the goals they set," Mrs. Godfrey said in agreement.

The words went straight to Alex's heart. "I know I've been guilty of that, but hopefully no more."

"Alex, I wanted to talk to you without anyone else around. I know you're struggling with a great many issues right now. I realize there is pressure to find out exactly what happened that night with your father. Given this and everything else, I feel I must require you to take a few days off. I know you wanted to keep working. I know, too, that there was no real love lost between you and your father, but I see a weariness in you—a state of mind that would benefit from rest."

Alex eased back in the chair and considered Mrs. Godfrey's words. "I suppose you would know better than I would." The idea of a rest didn't seem so bad. "I thought keeping busy would help, but it hasn't."

"I presumed as much. Do you feel like talking about it?"

Alex appreciated her motherly concern. "I've tried to talk with my mother, but she's not of a mind to listen right now."

Mrs. Godfrey nodded, her tightly curled gray hair barely moving with the motion. "She's no doubt consumed with her own emotions. I'd like to help if I can. You girls are like daughters to me. I never had children, and after my husband passed on, I always longed for a daughter to give me companionship. Now I have a dozen or more at times and I find I love the camaraderie."

Alex smiled. "You've been a good friend to all of us. And believe me, if I knew how to put my feelings into words, I would. But I find myself a mix of emotions—from guilt to frustration to sorrow."

Mrs. Godfrey's sympathetic expression put Alex at ease. Where her mother had clearly closed the door to communication, Mrs. Godfrey seemed eager to help. "I've been praying for your peace of mind. I know that your father was less than helpful in your life. I know he grieved you on many occasions. But he's gone now. He can't hurt you anymore."

"But that's just it. He is hurting me. His death is unresolved and my mother stands at the center of controversy once again. It's almost as if he's still determined to torment and torture her further."

"Have you spoken with your mother about what happened?"

Alex sighed and cast her gaze to the ceiling. "I've asked, I've cajoled, I've begged, and I've pleaded. She won't talk to me about what happened. She knows full well what occurred. Of this, I'm convinced.

"We were planning Father's funeral this morning and I tried to reason with her. They'll take her to jail in Williams if they can't find any conclusive proof to show she's not responsible for this." Alex brushed aside the tears that came unbidden. "She's going to go to jail, Mrs. Godfrey. And all because she's protecting someone else."

"But who?"

"That's just it. I have no idea." Alex met her supervisor's

gaze. "I have no idea and because of that, I am helpless. Besides those involved, God alone knows what happened that night. And He sure isn't saying a word about it to me."

"I understand. Just know that I'm here to talk to," Mrs. Godfrey encouraged. "I care a great deal about you, Alex. I know your days here are probably numbered. Your mother will need you now, no matter the outcome of this matter. You'll go your way . . . but just know how much I care."

Alex smiled in spite of her tears. "I do know, and I very much appreciate it."

That evening, Alex milled about the grounds, her spirit restless in her idleness. She'd worked so hard over the past four years, she'd scarcely taken time for herself. There were occasional outings with Luke or some of the other girls, along with trips home from time to time, but over all, she'd chosen to work.

"I worked because I wanted to free my mother from her misery, and now . . ." She let the words trail off as she suddenly realized she was speaking them aloud. "My goal blinded me to so much."

Looking out over the canyon, Alex wondered silently about the days to come. Everyone here at the canyon, including the rangers, seemed very protective of her mother. They'd certainly gone the extra mile by allowing Alex to seclude her mother away from the crowd. They'd spoken to the reporters, who had reluctantly agreed to leave the woman alone. The matter had only been helped by the death of President Harding. The smaller news of her father's death paled in comparison to the pain of the nation.

Turning to gaze back on the structure she'd called home for four years, Alex sighed. Her life here at El Tovar had been a good one overall. She'd made friends and she'd always felt safe, unlike her life at home.

People were gathering in front of the steps of El Tovar's main entrance. Alex had learned that Mr. Jastrow and Senator Winthrop were going to announce an end to their festivities and a postponement of their bids for the Democratic nomination for president. She was surprised, but pleasantly so. She reached into the pocket of her skirt and lightly fingered the envelope from Senator Winthrop. Perhaps they weren't all such bad people. Maybe Valerie was spoiled and self-centered, but she was only portraying what had probably been acceptable behavior for all of her life. Alex felt her heart soften a bit in her thoughts of the entourage. The only exception was Joel Harper. She knew him to be the snake he appeared to be. She could only pray he'd be caught red-handed at his schemes. She knew no one would ever believe her if she told them what she knew. After all, she'd tried and the investigator and sheriff had merely laughed her off.

Then there was the issue of her father. She could still hear Joel's comments on how much she was like him. *I am headstrong and determined. Although,* she reasoned, *those could be good qualities if used properly.* Her father's actions, however, always bordered on cruelty.

Oh, God, I don't want to be like him. He broke my mother's heart, and mine as well. When other girls were strolling hand in hand with their fathers, when they played together at picnics or went to the fair—oh, how I envied them! She looked back at the canyon and let the colors blur together, not really seeing anything in particular. *I know I have you, Father, but was it wrong to desire an earthly father too?*

"Penny for your thoughts."

She turned and met Luke's smiling face. Just seeing him

here, all dressed up in his finest suit of brown serge, gave her heart a start.

"Why are you dressed to the nines?" she asked, trying to put her introspective thoughts aside.

"I was invited to attend the gathering tonight. I wanted to find you first, however."

"Why?"

"The invitation came from Miss Winthrop." Alex frowned but said nothing as Luke continued. "She's been asking me about God, Alex, and I think she's sincerely seeking."

Alex put aside her twinges of jealousy and smiled. "I hope she is."

"Besides that," Luke continued, "I want to talk to her about Harper. I figure if anyone can help us to figure out his part in your father's death, it will be Valerie. I also want to watch Harper. I had a long talk with my ranger friends this afternoon. I told them what you'd shared with me and that I thought there was merit in checking it out."

"And did they listen?" Alex asked hopefully.

"To a point. They said they'd keep on the lookout for anything unusual, but that just because Harper spoke in such a manner didn't mean he meant to act on it. He might have been trying to impress your father."

"I know what I heard. It wasn't a matter of impressing anyone."

"I believe you," Luke said, reaching out for Alex's arm. "Now, I want you to believe me when I say you have nothing to worry about in regard to Miss Winthrop." He pulled her toward him and began to walk along the rim path. "I'm not the least bit interested in what she has to offer, but I am interested in you. Have you been thinking about us?"

"A little," she answered honestly. "Frankly, the events of

the past few days have rather overwhelmed me. I can scarcely think of anything but the fact my mother is protecting someone with her silence."

Luke stopped and looked at her long and hard. "Keep praying about it, Alex. The truth is bound to come out."

"I know. I just hope I can bear it when it does."

He smiled. "God won't ever give you more than you can bear. Just remember that. You once told me the same. Now I'm going to join Miss Winthrop, but my main desire is to keep track of Joel Harper. I don't want you in any danger, but perhaps you could keep focused on Jastrow and where he is at all times."

"That should be simple enough."

"Good. I'm confident we can figure this out together," Luke said, then surprised her by leaning over to kiss her forehead. "This will have to do for now."

Alex felt a ripple of excitement course through her as his lips touched her skin. She longed for a real kiss but knew such a public display would be uncalled for. Especially at such a time as this.

Alex watched Luke stalk off across the lawn, wishing he would remain at her side. She understood his plan, but nevertheless, his absence was sorely felt.

"Alex!"

It was Michaela, and the look on her face told Alex something was wrong. "What is it?"

"Your mother is gone. She's not at the cabin and neither is her guard."

"What? How can that be?"

"I went there to take them some supper, but they're gone. I asked the first ranger I caught sight of, but he didn't have any idea what had happened either."

Alex went cold inside. Surely they wouldn't have taken her mother to Williams without telling her first. Convinced that something more sinister was afoot, Alex insisted, "We must search for her."

Michaela nodded. "I'll let the others know."

Alex was frantic to reach Luke, but the speeches had already begun and Bradley Jastrow was expressing his regret over the death of President Harding. Alex moved toward where Luke stood with Valerie Winthrop when she found herself halted by Joel Harper.

"Miss Keegan, I'd hoped I might run into you. You see, there's a matter I think we should discuss."

"I haven't the time or desire, Mr. Harper." She tried to jerk away from his ironclad grip, but he held her fast.

"It would be most beneficial if you were to speak with me," he said in a whisper. "Beneficial to you and to your mother."

Alex felt her eyes widen, fear raced through her body like a wildfire. "Where is she? Where have you taken her? If you've hurt her . . ."

"Hush," he said, motioning toward Hopi House across the street from the gathering.

Alex allowed him to lead her to a more secluded spot but made sure they were still in sight of the crowd. In spite of their isolation, Joel leaned in close. "Now, my dear, what did you say to the sheriff about me?"

"I don't know what you're talking about," Alex replied nervously.

"You said something to him because he's hinted at it. He's told me he wants to speak to me about threats I made. You're the only one who knows about any such threats."

"I seriously doubt that," Alex said, trying hard to stand

her ground. "Your Miss Winthrop knows plenty, I'm sure. Not only that, but there are also those lackeys you hire to do your dirty work."

"Nevertheless, they've not spoken to the sheriff and investigator hired by the senator. You have."

"I have nothing to tell you, Mr. Harper. I simply want to know what you've done with my mother."

Harper laughed softly. "I'm sure you do."

Luke could barely concentrate on the speeches, for he'd seen Harper approach Alex and then drag her off to Hopi House. He'd almost gone after them when Harper stopped abruptly, still within Luke's range of vision, and began talking intently to Alex. So long as he could see her, Luke decided against going after them.

The speeches concluded and people were encouraged to linger and talk if they desired. Jastrow was immediately surrounded by a throng of supporters, as was Winston Winthrop.

"It was hard on Daddy to hear of the president's death," Valerie said. "He loves a good competition, but he always wants a fair fight."

"And this one isn't a fair fight, is it?"

She paled and began to stammer. "I . . . don't . . . well, that is . . . I can't . . ."

Luke took hold of her elbow and led her away from the others. "I just want to ask you one thing, and I need an honest answer."

Her eyes widened in fear and Luke felt sorry for her. He knew he sounded gruff, but their time was running out. "Is Joel Harper capable of murder?"

"You shouldn't speak of such things," Valerie said, lowering her gaze. "You mustn't."

"I'll do whatever I can to protect you, but you have to tell me the truth."

She returned her gaze to his face. "It's too late to protect me."

Luke shook his head. He had to find a way to reach her. He felt the urgency of it even as he glanced over his shoulder to find Harper still with Alex. "What about your father, then? What about protection for him? You told me you wanted to hire me as a bodyguard for him. Are you still extending that offer?"

Valerie began to sob softly. "I don't want him hurt. He's a good man. He knows nothing of Joel's scheming."

"Then tell me about it so we can put a stop to it."

She looked at him, her face blotchy and tear streaked. She seemed to be sizing up the situation, reasoning within her mind what was to be done.

"If I tell you everything and he finds out . . . he'll kill us both."

CHAPTER TWENTY-FOUR

Joel thought to further grieve Alex Keegan when he spotted Luke and Valerie in a close-knit conversation. Rage welled up within him. She'd been after Toland since they'd arrived at the canyon.

"It would seem your friend doesn't know when to leave well enough alone," he muttered.

Alex moved away from him and turned to look back at the crowd. "They're talking."

Joel laughed bitterly. "For now. But knowing Valerie as I do, they'll soon be involved in much more."

"Well, knowing Luke as I do, she won't get that far with him."

He turned to Alex and shook his head. "For one so beautiful, you're quite naïve. Money, power, and charm can get whatever it desires."

"It didn't buy you what you wanted," Alex replied brazenly. "It didn't buy me."

"Ah, but you'll come around in time. I'm not used to having to battle women of virtue, you see. I find those steeped in their religious nonsense to generally be avoided, but with you, I couldn't help myself. Now you're a challenge."

"A challenge you cannot hope to win," Alex answered. "You disgust me. Your money and power are false gods that give you deceptive confidence in what can be had. Not everyone can be bought at a price."

Just then Joel saw Luke put his arm around Valerie and actually pull her into an embrace. "Of all the nerve. So your cowboy won't succumb to her charms, eh? Just have a look."

Joel watched Alex as she scanned the crowd to again take note of Luke and Valerie. There was none of the jealousy or anger he anticipated, however. Her countenance remained calm, almost tranquil. But just as quickly, she turned back to him and frowned. "Luke can take care of himself, just as I'm sure Miss Winthrop can. I want to know where you've taken my mother. If you don't tell me, I'm going to the authorities."

"You won't go to the authorities," Joel said snidely. "You won't go to them because I have proof of what really happened the night of your father's murder. Your mother killed him just as sure as we're standing here. I heard them argue, you see. A little matter of an illegitimate child born to your father and one of his many women."

He watched the color drain from Alex's face. *Good,* he thought. *Let her be shocked and dismayed. Let her believe the worst—that I have the power to put her mother away forever. Let her see me as her salvation—then she'll be mine.*

"I don't believe you." Her voice was considerably less brazen than it had been only moments ago.

Joel smiled. "I don't suppose it really matters. The truth is the truth. The woman and her child were the final straw for your mother. She came here for a divorce because she could no longer deal with the matter. She argued with your father and told him to marry the woman if he chose, but to give her a divorce and let her be free. I believe she wanted to go away with you—to live elsewhere, just the two of you. At least I heard something to that matter."

"My mother didn't kill my father."

"Poor thing. The truth is really just too much to bear, isn't it?"

"I won't stand here and listen to your lies for another moment." Surprising him, Alex set off across the lawn.

This action, in turn, brought Joel's attention back to Luke and Valerie. They were still together, she still in his supportive embrace. Enraged at the public humiliation she continued to bring upon him, Joel marched across the grounds to take his fiancée back in hand.

They watched him approach, and Valerie appeared to have the good sense to pull away from Luke's hold. Joel seethed. He would teach her a lesson once and for all.

"What is the meaning of this?" Joel hissed in a low, menacing voice.

"Mr. Toland and I were merely talking. I got rather emotional and he comforted me," she offered.

"I need to speak with you alone," Joel said, reaching out to take hold of Valerie's arm. "Now."

Luke surprisingly said nothing. Joel had been prepared to do battle with the man, but he remained silent as he pulled Valerie away.

"Didn't I warn you? Didn't I tell you that I wouldn't tolerate your flirtations? I would think, given what happened between us in your room, you wouldn't risk annoying me further."

"He was merely comforting me," Valerie protested.

"There was nothing flirtatious about it. Good grief, Joel, look around you. People are weeping and miserable over the news of the president. They may not have liked the man, but the shock and sadness of it is overwhelming. Have you no feelings whatsoever?"

"The feelings I have or don't have are really of no concern to you. What does matter is that we have a job to do and I intend for you to uphold your part. Otherwise, some very unpleasant things are bound to happen."

"You don't scare me anymore. You've already done your worst," she said hatefully.

"You'd like to believe that, I'm sure. But, as I've told you, there are far worse things to come if you fail to cooperate."

She shook her head, as if uncertain. He could sense her apprehension and smiled. Sometimes the less said the better. The imagination was a powerful weapon. Given a chance to think about it, she would imagine far worse arrangements than he could dream up. Well, maybe not worse, but just as bad.

Luke watched the couple, wondering momentarily what had happened to Alex. She seemed to be nowhere in sight. The thought worried him, but so long as he had Harper in his sights, surely Alex would be safe.

He tried to appear interested in the conversation of those around him, while watching Joel Harper. He talked in rapid-fire to Miss Winthrop. She shook her head ever so slightly; he said something else, and this time she fervently shook her head. Whatever he was saying, Luke felt certain it had to do with Harper's plans to eliminate his competition.

Finally he saw Valerie acquiesce. She nodded and dried

her eyes on a handkerchief given her by Harper. With this done, she moved away to join her father. The senator smiled broadly and welcomed her with a hearty embrace. There was no doubt in Luke's mind that the man loved her a great deal.

Continuing to watch, Luke saw Valerie lean toward her father's ear. She appeared to be whispering something that met with his approval because the senator nodded enthusiastically and allowed her to take hold of his arm.

Senator Winthrop and his daughter mingled through the crowd of well-wishers and stun-faced supporters. They didn't stop until they reached Bradley Jastrow. For several moments they talked, just the three of them, and then the senator took his leave and it was just Valerie and Jastrow. Several times, other supporters came up to them, but Jastrow dismissed them. At one point, he led Valerie to the rim walk and pointed something out across the canyon.

Every nerve in Luke's body grew taut. It would be a simple matter to push the man over the edge. Perhaps Harper had threatened Valerie into doing just that. Scanning the crowd for Harper, Luke discovered he was nowhere to be found. Neither was Alex. His heart began to pound an anxious rhythm. *Help me, Lord,* he prayed. *Help me do what must be done.*

Luke moved away from the crowd to both search for Harper and try to keep track of Valerie and Jastrow as they moved down the rim walk.

"Mr. Toland, I would have a word with you."

Luke looked up to find Valerie's father making his way across the lawn. "I don't really have time right now, sir."

"Nonsense. This is important." The senator planted himself between Luke and the walkway. "I want to discuss the canyon with you. Valerie said you were quite knowledgeable."

Luke had no desire to discuss such things with the man.

Not when the lives of so many might well be on the line. Luke narrowed his eyes. "Did Valerie also tell you that your campaign aide is systematically killing off your competition?"

Winthrop looked completely shocked at the suggestion. "My good man, how dare you slander one of my staff?"

"I dare to because it's true, and right now you're detaining me from preventing him from killing again."

"I don't believe you."

"I don't much care. The fact of the matter is, your daughter filled me in on a great deal."

"I believe she's just suffering from the heat and the news of the president. I'm sure she didn't mean anything by it."

"She's suffering all right," Luke said, resolving to give the man whatever truth he needed in order to get the job done. "She's suffering because Joel is threatening her with your downfall and even death if she doesn't remain silent and cooperate with his schemes."

Winthrop looked stunned, his face contorting and changing colors until it remained a mottled purple. "You lie!"

"I actually wish I were," Luke said sadly. "Valerie needs you to prevent any more of this from happening. Apparently Harper has killed before and plans to kill again. She believes he even masterminded a plot that resulted in President Harding's death."

Winthrop began slowly shaking his head from side to side. "This can't be."

"What proof can I offer you? I only have your daughter's word and the word of another who overheard Harper plotting."

"It's just unheard of. Why would Joel resort to such things? I'm a popular candidate. I have a strong backing of supporters." He hooked his thumbs into his vest pocket and tried to appear under control, but Luke could sense he was anything but. "I believe you're making this up."

"Listen to yourself, Senator. This is your daughter we're talking about. Would she lie about such a thing? What would she have to gain from that?"

Winthrop considered the question for a moment. "She doesn't wish to marry Joel Harper. She would probably do anything within her power to keep that from happening."

"Then she's lied about the death of a dear friend named Andrew, as well."

"The banker's son? The boy drowned."

"Yes, I know. Valerie told me that Joel admitted to arranging the entire thing. Now we sit here with Keegan and the president dead, while Bradley Jastrow walks the south rim path with your daughter."

Winthrop's expression took on one of complete defeat. "You must save her."

"I'll do what I can," Luke replied. "You go to the authorities and tell them where we've gone. I've no idea what Harper has in mind, but my guess is he plans to eliminate Jastrow—and even Valerie if she's too much trouble."

Alex had no idea where Luke had gotten off to, but seeing Valerie move down the rim path with Bradley Jastrow on her arm, Alex knew she had to follow. She pushed aside Mr. Harper's threats to her mother and herself, pushed aside her fears of what she might actually bear witness to. She had to keep Joel Harper from reaping more harm. If that meant she put herself in an uncomfortable position, then so be it.

Following at a discreet distance and using the hotel to hide her movements, Alex observed Valerie and Jastrow as they talked and walked at the canyon's edge. They appeared to be moving in the direction of the Lookout. Alex wondered if they would go there or perhaps move on past to the more secluded studio cabin to the west. There were trees and a good deal of cover for someone who might wish to be left alone.

As they moved past the Lookout, Alex knew she could no longer stay under cover. She hurried away from the hotel and toward the patch of trees to the south. If she could make it there unnoticed, she could hide and move through the shadows until she reached a place where she could watch the path or even the studio.

Gasping for breath as she pushed herself to run faster, Alex nearly collapsed as she reached the first tree. The heady scent of pine and juniper filled the air. She leaned against the trunk of one tree, hoping to catch her breath before pursuing the couple. She had no idea how she might stop the turn of events, but she had to try. Visions of her father going over the edge haunted her imagination. It was such an awful way to die—to know for those last few moments that you couldn't stop the motion of events that would take your life. To endure seconds that would seemingly last an eternity.

She pushed away from the tree and pressed through the underbrush. She had to reach them—had to save the innocent.

Without warning, however, someone reached out to take hold of her. One hand clamped firmly on her arm and another went over her mouth and pulled her backward against a rock-hard chest. She screamed, but the sound was lost in the smothering hold.

CHAPTER TWENTY-FIVE

Alex met Luke's warning glance as he turned her in his arms. She'd been almost certain she would find herself face-to-face with Joel Harper, and she fell against Luke in relief.

"I thought . . . I . . ."

"Shhh. Look," he whispered and pointed to the rim path. Harper walked at a rapid clip along the narrow path. Luke pulled her close to him and added, "I saw a rough-looking character give him something. I've no idea what it was, but I'm figuring it has something to do with putting an end to Jastrow's life, and maybe even Valerie's."

"What can we do?" Alex questioned, pushing away from Luke to better see where Jastrow was headed.

"I'm not sure. I guess we follow him."

"He's not stopping at the Lookout, so maybe he's going to the art studio. It would be deserted at this hour."

Luke nodded. "Come on, but stay quiet."

They pushed through the trees as quietly as possible, Alex clinging tightly to Luke's hand. She thanked God silently for the support of Luke's presence. No one else in the entire world could give her the feeling of strength and security that Luke gave her. Yet what did it mean? Was this another sign that she was really in love with Luke?

"There they are," Luke said, pulling Alex to his side. His arms about her felt warm and protective and Alex had no desire to resist him. Instead, she looked through the brush to see what was happening.

She could see for herself that the trio stood just outside the studio. Joel pulled something out of his pocket and waved it in front of Jastrow. Alex put her hand to her mouth, realizing Joel held a gun.

"Shhh," Luke warned. They watched in silence for several moments before Luke motioned to the right. "We need to get closer."

Alex knew they could do nothing from this distance, but she didn't want to see Luke risk his life. There was a part of her that wanted to beg Luke to stay where he was or even turn back, yet at the same time, Alex felt overwhelmed with the need to know the truth.

They cautiously moved nearer, almost behind the three, stopping no more than eight feet from where Valerie stood.

"Please, Joel. Please don't do this." Alex could easily hear Valerie Winthrop's pleading.

"We agreed this was for the best. You don't want to see something else go wrong, do you, Val dear?"

Jastrow's expression looked like he was sizing up the situation. For a moment, Alex thought he might jump Harper, but Joel apparently realized his intentions and waved the man back. "Sit down on that rock. Now! You may have held the Huns at bay, but you'll find it another story dealing with an American."

"Mr. Harper, I fail to see . . ." Jastrow tried to speak in protest, but Harper pushed him back.

"Sit!" Joel commanded again.

Jastrow did as he was told while Joel Harper fished something out of his pocket and handed it to Valerie. "Take this syringe and load it."

"I don't know how," Valerie protested.

"It's simple enough. Even you can do it."

Alex watched Val take the vial in hand. "You do it, Joel."

"Pop the cork on the vial," Joel commanded. She looked at the bottle, then slowly pulled the cork from the top.

"Just put the needle down in there and pull the back on the top. It will suck the contents right up into the syringe," Joel said, smiling. "As for you, Mr. Jastrow, well, let's just say that by this time tomorrow, the nation will be mourning more than just the president's passing. We shall also be mourning the passing of a great war hero."

"And how is it you plan to kill me?" Jastrow questioned calmly.

"Haven't you figured it out?" Joel questioned, sounding almost indignant. "You're going to take an overdose of morphine. The pain you're suffering has become unbearable, coupled with your horrid memories of the war. It's just too much for you to endure. Death will be a welcome release."

"No one is ever going to believe it," Jastrow said quite seriously. "I've never been the type to give up."

Valerie began to cry. "Please don't do this, Joel."

She reached out to touch his arm. He pushed her back. "Don't whine at me. You know what I'm capable of."

"But Mr. Jastrow doesn't have to die. You could just threaten him and get his promise to drop out of the race for president. You'd do that wouldn't you, Mr. Jastrow?"

The man looked intently at Valerie and then Joel. "Is that what this is all about?"

Joel laughed. "You're a liability in my boss's campaign.

You're young, handsome, popular with the women—a war hero, for pity's sake. It's difficult for the senator to contend with such things."

"My father knows nothing about this," Valerie assured Jastrow, then turned to Joel. "You know Father would never want this. He's a man of honor."

"He doesn't know how things get done in this business. When he first ran for the senate in South Carolina, people still remembered the Civil War. He could appeal to other southern gentlemen who'd suffered as his family had suffered. That's not the case with the presidency."

"If that's all this is about, you should know that I've already reached a decision to pull out of the race," Jastrow said. "I had a talk with my staff this morning. I've decided to get back in the family business."

"I thought you weren't the type to give up," Joel said sarcastically.

"It's not a matter of giving up. I was merely testing the waters regarding the presidency. In weighing the situation, I simply made a logical choice to put off my candidacy until another time."

Joel frowned and Alex thought for a moment that he'd change his mind. He lowered the gun and bit his lower lip. Alex had never seen him quite this indecisive. Perhaps he would put aside his plan and let Jastrow go.

"See there, Joel," Valerie said, her tears still flowing. "He doesn't even plan to continue the race against Daddy."

Joel squared his shoulders and raised the gun again. "It doesn't matter. He knows too much now. Get that syringe loaded. Do it now!"

"Please, Joel," she began to sob in earnest, her hands

trembling as she held the syringe and bottle. "Please just stop before it's too late."

"If you don't do as you're told, you'll end up like Mr. Keegan, over the edge without so much as a prayer."

Valerie paled and shook her head. Alex nearly gasped aloud at this, feeling certain Joel was the one responsible for her father's death.

"So you did kill him," Valerie cried.

Joel smiled. "No. I actually wish I could take credit for it. The man was a dense-headed bore who held an overinflated image of his own self-importance. He deserved to die." He looked to Jastrow. "Unlike you, our most heralded war hero. You're simply in the wrong place at the wrong time. Or from my point of view, the right time. Your death will be mourned by thousands—maybe even millions. I sincerely doubt Keegan has so much as his wife to shed a tear over him. It's for certain his daughter won't."

Alex felt something move beneath her feet. A deer mouse skittered across the toe of her shoe, causing Alex to shriek without thinking. She looked to Luke, knowing the damage she'd done, and unable to utter so much as a whispered apology before Joel Harper demanded they show themselves.

Katherine Keegan stood before the men who held her life in their hands. They looked at her with skepticism and a hint of confusion. Looking to the man who'd been her guard for the last few hours, she nodded. The man handed her a basket, then reached into his pocket and handed his superior a folded piece of paper.

The ranger in charge took the paper and read the contents. "What's the meaning of this?"

Katherine Keegan reached into the basket and pulled back a cover to reveal a very small infant. "This is my husband's son. My husband's and Gloria Scott's. The woman whose letter you now hold."

The sheriff eyed her suspiciously. "What does this have to do with anything? Your message to us said that you were ready to talk about your husband's death."

Katherine nodded. "And so I am."

"Then what's with the kid?" he asked gruffly.

"The baby is the reason I came to Grand Canyon to ask my husband for a divorce. I'd just learned from Miss Scott that she'd had an affair with my husband, and this baby was the result. She had come to me seeking help. She had actually threatened me with public humiliation, but of course I assured her that was already a daily fact for me."

Katherine looked down at the sleeping infant. Her heart ached for the suffering and misery her husband had caused this child and his mother. It seemed most unfair that even one more innocent person should pay the price for her husband's indiscretions.

"I still fail to understand what any of this has to do with your husband's death," the sheriff replied.

"I must admit, Mrs. Keegan," Winthrop's private investigator, Mr. Stokes, said. "I am rather confused, as well."

Katherine looked back to the men who eyed her as if she might disappear from their sight at any given moment.

"I was very angry when I came here," she admitted. "I confronted Rufus about the baby and about his affair with Gloria Scott."

"And?" the sheriff demanded impatiently.

"And he laughed it off. Said there would be no divorce. Threatened me and our daughter if we should so much as hint at my desire to leave him."

"So he was mad and threatening, and you felt that you had no other choice but to kill him," the sheriff announced. "Is that what you're trying to tell us?"

Katherine shook her head. "No. That's not at all what happened. But if you'll bear with me, I'll tell you what did take place that evening."

CHAPTER TWENTY-SIX

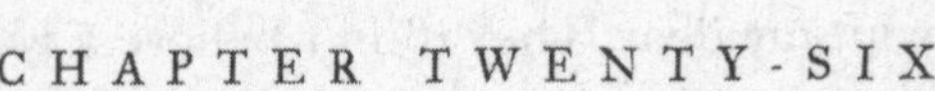

"Well, this is quite a mess, isn't it?" Joel stated, more than questioned, as he motioned Alex and Luke to come out from the clearing. He was careful to keep Jastrow and Valerie in his sight the entire time. Waving his gun, he motioned to Luke. "You, over there with Jastrow." He reached out and grabbed hold of Alex. Putting the revolver to her head, he smiled. "And you stay here with me."

"Let her go, Harper!" Luke demanded, taking a step forward.

"If you want to keep her alive, you'll do what I say and stay there. I've no desire to end the life of one so sweet," he said, pulling Alex backward against him, "but I'll do what I must."

Alex fought against his hold until Joel put his arm around her neck and pulled back hard. For a terrifying moment he cut off her air. Alex became still, knowing he meant business.

"Why not fight this out like a man?" Luke questioned.

Alex could see the anger in Luke's expression. The tick in his cheek, his clenched teeth, and the narrowing of his eyes were sure signs he was beyond mere fear and annoyance. Now he was enraged. She wanted to keep the situation under control, and her mind raced for something she might offer to neutralize the sparking emotions.

"Mr. Harper, this isn't the way to accomplish anything. You know the authorities have already been notified. They're on their way, even now."

"I don't believe you, my dear. They didn't believe a word you said to them. The sheriff had a good laugh when he told me that you'd suggested I might have murdered your father."

"You seemed a logical suspect," Alex said, hoping if she kept Joel talking and preoccupied with their conversation, someone else might actually think of something to do. "After all, my father was causing you some discomfort."

"How do you know that?" Joel questioned.

"Because my father caused everyone discomfort," Alex said, trying hard not to move lest Joel tighten his hold around her neck.

Luke shifted from one foot to the other, immediately catching Joel's attention. "Sit down next to Jastrow," he commanded. "I want you both where I can see you."

Luke studied him for a moment as if to ascertain the seriousness of his demand. Joel drew the revolver level with Alex's head. While his right hand steadied the gun, his left tightened against Alex's throat. For a moment, Alex panicked. She feared he'd kill her, if for no other reason than to lessen the odds against him.

"Joel, please stop this. You must stop now," Valerie pleaded. "These people have done you no wrong. They've shown only kindness to Daddy and I, and we've sorely misused them. Let them go."

"You simpleton. Don't you see?" he questioned. "They plan to destroy us. To destroy me. I've worked too hard, Val.

I've worked my fingers to the bone for your father. I've rearranged too many affairs to go down without a fight. Your father must be the president, and I must be at his side."

Valerie stepped toward him. "But if you kill us all, Daddy will never continue to run. He wouldn't run if I were dead. He would despair of even living."

"I won't have to kill you in order to keep you cooperative."

Valerie shook her head. "That's where you're wrong. I won't cooperate with you anymore. You've left a trail of death and sorrow behind you, and no matter where you go, those demons of the past will follow. I won't let you go through with this. I won't."

Alex thought Valerie Winthrop had never looked more determined. Not when pursuing Luke. Not when trying to bring a room full of strangers to their knees. No, this time Miss Winthrop knew she was playing a life-and-death game.

"Shut up, Val, and load the syringe."

She looked down at the items in her hands and Alex strained to watch. Moving even that small bit, caused Joel to tighten his hold once again. Alex had to press back against him to keep from losing consciousness. The idea intrigued her as Joel loosened his hold. If she pushed back against him with all her might, she could very well knock them both to the ground. It would be a risk as to whether or not the gun would go off, but it might be a risk worth taking.

She looked to Luke, who seemed to sense what she was thinking. He shook his head ever so slightly and Alex got the distinct impression he was telling her not to do anything at all.

"Put the needle into the vial and pull back on the top of the syringe. When you've managed to empty the contents of the bottle, I want you to take the syringe and inject Jastrow."

"Why?" Alex couldn't help but ask. It seemed such a logical question.

Joel laughed and pressed his lips against her ear. "Because, my dear, that's the way this plan works." He kissed Alex playfully on the lobe of her ear, causing Luke to take a step forward.

"As much as I would hate to bring any attention upon us, I will use this gun if necessary. Given this setting, I could most likely shoot the three of you, and Valerie and I could be well away before anyone figured out where the shots were fired from."

Valerie began to cry again. Alex could see that she'd done as instructed and now stood with the full syringe, looking for all the world as if she were frozen in place. Except for her tears, she didn't move. She scarcely even appeared to be breathing.

Joel turned slightly, nearly sending Alex off-balance. "You see, Mr. Toland, Valerie has morphine, Mr. Jastrow's dearest friend—his constant companion since the Great War. When Jastrow overdoses on the very drug he uses on a daily basis to control his pain, people will automatically assume he was unable to deal with the pain any longer and took his own life."

"Out here? Wouldn't it make more sense to seek the privacy of his room?"

Joel seemed to consider this for a moment. His hold on Alex loosened considerably. "It would have been more ideal. I had hoped that Valerie would work her wiles on the man and get him to take her back to his room, but it didn't work out that way. People seem to always be thwarting my plans."

"No one is ever going to believe the man came out here to take an overdose of morphine," Luke said, pushing his hair back ever so slowly. "You have to rethink this, Harper. His murder is going to be very evident."

"No. No, it won't. Valerie will tell them all how he told her he wished to die."

"No, I won't," Valerie said, coming toward Joel. "I won't do it. I'll tell them all exactly what has happened here."

"You wouldn't dare," Joel said, laughing nervously. "You're the one who will administer the deadly dose. You'll be guilty of murder."

"Then so be it," Valerie said, looking Joel dead in the eye.

Alex could feel Joel tense. "I think I'm going to faint," Alex said softly. She could only hope that Joel might be taken by surprise enough to forget the gun momentarily. Faking the faint, her knees buckled and she started to slide down to the ground.

"No!" he declared, trying to pull her back up by the hair.

"I'm sorry," Alex murmured, even as Joel tried to steady her. She landed on her knees, kneeling on the hard rock path.

Joel took hold of her by the hair and at the same time pointed the gun at Luke. "Don't take a single step. Valerie, do what I told you to do. We've got to be done with this before someone comes looking for us." Alex felt a grave sense of urgency. Her ploy had failed. What could she do to help now?

Valerie stepped forward, but at the last minute she turned and lunged for Joel with the syringe held like a dagger. He dropped his hold on Alex and managed to narrowly avoid the needle.

"You traitor!" he screamed, slapping her back. Whether she let go on her own accord or had no choice due to the force of Harper's blow, Valerie dropped her hold on the syringe and let it fall. Hitting hard against the stones, the syringe shattered and the contents spilled out.

"No!" Joel screamed, pushing Alex aside.

Luke sprung into action like a mountain lion to the kill. He rushed Joel and sent him sprawling backward. Alex hurriedly got to her feet, determined to help Luke in whatever way she could, but instead found Jastrow at her side, pulling her and Valerie back up the path.

"You ladies must get out of harm's way," he told them.

"But he has a gun," Alex protested. "We have to help Luke."

"I'll do what I can, but first I must see you safely away from this area. Go for help."

Alex looked to Valerie, who nodded. "We can get help," Valerie said as if to assure Alex it was for the best.

She looked back at the men who were fighting. "Please help him," she said, turning to go up the path with Valerie. They'd only gone a couple of feet, however, when the sheriff, followed by several rangers, Mr. Stokes, and Senator Winthrop, appeared on the trail.

"Down here!" she called. "Help us—Mr. Harper has a gun." Just then a shot was fired. Alex gasped for breath and turned on her heel, her hand at her throat. *Dear God, don't let Luke be hurt,* she prayed.

The sheriff and rangers rushed past her to take the matter in hand. Valerie began to cry anew and Alex thought for a moment she might join her.

"Neither one is shot!" the sheriff called out.

Alex watched Luke get up and dust off his clothes. She longed to go to him, to feel his arms around her.

"Alexandria? Are you all right?"

She looked behind her to see her mother coming behind

the senator and nodded as the senator hurried to take Valerie in his arms.

"What of you? Are you hurt?" he asked his daughter.

"Oh, Daddy, I'm fine now. Now that I know he can't hurt you."

The senator's expression grew stony. He put Valerie at arm's length and looked her over. "I'm so sorry for what I've put you through."

Alex's mother took hold of her and hugged her close. "Oh, my darling, I feared the worst."

"You had good reason to," Alex admitted. "Harper planned the worst." Then remembering she'd confronted Joel only a short time earlier about her mother's whereabouts, she questioned. "Where did he take you? He didn't hurt you, did he?"

"Who?" Katherine looked confused.

"Joel Harper. Didn't he find you in the cabin and take you from there? Michaela came and told me you were missing. I was afraid, and when Mr. Harper made some comments to me this evening, I presumed he was the one responsible."

"No," her mother replied, shaking her head. "Not at all. Something came up, and with the help of my guard, we settled the matter quite readily. No, Joel Harper had nothing to do with me leaving the cabin."

"I'm so glad, Mother. I've only wanted your safety—your happiness."

Katherine Keegan reached up and gently touched her daughter's cheek. "I've wanted no less for you, child. You're safe now. That's all that matters."

Valerie began to sob loudly. The senator stepped back, appearing uncertain as to what he should do. Alex saw her mother's expression and knew the compassion she felt for the younger woman.

"Maybe you could talk with her, Mother. Her own mother died, and I can speak from experience—you never outgrow the need for your mother."

Her mother smiled and nodded. "I'll see what I can do." Katherine went to Valerie and embraced her. The debutante seemed to fall apart at the motherly touch.

The senator went to Bradley Jastrow and shook his head. "I can't begin to extend my apologies for what my aide perceived as acceptable politics."

Alex heard little else. Luke approached her with a look of grave concern. "Are you all right?"

"I am now," she said in a barely audible voice.

Luke pulled her close, wrapping his arms around her. "I thought he would kill you."

"He would have. There's no doubt about that." She looked up to meet his gaze. "I thought he would kill you. I could hardly pray."

"He can't hurt anyone now." He held her tight and Alex realized she loved this man more than life.

"I couldn't have endured it if he'd killed you," Alex said softly. "I . . ."

"You don't understand! They have to die. They know too much!" Joel screamed as the sheriff and one burly ranger forced him back up the path. "It's too late now. Too late. They have to die."

Alex pulled away enough to see Joel's crazed expression as he came to a halt in front of the senator and Bradley Jastrow. "You don't know how hard I've worked," he said to the senator. "I've done all of this for you—for us. We must go to the White House. We must be president!"

The senator shook his head. "No, Joel. All that's over with. I'm resigning from the election. My daughter needs me now."

"You can't! I've done too much to make this happen. I've . . . I've even . . ." His expression grew wild and he lunged forward as if to harm the senator, but the sheriff and rangers held him fast.

Half dragging, half carrying Joel Harper, they moved off toward the hotel. The remaining ranger turned to the party. "I'll need to talk to you all."

A loud commotion could be heard at the top of the walkway. Alex strained to see what was happening, but when flashes of light exploded in the dimming evening light, she knew full well the newspaper reporters had found out the truth. Or at least their version of it.

Several of them came rushing down the path toward where the senator stood beside Bradley Jastrow.

"Senator! We need a statement. Is it true that your aide tried to murder Mr. Jastrow?"

"Did he also kill Rufus Keegan?"

They seemed to momentarily forget Alex and Luke. Valerie went protectively to her father's side, as if bolstering her own strength in order to protect him.

"Leave my father alone," she demanded.

Katherine came to Alex and Luke. "There something I need to speak with you about. Something you must see for yourselves."

"What is it, Mother?"

Alex looked to Luke, but he shrugged. "Yes, what is it?"

Katherine drew a deep breath. "Let's go to Mrs. Godfrey's office. I can tell you all about it there."

CHAPTER TWENTY-SEVEN

Alex settled into step beside Luke, while her mother took the initiative and led the way back to El Tovar. Alex felt Luke reach for her hand and she smiled. Looking up to meet his gaze, her smile broadened. How right it felt to hold hands with her best friend in all the world—to love him and care about him as she did. She looked away, wondering what had caused her mother to suddenly take leave of her protective cabin.

"Do you know what this is about?" Alex asked Luke softly.

"No, I was about to ask you the same question."

Alex shrugged. "Guess we'll find out soon enough."

She looked up at El Tovar in all its glory. The chalet-styling looked foreign against the canyon setting. With the sunlight all but gone, the place loomed like a brooding hulk. *I'm tired,* Alex thought. *I'm tired of this place and this job. I'm tired of the things that Arizona represents to me.* She had never thought it possible that she'd feel this way. She'd loved the canyon since she was a child and now she only wanted to leave.

Luke's giving me a way out, she thought as she continued

her self-reflection. Marriage . . . a home . . . a family of her own. She could have it all with this man, if only she'd put aside her fears. Luke wasn't like her father. He wasn't like Joel Harper. In fact, Luke was unlike any man she'd ever known. She looked to where her mother stood waiting at the porch entry to the hotel.

She smiled at the approaching couple, and Alex wondered what her mother might say to her concerns. Perhaps she'd get the chance to ask her later.

"Can't you just tell us what's happened?" Alex questioned.

"You'd better see for yourself," her mother replied. "I think such a monumental moment merits a face-to-face experience."

Alex couldn't begin to imagine what her mother had planned. She could see her mother's peaceful countenance, however, and knew that whatever the news, it must be good.

They made their way down the employee hallway and turned toward Mrs. Godfrey's office. Just then, Alex heard the unmistakable cry of a baby. Her mother opened the door before she could question the matter and revealed Michaela holding a squalling infant.

At first, Alex wondered if this had been the real reason Michaela had gone away on vacation. She'd left rather abruptly, surprising everyone with her temporary resignation. She'd been gone long enough to have given birth.

"Oh, Mrs. Keegan," Michaela declared, "I'm so glad you're back. He won't settle down. I tried feeding him as you suggested, but he just isn't interested."

Katherine smiled. "Alexandria, I know this will come as a shock to you, but this is your little brother."

Alex felt her mouth drop open. Her eyes widened as she looked to Luke. He appeared just as shocked as she was.

"How . . . I mean who . . ." She let her question trail off as she searched her mother's face for an answer.

"Sit down," her mother instructed. "I need to tell you the whole story."

Michaela got up. "Here, sit here. You can hold him. I think if I live to be a hundred, I'll never want a child of my own."

Alex took Michaela's chair and, without even knowing why, did just as Michaela directed. As her friend placed the baby in arms, Alex couldn't help but smile. "He's so tiny."

"Tiny, but loud," Michaela said, heading quickly to the door. "If you need help with him, maybe it would be better to call Bernice. She has a whole collection of brothers and sisters and probably knows better what to do than I would." She hurried from the room, pulling the door closed behind her before anyone could offer a comment.

But there was no need for comment. The baby had calmed in Alex's arms. He looked up at her with deep blue eyes, warming Alex to the bottom of her heart.

"I think he likes you," Luke said, coming to stand beside her.

"What's his name?" Alex asked her mother.

Katherine took a seat directly across from Alex. "His name is Brock. Brock Scott. His mother was Gloria Scott."

"Was?" Alex asked. "Is she dead?"

"Yes, I'm afraid so," Katherine replied. "But I'm getting ahead of myself. Let me start at the beginning. You see, shortly before I came to El Tovar to tell your father I wanted a divorce, Miss Scott showed up at the house in Williams, with Brock in tow. I didn't know who she was, but it was dreadfully hot that day so I invited her in. Once we sat down, she informed me that Brock was Rufus's son and that she had come to insist we help her out financially."

"Oh my," Alex said, knowing how much this woman's appearance must have wounded her mother.

"I'd never had to confront one of your father's women, and I'd certainly never had one of them share such news. I was stunned to say the least."

"And hurt," Alex said, feeling for her mother.

"Yes," Katherine nodded. "I was hurt as well. This revelation was the final straw. It was as if my eyes were suddenly opened to the truth. There was no hope for Rufus and me. Here was a young woman with a new baby and the need for a husband and father for her son. I figured Rufus might as well divorce me and marry the poor woman and give the child a name."

"Oh, Mother, I'm so sorry." Alex met her mother's gaze and saw the pain reflected there. Her expression pierced Alex's heart, reminding her yet again of her father's cruelty. Without thinking she said, "I'm glad he's dead."

"Alex, don't be bitter about the past. Your father was a lost soul. He never knew what was missing in his life because he was so certain his money and power could fill all those empty places. When it didn't, he tried to fill it with women. When that didn't work, he just became angry and hateful. You don't want to be like him."

"But I am like him," Alex said, shaking her head. She looked back to the baby who was falling asleep. "Joel Harper reminded me of that very fact. He said I had my father's independent nature, his determination, and his judgmental attitude."

"I disagree," Luke said softly. "You may have an independent nature and determination. You may even be a bit quick at times to assess a situation and see it in the wrong light—but you are nothing like him."

"I agree," Katherine replied. "Rufus did everything out of selfish need. He wanted the best—not for his family, but for himself. You've been patiently working this job for four years and during this time you've told me off and on that you were saving your money in order to take me away from my misery. That isn't the act of a selfish woman."

Alex felt a tear slide down her cheek. "I wanted to be a good Christian where Father was concerned. And how I wanted to respect him and honor him as the Bible said. But I feel I can't mourn his passing now because I've mourned his absence all my life. I watched him with one woman or another since I was a small girl. I always envied those women because they were laughing and having such a marvelous time and Father was laughing too. I always wondered why he didn't laugh with me?"

"Oh, my darling, I know. I know your pain so well. I tried hard to shield you from his actions. I knew you longed for him to care—to just once tell you that he loved you."

"And now he never will."

"No. He never will. But neither will he ever hurt us again." Katherine's words were firm. "I mourn the man I first married. The man I loved. But like you, I mourned that man's passing a long time ago. Losing the ugliness and sin of the man who'd become Rufus Keegan is not a sorrowful parting. Still, I won't speak ill of him. He was a troubled man who was hopelessly lost without God. He has condemned himself. Therefore, I don't need to, and neither do you."

Luke offered Alex a handkerchief. His expression was sympathetic, understanding. Alex felt certain he knew full well how confused her heart and head were over the entire matter.

"I know you're right," Alex said, cradling the baby close.

They sat in silence for several moments before her mother picked the story back up. "Gloria told me she would bring the baby to the newspaper office and tell her story if I refused to help her. I told her I had no idea of where Rufus had taken himself off to and had no way of dealing with the matter myself. I gave her a small bit of money, just what I had in the drawer for household expenses. I told her I would find Rufus and discuss the matter and see what was to be done. She left and shortly after that the invitation to join your father here at the Grand Canyon came from the Winthrops. I knew what I had to do.

"When I confronted your father about the matter, he would hear nothing of it. I tried to talk to him on several occasions, and always he'd either laugh it off or dismiss my concerns. I told him it was unfair for the child to suffer simply because its parents had been less than prudent. He told me to stay out of it, that he would deal with Miss Scott when the time came."

Katherine folded her hands and sighed. "Only the time came much sooner than he expected."

Alex noted the change in her mother's spirit. "What happened?"

"I hadn't realized it at the time, but Miss Scott had followed me to El Tovar. She lost no time in seeking us out. Rufus was livid. He threatened her and the child, then seeing that was getting him nowhere, offered to meet her later to discuss an arrangement."

Alex began to get a sick feeling in the pit of her stomach. "Gloria was the one on the rim that night, wasn't she?"

Katherine met her daughter's eyes and nodded. "I wasn't to go there. I wasn't to share in this meeting, but I felt compelled to be there. I talked to your father prior to the meeting. I begged him to divorce me and marry Gloria, but he was still adamant. He was sure it would ruin his chances with the Winthrops, and he was probably right. Nevertheless, I told him the child was more important than a lifetime of appointments in Washington. He only laughed at that.

"I had planned to remain in my room, but your father insisted I come to the lawn party. He felt I could boost his chances for appointment with the senator. I argued with him about it but finally agreed. He went down ahead of me and after I dressed, I joined him. He'd been drinking, there was no doubt about that. Someone had managed to get him exactly what he needed to bolster his courage." She shook her head. "Would that he could have turned to God the way he did to drink." She sighed again.

"But I digress. I went to the party and then, when he slipped away to meet Gloria, I couldn't help but follow him. I stayed hidden, not wanting to further anger him. I watched as they met on the canyon rim. She didn't have the baby with her and this seemed to make Rufus quite enraged. I heard him telling her to go get the infant immediately and meet him back there, but she refused. I believe now he intended to push them both over the edge and eliminate his problem."

"But why? Why would he act in such an irrational manner? Father never worried about his affairs. Why now?" Alex asked, shuddering at the thought of her father being a murderer.

"I don't know. When Gloria refused to go get the baby, Rufus slapped her hard. He lunged for her as if to send her over the edge but Miss Scott was prepared for this. She sidestepped him and pushed him away. Unfortunately, she pushed him off-balance and he stumbled backward into the canyon."

Alex sat in shocked silence. The clock on the wall ticked

away the seconds, but she found no words to speak. The picture in her mind filled in all the missing pieces. Luke tenderly squeezed her shoulder, causing Alex to raise her gaze to his. The look she found there gave her hope and filled her heart with the assurance that no matter what else happened, she would always have Luke.

"I screamed and ran to where Rufus had gone over," her mother continued. "Gloria screamed when she saw me and ran for the hotel. Moments later Luke appeared. I collapsed on the path, unable to even comprehend what I knew must be true. I knew Rufus was dead, but I just couldn't believe what I'd witnessed."

"Oh, Mother, I'm so sorry. I knew you hadn't pushed Father. I knew you would never do such a thing, but I couldn't understand why you'd protect the person who had. I feared the guilty party was threatening you or threatening me. I was so afraid you were protecting someone else so that they wouldn't hurt me. I couldn't have lived with it if you'd gone to jail to protect Gloria Scott."

"I wasn't protecting her," her mother replied. "I was protecting him. He didn't deserve to end up orphaned."

"But what of his mother?" Alex said, gently stroking the baby's dark hair. "You said his mother ran for the hotel. What happened?"

"After everyone learned Rufus had died, I figured I'd heard the last of Gloria Scott. I knew I couldn't prove what had happened and I honestly thought that if it kept mother and child together, it would be better for me to be blamed for Rufus's death. I prayed about the matter and decided it would be best to keep my mouth shut. No one knew about Gloria except me. I mean, I figured someone on the train might have remembered her, but I had no idea where she was staying, and it would have been very difficult to prove what had happened."

"But it was an accident," Alex said, realizing for the first time that her father hadn't been murdered at all. "The poor woman was simply defending herself."

"Yes, but no one but me knew that, and Gloria had disappeared. She wasn't registered at El Tovar, and I had no way of locating her without exposing her part in the matter."

Luke shifted beside Alex and asked, "So what happened?"

"Alex arranged for me to be moved, as you know. I felt better knowing the reporters wouldn't be hounding me and trying to break down my door to get answers. I also felt that the privacy would allow me a chance to actually find Gloria. I wasn't sure how, but I knew my guard would have to sleep sometime. But instead, Gloria left a note and the baby at the front desk. The note only said that this child should be delivered to me and that I would know what to do. The people there knew the rangers had me under their protection, so they delivered the baby to the rangers and they in turn brought the baby to me. What no one knew, until I'd taken the baby out of the basket, was that there was another letter under the baby's blanket."

"What did it say?" Alex asked anxiously.

"Gloria told me she couldn't live with the guilt of what she'd done. She knew she was responsible for Rufus's death and figured no one would believe it was an accident. She feared for the child and begged me to make a home for him so that he wouldn't end up in an asylum somewhere. She concluded the letter by stating that she planned to end her life. She gave directions as to where the rangers could find her, and sure enough, she had committed suicide."

"Oh, how awful." Alex continued to stroke the baby's

head, saddened to think of his mother deserting him at such a tender age. "And now he's orphaned."

"He doesn't have to be."

Alex looked to her mother. "What do you mean?"

"I mean you could raise him. It's obvious you have a way with him."

"But, I know nothing of raising a child. I'm not even married." She looked to Luke as if he could verify that one detail.

He smiled and reached down to touch her hand where it rested on the baby's head. "You could give me an answer to my question and sew things up rather neatly."

Alex felt overwhelmed by the moment. She knew she loved him. Knew that she didn't want to lose him. So why couldn't she give him the answer he wanted to hear?

She got to her feet and handed him the baby. "I need to think and to pray. I need time to sort this out."

Luke said nothing as Alex walked from the room. He looked down at the sleeping baby and then to Katherine Keegan.

"She'll do the right thing," Katherine said softly. "Not only by him, but by you as well. She loves you, of that I'm certain."

"I know it too," Luke admitted, "but she's scared."

"Of what?" Katherine asked, seeming surprised by his statement.

"She's afraid all men are like her father and his friends. She's afraid that fidelity isn't a possibility for any man. She's afraid to love and afraid to trust. And until she can come to terms with that, I know she can't marry me."

Katherine nodded. "Rufus hurt her badly. While other little girls had fathers to be proud of, Alex hid her parentage at every turn."

Luke took the seat Alex had just vacated and eased the baby onto his shoulder. Brock didn't so much as stir. "He's so tiny," Luke commented.

"Yes. He's only a few weeks old. Far too young to be without a mother and father."

Luke nodded. "I'm buying a ranch in Wyoming. It's a small place, but large enough for all of us. If Alex will marry me, I'd like you to consider coming with us."

"I appreciate that, Luke. You've been more than kind to me. I've always been reassured to know you were there for Alex. I know at first it was only in friendship, but I think that's what will make your marriage work. You were friends before the idea of falling in love ever came to either one of you. Maybe then, if the feelings fade, you'll still be friends and still have a foundation for your marriage to grow on."

"I'll never stop loving her," he said softly. "Even if she says no to my proposal. I'll never love anyone but Alex."

CHAPTER TWENTY-EIGHT

Valerie Winthrop looked to her father in complete dismay. "But, Daddy, everyone knows this affair was all Joel's fault. No one blames you. Why are you withdrawing from the campaign?"

The senator, looking older than his years, cast a sorrowful gaze upon his daughter. "I can hardly ask the country to allow me to keep their affairs when I can't keep my own in order."

"But Joel was underhanded and conniving," she protested. "He never let any of us know what was going on until it was too late. Why, I didn't even know about some of it until just a week or so ago."

"Exactly my point, Valerie. I had no idea what was going on under my own nose. I should have seen it. I shouldn't have had my sights so fixed on the presidency that I missed what was happening right in my own office—my own house. I will always blame myself for how Joel treated you. I can overlook his greed and ambition, but I will never forgive him for hurting you."

Valerie reached out and touched her father's hand. "There is no merit in holding anger toward him. Mrs.

Keegan told me that such things will only fester and allow for a hard and embittered heart. And she should know, given what she had to endure with Mr. Keegan."

"She's a lovely woman, gracious and soft-spoken. Just like your mother."

Valerie nodded. "She reminded me very much of Mother when she comforted me. I think her advice is most beneficial. She speaks as one who knows, and that will help others to listen and heed her word."

He looked to her and Valerie could see the tears form in his eyes. "I've been very wrong to subject you to all of this. Will you forgive a silly old man his ambitions?"

"Oh, Daddy, you didn't hurt me. I wanted you to run for president. I thought it would be marvelously exciting to play hostess in the White House."

"That will never happen now. The papers are running rampant with the scandal. Even Jastrow is backing out of the race. No doubt we'll be left with that rascal John Davis for a Democratic contender." He paused and shook his head. "No, by the time this scandal subsides, it will be too late for me to consider running for anything, much less president."

Valerie picked up her fork and toyed with her breakfast. "Perhaps you could write a book about all of this. Since scandal sells so well, maybe you should share with the public how you were a victim to Joel Harper, just as much as the next man. I wouldn't be surprised if you didn't have publishers clamoring to print it."

"It's a thought, I suppose," her father said, picking up his cup of coffee.

They were alone in the private dining room, tolerant only of each other's company. The press had hounded her father morning and night for exclusive interviews and always the senator declined. Valerie saw the toll it had taken on him, and she was secretly glad he'd decided to call off the campaign plans. He needed to rest. He needed to know she was well and safe and that Joel hadn't harmed her beyond her ability to recover.

"I know it would go over big. Why, we could even contact this one publisher in New York. I'm friends with the owner's daughter. I would be willing to wager money they would come all the way to South Carolina to talk it over with you."

The senator took a long drink and seemed to perk up a bit. "There are a lot of details that could benefit those in the business of politics."

She smiled. "Of course. There are businessmen who would most likely benefit as well. Then, if told in the right manner, you might even attract quite a few women readers."

"I could start with my early days in business and move into the political arena," he said, nodding. He looked to her and smiled. "You're good medicine for this old heart. Just like your mother used to be. I miss her a lot, you know."

"Yes," Valerie said, reaching out to cover her father's hand. "I miss her too. She made us both feel very loved."

"Indeed," he replied with a sigh.

Valerie gave his hand a squeeze and then picked up her fork again. With a forkful of eggs halfway to her mouth she said, "I would want to help you with the book, but there is something else I'd like to help with first. Maybe you'd like to be involved as well. It's a very good cause."

Her father seemed surprised. "Do tell. What has caught your attention this time?"

"Mother, I really need to talk to you," Alex said as her

mother cuddled Brock and talked to him in animated tones.

"You know you can discuss anything with me." She looked up to meet Alex's gaze.

"You're so kind to him," Alex said, motioning to the baby. "How can you abide him? I mean, surely he reminds you of your bad times with Father."

Katherine looked taken aback. "Well, it's hardly his fault that his parents had no concern for their actions. This baby is innocent. Completely and totally innocent. He must be allowed a fresh start."

"I agree. I'm just not sure that start should begin with us."

"But why?"

Alex sat down on the foot of the bed. "It's just that I wouldn't want this baby to be a reminder of all you suffered, a living memory of the things that happened the night Father died."

"Alex, you're worrying for nothing. I look forward to grandmothering this infant. I don't have the stamina to raise him, but you do. You would make a good mother for this child. He's flesh of your flesh. He's your father's son. We can't let him go to strangers. Could you really abide that? Knowing that your little brother was out there somewhere with someone not of your choosing to raise him?"

"No, absolutely not!" Alex declared, feeling a fierce protective nature toward the baby. "But you are uppermost in my thoughts. I'd hate to see you hurt again. We'll be burying Father in four days' time. I'd like to be able to bury the pain of his actions as well."

"This baby will always be with us," Katherine stated matter-of-factly. "You can't bury everything about your father's indiscretions. But God can make smooth the rough places. He can bring sunlight to the shadows and change night into day. A God who can do all of that can surely heal the hearts of two women."

Alex smiled. "Luke once accused me of thinking God couldn't handle everything. That some things were just too big."

"And was he right? Did you feel that way?" her mother asked softly.

Alex chewed on her lip for a moment before responding. The way she'd felt only weeks ago seemed so very different than the way she felt now. "I suppose I did in some ways," she finally said. "I didn't mean it in the literal sense, because I know nothing is too big for God. But it seemed too big."

"And now?"

"Now I feel confused by the sudden change of many of my feelings."

Her mother smiled and gently laid the baby on the bed. "Luke?"

"For one," Alex admitted. "I love him."

"Yes, I know."

"And he loves me."

"Again, this is not news to me." Her mother reached across the baby to touch Alex's knee. "What are you going to do about it?"

"He wants an answer to his proposal of marriage. He's bought a ranch in Wyoming and would have us live there with him. All of us. Me, the baby, and you."

"He said as much."

Surprised, Alex rose from the bed. "When? When did he tell you about this?"

"Yesterday, after you left to go think and pray."

Alex paced the floor at the end of the bed. "Mother, it's

so hard to know what's right. My heart tells me one thing, but my mind . . ."

"Reminds you of the past and of the bad things done to you," her mother interjected.

"Yes. Yes, the past is haunting me. I couldn't face Luke if he took lovers as Father did."

"He won't."

Her mother's voice held such certainty, but still Alex wasn't convinced. "He's just a man, Mother. He's flesh and blood. He'll be tempted."

"Maybe tempted, but he won't cheat on you as Rufus did with me. I feel confident of that."

Alex shook her head and stopped directly in front of her mother. She wanted to believe her words, but fear bound her in a way that nearly choked all hope from her. "How can you be so sure? What guarantee can you offer me?"

"Alexandria Keegan, you know full well that life comes without guarantees. However, you also know that God has promised to be with us through the thick and thin of it. How can you doubt that He would protect you and help keep Luke faithful?"

"But God didn't keep Father faithful."

"Your father didn't desire to be faithful. Not to me, nor to God. Your father had his own plan and always at the center of it was Rufus Keegan. Luke loves God."

"I know he loves God, Mama," Alex said, falling to her knees in front of her mother. "But he's only human."

"As are you. What makes you so sure you won't be tempted to cheat on Luke? After all, you'll be stuck out in the middle of nowhere on a ranch without too many other people around. Those who are around will most likely be men—ranch hands."

"That's silly. I could never look at another man as I do . . . Luke."

Realization began to sink in. Why should the same not be true for Luke? Why couldn't he be just as faithful as she? Why couldn't Alex trust that he would push aside any seemingly tempting moments in favor of his love for Alex?

"I'm being really ignorant, aren't I?" she asked her mother.

Katherine reached out and gently stroked her daughter's wavy brown hair. "It's the first time you've been in love. You're entitled to not have all the answers."

"I really do love him. When I wake up in the morning, he's the first person I think of. When I go to sleep at night, I always do so with something he said on my mind. He makes me laugh—he makes me feel safe and protected."

"And he loves God," her mother added. "What more could you possibly want?"

Alex shook her head. "Nothing. He's everything."

"So what are you going to tell him?"

Alex smiled. "I think you already know the answer to that. But what about you? Will you come live with us?"

Katherine looked to the baby and shook her head. "No. I have plans."

Alex pulled back. "Plans? What plans?"

"I want to sell the house in Williams and dissolve all of your father's business dealings. When this is completed, I want to move to a larger city—I'm not sure exactly which one. Maybe Denver, so that I could be close to you."

"What would you do there?" Alex got to her feet and pulled a chair up close to her mother's bedside. Sitting down, she waited for her mother to explain, seeing a light in her eyes that she'd not seen before.

"I want to buy a big house with lots of rooms. I want to open a home to women who have suffered as I have—as Valerie has."

"Valerie Winthrop?" Alex still prickled at the name. "I'm still working on my feelings toward her. She was always flirting with Luke and lying to me."

"Don't blame her, darling. She has suffered unimaginable horrors in her life. You two have more in common than you would imagine. While her father thought she hung the moon and stars, he was always busy. Too busy to guide her actions. She was spoiled and encouraged to be flirtatious and do whatever she had to in order to get the attention she wanted."

"But at least her father loved her."

"Yes, but an absent father is still an absent father, and a child growing up without the loving guidance of such a parent will still suffer. Just as you did, but for entirely different reasons."

Alex felt overwhelmed with guilt. "I'm sorry I've judged her harshly."

"I hope you will put the past aside," her mother said gently. "Valerie decided to trust the Lord and follow His will—just last night. She and I had a long talk."

"Really? Well, that is good news," Alex said, not exactly sure how to deal with the issue. It was hard to just automatically switch from feeling a measure of contempt to joy, yet this new information really did change everything. *Oh, God, forgive me for my hardheartedness. I thank you that Valerie Winthrop came to you. I'm glad you're there for each and every person, not just the ones I think deserve your mercy.* She felt deeply ashamed of her attitude. "Oh, Mother, I have so much to learn—so far to go."

"But we all do. As long as we're still here walking this earth, there are things the good Lord is teaching us—showing us—bringing us through. Valerie is no different. She just needed help to see the way."

Alex felt tears come to her eyes. She sniffed and nodded. "I'm so glad you were there for her. I'll make a special point to offer her my apology and my congratulations."

"You'll have ample opportunity. You see, Valerie wants to help me with my idea for the home to help needy women."

Alex was truly surprised by this. The Valerie Winthrop she knew was self-centered and . . . *I'm doing it again,* she thought. *I'm judging her by her old nature, not the new creation she is in Christ.* Meekly Alex questioned, "She does?"

"Yes. Not only that, but she's going to talk to her father about putting some of the Winthrop money into the effort. With that kind of backing, we can do something truly wonderful. We'll be able to buy a very large place, furnish it nicely, and even bring in some staff to help keep it up. Maybe we can offer programs to teach women various things that can help them to be more self-sufficient."

Alex laughed as she wiped away her tears. "You have this all figured out, don't you?"

Her mother smiled and nodded. "I've had a lot of time to think. Ever since your Father's indiscretions became more frequent, I wished there might be something out there for me. Then when he died and I was left alone while the investigation went on, I began to pray in earnest for how I might make a difference. I knew Rufus couldn't atone for his sins, but perhaps I could atone for mine, as well as serve other hurting women."

"I think it's a grand idea, Mother. If anyone can make such a thing happen, you'll be the woman for the job."

"I'm glad you approve."

Alex saw the joy in her mother's expression and it warmed

her to the innermost part of her being. "How could I not? I only want happiness for you. You deserve it."

"So do you. So are you going to go find that cowboy and tell him how you feel?"

Alex smiled. "I think he's waited long enough for an answer—and for my complete trust."

"I think you're right."

As Alex got to her feet, her mother did likewise. Embracing her daughter, Katherine Keegan said, "Trust God first and foremost. The world will always disappoint you, but God never will. His love is never ending. He will see you through, even when things seem grim and dark. Even when the morning seems as though it will never come, He is your light. Don't put that job off onto Luke. He'll never be able to live up to it, and you'll be disappointed in him. Just remember, it's not his duty. As you said, he's only human."

Alex hugged her mother tight. She could only pray that she might gain insight and maturity from her mother's words.

A knock on the door interrupted their moment, but Alex knew she would carry their conversation in her heart for the rest of her life. Allowing her mother to answer the door, Alex finished wiping her eyes.

"Ah, here's where my best gals are held up," Luke announced as he came in. His loud voice woke the baby, causing Brock to whimper and fuss. Without a word to the ladies, Luke strode across the floor and picked the infant up and rocked him back and forth. "Guess I'm going to have to learn to be a little more quiet when I enter a room, eh, Mrs. Keegan?" He grinned at Alex's mother.

"When you have a baby in the house there are all kinds of concessions to be made," her mother answered.

Alex thought it rather amazing that Luke should feel so at

ease with the child. Alex felt her cheeks grow hot when Luke looked up to catch her watching him. He winked and gave her a smile.

"We were just talking over our plans for the future," Katherine told Luke.

Alex nodded and tried to steer the conversation away from anything too personal. She wanted to wait until she and Luke were alone in order to discuss their own plans. "Mother plans to open a home for women who've been hurt or abandoned. She might move to Denver, and Valerie Winthrop is going to help her."

"Miss Winthrop? Really?" Luke seemed just as surprised as Alex had been.

"Yes," Alex replied. "Last night Mother helped Miss Winthrop see her need for the Lord."

"Well, I'll be," Luke said, nodding in approval. "Just goes to show those folks I would have given up on, God has a plan for. Good thing I'm not in charge."

Katherine smiled, looking more youthful in her appearance than Alex could ever remember. "I think we would all fail miserably at His job."

"Well, I know I don't have a big house yet, Mrs. Keegan, but you'd be welcomed to come live on our ranch and bring your wounded women too." He chuckled softly. "Hey, I might even put them all to work. After all, I'm going to need ranch hands."

Katherine and Alex shared a smile before Katherine crossed the room to take the baby from Luke. "You watch out, Luke Toland. I just might take you up on the offer." She rocked the sleeping child a moment before looking back up to Luke. "You know, you're quite good with children. I hope you'll give me lots of grandchildren. You'll no doubt be a wonderful father. We'll have to work on that Mrs. Keegan thing, however. I don't think I'd want you calling me that if we're to be family."

This time Luke blushed a deep crimson. Alex watched the color climb from the collar of his shirt and fan out across his cheeks. Even his nose turned red. "Well . . . uh . . . you know, I haven't had an answer from your daughter regarding that matter."

Alex knew the time had come to talk to Luke about her feelings. Looking to his broken wrist, she questioned, "Luke, do you suppose you could handle a horse? I mean for a ride?"

Luke looked at her with a bemused expression, seeming to forget his embarrassment. "Handle a horse? Can I handle a horse?" He looked to her mother. "Did you hear what she asked me?"

Katherine laughed and Alex reached out and grasped Luke's arm. Pulling him toward the door, Alex called back over her shoulder. "We're going for a ride, Mother. We shouldn't be gone long."

She could still hear her mother's gentle laughter in the hall as she led Luke toward the stairs.

"Can I handle a horse? What kind of question was that, Alex?"

"Better mind your manners, Mr. Toland, or you won't get an answer to the question you've been pestering me with of late."

Luke stopped short, and Alex couldn't help but laugh at the serious expression on his face. "Yes, ma'am," he said with the briefest nod. "I surely wouldn't want to jeopardize that."

"I didn't think so," Alex said with a smile.

CHAPTER TWENTY-NINE

Alex finished with her horse, slipping three fingers between the cinch strap and the horse's belly to make certain it was tight enough. Satisfied with her job, she couldn't help but smile at the memory of Luke first teaching her to saddle a horse. She was just about as green as a girl could be when it came to dealing with livestock. She'd lived a sheltered city life, and the idea of having to deal with a horse was not only foreign to her, but scared her as well.

"What's that smile all about?" Luke questioned.

"I was just remembering when you first taught me to do this."

"You haven't done it all that much even in the four years since you've been here. I'd better inspect your work." He took his horse's reins in hand and wrapped them around the fence post. He went to Alex, looked over her work, and nodded. "You always were a quick learner."

"I had a good teacher," she threw back.

Alex raised the split skirt just enough to bring her booted foot to the stirrup. This accomplished, she grabbed for the horn and gave a couple of bounces to hoist herself into the saddle. Luke helped by giving her a push. He adjusted her stirrups to the proper length, making certain she was comfortable.

Handing her the reins, Luke let his hand linger on hers. "See, I told you I could handle a horse."

She grinned. "We haven't even started the ride yet. I wouldn't be boasting until after we return."

He laughed, gathered up his own reins, and vaulted into the saddle. Alex thought he made it look so easy. She always felt as though she were raising her leg straight up in the air just to put her foot in the stirrup.

They moved away from the stable at a leisurely pace. Alex eyed Luke's cast and thought again of his injury. "So how is the arm? Is it hurting much these days?"

"Nah, it's mostly just an inconvenience now. I can't believe I have to wear this cast for another few weeks. Seems like bones ought to knit faster than that."

"Too bad your patience suffers just as long in coming," she teased.

"I have more patience than you know of. I've been mooning over you all spring and you didn't even notice me."

Alex felt her stomach do a flip. "I noticed you, but I didn't notice you like that. I thought you were just—"

"A good friend," Luke interrupted. "I know. I came to hate those words."

She laughed and took the lead on the trail as it narrowed. They rode for some distance, neither one talking. Alex knew Luke was waiting for her to speak up and tell him what he wanted to hear, but frankly she was nervous. Her hands were shaking even as she gripped the reins. Her horse whinnied softly, sensing her state of mind. *It was probably not a good idea to suggest the ride,* Alex thought. She knew horses were very sensitive to their rider's dispositions.

The trail widened again when they reached the place where it headed into the canyon, but the widening was brief. The path quickly narrowed as it dipped at an incline. The canyon spread out below like a rich tapestry of browns and golds, greens and reds. It was God's handiwork and God's alone.

Instead of going into the canyon as Alex had suggested earlier, she reined back on the horse. Luke came even with her and frowned.

"What's wrong?"

"I think I'd like to talk to you here. My hands are shaking so hard I can hardly hold on to the reins."

Luke grinned. "Shaky hands make it sound like things just might be going in my favor."

She cast a gaze toward the skies above. "Doesn't everything go in your favor?"

"I sure hope so—especially in this case."

He dismounted and Alex did the same without waiting for his help. Kicking free of her stirrups, she slid over the side of the horse and landed with a thud on the rocky path. She was going to have to get a whole lot better at this kind of thing if she was to become a rancher's wife.

She pulled the horse along and went to stand not far from the path. "So what's wrong with being friends?"

The question took Luke off guard. In a flash she saw his expression change from humored to very serious. "There's nothing wrong with being friends, unless you want more." He came to stand beside her. "And I want more."

His horse whinnied and bobbed his head up and down against Luke's hold. They couldn't help but laugh at his antics.

"See," Luke said. "He agrees."

"So do I," Alex said softly. "About that and so much more."

Luke reached out and pushed back an errant strand of brown hair. "I love it when you wear your hair down. Did you know that?"

"No, I don't guess I did," Alex replied, feeling her heart pick up its beat. Her breath caught in her throat.

Luke gently stroked her cheek. "So what more do you want?"

"Hmm?" she asked, feeling a million miles away, mesmerized by his touch.

"You said you wanted so much more."

She nodded and looked back to the canyon. This piece of ground, this phenomenon of nature had played such an intricate role in her life. Even now, it was the scale on which she measured her next words.

"I want to receive enough love to fill up this canyon. I want to give that much love in return." She turned to see Luke's thoughtful expression. This time she was the one who reached out. She touched Luke's cheek, feeling the warmth of his skin beneath her fingers. She rubbed her thumb along his jawline, the stubble scratching against her touch. Luke said nothing, although she could feel him tremble.

"I want to wake up every morning with my best friend at my side. I want your smile to be the first thing I see every day."

"I'm kind of a bear in the morning," he admitted. "You might not get a full smile out of me."

Alex laughed. "Well, if Daniel can brave the lion's den, then I suppose I can brave a bear in my bed." She raised a brow as if considering something important, then added,

"And if it becomes too difficult, I'll simply have one of our children wake you up."

Luke reached for her and pulled her close. The reins of his horse slapped gently against her arm. "I like the sound of 'our children.' I like even better the idea of waking up next to you every morning."

"Oh, Luke, I love you more than I thought possible. The idea of giving my heart to someone has frightened me for so long that I couldn't imagine ever getting beyond that hurdle. I truly figured to be alone for the rest of my life—or at best to be living with my mother."

"Ah, darlin', I could never have let that happen. My life isn't worth a plug nickel without you. Spending most every day seeing you here at the canyon proved that to me. Every time you went away, I felt like a big chunk of my heart went too. I love you, Alex. I'll never love another woman. I told your mother that, and now I'm pledging it to you."

"What about Brock?"

Luke's brows drew together. "What about him?"

"What about us keeping him and raising him? It won't allow us to go into marriage on our own. We'll have a ready-made family."

"I don't mind one bit so long as you're a part of the arrangement. That baby doesn't appear to have anyone else standing in line to make him a home."

"But can you love him?"

"Can you?"

Alex nodded. "I wouldn't have asked if I didn't already have it in my heart to love him."

"Then give me credit for feeling the same way."

"You truly are a treasure of a man," she said, wrapping her arms around him. Lifting her face to him, Alex remembered the thrill of his kiss and hoped he'd seal the deal with another just like the first.

"So are you saying yes to me?" he asked, his mouth just an inch or so above hers.

"Yes," she breathed. "I'll marry you."

"When?"

She laughed. "Are you going to kiss me or not?"

He grinned at her playfully. "First answer my question. When are we getting married?"

"Probably sometime after my father's funeral. Knowing my mother, she's already planning the wedding. Will next week be soon enough?"

"I suppose if I have to wait until then, it'll have to do."

Alex tightened her hold on him. "Now kiss me."

"Yes, ma'am." Luke pulled her tight and lowered his mouth to hers. As his lips claimed her, Alex thought she might burst from the sheer joy of the moment. The emotion from their kiss warmed her from head to toe. Life with Luke Toland was going to be quite the adventure, she decided.

"Is this part of the park's new attractions?" a familiar voice called out.

Luke and Alex separated and pulled back to find Clancy leading a small group of mules and riders. He motioned to the group. "We're going to have to charge extra if this is going to be a regular show."

Luke kept his hold on Alex and nodded. "This is going to be a regular thing, but not here at the canyon. We're getting married and moving to Wyoming, just as soon as I get the details sorted out on the ranch I'm buying."

"That's why it's particularly fortunate that we've run across you here," another man called out. Bradley Jastrow dismounted from his mule and came to where Alex and Luke stood. "I was hoping to speak to you before I left the canyon tomorrow, and here you are."

"I didn't know you were still here, Mr. Jastrow," Alex commented. "I'd heard your party had pulled out."

"Most of them have," the handsome man admitted. "I dismissed my staff as soon as I gave the press the word that I was pulling out of the race for president. But I stayed on because I wanted to arrange something special. I haven't gotten all the details worked out, but I want you to have this." He reached into his pocket and pulled out an envelope. "Consider it thanks for saving my life."

Luke took the envelope, but shook his head. "No thanks are needed. Like I told you before, Alex is the one who had most of this figured out. I just kind of followed her lead."

"I'm grateful to you both. And in speaking with Miss Keegan's mother, I understand there might be reason to celebrate soon."

"That's right," Luke said, loud enough for Clancy to hear. "She just accepted my proposal of marriage."

"Well, pardon my sayin' so, Miss Keegan, but it's about time. I figured him a goner if you didn't give in soon."

Alex laughed, watching the grin broaden on Luke's face.

"I might say the same about you and a certain red-headed Harvey Girl," Alex teased Clancy. "I've seen the way you two look at each other, so don't think you're fooling me."

Clancy turned scarlet and looked away, muttering, "A fella has to think these things through."

Alex and Luke laughed, knowing that Bernice just might have her work cut out for her with Clancy Franklin.

"You both have my congratulations," Jastrow said, bringing their attention back to him. "Please consider this a wedding gift if you figure my thanks to be otherwise unnecessary."

Luke opened the envelope and studied the paper for a moment. "I can't accept this."

"Mr. Toland, please understand, I'm a wealthy man and this is one way I can show my appreciation. I know that there is no amount of money that could equal my life, but rest assured when I say this is but a pittance, and I truly want you to have it."

Alex couldn't wait any longer. "What is it, Luke?"

Luke handed her the paper. "Mr. Jastrow is arranging for us to take ownership of a nine-hundred-acre ranch, complete with herd and house."

"What!" Alex couldn't believe it. "Mr. Jastrow, that's much too generous. We could never accept this."

"Please. You saved my life, and I have it in my means to help you with your new start in life. I know you didn't save me because of what you could get out of me. That makes it all the more important that you let me do this. You helped me out of the goodness of your heart—out of a belief that life is sacred and that people should stop injustice where they find it. You were a blessing to me, now let me bless you in return. This entire matter has given me a new outlook on life. It's really changed everything for the better."

Alex looked to Luke and shrugged. "We've had worse thrust on us."

He laughed out loud at this. "Indeed we have. Well, Mr. Jastrow, I suppose we could allow you to impose on us just this once. But there must be a provision."

"And what would that be?" Jastrow asked.

"That you come out and visit us sometime. I know Wyoming is a long ways from Alabama, but a man of your means shouldn't find it too difficult."

Jastrow smiled and when he did, his entire face lit up. "I should say not. I would be most honored to visit you and your new bride in Wyoming. We'll set up the arrangements in a few months—after you've had time to settle into a routine."

"Oh, there will never be anything routine about living with her," Luke said in a teasing tone. "That's what I like the best."

Alex finished with her packing and made her way to the kitchen to say good-bye to everyone. It wouldn't be easy to say farewell to Michaela or Mrs. Godfrey, or even Bernice. Alex had come to care a great deal about each and every one of the girls, but especially those three people.

The plan was to return to Williams with her mother and to hold the funeral for Rufus Keegan on Friday. The fact that her father was truly dead still didn't register or ring true. Alex kept waiting for him to walk through the doors of El Tovar with his latest conquest at his side.

"I wish you weren't going," Michaela told her as she approached the salad preparation area.

"I know. I'm going to miss you all so much. But you'll come visit me on your vacations, won't you? I plan to have a big house with lots of guest rooms," Alex said enthusiastically. "I want lots of visitors, especially at first, because I know nothing of being a rancher's wife and everyone tells me it's very hard and very lonely."

Michaela laughed and tweaked Alex's cheek. "You'll never be lonely with that cowboy of yours."

Alex knew she spoke the truth. She couldn't begin to

imagine herself lonely with Luke in the same house. "Then there's Brock. We're adopting him, you know."

"I'd heard that, but to tell you the truth, I thought you were crazy."

"But he's my brother—he's family. I couldn't send him out to be taken in by strangers. What if they failed to teach him about God? What if they were mean and heartless people?"

Michaela patted her arm and nodded. "I know. I know. I completely understand. I only thought you were crazy because you'll have no time to be alone, just you and Luke."

"We'll make up for that," Alex said confidently.

"Alex!" Bernice called, bringing in a tray of dirty dishes. "Are you leaving now?"

"On the evening train," Alex replied. "My father's funeral is Friday and my mother wants to prepare the house in case people stop by."

"But of course they'll stop by," Bernice said, taking Alex's hands in her own. "I wish we'd had more time to know each other. I already feel we're the best of friends."

Alex felt a special warmth toward the girl. They'd shared the horrible scene of Rufus Keegan's indiscretion, yet Alex had never known a gossipy word to come from Bernice on the matter. She valued and trusted the girl.

"We are the best of friends," Alex agreed, "and as I was telling Michaela, you must come and visit me soon. I'll send Mrs. Godfrey my Wyoming address."

"I've already checked into it," Bernice admitted. "We can take the train from here to Williams and head to New Mexico and up through Colorado. We have to change trains a couple of times, but then we head to Cheyenne and over to Laramie. It's really quite easy."

Alex laughed. "It sounds like you have it pretty well figured out."

Bernice nodded. "I don't have too many friends, so I'm not about to lose the ones I do have."

Alex left them to go in search of Mrs. Godfrey and found the woman in her office. "I've come to say good-bye. We take the evening train to Williams."

"Yes, I know," Mrs. Godfrey replied. "I'm going to miss having you here. You're my number one girl. In the four years since you came to El Tovar, I've never had a moment's trouble with you."

"Until the last month," Alex teased.

"No, even then the problems weren't of your making. You were merely caught up in the games that were played out around you. You were never to blame." Mrs. Godfrey extended an envelope. "Here is the pay owed you."

Alex took the envelope and tucked it in the pocket of the green skirt she wore. "Thank you."

"And this is a little something from the girls and me," Mrs. Godfrey said, pushing forward another envelope. "We all wrote a little note to you so that when you feel the need for company you can open this letter and have all of us with you."

"Thank you," Alex whispered, her voice cracking. Tears slid down her cheeks. "I'll cherish this. You truly were my family here."

"How is your mother taking all of this?"

"She's doing remarkably well. Who would have guessed that there was such a bold, adventurous woman buried beneath that tiny frame? She's already contacted a real estate company in Denver. She's to look at four estates the week after next."

"When do you plan to marry?"

Alex grew thoughtful. "I didn't want to do anything that seemed disrespectful to my father. I figured to wait several weeks, but my mother insisted we go forward with the wedding as soon as possible. We'll probably marry in Denver, although I wish it could be here with all of you. What a very special ceremony that would be."

"It will be special no matter where you have it," Mrs. Godfrey insisted. "We'll all be with you in spirit, if nothing else."

The clock on the wall chimed and Alex realized the hour was getting away from her. "I'd better go. I need to find Luke and make sure he knows how to find us in Williams. He won't be able to join us until tomorrow."

Mrs. Godfrey got to her feet and came around the desk to give Alex a hug. "God be with you, child, and if you ever want to come back to work for Fred Harvey Company, you know you have a job."

"I'll remember that," Alex said, kissing the older woman's cheek. "Thank you. For everything."

CHAPTER THIRTY

"Goodness, Mother, I've never seen you so worried about catching the train," Alex said as her mother bustled around the room. "Where is my traveling dress? I laid it out before I went downstairs."

"I packed it away. I have a special dress for you to wear," her mother said, pulling a box from under the bed.

"Mother, is this new?" Alex questioned. She opened the box to reveal a beautiful creation in crepe. Pulling the dress out, Alex gasped. "Mother, this is incredible. Where did you get it?"

"I have my sources," she said smiling. "I just think it would be to our benefit to look our best when we return to Williams. We've lived in shame for too long. Now we can return with our heads held high."

"But what about Father and mourning? This gown is the palest lavender I've ever seen. It's almost white. And silk hose and matching shoes! I can't believe it. This is far too rich for the likes of me."

"Nonsense. You're a Keegan, and your financial situation is not such that you should dress as a pauper. Now, hurry. I want to be ready to leave in exactly half an hour."

"But, Mother, that will put us waiting at the station for at least an extra thirty minutes."

"I don't care. That's the way I want it. Now you dress. I need to finish with my jewelry. Brock is sleeping, so he shouldn't be a problem for either of us."

Alex nodded. There was nothing else she could do. Her mother had made up her mind and Alex hadn't seen her this animated in a long, long time. Maybe never. Putting the gown back into the box and taking it with her into the private bath, Alex began the transformation.

Peeling off her old blouse and skirt, Alex took up the new dress and marveled again at the silky feel. The delicate handkerchief hemline was scalloped and trimmed with a fine lace. Alex pulled the dress on over her head and marveled at the feel of it against her skin. She adjusted the top and smoothed the low waistband across her hips. Looking in the mirror, Alex thought the color was marvelous. The pale lavender reminded her of the orchids that sometimes were brought in to grace the Harvey tables.

"Arrive in style, eh, Mother? Well, we will certainly be doing that."

Alex added the hose and shoes of the same color, then wondered about what she should do with her hair. Pinning it carefully, she looped and twisted her wavy curls until she had managed to pile it all atop her head. She would have to wear a hat, of course. No decent woman would travel with her hair bare, and this style would allow her to wear even the closest-fitting hat. Then it dawned on Alex that she didn't have a hat worthy of this dress.

Running her hand down the material of the long sleeve, Alex smiled. She had planned to locate Luke and tell him good-bye. He would be so surprised to see her in this. The smile stayed on her face even as she came into the bedroom. "Well, how do I look?"

Her mother turned from where she was fussing with the baby. "Oh my!" She put her hand to her mouth.

Alex twirled around in a circle. "I don't know how you managed this, Mother, but thank you. It's lovely."

"Well, actually, I did have some help. I hope you don't mind. The dress has never been worn, but it did belong to someone else—Valerie Winthrop."

Alex paused a moment and waited for some ill feeling to surface. But there was none. Smiling, she shook her head. "I don't mind at all. I hold Valerie no malice. Especially now that she will be working with you on the house in Denver. No, my only regret is that I don't own a decent hat to wear with it."

Her mother went to the far side of the bed and held up a hatbox. "You do now." She smiled. "I hope you don't think me silly, but I really wanted things to be perfect."

Alex laughed and pulled out the cloche hat of the same pale color. It dipped low on one side and flared out ever so slightly on the other. "Oh, it's charming." She hurried back to the bath where she tried the hat on while looking in the mirror. "It's perfect, Mother."

"Wonderful. Now we really must hurry. I have the baby ready to go. I've asked Michaela to come and help us." A knock sounded at the door and her mother hurried to answer it, even as Alex came from the bath. "And here she is."

Michaela took one look at Alex and began to clap. "My, but don't you look marvelous. The picture of grace and elegance."

"My mother gave me this wonderful outfit. Believe it or not, it's one of Valerie Winthrop's. Apparently she purchased it, but changed her mind." Alex twirled in girlish delight.

"Mother said it's never been worn."

"Until now," Michaela replied. "And worn quite well. Luke's eyes will pop out when he sees you."

"Well, that's provided I can find him. I looked all over for him earlier. He promised to come to the station with us."

"Then I'm sure he will," Michaela declared. "Here, Mrs. Keegan, I'll take baby Brock." She took the baby in her arms and cooed at him. Brock seemed captivated with her murmurings and watched her silently.

"I can carry him," Alex said, reaching out for the baby.

"You'll get to play with and carry him all the time," Michaela replied. "It's my turn for now."

Alex laughed. "I thought you weren't interested in children."

Michaela jostled the baby in her arms and replied quite seriously, "I can't imagine what you're talking about. I'll probably have at least ten." She giggled then and stuck her tongue out at Alex. "Oh, you're right. I'll probably never have any, but I don't mind carrying Brock just now."

"What of the luggage, Mother?" Alex asked.

"The bellboy was coming up right behind me," Michaela replied. "So we needn't worry about that. Come on. I'll walk with you."

Alex chatted with Michaela and her mother about the days to come. Michaela promised to come to the funeral and offer her support, and Alex blessed her for her concern. They descended the stairs, Alex knowing in her heart it would probably be the last time that she'd do this. She looked around her as if to memorize every feature.

"Funny," she told her companions, "I've lived here for four years and never really thought about the day I'd leave."

"Will you be sad?" her mother asked, her tone quite serious.

Alex shook her head. "No. Not at all. I'll have Luke and the baby, and one day we'll have children of our own. I'm bound and determined to prove myself a good rancher's wife. I'll buy books or take lessons or whatever it takes so that I'm just as useful to Luke as I can be."

Michaela laughed. "Oh, you'll be useful to him. On those bitterly cold Wyoming nights, he won't even need to take a hot water bottle to bed with him."

They laughed at this and proceeded through the lobby to the porch. "Well, this is it," Alex said as they descended the steps. She turned to say something else and forgot her words as she gazed across the lawn to the south rim and found Luke and a multitude of others gathered.

"We wanted to surprise you," her mother said when Alex turned a questioning gaze upon them. "I didn't want you to have to wait for a funeral in order to have a wedding."

"I don't understand," Alex said, looking from her mother to Michaela.

Michaela laughed and shifted the baby. "This is your wedding, silly. We hope you don't mind that we took liberties, but what's done is done. You can't leave the man waiting at the altar, so pick up the pace."

Alex looked across the lawn again and met Luke's gaze. He was dressed impeccably in a dark blue suit that she didn't recognize. Maybe it, too, was compliments of the Winthrops.

Her hands trembled as she turned to her mother once again. "You planned all of this for me?"

"I'm sorry if I've overstepped my bounds. A woman should plan such things for herself, but I couldn't bear the idea of a hurried wedding in Denver. Your friends are here. Why not have it here?"

"I'm delighted. Stunned. But nevertheless, delighted."

They made their way across the lawn, and Alex found Mrs. Godfrey nodding in approval and wiping tears from her eyes as Alex joined Luke before the preacher.

"You look . . . well . . . there aren't words," Luke said as he took hold of her hand. "I'm completely captivated."

Alex smiled. "I'm rather taken aback, myself. You cut quite the figure in that suit."

Luke pushed back his sandy hair and grinned. "The collar itches. I can't wait to get out of it. It's sure not what I'm used to."

Alex giggled. "Me neither. The Harvey uniform was good enough for me."

"Shall we begin?" the preacher asked.

"Yes, we have to hurry," her mother said, coming to stand beside her daughter. "The train leaves in thirty minutes."

Alex looked to Luke. "It's not what we planned, but do you mind?"

"I don't mind at all. This way I know you're mine—I know you won't change your mind before I can join you in Williams."

"I wouldn't change my mind anyway, Luke Toland. You're stuck with me through thick and thin."

"Just the way I want it."

The sun had moved to the west, but it still shone across the canyon in a glory of color. Alex marveled at the wonder of it all. The way the clouds played across the blue skies, the way the shadows below danced in and out of the crevices. Alex knew that as long as she lived, she would always stand amazed at what God had done here.

"Are you ready to do this?" Luke asked. She nodded, feeling the thrill of his smile go clear to her toes. He turned to the preacher. "Let's get to it."

Twenty minutes later Alex was announced as Mrs. Luke Toland. Everyone pelted them with rice as the first warning whistle sounded from the train in the station.

The party moved en masse toward the station but held back, giving their good-byes before reaching the platform. When only Luke remained, he took Brock from Michaela and crossed the platform with Alex at his side. Katherine took the baby from his arms and moved to board the train.

"I'm blessed to have you for a son," she told him as he helped her aboard the train.

"I'm blessed to have you for a mother," Luke replied in turn. "Mine has been gone for a very long time, and I think it will be pretty nice to have you around from time to time. Are you sure you don't want to come and stay with us for a while?"

"Not just yet. There's so much work to be done. I want to stand before the Lord and feel I did my best for Him."

"That's all any of us want," Luke agreed. "I have a feeling you'll more than satisfy the Lord in your love for others."

Katherine smiled. "I have no doubt the same will be true for you. I know what you did for Valerie. She told me about your kindness to her, talking to her about God despite her brazen actions toward you. You have a good heart, Luke." She smiled at Alex, who stood only a few feet away, listening to their exchange. "Now, you go give your wife a proper good-bye and we'll see you on Friday."

Luke nodded. "Yes, ma'am." He tipped his hat and waited until Katherine had disappeared before turning to Alex.

"You said some very sweet things to my mother," she told

him as he took her in his arms. As he pulled her close, Alex put her hands on his chest. "Behave yourself—we're in public, Mr. Toland."

"Yes, Mrs. Toland, but I'm a newly married man and I won't be able to hold my wife again until . . . well, it seems like it will be forever. As soon as I finish showing the new crew the ropes, I'll be back, and then I'll never have to let you go."

She smiled and lifted her hand to touch his face. "I know. I feel the same way, even if it is only until tomorrow."

He kissed her sweetly on the mouth, then trailed kisses on her cheek and nose and eyes. "Don't forget me," he whispered just before he kissed her mouth again.

Alex pulled back and smiled. "I could sooner forget to breathe."

The train whistle blasted and the conductor called the final board.

"I have to go," Alex said, pulling away from Luke's protective hold. "I'll pick you up at the station tomorrow. Don't miss the train."

"I won't. I'll be there before you know it. You'll see."

He walked her to the train and let the conductor help her aboard. "I love you," he whispered.

She replied in like manner, but the train whistle blocked out her words. They laughed and Alex found herself pushed up the stairs by the insistent conductor. She waved as the train pulled out, joyous in her newfound feelings of love and contentment. There was no fear of whether he'd come back to her. No fear of what might happen in her absence. God had melted away her fears—He had taken away the shadows and put sunshine and hope in their place.

EPILOGUE

August 1925

Alex laughed at the antics of two-year-old Brock as he toddled around the corral where his father worked to pick out the horse stock he would sell in Laramie.

"He'll be climbing that fence before you know it," Luke called out as Alex pulled Brock away from the fence.

"Don't I know it. He already climbs everything else. I'm always finding him up on the table," Alex replied.

It was their second-year anniversary, and Alex couldn't help but wonder if her husband would remember. She had a very special gift for him, but she hated to mention it for fear he had forgotten. She certainly didn't want to make him feel bad.

Luke continued with the stock, pointing out this one and that one among some thirty horses. Clancy, who'd joined them from the canyon recently, marked the horses in order to separate them out later.

Brock fussed in Alex's arms. "What's the matter, little man?"

"Wanna horsey. Wanna ride horsey."

"You can't go riding just now. Papa will take you later," she said softly and kissed his dirty cheek. The boy squirmed and fussed until she put him on the ground. "Why don't you go play with the puppies?"

"Pubbies!" Brock clapped his hands and headed to the porch where their collie dog, Mollie, kept her rapidly growing brood of six pups.

Two years of marriage to Luke. Two marvelous, love-filled years, she thought as she dusted the dirt from her apron. She'd been happier than she'd ever dreamed possible. Happier still when Clancy showed up to hire on with the announcement that he and Bernice would be getting married the following October. They had all agreed that Clancy and Bernice would need their own little house, so he and Luke had begun immediately to put something together. Alex was delighted with the news that Bernice would soon be her ranch companion. The company of other women was generally reserved for church on Sunday or those rare occasions of visiting.

The men came from the corral and Clancy nodded and took the paper from Luke. "I'll see to this, boss. Don't you worry a thing about it."

"With you on the job, Clancy, I never do."

Luke crossed the yard to where Alex stood. "I have a surprise for you. Will Brock be all right for a few minutes?"

"Oh, sure. He's with Mollie now." She pointed to where Brock patted the mother collie on top of the head with rather strong-handed pats. "Be gentle, Brock. Don't hurt Mollie."

"I see pubbies," he said, moving from Mollie to the babies.

"He'll be busy for a few minutes—but only a few. He'll soon figure out that he needs to be off doing other things."

Luke laughed. "Then come with me to the barn. I want to show you something."

"All right."

Alex looped her arm through his. "So what's the occasion, Mr. Toland?"

"You know full well the occasion, Mrs. Toland. It's the same occasion that caused you to bake a cake this morning." He looked at her and laughed. "You thought I'd forgotten our anniversary, didn't you?"

"I didn't think that at all. I just didn't want you to feel bad if you had."

"Well, I didn't forget. In fact, I've been thinking about it for weeks. I got Clancy to help me with your gift."

"Really? What is it?"

"You have to wait and see. Now close your eyes and I'll lead you."

She laughed and did as he bid her. Leading her into the barn, Alex felt the warmth of the sun diminish and the shadow of the interior fall upon them. It was a bit cooler here, but only marginally. But instead of stopping and having her open her eyes, Luke led her back outside. Alex could only imagine that he'd taken her completely through the barn.

"Okay, you can open your eyes now."

Alex did so and found herself standing in front of a car. "You bought this for me?"

"Well, for us, but I figured it was time you learned to drive. You never know when you'll need to take yourself to town when I'm too busy to drive you."

"Oh, Luke, you're a very thoughtful husband."

He turned and studied her for a moment. "Do you really like it? I know you've never been all that fond of automobiles, but they really are the way of the future. The horse and buggy days are all but behind us. Especially in the cities. I figure the day may even come when we want to drive to Denver and visit your mother."

"I'd like that," she admitted. "Yes, it's the perfect gift."

He smiled and kicked at the dirt. "Glad you like it." He paused for a moment. "So what did you get me?"

"Well," Alex began, "you can't have it just yet."

He frowned. "Why not?"

"Because it won't arrive here until about six months from now." She grinned and felt overwhelmed with the joy of her news. "We're going to have a baby."

He stared at her in disbelief. "We're what? Are you serious?"

She giggled. "Yes, I'm quite serious."

Without warning he lifted her in the air and circled her around and around. Putting her back on the ground, Luke pulled her into a crushing embrace. "I couldn't be happier. This is the most wonderful news I've had since you agreed to marry me."

"I thought you'd be pleased," she said, seeing the pure joy in his expression. "I know I am. I'm completely in love with the idea of having your babies."

He set her away from him just a few inches and put his hand to her stomach. "Do we really have to wait so very long?"

"Good things take time. You worked for four years to get me," she reminded him.

"I know, and it seemed to take forever."

"Well, this baby will be with us before you know it."

"God has been so very good to us," Luke said, putting his arm around her shoulder. Together they walked back to the house where Brock was still consumed with his puppy visit. "Brock will be excited, that's for sure. He sometimes seems kind of lonely."

Alex nodded. "I know, but soon he'll be patting the baby

on the head instead of Molly." She smiled and leaned against Luke, her head nestling against his shoulder and neck. She had never wanted anything more than what she had with Luke. Gone were the nightmares of the past, her anger with her father. Yielding it to God seemed the only way to have true happiness.

"I wanna ride horsey!" Brock declared, seeing them standing there watching him.

Alex smiled and turned to her husband. "Well, I suppose you and the boy should take your daily ride."

"I suppose we should," he said as Brock came plowing across the porch and jumped off the edge. Luke caught him and lifted him high in the air before settling him on his shoulders. "The boy is fearless."

"So are you," Alex said with great pride.

"That goes the same for you, my darlin'. I think you're probably the bravest one of us all."

"It comes with knowing where to place your trust," Alex said, knowing Luke would appreciate her meaning.

He leaned over and kissed her forehead. "I couldn't have said it better."

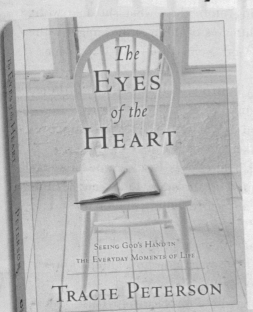

Tracie shares her thoughts on why she writes non-fiction:

> *I really didn't set out to write non-fiction. I find it to be so very personal—leaving me feeling rather vulnerable and open to inspection. But even with these concerns, I couldn't ignore the call to write non-fiction. Taking stories from everyday life, however, allowed the fiction writer in me to have some say over the non-fiction elements. I think people are often confused and put off by some types of non-fiction material. I often hear readers say that some non-fiction leaves them feeling overwhelmed because of their inability to comprehend the theological dynamics or scholastic reasoning. For this reason, I've created my non-fiction as just a simple collection of stories from everyday life. My goal is to show that God is very much alive and at work in the most minor of daily details, and that He cares for us, even when we cannot perceive Him in the mix. I hope you'll be blessed by the stories I've shared. Ultimately, I pray that your eyes will be open to God's presence in your daily life.*
>
> *Tracie Peterson*

Turn the page for a preview of Tracie Peterson's *Eyes of the Heart.*

Introduction

As a child I always thought people saw life the same way. I thought boys, girls, men, women, everyone had the same gifts and vision for the world around them. I was wrong. As I grew up, both spiritually and physically, I came to see the uniqueness of each individual. I don't think this lesson was driven home any more clearly than when my sister, Karen, commented to me that she couldn't string two words together and have them make sense.

How could this be? I thought. Didn't everyone possess the desire to write—and the ability? I figured writing was one of those original three basics you learned in school; how could she stand there and tell me she didn't have what it took to do this? Gradually I heard other people say the same thing. And silly as it sounds, that was when I came to better understand that God's gifts and the talents He gives are uniquely designed for the person He desires us to be.

With this in mind, the concept for this book was born. I came to realize that some people find it easy to see God in everyday life, while others struggle with the burdens they carry, unable to see much of anything. Sometimes obstacles keep them from seeing the truth. And sometimes the truth is the very last thing they want to see.

Having been in both places, it has become my desire to share with you how God opened the eyes of my heart. I want to share this, because these lessons changed my life. And like a very special party where everyone is going to have a marvelous time, I didn't want you to miss out.

So settle back and view the world through my eyes, if you will. Open your heart to the wonder of God's picture lessons. Let the eyes of your heart be enlightened that you might have hope. Hope that comes not from a book, or from me, for we will both fade away to dust. No, let the hope come from the King of the Universe, who loves you now even as He loved you on the cross.

Oh, and by the way, my sister, Karen, has a marvelous ability with numbers. She can do algebraic expressions in her sleep—a talent God did not see fit to bless me with. Unique in the Lord? You bet. Ah, the wonder of God!

—Tracie

4

Charred Sticks and Stones That Roll

On a trip to Yellowstone National Park, I was amazed and overwhelmed at the beautiful landscape. The geysers were fascinating, the wildlife amusing and a little frightening, and the people wonderfully animated.

But just when I thought I had the big picture in mind, God took me in a totally different direction, and the lesson He taught me there was most valuable. Amid the beauty of this national park were thousands of acres of fire-scarred land. The area was stark: a mournful reminder of tragedy.

Tall, blackened sticks rose out of the earth. Nothing grew on them. They were lifeless. The scene went on for miles and miles and left me feeling sad. Then to my surprise, I noticed other things: little flowers growing in between the blackened columns. Smaller, green trees, lush with life, struggling to rise from the ashes. The forest wasn't dead, but the overwhelming evidence of the tragedy that had struck so many years earlier was shadowing the truth. The worst that could happen to a forest had happened, and the scars were still there. But beyond that, growth and renewal were also evident, and it was here that I saw my life lesson.

Not so long ago I experienced a tragedy too. And like that mighty forest fire, the destruction swept through and destroyed the lush green growth that had been my life. When the fire died out, I felt there was little left but black stubs and vast, charred wastelands. I felt ugly and useless. Nothing seemed right, and though I refused to give up hope in God, I felt perhaps He might have been a tad overworked on the day that brought my blackest hour. Maybe He'd been a bit too busy to notice what had happened to one of His children.

It was easy to see the charred remainders. It's easy to see them now. What's not so easy to recognize is the growth that has come from the fire. The little things. The love of good friends and family. The unexpected help that nurtured me.

There are flowers growing, and saplings are striving to push up past the ashes. There is life amid death. Hope in the midst of adversity. But it's so much easier to see the dead trees.

I think of Mary and Martha and all the friends who'd gathered at the tomb when Lazarus died. Their grief was more than they could bear. Their hope had been that the tragedy would be averted. They had, after all, sent for Jesus. They knew He could keep this horrible thing from happening.

But He hadn't come. At least not in time. Death had marked their family—robbed them of their loved one and betrayed their hope. Now there was nothing but cold stone and black stubs. Desolation and death were all they could see. And even when Jesus showed up, all they could say was "If you'd only been here . . ."

They could see nothing but death and its finality. They didn't recognize the fact that Jesus causes life to sprout anew. They knew that they would all be together again someday. But right now that big stone across the tomb was more than they could contend with. It cancelled all other possibilities. It overwhelmed their hope.

I've always been impressed with the story of Lazarus. Not only for the obvious show of Jesus' ability to raise the dead; not even for the fact that Jesus wept. There was another aspect of this story that caught my attention. Before Jesus commands the dead, before He brings Lazarus back to life, He tells the people to take away the stone.

He could have supernaturally moved the rock himself. He could have raised His hands and blasted it into a million pieces. He could have caused Lazarus to walk right through it. But He didn't. Have you ever wondered why?

I think I know. At least I want to venture a guess.

I think many times in our lives we need resurrecting. We need to come out of the tomb and back from the dead. Sometimes we need it for ourselves, and sometimes we need it for someone we love. Either way, I believe we have to be willing to *remove the stone.* Sometimes we have to be willing to take out the black stubby pieces and cast them aside. To see beyond the burn. Sometimes we have to let go of the past and be willing to look to the new life of the future. Easy task? No way!

I think Jesus knew the people well enough to know that they would argue with Him. And, of course, they did. "He's gonna stink, Lord. He's been in there four days now."

Then Jesus asks them, "Did I not tell you that if you believed, you would see the glory of God?" (John 11:40).

Do you know what they did next? They acted on faith they could only hope was valid. They took away the stone, and Jesus raised Lazarus from the dead. But as important as it is that Lazarus was resurrected, I think it is crucial that the people removed the stone first.

Maybe something bad has happened to you. The horror of it has left you defeated and overcome with grief. Maybe you're even saying to God, "If you'd only been here . . ."

The blackened fields stretch out around you; the charred stubs stand as lifeless reminders of what was once beautiful and fertile ground. Maybe your husband has announced he wants a divorce. He's found someone else. Could be that job you loved suddenly went up in flames. You find yourself laid off, let go in the wake of downsizing. Maybe your child has experimented one too many times with drugs, and now the police want you to identify her body at the morgue.

You stare out at the devastated land—the cold tomb. "If you'd only been here, God," you say. "If you'd only seen and cared enough to stop this before it got this far."

But He was there. And He is here, and He does care.

It's easy to see the negative, the horrible bits left behind. The scars are ugly and the eradication complete. But what He showed me in my own life is that I'm not alone, and that I have only to believe and to act on that belief. To take away the stone so that I might see the glory of God.

God is still in the business of resurrecting lives. It's not something we have to wait for until the end of time. He does it on a daily basis. He does it in ways that bring life out of the ashes of death.

That woman you know who lost her child and husband in a car accident. The man who can't seem to quit gambling. Those sad, lost souls who are only going through the motions of life but have no direction, no hope. He can bring them back to life. He can bring them out of the tomb.

But we have a responsibility. We must be willing to take away the stone. We must act on what we profess to believe. If we leave the stone in place, we won't see God at work. If we wrap ourselves up in the charred reminders of what might have been, of what once was, we might fail to see the new growth that springs up right beneath our feet.

What stones are you refusing to let go of? What stones are you refusing to move?

Think about the sorrow you've experienced, the hopelessness you've known. Do you need to be resurrected? I know just the one who can help.

Gather up your courage, put a little spit on your hands, and give a mighty shove. Move that stone. See beyond the fire and the charred remains of what might have been.

God's glory is just around the corner, and He wants to share it with you. He's in the business of bringing life out of death. Let us be in the business of moving stones.